Scars of the Golden Dancer

NightEyes DaySpring

Dancing Jackal Books

Scars of the Golden Dancer

Copyright © 2022 NightEyes DaySpring

First Edition Paperback, 2022

ISBN 978-1-957364-00-1

Dancing Jackal Books
Tallahassee, FL
www.dancingjackalbooks.com

Cover illustrated by Hibbary – *www.furaffinity.net/user/hibbary/*
Interior map illustrated by Teagan Gavet – *www.teagangavet.com*

*To Othello, who supported me through this project with
all its ups and downs and kept asking me when.*

Content Warning:

The following work contents scenes of explicit male/ male sex and deals with topics such as prostitution, abuse, violence, loss, and post-traumatic stress. This book is intended for adults only, and reader discretion is advised.

Table of Contents

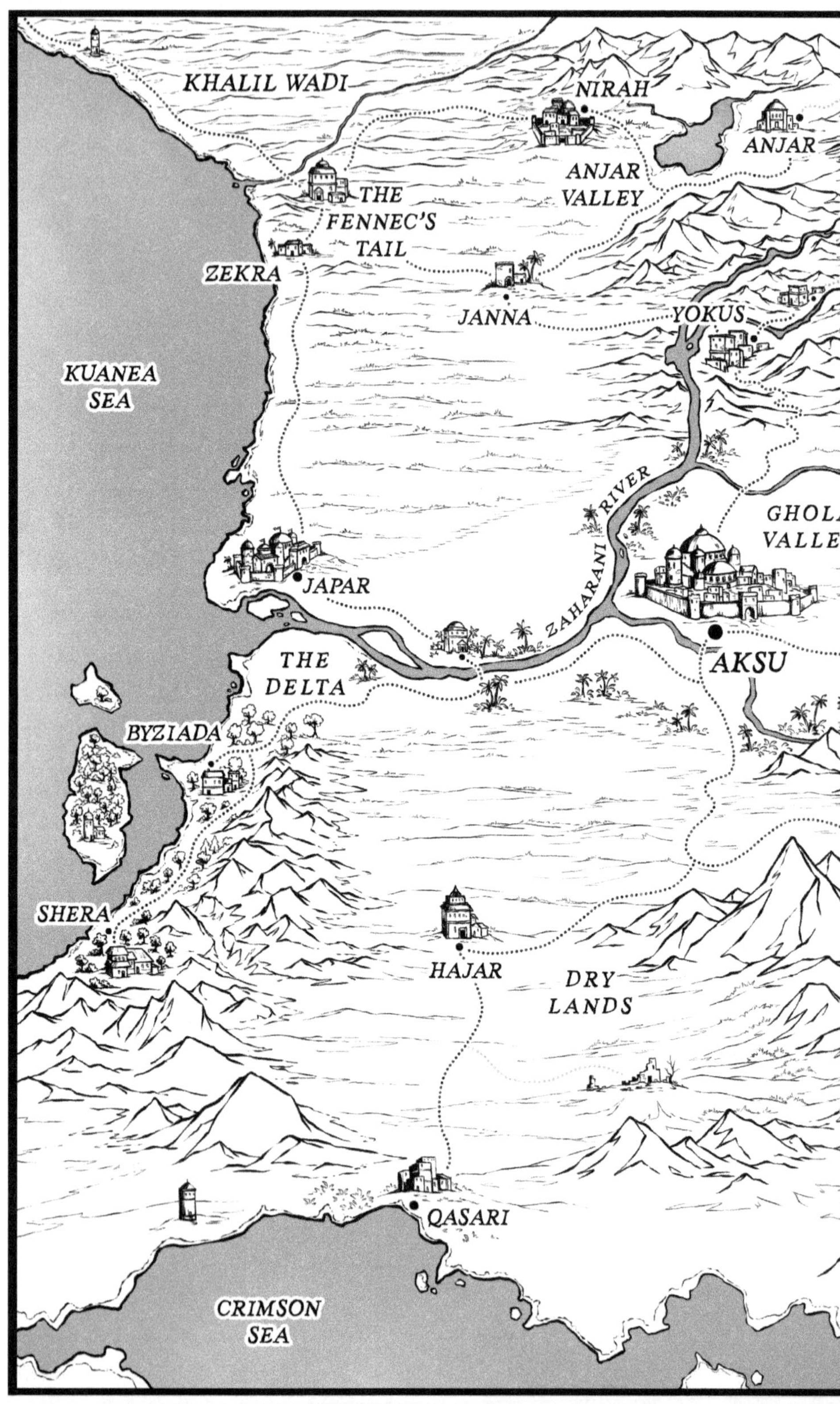

KHALIL WADI
NIRAH
ANJAR
ANJAR VALLEY
THE FENNEC'S TAIL
ZEKRA
JANNA
YOKUS
KUANEA SEA
ZAHARANI RIVER
GHOL VALLE
JAPAR
AKSU
THE DELTA
BYZIADA
SHERA
HAJAR
DRY LANDS
QASARI
CRIMSON SEA

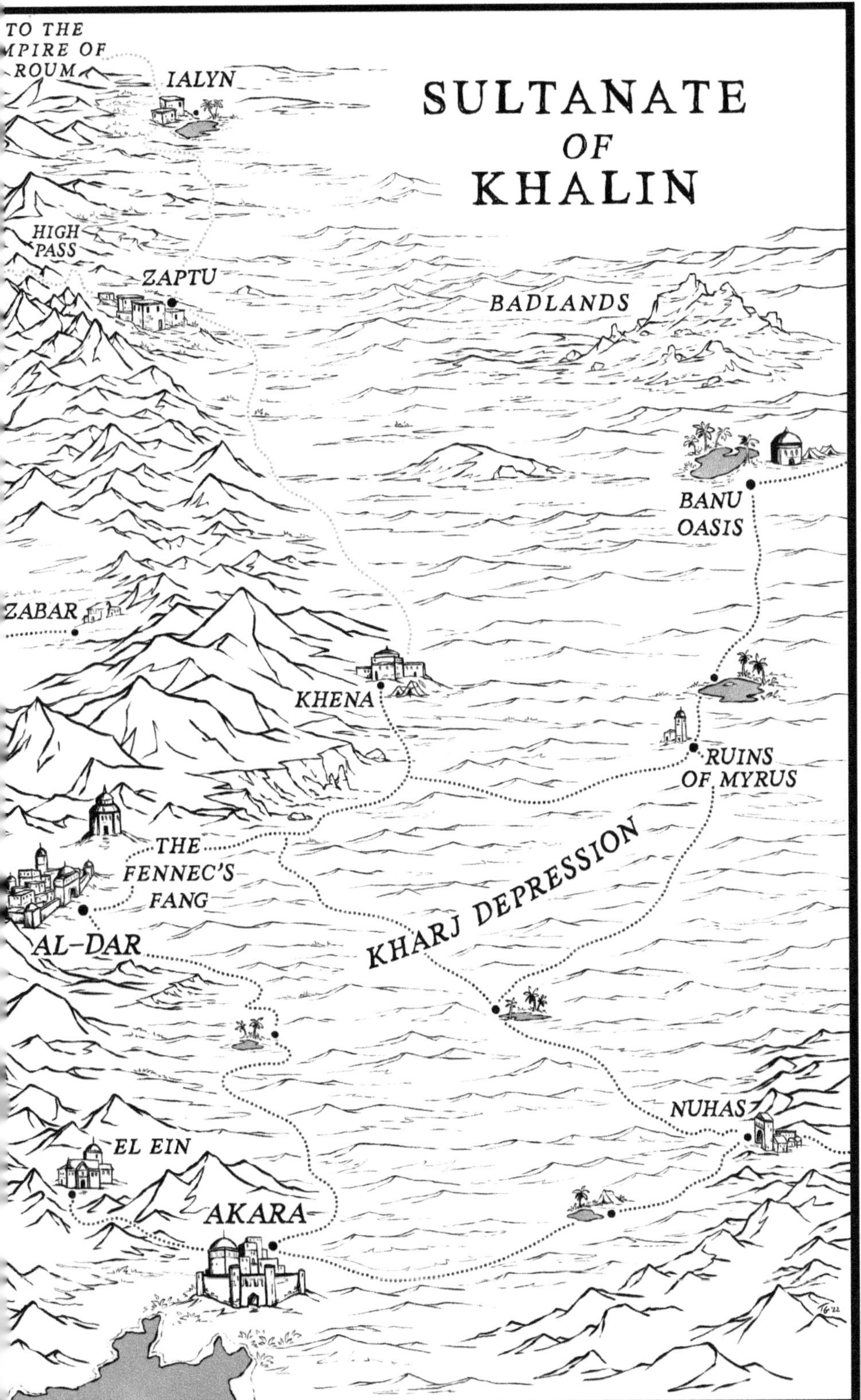
TO THE
EMPIRE OF
ROUM
IALYN
HIGH
PASS
ZAPTU
BADLANDS
SULTANATE
OF
KHALIN
BANU
OASIS
ZABAR
KHENA
RUINS
OF MYRUS
THE
FENNEC'S
FANG
AL-DAR
KHARJ DEPRESSION
NUHAS
EL EIN
AKARA

The Caravanserai
(Naji)

The desert moon shines like a jewel in the night sky, full and bright, watching over the caravan town. Now that the sun has set, the dry air is cool, and the wind shifts lazily over the dunes, ruffling my fur. With the stifling heat of the day fading away, it's refreshing to be outside.

I've never been here before, so I didn't know what to expect. This village of Zaptu is off the main caravan routes through the desert, and it's little more than a cluster of mud-brick houses on the road leading to the local caravanserai. In the center of the houses there is a small square with a cheap inn, which is where I decide to stay. The rest of the structures in town are just residences. I've been to more remote places in my travels, but Zaptu is one of the smallest caravan towns I've seen. If the shortcut through the mountains doesn't prove useful, I doubt I'll ever come back through here.

The innkeeper suggested I go to the caravanserai since they're having a festival tonight. While I want to sleep, the ghosts of my past are haunting me. After traveling straight across the desert for five days alone, camping out in the open, I need the company of others to bring me back to the present.

My body is worn from hours of climbing over sand dunes, and my paws ache from stepping over jagged rocks, but I have been alone with my thoughts too much. Even if I just stand quietly off by myself, it will be a nice distraction. I will feel relieved to be a part of society again.

As I approach the stone compound, it looms over me. It has only a single gate. The walls are nondescript, but the gate's archway is eloquently carved with inscriptions and ornamentation, a sign that appears to reflect more the town's past wealth than its current. The door under the arch is open, with a lone caracal standing guard outside. He waves me over as I approach.

He takes a moment to appraise me before he speaks. "Have you come to see the dances tonight, traveler?" he asks.

"Yes," I say. The innkeeper didn't specify what was going on, but I gathered it would be a show of some kind. He said I would find it very entertaining, but I didn't have the heart to tell him I likely wouldn't find what interests me there. I did take his advice to at least come and look. Spotted hyenas like me aren't common in this area, yet that's not where my reservations come from.

The caracal nods. "Things have already started, but there is still some entertainment left for the night. What's your name?"

"Naji."

He smiles and spreads his paws out. "Welcome to the caravanserai of Zaptu, Naji."

I smile back and head through the gate. While the outside is simple with only one entrance, the inside has everything a traveler or caravan would need in one building. The narrow tunnel from the entrance opens into a large courtyard in the center of the complex. Small shops and storefronts are set along the courtyard's edge while the high exterior wall protects the complex from raiders. There are rooms for rent and booths for passing merchants wishing to sell some of their wares. I realize I could have stayed here, but there's no need. Any room with a clean bed beats sleeping on the ground.

On one side of the courtyard, a small crowd has gathered, and music is playing. People are standing in groups or sitting on carpets watching. Getting closer, I catch sight of a female striped hyena dancing alone in the center of the gathering, and my attention is drawn to her. A long piece of fabric is fluttering around her body, clasped in her paws. Other performers are waiting their turn off to one side, but the hyena captivates the audience with her performance.

She comes out of a twist and drops the fabric in front of herself. As the music begins its crescendo, she plants both feet and starts undulating her body. The muscles under her fur cause her stomach to ripple back and forth. Quick movements are followed by soft sensual motions, her actions precise and carefully timed. The drumbeat quickens as her dance hits its climax. As the song thunders to its end, she reaches down to the shift she's wearing and pulls it. The next moment, she's wearing only her top as the fabric around her waist falls away. As the final notes sound in the song's finale, she lifts her top and pulls it off. Now completely naked, she gracefully bows low.

The audience explodes with hooting and catcalls. I clap myself, appreciating her form and moves, but surprised at the boldness of the dance. A cheetah comes forward, wearing a long kaftan, and stands next to the hyena, waiting for the applause to die down before he speaks. "Thank you, Sahar, for your beautiful dance," he says, pausing to chuckle, "and the wonderful flourish at the end. If you liked Sahar's routine, please don't be stingy now." He pauses, and the crowd applauds again. "Who wishes to buy the lady's attentions for the night? She's as good between the sheets as she is at dancing."

"A silver dirham!" someone shouts.

"A silver and ten copper fals," comes another call from the crowd.

I understood what the innkeeper was suggesting when I came here, but it still surprises me to see people bid in public like this. In Aksu, where I live, when you see dancers on the street, they always belong to an acrobat troupe. I had never seen whores dancing to advertise their wares in public like this, not that you can't find them in the back alleys. The people of Aksu are not very rigid in their morals toward prostitution, but they are more reserved where they let it reside. Then again, in a city with a thousand courtyards, discretion is much easier to achieve than here.

Everyone here seems to be enjoying the spectacle, and the bidding is very lively. Many of the bidders appear to be travelers, still wearing their dusty robes like I am, but a few people wear finer clothing. The bidding ends, and the hyena's attentions go for four silver dirhams to a scrawny wolf wearing a worn cloak fashionable with people to the north. I feel out of place standing here by myself, the only one of my kind in the crowd, but before I can leave, the next dancer is stepping forward. I'm ready to turn to leave when the glint of steel catches my eye.

A male golden jackal steps up with a swish in his step, carrying a kilij. The curved sword is unsheathed, and the blade glints in the light. Loose sheer fabric hangs off his hips, with a sash around his waist. An open vest on top of a tight shirt completes the ensemble. Like the woman before him, he's here to sell his wares, but his is a different kind of attraction. He looks quiet and reserved as he stands in the middle of the audience and kneels, holding the sword out in front of him, the tip in the dirt. He focuses on the point of the sword in the ground, waiting for the music to begin.

"And now, Zayn," calls out the cheetah. The applause is muted as he steps back to the stand next to the musicians.

The music starts slow with a flute. At first, the jackal just lets it drift, staying still, but when the strings join, he comes to life. Zayn swings the blade out before him and twists his body as he brings it to his side. He moves gracefully, stepping quickly with his feet and sweeping the sword in wide motions. He catches the dull edge of the blade with his free paw so he can pivot while holding it above his head before he lets go as he swings it out again. Slowly the music builds up pace, and Zayn moves faster, pushing himself into the song with eagerness.

When the drums begin, he rolls his stomach suggestively to the beat, while holding the sword above his head. He drops to his knees, balancing the sword on top of his head, and the blade barely wobbles.

He is one of the best dancers I have ever seen.

He leans back, holding the sword on the ground, till his head is touching the earth, twisting his belly and body to the beat. Then in a flash, he is back on his feet swinging the kilij.

His movements are intoxicating, and he is beautiful. As I'm watching him perform, I find myself wondering what he would feel like under my paws. His performance is powerful, seductive, and leaves me breathless. With the music at its crescendo, he spins around, holding the sword. He steps to the left, and the blade is a blur as he swings it wide. Zayn spins again, stepping back to the right, the blade slicing through the air with precision where he stood a moment before.

He finishes his dance with his footpaws close together, chest heaving from exertion. He has put his heart and soul into this, and while the audience applauds his efforts, they are not fired up like they were with the girl who danced previously.

The cheetah comes up smiling, pats Zayn on the back, and shakes his shoulder. "Passionate as always," he declares to the audience. "Who wishes his attentions for the night?"

There is no response from the crowd, only a gentle mumble.

"No one wishes for his attentions this night?" asks the cheetah.

"Two coppers for his muzzle," says someone in the audience. The jackal looks toward the speaker, his ears drooping instinctively.

Someone else laughs at the ridiculously low offer.

"Four coppers for his tail," someone else calls out. The jackal huffs, not amused.

"He won't even give you a hand job for four coppers," says the cheetah to the audience. "Has not his dance earned him at least a silver dirham? Be generous now."

Nobody speaks up. I hear a whispered comment of "not buying in public" from someone near me. The jackal looks away from the crowd, dejected. His lively ears and tail are drooping even though he is still panting heavily from the exertion of the dance. He's a great dancer, I can tell that, but he belongs in an acrobat troupe, not out here selling himself to travelers. Glancing around at the audience, I can see many of them want him with hunger in their eyes but are too shy to speak up. A few are licking their fangs.

He turns away from the center of the dancing area, tail dragging behind. All that passion and drive he showed is gone, replaced by despondence. I can't deny I wonder what touching him feels like, but I also feel a connection to him, an understanding. I know what that look is; I know what being alone is like. I'm reminded of rosetted fur from a ghost in my mind that followed me across the desert for five days, of days past, and days that could have been. And deep down, I want to feel the lithe frame of the jackal, with his powerful muscles, under my paws.

"Three silver!" I call out, going high. There is a palpable gasp from the crowd as many of them turn to gawk at me. A few give me jealous looks. I don't care what any of these people think of my tastes. I stand up straight, letting them stare. The jackal has frozen in mid-step and isn't moving. Even though I'm paid for my skills with the sword, I can feel all the eyes on me, and it's a little frightening.

Did I just buy the attention of a male whore for the night? Have I been alone for so long I'm willing to pay and pay well for companionship? The job that sent me across the desert only paid twenty silver dirhams, so this is a good chunk of what I just earned.

"Three it is," calls out the cheetah.

Why yes, I did.

&

Zayn is standing off to the side next to the musicians as I approach him, money in my paw. He's leaning against the wall of the courtyard, waiting. His ears perk when he sees me. There is already another dancer entertaining the crowd, so no one is paying any attention to us now. He's still wearing his dancing clothes, but he doesn't have the sword anymore.

"Three silvers is most kind of you, sir," he says meekly, looking down.

This submissive action surprises me. It's different from how I thought he'd act. I much prefer the drive he showed dancing and the fiery personality I suspect lies within. I reach down and gently tilt the jackal's muzzle up, so he is looking at me. "You are an amazing dancer." When he doesn't respond, I continue. "Are you not worth three silver?" I ask him.

"Oh yes, but some nights the crowd is shy. Not everyone is as discerning as you are," he says and then grins, tongue lolling out.

"I appreciate anyone who can swing a sword like that."

That gets me a small chuckle in return. He puffs up his chest. He has a slenderer build than I do, but he's only a few inches shorter than I am. I'm rather broad-chested, but hyenas are usually stockier than jackals. "I will not disappoint you."

His scent is strong from the exertion of dancing, but beneath his musk, I can smell the enticing hint of frankincense. I'm forced to smile at his enthusiasm. "I don't think you will," I say, slipping the money into one of his paws.

He looks down to check the money before he sequesters it away into a small pouch. Pleased, he asks me, "You are staying here in the caravanserai?"

He's very down to business. I guess in his line of work, people don't pay you to talk, but I want to know more about him too. I want to know what makes this lanky canine tick. He doesn't know that, though. He thinks I'm just paying for his body, which I suppose I just did.

"I'm staying at the inn on the other side of town."

"Ah, that's fine. The rooms there are nicer," he says before he smiles, flashing a little fang. "Shall we sojourn?"

I do want to go, to explore his lithe frame, but first, I want to introduce us formally, even though I already know who he is. "What is your name?"

"Zayn," he says, bobbing his head softly. He pauses, considering. "What is yours?" he asks, finally.

"Naji," I say.

The jackal nods, wagging his tail softly and doesn't say anything else. I want to ask him something to keep him talking, but he's waiting on me to move.

"I've, uh, never done this before," I confess.

"You take me back to your room."

"I know, I'm just…," I know what drives someone to this type of work. "I'm sorry."

His expression hardens. "I'm not giving you your money back."

"I wouldn't ask for it."

"Then why bid with your coin?"

I shrug. He wouldn't understand, and I'm not sure I do either. "Spur of the moment, I guess."

"You find me attractive, do you not?"

I nod. "Of course, but I have always been mithly."

"You are the same as me then," Zayn says, before pointing a finger toward the crowd. "Not many of us here with that preference, but you never know who passes through town."

"I imagine that doesn't make your work easy."

He shakes his head. "No, it doesn't, but I survive." He yawns. "You sure you don't want to get what you paid for?"

"I'm good. It's—" A paw touches my arm to stop me from talking.

"It's okay, really. I don't mind," he says.

My ears lower. "It wouldn't be right."

He looks toward the current dancer, a fennec fox, bounding around the stage. "Life isn't always right, but we keep on living anyway. Shall we go?"

There's nothing I can think of saying to that, so I turn to lead him out, and he wraps an arm around mine. His paw is warm, and the pads on his fingertips tease the fur on my arm. No one watches us leave as we walk out of the caravanserai, and I'm struck by how casual this feels as we head out into the night.

The caracal guarding the gate waves and smiles. "Glad to see you found something of interest to do with your time here," he says.

I just mumble a thanks and walk down the road, the jackal holding onto me. His musk has taken on the subtle scent of arousal, and it tickles at my nose. The air doesn't feel oppressive in the cool night, but the anticipation of what's to come makes my fur tingle.

⤳

The innkeeper barely looks up from his reading when I return with Zayn. This inn is a small building, and the entranceway opens into a modest tiled courtyard with a single date palm growing in the center. I pause in the courtyard to light a lantern and lead Zayn to my accommodations for the night. There are a few lamps set up around the inn, but in my room, it's dark. Halfway up the wall, there is a large metal hook, and I hang the lantern on it.

The room itself is simple. It contains a small, low, wooden table on one side with a washbasin on it and a narrow wood frame bed. The accommodations are basic, but there is decorative stone latticework high in the wall that lets fresh air in from the courtyard.

Even as I'm closing the heavy wooden door behind us, Zayn is stepping into his role. He walks up behind me to press himself against me, running his paws across my stomach. His touch is gentle as he ruffles my fur. I turn around.

"You waste no time," I say to him.

He laughs, lightly toying with my pants. "I know how to handle someone like you."

I smile at that comment. I'm not sure comfortable is the right way to describe what I'm feeling. I already feel a little flush being in this little room alone with him. I wonder if he's really as excited as he seems or just good at this. The vest I'm wearing is buttoned up the front, and the moment I go to start undoing them, Zayn starts to loosen my pants. He has them down at my ankles before I undo the last button. He looks up at me, obviously trying to guess what I want to do first. The look in his eyes is plain: do I want to have him get on his knees, or do I plan to lead? Before he can take some action, I step away from the door, leaving my pants on the floor, and brush past him.

"Come," I say, going over to the bed, trailing a paw across his chest. I slip the vest off, and I pull off the shirt I am wearing, tossing it aside. The bed is small, but the inn at least provided me with some pillows for it. Zayn takes off his sash and pants, carefully folding them before he places them on the table. When he's done, the jackal comes over and gets on top of me to straddle me as I recline on the pillows. I'm already aroused, but I can feel myself stiffen further.

Slowly, he pulls off his vest and the undershirt while on top of me. His body is beautiful, and his shaft is already starting to peek out of its sheath. I stroke my large paws through his fur. My need aches with him sitting on my hips, and the jackal quivers at my touch. Yet, the moment I put my paws on him, things feel wrong. The jackal's fur is coarse, and yet underneath it, I can feel the tracing of scars against the flesh. Old scars and wounds cover his body on his back and sides. I frown to myself as I ruffle his fur.

"Are my attentions not to your liking?" Zayn asks. He's noticed the change in my demeanor.

"They are very much to my liking," I say. I run my paw up his back, feeling the subtle way the skin has been ripped up and healed, hidden by the coarse fur. "You have been whipped before?"

Zayn looks away the moment I ask the question, and his ears lower quickly for a second before he looks back at me. "Once, yes."

I stroke my paw carefully through the fur. "Why?"

Zayn tickles my tummy, making me squirm, trying to distract me. "It was a long time ago; I had a rough time growing up."

I close my eyes and rub up and down the jackal's side, making Zayn squirm. I trace over the scars again before letting go. "You had such a rough time growing up so that you were whipped multiple times?" I ask when I open my eyes and look straight up at him. There are too many scars for this to be a single occurrence.

Zayn growls at me. "I don't have to be here. If my body does not please you, I can leave."

"These are not the scars of a prostitute," I respond.

Zayn sighs and looks away again, thinking before he looks back at me. "It was a long time ago and not something I want to talk about." The jackal leans down to lick my nose. "Now, will you stop asking questions and let us continue this? You're going soft on me."

There is something more to him I don't know. "You don't have to do this," I whisper. "We can just talk." The scars tell a story I want to know.

Zayn chuckles. "I want to," he says. I wonder if his reassurance is real or part of the job. He doesn't give me long to question that, because he quickly draws me into a kiss. When I press my tongue up against him, he deepens the kiss and lets me explore his muzzle. I can feel his fingers starting to wrap around my cock, running up and down it. I shift my weight underneath him, and when he breaks off the kiss, I reach up to trace the line of his muzzle.

He smiles down at me before he sits up in my lap, leaving my hardening cock pressed against his rear. Lithe, powerful, and seductive, he's beautiful. Looking over the jackal's tawny pelt, I can almost forget what lies underneath it. I gently trace my paw down his thigh, toward his groin, and along his cock. He whines with need and presses himself back harder, paws going up behind his head to show off his stomach. I squeeze his shaft a little to see what type of response I get out of him.

He shivers, letting his stomach muscles roll. "See, isn't this better?" he murmurs. He lifts himself up a little and sits down, forcing my hardness to trace the cleft of his ass, his tongue lolling out of his muzzle. What he is doing is just making me want him even more; I need to feel him wrapped around my cock. He senses that, because as if on cue, he's reaching back behind himself. I don't even see where he gets the oil from with him balanced on my chest, but I can smell it. The next time his paw touches me, he's stroking my shaft with the lubricating oil. I feel myself gasp at his touch, but that only causes him to start smirking.

The jackal pushes up and positions himself so that I feel myself pressed up against his hole. A split second later, I'm sinking into him as he sits down. He consumes all of me with no restraint then pulls himself up to start a riding rhythm. All I can do is grab his hips and hold onto him as he starts bouncing on my slickened member. I close my eyes and just feel him work me. It's everything I thought he would be.

The sensation is wonderful. Each stroke is like heaven, and the room fades out of my perception. All I can feel is Zayn, and I don't want to let this moment go. The bed is groaning loudly in protest, but I barely notice. I find myself panting hard as I rise up to meet his body. He's hot against me, and each stroke pushes me closer to the edge of release. It stretches on seemingly forever, but finally, I feel a quickening in my own pulse and his rhythms. I press myself into him as hard and deep as I can, and I feel myself explode. He stiffens at first and then lets his body relax as I settle back on the bed.

As I collapse spent, I realize he hasn't come yet, so I wrap my fingers around his cock again. He squirms a little and gives off a needy moan. With one paw holding his thighs down, I work my hand over his hard canine knot, grinding my spent shaft against his rear.

He barks a little and screws his eyes shut. It doesn't take much effort on my part until his tongue is lolling out of his muzzle. With a yip, the jackal shoots onto my stomach, almost hitting me in the face.

"Someone enjoyed that," I say, spent and exhausted.

He pants, out of breath. "Yes."

We stay this way for a few minutes, sharing the afterglow before he gets off of me. Cleaning up with a towel and a small jug of water Zayn fetches for us, I wonder if he's going to leave now, but he doesn't make any effort to. Afterward, we lie on the bed with him on top of me. I run my claws through his fur as I breathe in his scent. He's warm, and I have my muzzle buried between his ears. We're both tired, but I still have questions. Idly I've been tracing the scars across his back.

"Really, how did you get these scars?" I ask him.

He doesn't say anything at first. I wonder if he has fallen asleep, but then he speaks.

"I was paid well by a traveler passing through town who enjoyed using the whip. He beat me pretty badly, and at the end of the night handed me a purse full of gold. I spent the next few weeks recuperating."

I shake my head. "Some people think only of themselves. I'm sorry that happened to you."

"Yes," he responds coolly, "but I'm not the only one with scars under their fur either. How did you acquire a jagged scar like the one on your flank?"

I'm a little surprised he noticed that, but I tell him the story. "Knife fight. I got ambushed while working as a guard back in Aksu. My assailant was quick and managed to slice me open good, but he wasn't quick enough once I pulled my sword. He ended up dead."

I feel him stiffen. "What is it you exactly do?" he asks me.

"I'm a hired swordsman. I generally do guard work, but I've also done caravan work before. I try to be discerning about who I work for."

I feel him relax a little. "Of course. You have to be with that type of work."

I want to talk to him more, but I'm tired, worn from traveling and worn from what we just did. Instead, I just hold him. We drift off to sleep together shortly after that.

Sunlight is filling the room as I recheck my pack. It's getting toward mid-morning as I finish getting my gear together. Zayn left at dawn, wishing me well on my journey, and since then, I have been alone with my thoughts. I went out to buy supplies for the last leg of my trip before returning to get my things together. I am trying not to dwell on the jackal, but my mind keeps drifting back to him. The old road up to the pass will take me away from here and back to Khalin on the other side of the mountains. I may never come back through this town again. If so, I would never see Zayn again, and for some reason, that bothers me.

Absently, I stroke my left flank, feeling the scar there. It was a very deep cut, and the fur has a subtle way of not growing right over the wound that slightly mars my pelt. I can still mentally feel the scars under his fur as I think back to touching him. Zayn has been whipped so that his fur wouldn't bear the marks of the beatings, yet the skin underneath carries the wounds. Whoever did that was careful not to ruin the jackal's looks.

I shake my head. Something about the story doesn't sit right with me, but who am I to judge? We've all got scars we don't want to talk about, including me. Lucky for me, not all of mine are visible.

"You're growing soft, Naji," I mutter, as I stand looking over the items I have with me. Years of working as a hired blade and I would think something like this wouldn't bother me. I've killed people before, but I try to maintain a sense of honor about my work. Some of the jobs I had to take when I first started out made that impossible to do. Now that I've established a good reputation, I no longer do that kind of work.

I sigh to myself. Crossing the desert without a camel has been very draining, and being alone out in the sand can play tricks on your mind. I did a lot of thinking on my way here, and I'll do a lot of thinking on my way to Aksu. I've done a lot of hurrying from place to place in my life, always moving, always keeping busy, looking for my next job. It's kept me going, and it's kept me alive, yet it's getting harder to keep things in the past behind me.

Maybe I should give myself a little time to breathe right now. I can leave tomorrow; there's no pressing reason for me to be back in Aksu immediately, and just maybe, I can see Zayn again.

A Repeat Customer
(Zayn)

The weight of the silver dirhams feels good as I play with the coins in my hand. Three silver is an excellent night for me. Sometimes, in the middle of summer when the heat is at its hottest, I am lucky to make that in a week. Making that in a single night? That is a blessing.

The coins are new too. They barely have any wear on them at all. Most of the money we see out here is old and worn. You only get coins this new if you trade in the markets of Aksu, but most of the caravans headed for Aksu pass south of us, traversing a low pass in the mountains to get to the great city. Some do stop here first to trade, but the majority of the traffic we see is from caravans heading north that wish to bypass the Sultanate of Khalin. I've always wondered what Aksu is like, but these coins will be the closest to that great city I ever get.

I close my eyes as I lay on my bed, head dangling off the side. I am transported back to last night. I remember the concern on the hyena's face as he traced his paws across my scars. Few of my clients notice them. Even fewer care. It's nice to occasionally have someone who does.

I can also remember the feeling of his hard cock pressing into me, the heat of his need warm inside me. I vividly recall the way his paw pads against my shaft made me quiver. The fact he actually made me cum? It's touching. Almost no one cares if the sex is pleasurable for the whore.

I open my eyes, and I'm back in the present. My shaft is peeking out of its sheath, and I'm lying on the bed I often conduct business on. The light coming through the opened shutters is soft and fills the barren room. The bed is the center-piece of the space. The majlis the bedroom opens onto is just a place for me to entertain my guests before things get serious. Their comfort is what matters, not mine.

I roll over on the broad bed, sinking back against the pil-lows. The faded scent of encounters past filters to my nose. The rich fabrics are perfumed with jasmine and amber to hide any lingering smells, but I can still sort out the scents if I con-centrate.

I make my living servicing the needs of men like Naji, but it can be hard to always have enough money to buy food. While the hyena was a good customer, I doubt very much I will ever see him again. I do have some regular customers I see when they pass through town, but I can tell the hyena isn't going to be one of them. He's not a trader, so it's unlikely he'll come this way again.

I put the coins back into my purse. I should be okay for a bit. I have enough right now, and I can actually give myself a day off. Standing up, I look myself over. I cleaned up when I came home, but I could use an actual bath. It's a luxury I rarely can afford, so this will be a real treat.

The next dance won't be for a few days anyway, so unless a caravan passes through today, I won't have any customers. Usman, the cheetah who arranges the dances, will let me know if anyone needs my services. Tomorrow I will get back to plying my trade, but today is a day for just me.

≈

The smell of meat grilling makes my muzzle water.

"How much for a kebab?" I ask Amare, the wolf who runs the stand.

He looks up from the charcoal fire, finally noticing my presence. A small frown lights on his muzzle. We go back a few years, but it's not always been pleasant. We used to be friends once, before I started dancing. Since then, he's been distant to me, but sometimes he comes to my house at night, desperate for what I can offer him. As far as I know, he's never ever visited any of the girls in town.

"Three copper," he grunts.

"Three? For what little you paid me last time, you expect me to pay even two?"

He coughs. "If you want, I can charge you four."

"Amare…"

He shrugs. "No one has brought chickens to town this week. Kebabs are three coppers today."

"How about two for five?" I ask hopefully.

The wolf considers. "I can do that."

With a quick exchange of money, he hands me over two kebabs of seasoned chicken. I take them, thank Amare, and leave him where he is set up in the small square at the center of our village.

While I walk over to the caravanserai, I nibble the tender meat carefully off of the kebabs. The seasoning is rich and flavorful with paprika and cumin playing across my tongue.

At the gate, I wave to the guard. The jackal who is on duty nods as I head through the narrow gate into the courtyard beyond. Zaptu is small, and everyone knows me here. Sadly, some of the villagers tend to shy away from me. There are no secrets here, but not everyone approves of what I do. They think it makes me less of a man. A few of them do partake in my services, but most of my business comes from people passing through.

On a day like today, it's quiet. Last night's travelers have already taken to the road, and without a major caravan in town trading, mid-morning at the caravanserai has lapsed into a sleepy daze. A few merchants are out, hawking their wares under awnings above niches built into the courtyard's walls. Most seem bored, but in the back, an old, female golden jackal is vigorously haggling for spices with a fennec.

The sun, still climbing into the sky, will keep down traffic until the heat of the day starts to fade. After my bath, I plan to return home to sleep away the afternoon heat.

The small hammam inside the caravanserai is located in the back of structure. It's deserted when I arrive. I pay the attendant half a silver dirham for the treat and then wait while he draws water from the well and perfumes it for me. Finally, I get to slip into a small tub of warm water and let myself settle to the bottom. I'm told our small bath is nothing compared to the ornate baths in Aksu, but I greatly appreciate that I have the option to soak and scrub my fur when I can afford to.

Slowly and methodically, I work my paws through my pelt with the soap, flushing the dust and dirt out of it. I let no spot go untouched, and when I finally get out the tub, the water has turned murky from the accumulated dust and sand that's come off of me. Afterward, I towel down and proceed to gently brush out my fur. I have to push the comb through my tail repeatedly before I can get all of the tangles out of it. It has been a while since I've had the spare coin, but the tedious task of brushing myself makes me feel relaxed and puts some wag into my tail. I am completely dry by the time I put my clothes back on, a large clump of sandy-colored fur on the ground the result of my efforts.

It's getting towards early afternoon when I leave the hammam. I buy a sweet pastry from one of the vendors and sit by the well in the corner of the courtyard to eat.

I hear footsteps approaching me. "I saw your dance last night, Zayn," says a familiar voice, as I'm finishing the pastry. "You keep getting better."

I look up and smile at Nawra. The jackal is wearing a long robe of rough wool cloth with her dark tan tail wagging behind her. She has her six-month-old daughter in her arms, a spitting image of her mother.

"I am still not as good as you."

She shrugs and sits down next to me. With her is Farida the cheetah, Usman's wife. She's wearing a kaftan of rich red fabric. She always has first choice of the fabrics her husband purchases, and she makes good use of that selection to dress well.

"I think you've mastered everything I could ever hope to teach you," Nawra says. "You even have learned some things I don't know. I am increasingly impressed with what you can do with that sword."

"Only under your tutelage have I been able to get this good."

She smiles. "You flatter me, but I won't be dancing anymore."

Farida laughs and sits next to Nawra. "Not with a kit this rambunctious. You won't have time!" She holds out a hand and the pup grabs at her finger, cooing happily.

"Amal is well behaved."

"This is the easy part," says the cheetah. "Wait till she gets older."

Nawra tilts her head. "Where are your two cubs anyway, Farida?"

The cheetah looks up and glances across the courtyard towards Usman's stall. "I left them to terrorize Usman." She squints. "It looks like it's working."

I laugh. "He loves those two."

"Not when he's trying to sell, but I get tired of chasing them."

Nawra bounces her daughter on her knee. The pup squeals in delight. "I appreciate you making the blanket for Amal, Farida."

"Oh, don't think anything of it," she replies. "You would have done the same for me."

"Still, you didn't have to. I could have gotten some wool and homespun some cloth."

The cheetah shakes her head. "Cotton is better when they're young. She's a growing pup anyway. You'll have plenty of other garments to make for her."

"Speaking of sheep, how do you like the life of a shepherd instead of the one of a dancer?" I ask Nawra.

She frowns and glances toward the stage area in the courtyard. "The flock is doing well, although we'll need to move them soon to find better grazing. I miss the dancing, but I don't miss the men. Sina and I aren't rich, but I think we're doing okay." She shrugs. "I made what I could from it," she says, rubbing one of the silver bangles she's wearing. "You can't do it forever."

"That's true," says Farida. "Someday you will stop dancing yourself, Zayn. It is not an easy path."

"No, it's not," I say. The scars on my back prove that.

"Speaking of the dances, Usman still has your sword," the cheetah adds.

"Yes, and I need to settle up with him for last night." I get up. "I will see you both later."

"Have a good day," says Nawra.

"Make sure the kids aren't driving Usman crazy," says Farida, before she turns back to Amal to coo at her. The puppy smiles big.

I make my way across the courtyard to the far side where Usman's stall is. He always holds my sword for me when I go off with a client after the dances, and I need to give him his cut for last night's work. He's sitting in the shade of his stall, going over some records when I walk over.

"Where are your cubs?" I ask him. "Farida said she left them over here for you to watch."

"Ha!" he says, pointing to the two of them as they run past playing tag. "You can see how well telling them to sit still is going."

I chuckle. "They're only four."

"I know, but sometimes it feels like only yesterday that they were born."

"I guess. The passage of time has been much slower for me." I've been working the dances for three and a half years now, and it's hard to remember sometimes what my life was like before I did. Usman's kids were still infants when I started. I decide to change the subject. "How's business going since you are stuck watching the cubs?" I ask.

He shrugs. "The usual. There was a little business in the morning, but mostly it's quiet in the afternoon. That said, you look quite happy today, I see."

"I treated myself to a bath," I say, pulling out a half silver coin and handing it to Usman. "Also, your share from last night."

He takes the coin and pulls out my kilij from where it is tucked in the back of his stand. The scabbard that protects the sword glints as he hands it to me. "You're always the most reliable of my girls."

"Of course," I say, with a wink. When I was still growing up, I used to run errands for him, picking up his fees from the dancers. Now that I dance myself, I always make sure he gets his cut. With him being one of the few friends I have, I make sure we're always on good footing. "I just wish I could earn more."

He smiles a little sadly. "Not everyone appreciates what you have to offer, but you are the most skilled of the group."

"Coming from you, that means a lot. Are there any caravans expected?"

"I have a reliable tip from one of the traders who passed through last night that one should be along in two or three days. That should bring you some business."

I grin. "Send any looking for the other side my way."

"Always," says the cheetah. "I should let you know," he adds, "your friend, Sarda, is passing through town. He said he has to head south quickly but was hoping you'd be available for a bit."

I feel my tail go still. Sarda is my most important client, and he pays me better than anyone. While I appreciate the money, sessions with him are always difficult for me.

"He came in last night?"

The cheetah nods. "He got in very late, well after midnight. He slept in so he can travel in the cooling night air. He went to see if you were available about half an hour ago."

"I see. I had best go and make myself available to him," I say with apprehension.

Usman looks at me for a moment before he nods. I can tell he wants to say something, but he's not sure what he should say. Usman doesn't know exactly what Sarda does to me, but he knows I don't take other clients immediately after the lion visits, sometimes for up to two weeks. If he actually knew what Sarda did, he would try and stop our sessions. I've debated telling him, but that much coin is hard to walk away from when you sometimes go hungry. Since Sarda arranges his sessions directly with me, I haven't had to tell Usman what I'm paid. The cheetah only asks for a cut for what people earn at the dances since he arranges them.

I start to walk off, but Usman finally speaks up. "Will you be by tomorrow?"

I pause and look back. "Probably not."

The cheetah purses his lips. "I know he can be demanding, but if you are not too tired, perhaps we can have tea in the evening. I bought some fresh tea from the east yesterday you might like to try."

I smile hollowly. "That would be great."

"Tomorrow, at dusk then?"

"I'll try and be there."

Usman knows I'm lying as I speak, because he squints at me. "You know—"

"Thank you, Usman. I'll be fine."

The look he gives me tells me he has begun to suspect what happens, but he won't stop me. "Tomorrow then," he says finally. "Take care of yourself, Zayn."

I nod and turn away, quietly padding out of the caravanserai. It is time to see my best client.

∼

I spot the lion before he sees me. He's sitting in the shade of my house, waiting patiently for me to return. His loose traveling clothes are dusty, but his mane is brushed out, glass beads woven into it. Sarda has broad shoulders, but he has developed a pudge as he's aged. Bits of gray have started to creep into his mane, and even though it's been less than two months since he last visited, I swear he is looking older and more worn.

He flashes his fangs though when he catches sight of me. He appears eager to see me, and I know what that means. Sarda outweighs me and is taller than me, and he uses that to his advantage in our encounters. "I was worried you would be out for the rest of the afternoon," he rumbles, pleased.

"You're back," I say to him. "I had not expected to see you so soon." I never know when he's going to pass through town, only that he does every few months.

"Indeed," Sarda says, tail lashing in anticipation for what is to come. "I did not expect to be back so soon, but I have business to attend to in Akara. Naturally, I couldn't miss an opportunity to see my favorite dancer."

I don't know if favorite is the right term for what we do, but he pays me more than anyone. I don't want to think of where I would be without him.

I pull out my wooden key, insert it into the lock, and lift the key so I can draw back the bolt holding the door closed. Retrieving the key, I let him inside before I close and secure the door. I set my sword down, hang the key on a hook, and light the lantern in the main room.

I feel Sarda's breath on my neck now that we are alone. He whispers into my ear. "You look well." Paws wrap around my shoulders.

I bob my head. "Money has been tight, but I've done well recently."

He ruffles the fur under my neck as he murmurs into my ear. "I trust you don't have any other appointments today?"

I shiver in apprehension and uncertainty. Sarda is always the dominant male when he's around me, but it isn't submission that makes me nervous. It's the lion himself and how he tries to break me.

"I don't."

A claw traces around one of my nipples. "Good." He slowly turns me around. "You never disappoint me," he says, hot breath on my face, as he holds up two gold dinars. "I hope you won't mind if I indulge tonight. Last time, I was too worn out to enjoy all that you offer."

I take the money. The coins are heavy in my paw, as I force a grin. "Of course not." Two gold dinars is a lot, even for Sarda. That's eight times what Naji paid me. There is no mistaking what he wants from me now. I already know Usman will be disappointed when I don't have tea with him tomorrow, but he can't know. He must never know for sure. If he complains, I will tell him the money was too good. Maybe he'll believe that half-truth.

Sarda smiles then, and it is not a kind smile, but the smile of one about to do something that he knows is wrong. "Good."

"Did you want some wine?" I ask him.

"Just a small glass if you don't mind. I find it dulls the sensations if I have too much."

I nod in submissive acknowledgment. "Of course," I say. When he releases me, I walk over to the chest where I keep a few bottles for my discerning clients. I pull out one of the better bottles and a clay cup. I uncork it, letting the pleasant smell drift to my nose as I pour some into the clay goblet. I can hear the lion moving around the room as I do this, and when I turn around, he's taken up residence on the divan. I walk over and bow, handing him the goblet.

"Your wine," I say.

He rumbles in thanks as he takes the goblet and brings it to his muzzle to lap at it. Afterward, he sets it down on the low table in front of my divan, his eyes looking at me hungrily.

I know the routine and start undressing without him asking. Any clothing I have on Sarda will destroy. Once I'm naked, I stand there, paws clasped behind my back, looking down at the floor.

Sarda gets up and walks around me, circling his prey. "You look so broken, Zayn. Is it because you know your place is under me?"

"I am just tired. I had work to conduct last night." I have limits on how far I'm willing to take Sarda talking down to me, and on this point, I am not willing to compromise.

"Always the industrious one," he says from behind me. I can hear the rustling of fabric as he pulls something out of his robes. He gets closer to whisper into my ear. "I like that about you," he says, as he begins to bind my hands together with rope. A paw traces my side and squeezes my rump roughly. "Shall we proceed? I do need to make good time today."

I steel myself for what is about to happen. "Of course."

He leads me into my bedroom where he pushes me down onto the floor. I can hear him whistling as he exits the room and takes his time getting ready. I wait for Sarda. I can hear the sound of the cup being picked up and set back down on the table. I know he delays so as to try and make me nervous, but I already know what he wants.

In a few minutes I hear his padded footsteps on my floor as he walks back in. I could turn to see him, but I don't bother. I know he doesn't want me looking back.

"As ripe for the taking as always," he says with a throaty growl. He cracks his whip, and my ears instinctively go flat. The beating he paid me to take is about to begin.

As the first crack of the whip falls across my back, I close my eyes. Sarda's money means I'll eat well for a month, even though it will take a week for the wounds to heal. When he's done savaging me, he'll fuck me, and then leave me here alone to lick my wounds. I grimace as another crack falls across my back. I wish I didn't have to do this, but Sarda is my bread and butter. He is my patron, and he gets what he wants.

As another stroke of the lash falls across my back, I cry in pain and pull against my bindings. Even though the money is good, I never have gotten used to doing this. It will be over soon. I just need to grin and bear it.

I'm sitting on the floor of my bedroom, gingerly leaning a shoulder against the wall. My back stings from multiple open wounds, and my rear feels like it's been through a long night of work. Now that Sarda is done, I just want to lie down on my bed, but my wounds are still bleeding. Instead, I lean for a bit.

"I must be off now," the lion says, walking back up to me after dressing.

"Of course," I groan. "Safe travels."

He kneels down in front of me. "When I finish, perhaps I can see you on the return."

I look up at him, trying to blink away the tears in my eyes from the pain.

He reads my expression and laughs. "We can do something less exotic then. I have some new rope techniques I wouldn't mind trying on you." He fishes something out of his coin purse and removes another gold dinar. "For being such a good companion. I know I pushed you hard today," he says, holding it up.

I reach up and take the dinar. Sarda leans forward to lick my nose and gets up. Without another word, he lets himself out of the house, leaving me alone.

I stay there for a while, clutching the gold coin in my paw. This is what my life is—an endless struggle to survive. Even when the times are good, I'm nursing myself back to health, always making sure I keep something aside for when times are lean.

Sarda was rough this time, and my body aches so badly right now it's almost unbearable. The extra gold dinar is to cover any lost wages, and extra income to cover the deep cuts in my flesh. I growl and fling the coin across the room. It hits the wall with a dull thwack, knocking loose plaster, and rolls under the bed. It might be dented now, but nobody will care when I go to spend it.

Slumping back against the wall, I rest, trying to get my strength back. I should get up and clean myself up, but I don't have the energy. The bath I took earlier today is now wasted. A few tears stain the fur by my eyes, but I wipe them away. I'm not going to feel sorry for myself.

My whole back itches and burns from all the little cuts. The whip Sarda uses doesn't maim my fur, but it cuts right through it to the skin. The poultice I have will help it heal once I get the energy together to use it. The scarring? Well, it comes with the line of work, I guess. Now that I know how to treat it, it doesn't seem to be getting worse, but after a session like this, I'll likely have some more.

The money will last for a month, and if I'm careful, I can stretch it out even longer. Nawra and Farida are right though. I can't dance forever. I know one day these scars aren't going to heal, and I'm going to be unable to work. What I'm going to do then, I don't know. Until then, I will survive.

Crimson Lines
(Naji)

It is a rare treat for me to have time to waste in my life. The innkeeper is kind enough to lend me a book of poetry, so I spend the heat of the day reading in the shade under the date palm in the inn's courtyard. It's an old book, but the words upon the pages are timeless. The poet speaks passionately about his beloved, and I take the time to savor his work.

It is only when the sun is starting to set that I head back up to the caravanserai. Long shadows cross my path as I walk, and I wonder if Zayn will be there. I don't know what type of schedule the jackal keeps, but he might be around. Even if he's not, I need to stretch and there's no other place in town to go.

The guard at the gate of the caravanserai is different from last night's guard. He's an older wolf with the broad stocky frame of a warrior. He nods at me when I approach and waves me by. Inside, things are quiet. There are a few merchants in one corner talking, while another is packing up his wares for the night. I wander around the courtyard, watching, as some people tend to a few camels. The crowd from last night has been replaced with the orderly process of business. I stop at one stall, run by a cheetah, to look over the goods he's selling. It looks like he's already packed a few things up in the back of the stall, but he's got some cookware lying out still. Nothing catches my eye that I would want to carry back home over the mountains.

"Ah, you are still in town, I see. I thought the caravan left in the morning," he remarks to me. It takes me a moment to place him, but I recognize him as the one running the dances last night.

"Oh, I wasn't with them. I've been traveling alone."

The cheetah gives me an appraising look. He's lanky and a little older with some gray in his black fur. "Not many lone travelers out there, but some people make the journey by themselves. I know it can be dangerous to travel the sands alone."

I shrug. "I tend to be more worried about raiders than the dunes themselves, but anyone who thinks I'm an easy mark will find that assumption wrong."

He nodded. "You heading north or south?"

"West actually, over the pass."

"Oh. Heading over the mountains would be the quickest way to Aksu. Not many take it because it's a steep climb. Negotiating the trail with pack animals can be a challenge, I've heard."

"No one from here takes it?"

"A few people do, but I haven't ever done it myself. There's nothing out that way until you cross the mountains. Then you see farming communities in the high valleys on the other side. There's no water until you reach the high pass."

"Thanks," I say. "I wanted to ask, are dances like last night very common here?"

"I usually arrange something once a week, depending on how many caravans are passing through town. Why, looking for more entertainment?"

"It hadn't crossed my mind actually," I say.

He shrugs. "As you wish. Just let me know what your taste is, and I can find you something different from last night."

"I'll remember that." I consider for a moment. Something doesn't sit right with me. "You arrange all the clients for the dancers?"

The cheetah frowns. "I only arrange the dances themselves, but I forward everyone business. We're a small town and sometimes there is no coin to be had for anyone. I've been through my own lean times, so I ask only for a small cut for myself after I pay the musicians."

"What about for Zayn?"

"What about him?"

My eyes narrow. "Well, he has scars…."

He blinks. "Scars?"

"On his back. He's got scars under his fur."

His eyes narrow and his whiskers twitch. "How many?"

"A number of them. I assume he was whipped before he came here?"

"Zayn was born in Zaptu. I knew his parents before they passed." The cheetah looks down at his shaking hands. "God forgive me, I should have known." He clasps them to try and keep them steady.

"What do you mean?"

"Zayn had a client earlier today, Sarda, who seems to favor him. I've not been able to figure out what he does to Zayn, but I never see him right after he visits."

"How rough is this guy?" I growl. "Have you never thought to ask?"

"I don't know," the cheetah says, his voice cracking. "Whenever I bring up Sarda, Zayn has always dodged my questions. I told Zayn when he started dancing the coin would not be as good as the others, but I was not going to take away his hope. He is stubborn and insisted on finding out himself."

I can feel my stomach turning. "So, this has been going on for a while?"

"I think so. I should have figured out this was what was going on. I told him he needed to be careful, but I had no idea it would come to this."

My paw falls to my sword hilt naturally. "Where are they?"

"They would be at Zayn's house, but Sarda may have already left. I know he likes to travel at night when it's cooler." He looks at my paw on the kilij. "I know you may be thinking of doing something rash, but I should warn you, Sarda is well connected."

I let go of the sword. "So, what are you going to do?"

He frowns. "I'm not sure there is much I can do right now. Sarda is a friend of the Emir. I need proof before I can petition."

I don't know anything about the Emir of Zaptu, but I know that connection makes this more complicated. The cheetah's words could fall on deaf ears. "Let me go for you," I offer.

"What good would that do? A wanderer from the sands has no say here."

"I can wait until Sarda is gone and talk to Zayn. I will find out the truth for you."

He considers, tail lashing behind himself. "Zayn will probably turn you away at his door, but he won't talk to me about this. He might talk to someone else. Whatever you find, nothing must happen to the lion. You aren't prepared for that kind of trouble."

I grit my teeth, but I know Usman is right. The politically connected are always dangerous to confront. "I promise nothing will happen to him."

"When you finish, no matter what happens, come back here and let me know. If I'm not here, talk to the guard at the gate. Tell him you have a message for Usman, and then let him know what you found. He's a friend of mine and will let me know what you say. Is this okay with you, yena?"

I nod. "I can do that for you."

"Good. I pray that my fears are wrong, but I fear that my prayers are for naught."

The cheetah tells me how to find Zayn's house. There is a great sadness in his expression as he does. I thank him and head off toward the golden jackal's house, unsure of what awaits me there.

⁂

It doesn't take me long to reach Zayn's house. As the cheetah described, it lies on the edge of town. The mudbrick home has a faded blue door and shutters, the paint flaking off in many places due to the sun. The house itself, while larger than some of the other houses in town, looks older. The squat structure is quiet, but in the growing dark of night, I can see light leaking from around one of the shuttered windows.

I pause by the door, considering what the cheetah said. If Zayn is still with Sarda, I don't want to disturb him and arouse any suspicions. Swiveling my ears carefully, I don't hear anything to suggest the lion is here, but I can't be sure. After listening for a minute, I finally knock, using the hanger set into the battered wood.

Inside, I hear a little shuffling. "Who's there?" Zayn calls out.

"It's me, Naji", I say. There is silence for a few moments.

"Why are you still here?" he asks.

"It's a long climb up in the mountains. I decided to take a day to rest. I thought perhaps you might like company."

There is silence again. It doesn't sound like he's moving to get the door. "Now?" finally comes the exasperated response.

Is he with his client the cheetah spoke to me about? "Is now not a good time?" I ask through the door.

"Now is certainly not a good time. Who told you where to find me anyway?"

"The cheetah who runs the dances told me when I pressed him. Should I come back tomorrow?" I inquire. "I was planning to leave in the morning."

He growls at me through the door. "Why the fuck did Usman tell you where I live? He knows I don't want more business."

"He told me that also."

"Then you can go tell Usman then I'm fine."

"It's hard to tell a man you're fine if you won't open the door. He is worried."

I don't get a response. After a moment of silence, I hear the sound of movement and the door opens inward. I step into the room and Zayn closes the door unceremoniously behind me. He looks displeased to see me. His scowl isn't what catches my attention though—it's the scents in the air. There is the distinct tang of blood in the room. I sniff to process what my nose is telling me. The smell of sex is there and someone else's scent too, but it is blood that permeates the space.

Zayn is standing before me naked. The fur is matted on the sides of his chest and stomach. A lantern is hanging in the back of the room, and as I study Zayn, I can see a crimson tinge along his flanks, mixed into his tawny fur. He starts to say something to me, but I reach out and grab his shoulders to turn him around.

"It's fine!" he yells at me, but I ignore his protest. His back is a mess, the fur matted with blood. I turn him toward the light, and I can see fine cuts underneath. Most of them appear to have closed, but a few are still oozing blood.

"What happened?" I ask him.

"I had a customer," he snaps, as he turns around to face me. "He's fond of the whip."

My heart sinks. "You said this happened only once."

His ears lower. "So, I lied," he says. "People are paying me for a good time. Usually they have me face down in a pillow or on my knees. It's rare for someone to notice the scars under my fur. If they ask, I tell them a half truth about it."

I'm shocked he willingly puts himself into this situation. What type of bastard does this to someone? "How often does this happen?" I ask.

He rolls his eyes. "Every few months when Sarda passes through town. He pays well. Two gold dinars usually. Generally, I don't make much at the dances. They pay less for men than woman. Plus, the work is intermittent. You're the best customer I've had in a month's time. This is the only way I've found I can guarantee I can afford to eat."

Usman said Zayn is independent, and I can see that. It's not just his body posture that tells me that, but the hardness in his gaze. He's clearly in pain, his paw is pressed to his side, but his eyes are clear and focused on me. He is stubborn. He doesn't want me interfering. "No one should be this desperate."

He snorts. "Spare me the sympathy. Life is not easy."

I gawk at him. "And this is what you call a life? Being beaten because of someone's whims?"

The jackal snarls at me, both in pain and frustration. "He's careful. He never whips me more than I can take, and he makes sure not to leave visible scars. You think I like being someone else's dark sexual gratification?"

"No, but this doesn't have to be your life," I say. "Usman can help you."

"Usman has already helped me far more than he should have. I need to be able to stand on my own, and this is the life I have here."

"You've got to find a better life than this."

He squints at me. "And who is going to help me do that? You?"

"I don't know, but this, this is not living. This is dying slowly."

"I'm sure there are men who would be happy to take me away from here to be their little house boy," he snarls, "but I will never submit to that. At least out here I support myself."

"At what cost? You know what this is doing to you. Those scars will only get worse."

He lifts his paw from his side where he's had it clutched. There is blood on his pads, and he studies it. "It's what I have."

"You can find work that doesn't require you to sacrifice your blood to the whip."

"If only."

"At least let me dress your wounds."

He considers for a moment before he says anything. "That would be good. There is only so much I can do back there on my own."

As he steps away from me to fetch something, I finally look around his house. It's very sparse. The first room is set up as a majlis. There is a lush divan covered with pillows and a low table for serving drinks, but little else. A single faded wall tapestry with geometric designs hangs over the divan. A rug has been placed before the divan, and while comfortable and inviting, it doesn't fill up the room. The rest of the room is bare besides a cabinet Zayn is pulling things from. The hearth looks cold and barely used. Only a few cooking utensils sit near it, collecting dust.

Zayn returns carrying some poultice in a jar, a clean rag, and a bowl with water. He hands them to me. "Here." He glances toward the couch piled high with pillows. "Let me lie down on the bed so you can put that on," he suggests.

I nod in agreement and Zayn walks through an arched doorway into his bedroom. The room also seems like it once contained more furniture than it does now. There is a trunk at the foot of the bed, and a table placed nearby. The bed itself is broad and pillows are stacked on one end against the headboard. Two ropes are hanging from the headboard. I want to ask about this, but I bite back the comment.

He gets on the bed after placing an old cloth on top of it and lies down on his stomach. I get on the bed after him. The mattress is softer than I expect it to be, packed with quality straw. I start by cleaning the scratches. The rag quickly turns pink from the blood on his back. Under my strong paws, he whines and growls as I rub poultice into his wounds, but only when the pain is too much for him. As I work, I glance back up at the headboard. How many other men have had him on this bed? Do they often tie him down, or are the ropes just for this special customer of his?

When I'm done, I sit back and look over my handiwork. The wounds look better at least. I get up from the bed and he follows my lead.

"Thank you," he says stiffly.

"You're welcome," I say. "Should I leave you to rest now?" I don't know what else I can do but tell the guard what I've found. Only time will heal his wounds.

He scratches at an ear. "Yes. Will you be leaving in the morning?"

"I guess. I need to set out at some point on the mountain road into Khalin."

"You are going to Aksu?"

"Yes. I am going home."

He closes his eyes and sighs. "You want to help me? You really want to help me?"

"If there is something I can do, yes."

He's quiet for a moment. "There's little left for me here, and if you think I deserve better, help me get there." He opens his eyes and stares at me. "Take me to Aksu. Show me where there is a job I can do that doesn't put me on my knees."

I open my mouth and close it. "Wh…at?"

"Take me to Aksu."

Aksu's streets are vibrant and full of opportunity, but they are not without their own challenges. "I can do that, but what will you do when you get there?" I ask cautiously.

His ears lower. "I don't know. Maybe what I do now? The coin would be better I imagine."

My mind races thinking. "I'm sure you can do better."

"Maybe, but I survive. It's what I do."

"You can do more than just survive."

He shrugs. "Well?"

This is not a development I expected. "You should talk to Usman first. I am in no particular hurry to leave town, but I do know once you leave, you may never return here. The journey is not dangerous, but it is not one you will want to make by yourself. Aksu is very different than Zaptu."

Zayn's gaze hardens. "As I said, I survive."

I know what desperation does to people. I've felt it myself, yet I don't know if this is desperation or if I am an opportunity to leave he's never had before. "If that's what you wish, I can help you. I have a friend, Fadel, who has connections. He even employs some entertainers himself. He will know what you can do, but you will need to sort out your affairs before we leave first."

His ears perk. "I can do that. I will talk to Usman first."

"Good."

He walks over to the door to let me out and pauses. ""Why did you come here?" he asks me.

"I told Usman about the scars."

He frowns. "I see. Well, he was going to find out at some point."

"Why didn't you tell him?"

"He already has done so much for me. I do not wish to rely on him for everything."

I'm not sure what I can say to that. Even though he is in pain, he stands up straight to carry himself with pride. Zayn reminds me so much of the close friend I lost it hurts. He too was proud and strong, but he is gone. Only the memories are what I have, and when you're alone in the desert, sometimes regrets are all you can think about.

"You know where I'll be staying," I say, and Zayn lets me out of the house. He quietly closes the door behind me, leaving me in the cool night air.

❧

I turn over what happened in my head all night and the next morning. When I run out of questions for myself, and with nothing better to do, I return to the book of poetry, the spiraling lines of verse echoing in my head. The sun is high in the sky before anyone comes looking for me. The small courtyard of the inn is deserted. The innkeeper is somewhere inside, hiding from the midday heat. The shade of the lone date palm in the courtyard is at least a welcome addition, and I sit under it on top of a carpet.

I am reading a passage I read yesterday that talks of the joys of pure love when I hear the click of paws on the tile. Looking up, I see the cheetah from the caravanserai coming up to me.

"I wondered if you would be hard to find, but I see that is not so. Zayn says you go by the name of Naji?"

I set the book down. "That I do, but I'm not trying to hide or anything," I say, looking up at him. "I'm surprised to see you though."

He waits, and when I gesture, he sits down on the carpet next to me. "I thought we should talk," he says.

"Zayn told you he wants to leave Zaptu?" I ask.

"Yes, yes he did. We had a long conversation last night about Sarda."

"Has he changed his mind?" I don't really expect the jackal to leave with me. I've thought about this, and while he might be better off in Aksu, this is his home. Usman, though, shakes his head.

"He told me it was better he leave. There are too many memories for him here."

I'm taken aback by this. "There are?"

"Generally, people only dance for a few years. He picked it up not long after he turned eighteen. It's not easy for a man to do that. People think it makes him less than a man."

"That's nonsense."

He chuckles, amused. "Oh, I know, but Zayn is only twenty-two. He's still got some of that youthful stubbornness going for him."

"I see. You don't approve of him leaving, do you?"

The cheetah leans forward. "I blame myself for not having the coin to hire him, but even if I did, he wasn't going to let me. Zayn followed an all too familiar path for me, and I know that no matter what he does now, people will remember." He lifts up his hands. "You see this gray here?"

"Yes."

"Age does this to you, but when I was young, I used to be quite a dancer myself back in the day. It's been years, but there are people here who still think I'm less than a man because of that. I even have two cubs, but that's all they see. I'm told that in Aksu, people don't have time to care about each other's personal lives."

"A few do, but there is a community of people like myself. We call ourselves mithly. If you know what the risks are though, why do you run the dances?"

"We are a poor town. We always have been, and we maybe always will be. The Emir collects taxes, but he has little extra after upkeep for the caravanserai. Our lifeblood comes from the caravans. I took over the dances so I could have some control, to try and create a better space than the one I used to work in." He sighs. "There are limits to what I can do."

"I gather there have been problems like Sarda before."

"There are always problems like Sarda, but he is going to be a particularly difficult one. I believe he lives in the town south of us, but I know he is a friend of our Emir. Sarda always favored Zayn, but his tastes are dark. I don't know what he will do if Zayn is not here, but the most I can do is warn the other dancers not to accept his coin. I don't have the ear of the Emir."

"It is not healthy to treat someone like that."

"Of course not, but Zayn always took coin for his lashings. Even if the lion wasn't the Emir's friend, that limits what recompense Zayn could seek."

That's not right, but I don't know what can be done. I am just a stranger here. "I have a friend who I believe can help Zayn find some work. He has connections. He won't have to sell himself."

He considers me. "I would ask you if he should trust you, but that is pointless. Only the most insidious of liars are willing to suggest they may be lying. Those are the people who can lie to you so blatantly and yet so convincingly that you still believe their lies."

My ears perk at that. It's a keen observation. "Wisdom does not come easy. It must be learned."

"Indeed. I must get back to my stand. Zayn has some business he wants to attend to today, but he told me he should be ready by mid-morning tomorrow."

I'll need to get some extra supplies for the journey then. "Then have him meet me at the gate of the caravanserai."

The cheetah nods and gets up. "I'll let him know." He holds out a hand. I get up and take the outstretched paw. We exchange cheek kisses.

"I wish you both a safe journey," says Usman.

"Thank you," I say, and he turns and walks away, leaving me alone in the courtyard with the book of poetry. I sit back down and pick it back up. I flip it open to where I had stopped reading. The destined lovers in the poem talk about how they were meant for each other, but is life ever like that? Is it ever so easy that two people will meet and fall in love and that all will be simple and good?

Maybe for someone else, but not for me. My fate is complex and ever changing, and right now my journey entails someone I hardly know.

❧

The guard at the caravanserai, the caracal from my first night, watches me for a while until he gets bored. He has dozed off a few times as the morning air warmed. Sitting in the shade of the caravanserai's wall, I play back the last day and a half in my mind. I didn't expect to be taking someone with me over the mountains when I came to Zaptu, but the company will be nice. What happens when we reach Aksu, though, will be interesting. I hope Fadel can help Zayn out.

Mid-morning passes, but the jackal still hasn't shown up yet. I wonder if I should go looking for him, but this is where I told Usman I would wait. As the minutes slip by, I wonder if Zayn has changed his mind. I purchased extra provisions for the jackal, so all I can do is wait see if he shows up.

Finally, with the noon sun having taken almost all of my shade, I see Zayn coming up the dusty road. He has a rough spun white kaftan on with brown pants underneath. In normal clothes he still looks handsome, his golden color fur bright against the neutral-colored clothing. On his hip he carries his sword, and on his back he has a pack.

"I'm sorry it took so long, but I wanted to have tea with Usman before leaving," he says. "I wanted to say goodbye to him, his wife, and their cubs."

"I understand. You two are close?" I'm not sure how Zayn really feels about Usman.

"To a degree. Usman has always been a father to me, but we've also had our disagreements. It was good to finally reconnect away from the pressures of life before I leave."

"He seems like he has his heart in the right place," I offer. Zayn just nods.

"Are you sure you want to do this?"

He looks back at the village, ears lowered. "Zaptu has been home, but it hasn't treated me like a home for a while now."

I remember leaving my home village the last time. I didn't realize at the time it would be forever. "Sometimes we outgrow the places we were born."

He turns back to me. "I guess I have."

"So, do you have room in your pack for supplies? Also, is that all you are bringing? I was wondering if I was going to have to try and buy a camel to make the climb with us."

"There is a little room still," he says, taking a wrapped bundle of food that's been sitting next to me. He puts the pack down to shove it in. "This is all that I have left."

He's really doing this. I keep wondering how serious he is about it. "You sold the house?"

"Usman gave me what he could for it. It's not much, but he'll find someone in town who needs it eventually. If I am going to do this, I might as well go all in."

I'm a little floored by the fact he just sold his house. "So that's it then. No turning back?" I ask, reaching for my pack and standing up.

"That's it," he says. "I have my father's sword, my mother's shawl, and my clothes. I'm going to build a new life for myself. Beyond Usman and Farida, there are just memories here now."

I look at my charge for this journey. His posture, even his composure, is different now that I'm not his customer. I'm not sure I would have trusted someone like me if I was in his situation. I feel the stirrings of the memory of what we did two nights ago, but that was just business. Now is not the time for such things, and there may never be a time again. We are barely more than strangers.

"I hardly know you, and you hardly know me, so I want to be clear on this before we leave. I'll take you to Aksu, and I'll help you find work, but I don't owe you anything beyond that. The road I walk in life tends to be walked alone."

He gives me a steely look. "I gathered that when you came to town by yourself. Don't worry, once I land on my feet, I'll be able to take care of myself."

I soften. There's no need to frighten him either. I can see the tentative tail wag he's doing. "Once you get used to it, I think you'll like Aksu. It took me a while to adapt to it myself."

"You weren't born there?"

I shake my head and pick up the waterskin I'll be carrying. "No, I'm from the savannas of the south originally. I live in Aksu now, though."

"I don't know much about that."

"Perhaps I'll tell you about it at some point." I look up toward the mountains. "The road up over the mountains will be rough, and we have to carry enough water until we reach the top. I'm told there is a spring high up in the gap the road passes through where we can refill. It will take two days to reach the pass. They said the trail should be pretty easy to follow."

Zayn takes a deep breath. "Then let's get going."

I start walking toward the dusty road that leads away from Zaptu toward the Sultanate of Khalin. Behind me, the jackal follows, his paws soft against the sand and stones.

Stone Roads
(Zayn)

All my life, I've had mountains to the west of me. I've watched the clouds pile up at the tops of them, and wondered what life was like on the other side of those peaks. I know life in the sultanate is very different than in Zaptu, but how is it different? I don't know, but I'm on my way to find out, climbing up into the mountains, following the tail of the hyena who will take me there. In the dark parts of my mind, I wonder how much of my already damaged dignity I will be able to maintain once I get there. A whore must always be cautious with whose company he keeps, but I've gone ahead and made a snap decision; I hope I've chosen wisely.

Two nights ago, as I stood in Usman's house, he'd told me I was being rash. "You need to think this through carefully. You do not know what awaits you in Aksu," he warned me, but he also didn't tell me I shouldn't leave either. I know I will always be the ostracized one in Zaptu until people forget. It's been over fifteen years ago since Usman danced himself, and they've still not forgotten.

Zaptu is nestled at the base of the foothills, above the desert dunes. The dusty trace of dirt and stone that is the road cuts over the dry hills. Behind us, the great desert, with its endless dunes, rolls away from us. As we climb up, Zaptu disappears from sight. It hits me then—this is really happening. I've been to the next town on the caravan trail south from Zaptu, but I've never gone up into the mountains before. Everything from this point onward will be new to me.

It's been two days since my session with Sarda, but I still feel the lingering itching and pain from the scabs under my fur. My muscles complain in protest from the hiking, and my footpaws quickly remind me I have not traveled since my mother died. The exertion of hiking up the road causes my skin to pull, and the feeling makes my wounds ache. Like so many times in my life, I put my own comfort aside, but this time it's not for another. It's for myself. I want to finally move on and find a real life for myself. It's time I started living.

The hike is tiring and draining. The sun is punishing, the air hot and stifling. After an hour we stop to drink some water.

"It should be cooler once we get to a higher elevation," Naji remarks, tongue hanging out. "The wind will keep down the heat."

I glance up toward the mountains. In the winter, the distant peaks are tipped in white. Currently it's late spring and only the very tops show any snow cover.

"I see why no caravans take this route," I pant, still trying to catch my breath.

Naji pants. "The low pass to the south is much easier, but this is a direct route. When I traveled out east, I took the low pass, but I've meant for a while to try this pass."

"You think it's better?"

He shrugs. "Just different. I headed directly across the desert toward Zaptu instead of following the main caravan route when it swings south, west of the Banu Oasis. You have to be willing to camp out in the desert to take that route, so for most, shaving off four days isn't a worthwhile trade. Some people want discretion, but since I was going to be returning by myself, I figured I'd take the quicker route."

I nod in agreement. I know my father used to travel south so he could reach the main caravan route. The few people I've ever met who traveled directly from the Banu Oasis to Zaptu say it's five to six days of rolling dunes without water. It's a great place for someone to disappear.

The hyena checks my wounds, and I take this opportunity to apply more poultice to my back. The relief it brings is welcoming. The pain goes down with that, and I can feel the tension I'm carrying in my back relax. It is still sore, and it will stay that way for a while. It always does. We rest for a bit. Eventually, Naji picks his pack back up. "Ready?" he asks me.

I nod as I pick up my own pack, and we are off again. The trail is a narrow path of worn earth that sometimes fades out. In places where the ground is stony or the trail exposed to a lot of wind, small cairns of rocks have been laid out to mark it.

"You've traveled a lot," I remark, as we pick our way up a hill.

"I go where the coin is, be that as a caravan guard, or as a bodyguard. Most people who want to pay me don't need me to hang out in one place."

I recall the scar he has. "It is dangerous?"

"It can be, but it's also sometimes quite boring. I do a lot of waiting around."

"It's work I guess."

"Yes. I kind of fell into it, and I've stuck with it. It's what I know how to do."

That, I understand too well. Survival is a universal need for us all, and the hyena needs to eat like the rest of us. As the itching in my back picks up, I'm reminded of the type of trades I have made for my own survival. I can only hope that Aksu offers a better path than Zaptu did.

And if it doesn't? Well, I'll figure something out. I'm a survivor. The sword strapped against my leg as I walk is a constant reminder of the fact.

☙

The first night on the trail we camp in a hollow between the hills. There is some dry scrub that Naji and I collected before the sun went down. We didn't have enough fuel to keep it going all night, but it is enough to bake some bread.

Naji mixes some flour with water and a little salt to make a paste. He then shapes two flat loaves of bread which he lets sit while he makes a bed of embers from the fire. He seals the bread against the coals before he buries the loaves under hot embers in a small depression dug out next to the fire. Once those have cooled, he uncovers the loaves.

"It's not very tasty, but it will keep you going." He fishes some dried mutton out of his pack and hands me some. "I can make actual good bread with an oven."

I bite into the loaf of bread. It is hard and tastes ashy, but it's warm. Gingerly I nibble at it.

Naji sits, listening to the crickets and cicadas sing over the sound of the wind. The temperature has already dropped, and it's become pleasant out. The fire is small, and it barely highlights his face, but Naji's eyes shine in the darkness. "I don't think there's anyone near us for miles," he says.

"There might be some shepherds out there with their flocks."

"Possibly. I didn't see much green when we hiked, but who knows where the rains have fallen."

I shrug. I know people would talk about where to graze their herds back in Zaptu, but I never was very interested in that. "There's an art to it."

"There is. Not my world, but it always surprises me what people can find."

I yawn, tired from the day.

"You can get some rest. I'll keep watch for a bit."

My ears dip a little. "You think that's necessary? We don't have raiders in these parts."

He shrugs. "Force of habit mostly, but you can never be too sure."

I guess he's right. I stretch out by the fire, using my pack to brace my head. The hyena sits nearby, watching the flames, ears flicking occasionally to pick up the sounds of the night. I want to ask him if he thinks we should take turns keeping watch, but even as the thought is forming, the soft light of the flickering flames helps lull me to sleep.

$\approx$

In the morning I wake cold and stiff to the rhythmic sound of metal striking metal in the predawn light. I glance toward Naji who is making some type of twisting motion with his hands.

"What on earth are you doing?" I ask him.

He looks up. "Oh, you're awake. I'm grinding coffee." He holds up a small brass mortar and pestle.

I yawn. "You woke me up."

His ears lay flat. "Sorry. I've got a routine when I travel like this."

"It's fine. I should get up. I'm surprised you don't travel at night though. Sarda did."

His ears flick at the mention of that name. "I have. If I'm on my own long enough, I may, but the towns function during the day. Back home, when we traveled great distances, we'd travel at night, but there were acacias for shade to sleep under during the day. I can't really sleep out in the dunes when the sun is high."

I don't have much experience with traveling, so I let the conversation lapse. Naji goes back to grinding the coffee while

I lie there trying to find the energy to get up. I'm stiff, and my back still hurts. The sun hasn't come out yet and started to warm the land, so the ground is cold against me. Finally, I get up and start stretching, adjusting my clothing.

"I'm not sure I will ever be used to sleeping on the ground," I remark.

Naji laughs. He's currently brewing the coffee over the fire in a small kettle. "Trust me, I much prefer a real bed than this. I am not the young pup I once was."

It occurs to me I don't actually know how old Naji is. He speaks as one much older than I am, but he doesn't look a lot older than me. "How old are you?"

"I turned twenty-eight this year."

"Only twenty-eight? From the way you talk, it sounds like you've seen a lot."

His ears droop. His tail, which was wagging, goes still. "Yes and no. It doesn't help that I don't like to stay still for too long."

I wonder if he's running from something. "Is there a particular reason you travel so much?"

The sun is finally coming up behind Naji and some of the light catches the tips of his fur. It highlights it well, but his face is dark and masked in worry. He looks vulnerable.

"Let's just say it's been a long road, but one worth traveling." He pours the coffee into a cup and then comes over to me so he can press it into my hands. The brew smells strong and bitter. "Drink, it will help return some of the feeling to your paws and tail."

I do, letting the warmth flow into my chilled body, and the moment the cup is empty, he refills it. I recognize the tradition as one my father told me about. After drinking my third cup, I shake it to indicate I didn't want any more and Naji does not refill it. They say it's good to carry some culture with you in the sands, it helps keep you grounded, and I am not one to argue that fact.

We are alone out here, but we are alone out here together. That is no reason not to remember our roots.

∾

The day is spent hiking in the heat. Naji talks about the terrain we pass, and when I confess I don't know much about desert camping, he gives me some important tips. It reminds me a bit of my father, and that only makes me realize how long it has been since he passed on. I get silent then, but when Naji stops to see if he's boring me, I tell him to go on. It's interesting enough, and I don't want to be alone with my thoughts.

As we continue up the slopes, the wind picks up. It's a relief from the oppressive heat of the day, but when we stop to camp for the night it becomes a problem.

In the evening, the temperature in the desert drops. Down at the bottom of the foothills where Zaptu is nestled, it makes the evenings pleasant. Up in the mountains, it makes the evenings cold. Once night falls, the wind gains strength, sweeping down the barren slope. The drop in temperature is more severe than last night and the wind is making it worse. After having climbed for a day and a half since leaving Zaptu, the pads on my feet are sore and my back is burning. Even Naji looks pretty worn from the day, and resting brings no relief to my fatigue as the wind robs my body of heat. After tending to my wounds, I huddle in the blanket I brought, shivering.

I'm not familiar with roughing it like this. My fur isn't thick enough for the chill, and the ground is hard. I sit miserably on the ground on the thin mat I brought while Naji busies himself making camp. My ears are pinned back to help keep them warm in the gusting wind.

"I have another blanket if you'd like," says Naji. He's lit a small campfire with some dried brush we collected before nightfall. Even at this elevation, it's still hard finding enough fuel for a good fire. With the wind right now, I'm not sure that's going to matter.

"I'll be fine," I say. I'm trying not to let him know how miserable I feel right now. It's going to be a restless night.

"You sure?" he asks, as the wind ruffles his fur. The small fire is too low to cook on; it just gives us a little light and heat to help with the chill. He pokes at the fire. It keeps sputtering in the wind and he's constantly having to tend to it.

"Will the wind do this all night?"

"Possibly," he says. "I guess we should have looked for a more sheltered spot to sleep before the sun went down. I didn't think the wind would pick up like this."

I grunt and lay down, curling up tightly in my thin blanket. I try and get comfortable, using my tail to help hold in heat, but the blanket isn't thick enough to keep me warm. I close my eyes. It's just one night. I can get through this, and hopefully at some point tonight the wind will calm.

"Take the blanket," says Naji, reaching to pull it out of his pack.

"What will you use then?" I ask him.

"I have my kaftan."

"It's your blanket. You should use it."

"We can share it," suggests Naji. "The fire won't last once I lay down."

I'm not big on us sleeping together tonight, but that's the best option. Extra warmth would be good, and the hyena is the only source of warmth besides the faltering fire. I don't want to give him the wrong opinion of why I went on this journey with him, but I won't sleep if I spend all night shivering.

I drop my gaze to the fire. "If you think that's for the best."

"I'm not going to touch you, if you're worried about that."

I look up at him and he shrugs.

"Just let me know when you are ready to get some sleep," I suggest. Hopefully that lets him know I'm not interested in being intimate with him.

"Sure," replies Naji. He yawns, scanning the darkness. In the meantime, I watch the flames. When the fire sputters again, Naji adjusts the rocks he put in place to protect it. After he is satisfied and feeds it some more brush, he digs into his pack and pulls out food.

"You should eat something to keep up your strength," he says, handing me some dates and dried meat.

I reach out and take the food. I pop a date in my muzzle, savoring the flavor.

"I guess it's too windy to bake bread." I remark.

"Yes. I can make some in the morning, if the wind has died down." He bites off a chunk of dried meat and chews.

I woof an acknowledgment. Hot food in the morning will be good. It will help give me energy for the day's exertions. We eat in silence for a bit, me still curled up on the ground while Naji sits, letting his fur ruffle in the wind.

"How long will the trip take?" I ask.

He swallows. "I'm not sure. Probably it will take a day more to reach the border. From there, we climb down into a valley that leads to Yokus."

I nod and we finish our meal in silence. He plays with the fire for a bit more, listening to the sound of the wind across the stony slopes.

After a while, the hyena lays his sleeping mat right next to me and gets the blanket from his pack. He curls up next to me, his back against mine. His body is warm against me, and his scent is familiar. It's not as sharp as mine, but it's still strong. To get more heat, I press my back up closer to him.

The light for the fire flickers for a little while, until the wind finally kills it. When it does, we are plunged into darkness, alone under the light of the stars. I curl up closer to Naji to stay warm, and he shifts his body against mine, our backs pressed together. The wind whips across the hill side, but I am no longer cold.

As I drift off, I wonder if I'm crazy for doing this. The blackness of night is all-encompassing. The moon, slowly retreating from its zenith tonight, provides pale illumination to the barren slopes. I gaze into the darkness thinking about what will happen. This time Naji falls asleep first, and I can hear him snoring. I lay awake for a while before sleep finally finds me too.

૱

The third day on the road is again spent climbing. As the morning wears on, the chill in the air gives way to a rising heat, and by mid-morning, my tongue is lolling from exertion. The road is just a dusty trail weaving across the slopes. We meet one traveler in the morning, a wolf farmer I'd seen before in Zaptu's caravanserai, traveling with two camels. One is loaded with chickens in cages, and the other has sacks with onions and flour. He stops and talks briefly with us before he sets off, looking to make the best time he can. He does tell us how to find the spring up ahead before resuming his journey down the mountain.

The scrubby vegetation dotting the mountain slope varies little as the hours wear on. My paws are sore from stepping on stone constantly, but at least my back doesn't complain as much as it did yesterday. Finally, in the late afternoon, we reach a small monument that marks the border, located just outside of the high pass. The stone monument is blank, except for the carved seal of the Sultanate of Khalin.

The pass is narrow. The road cuts between two mountains at the bottom of a steep ravine. Rock rises up on either side of the road. At points the mountains tower high above us, the path cutting through a crevice in the wall of rock. We follow that in the fading light, but before night falls, the crevice opens onto a high mountain valley. It is here, near the outlet of the ravine, where we find the spring the farmer mentioned.

The spring is a little trickle of water under an overhanging rock that collects into a pool cut into the stone by some traveler. The water is refreshing to our parched muzzles, and we take this opportunity to refill our waterskins. We decide to camp in a sheltered hollow near the spring, and since we have some time before sunset, I take this chance to sit and watch the water run into the pool. It's cold to my touch, unlike the well water in Aksu.

"Not used to seeing running water, are you?" he asks me.

I shake my head. "Never."

The hyena chuckles, amused, and goes off to find some brush for the fire tonight.

After a light meal, we turn in. The late spring weather up here is quite variable, and once again, I have to curl up against Naji to stay warm. I at least sleep better since we're out of the wind, although the temperature drops so low, I can see my breath smoke in the feeble light the waning moon gives us.

❧

Dawn on the fourth day brings a cold fog to the high valley. A dampness settles into my fur and chills my bones. When I get up, I must stamp my paws to get some feeling into them. A crust of ice has formed on the surface of the spring, and we have to break through it to get to the precious water. Everything is still and featureless, like the world has been muted around us.

We travel all morning through the high valley on the other side of the pass. It slopes downward, but the terrain is still rough and involves us climbing up and down various rises as we follow the road. At points, our paws crunch oddly against the cold ground. Naji tells me this is frost, and I stop to examine the frozen condensation before we continue on. As the day grows warmer, the frost melts into the hard, packed earth.

"Is this typical for the mountains?" I ask Naji, squinting into the gloom when we take our first break of the day. Even now that the sun has cleared the mountains, it's a hazy orb in the sky. The dead feeling of the land around us makes my fur crawl. The gray colors of the earth are muted, and the vegetation here is low to the ground suggesting it struggles to grow. Even the sound of our voices is deadened to my keen hearing.

"Yes," says the hyena. "At high enough elevations, you can get weather like this in the non-summer months."

The air is heavy, and I'm not used to that. "I've seen fog in Zaptu, but it has always burned off quickly."

The hyena glances around. "This may last all day."

"It can do that?"

He chuckles. "Of course. It rains up here too. That's why the lower valleys below are so fertile."

I shiver and pull my kaftan closer to me.

Even though the fog obscures much of the landscape, I can tell at some point we descend a ravine into a lower valley. I'm quick to notice there are trees sheltered in this valley, and I stop briefly to gawk at this. The landscape continues to change drastically around us as we travel, and soon it is much lusher than the high valley we just traversed. The trail becomes wider. Soon we're passing farms with orchards of apples and almonds, and around what I think is midday, we pass through a small village of timber and stone houses. At this point, the road improves from the rough trail we followed into a well-maintained track. Stone bridges cross gullies, and we see other travelers out on the road. Many appear to be farmers and traders with business to attend to.

Around one bend, a strange bubbling sound catches my ears. The road turns here and starts to follow a stream as it meanders down through the valley. I insist we stop at the water, and quickly scramble down into the gully it cuts.

"It's just a stream," Naji tells me from the road, as I trace my hand through the icy liquid, standing on the banks. The spring we camped next to was small, barely a trickle of water. Someone had to coax the water into a basin to make it useful to travelers. This stream flows unabated and undisturbed. The sheer volume of water in it is also surprising. Green spikey grasses grow next to the water. Never have I seen so much water in my life.

The scent of the water is clean and fresh too, and it's mingled with the scent of wet earth and vegetation. All these new smells are overwhelming, but I inhale deeply so I can commit to them to memory. It takes me a minute before I can respond.

"I know, but I've only heard of these before. I've never seen one." Only when it rains have I seen the dry wadi near Zaptu fill with water. These flows are only temporary, and soon they dry up again, sucked down into the hungry sands. The green grasses along the banks tell me this is not an occasional flow of water, but that it flows year-round.

He chuckles. "You do know a river runs straight through Aksu, right?"

"It does? Is a river much bigger than this?" My hand has gone numb from the cold water, but I don't care. My tail is wagging excitedly at the wonder of so much water.

"Yes. It's wider and deeper. You can even swim in it if you wanted."

I look up from the mesmerizing sight and sound of the water to where he's still standing on the road. "What do you mean 'swim'?"

"You get in the water, and since you can't touch the bottom, you have to keep yourself afloat to get to the other side."

I blink. "You mean like, in the water?" I look back at the water and stand up. Gingerly I step out into the stream, and immediately the cold water flows over my footpaws, making me shiver. "Something like this?"

He rubs a paw over the back of his head. "It's similar, but imagine the water being over your head."

I frown, looking at Naji, and I try to imagine what he's describing, but it seems impossible. I know the sea is supposed to be a vast expanse of water like the great desert, but a river can't be that big, can it?

He gives me a nervous laugh. "I guess you'll have to see it to understand. The Zaharani, the river in Aksu, is so big the only easy way to cross it is to use one of the stone bridges in the city."

What a strange place he is describing. I walk around in the stream, feeling the flow of the water and the sand underneath the surface under my numb feet.

"I guess. This is amazing," I say excitedly, kicking my paws through the water.

"I'm sure, but don't stay in there too long. The cold will make you sick."

I close my eyes, just feeling the pull of the water, inhaling its clean scent. What a strange, wonderful land the sultanate is. I hope I can find the future I've always dreamed of here.

I stay in the stream until my teeth start chattering and the hyena comes down and pulls me out. I am so mesmerized by the stream, I do not realize the fog has burned off at first. Tall mountains, some still tipped in white, hem us in on three sides. The land here in the upper mountain valleys is rugged, but green. Farms dot the slopes of the mountains until the green gives out to stone. I'm able to sun my chilled body on a rock and dry out the hem of my pants. It's an hour before we finally get moving again.

That evening we stay at a small inn in a little village. The innkeeper turns out to be friendly red fox. I've heard of red foxes before, but never seen one. Naji politely has to whisper into my ear that I'm gawking to get me to head into the bunk-room.

"Are there many of them here?" I ask, as we're walking away.

"There are a few in the sultanate," he says. "Mostly up in the mountains though."

The accommodations are a basic dormitory, but there is a straw bed instead of the hard ground. We have to share a room with two striped hyenas who are traveling merchants from a town called Yokus. I get my own cot next to Naji's and I curl up on it exhausted, worn out from the day.

Naji stays up talking to the other hyenas, but I only half listen to them. I quickly doze off from exhaustion. It's been a tiring trip.

The next day, the valley we are in connects to the much larger Ghola Valley that runs north to south. At the crossroads we take the southern path. Travel becomes very easy, and we're traversing through farmland planted for the summer growing season. Orchards of olives, figs, and apples cover the valley's sides while farms raising goats, vegetables, and grapes are on the valley's floor. I've never seen a land so rich and fertile. The rain that the mountains keep out of the desert to the east must fall here on the western slopes.

At the end of the valley we reach Yokus, a market town, on the eastern edge of the valley. Built on a hill, its paved streets cut diagonally up toward the summit. A wall protects the town, but a cluster of inns and stables are situated near the gate outside of the wall.

I'm in awe of the size of this place, so Naji and I stop to admire it where the road dips down toward the city.

"Are fortifications necessary here?" I ask the hyena.

"Not anymore, but Yokus is a very old town. It predates the sultanate."

"This place is huge," I whisper.

"There were what, about two hundred people in Zaptu?"

"A bit more, but pretty close to that."

"About ten thousand people live in Yokus."

That population seems beyond comprehension to me, but I can't deny what my eyes are telling me. When we descend the road and enter the town, my nose confirms this place is very trafficked. Scents of food, spices, and the people constantly vie for my attention. Some scents are familiar, but many are new. I try and get a good whiff, but immediately a new one takes its place. I can't sort all these smells out.

Naji notices me sniffing the air. "I should warn you, Yokus is a fraction of the size of Aksu."

Even though I know it has to be true, as we walk through the town, it's hard to believe bigger places exist. Yokus is bustling with merchants and traders, and I feel small and insignificant in this crowd. Farmers from across the valley come here to sell their wares. Even though it is only late spring, goods are already flowing through town's market. Honey, vegetables, and fruits are for sale. Casks of wine, now aged and ready to sell, are stacked in the market, and there is an entire street where the merchants only deal in wine.

"Never have I seen so much wine in one place," I remark to Naji as we're passing through the market.

"Some of the best vintages of wine you can get in Aksu come from the vineyards up here. The Ghola Valley is very fertile."

The wineskins I was able to get in Zaptu were expensive, and it was a delicacy I only served my most discerning customers. I never could afford to enjoy it myself, so the sheer quantity of wine for sale shocks me. They're also hawking it for far less than it costs in Zaptu. At the end of the market sits the inn Naji takes us to, its large wooden doors silently watching the bustle outside. The sun is setting behind the mountains as we enter. Large windows are set into the front of the structure, but they're already shuttered for the night. Instead, large lanterns are hung from the arched ceiling, and the last of the evening light filters through smaller windows further up to help illuminate the room. In the middle of the entrance there is a small table, with a caracal sitting behind the desk set with a lantern and an account book. The cat looks up from what he is doing when we approach.

"Welcome," beckons the innkeeper. "How can I help you?"

"I would like a room for the night," Naji says.

"As would I," I add.

"Two rooms then? They're a silver dirham each."

The hyena doesn't say anything as he fishes a silver coin out and glances at me. It takes me a moment to realize he's expecting me to pay for my own room.

"Give me a moment," I say, and put my knapsack down to dig out my coin purse from the bottom of the pack. It's wedged into the bottom, and I have to pull out the hefty bag and dig out two half silver coins and hand them over. The entire time, Naji and the caracal are watching me. When I put my coins on the counter, the innkeeper hands both of us wooden keys.

"In the back of the courtyard, on the other side past the fountain, there is an archway. Through there, you'll find two doors. Yours is the room on the left," he says to me, "yours is the room on the right," he tells Naji.

"Thank you," I respond.

Setting the coin purse back in my pack, I hoist it and turn to walk behind the desk toward the courtyard.

"I didn't realize you had so much money on you," Naji whispers, as we walk through a set of open doors into a paved courtyard. This inn is much nicer than the one in Zaptu. The courtyard is filled with green vegetation and the pillars decorated with geometric carvings.

I look over at him. "I tried to save everything I could, but most of what I have came from Sarda."

"You might want to carry some of that in a smaller purse, so you don't need to go digging for it like that. In the city, you never know who is watching you."

I never carried it all with me in Zaptu, but that's because I kept it hidden at home. "I've still got my small coin purse."

"Good," says the hyena. "The cities are different."

Just looking around at the beautiful tile work and lush vegetation growing in the courtyard, I know I'm in a different world. We cross to the arch on the far side and find the two doors the innkeeper spoke of against the back wall of the cloister. I take my key and unlock the door.

"If it's okay, I would like to take a nap," I say.

"I'll come get you when I am ready to get some food."

"That works," I reply, walking into the room and closing the door behind me. Hiking for five days has been tough on me, and my paws hurt badly. At least my back is starting to heal. I also never realized such a different world existed so close and yet so far from me.

The room is larger than I expected it to be, with shuttered screen windows in the back. I walk over and open the shuttered window to flood the room with the fading light. There's a quiet street outside with houses beyond.

The room is well appointed. There is a chest at the foot of the bed, and the nightstand next to it is carefully carved, but I don't take the time to admire the work. Collapsing onto the bed from exhaustion, I roll over and realize there's no hyena to press my back up against. I wonder why that feels like a loss, but I pass out asleep before I can ponder that.

❧

It's completely dark when rapping on the door to my room awakens me. I have to blink a few times before I can focus on my surroundings. Only faint moonlight coming in through the window lets me see where I am. It takes me a moment to remember exactly where this is. Getting up, I drag myself over to the door and open it.

The light from the lanterns in the cloister eases around Naji's bulky frame. The hyena looks at me.

"I would have woken you sooner, but I could hear you snoring. I wasn't sure if you wanted to eat or not."

I give myself a shake, letting my fur settle. "How long was I asleep for?"

"About two hours."

"Figures. After walking all day, that bed felt amazing. I didn't get a great night's rest at the bunkhouse. I think one of those merchants snored all night."

"Did you want to eat something tonight?"

"I should." The moment he suggested it I felt hungry. I am so tired; I hadn't even realized that.

"The inn has food," he offers.

I smile. "That sounds best."

Naji turns, and after locking the door to my room, I follow him back through the courtyard to a different part of the building. There are tables set up under a series of interlinked arches, and people are talking over food. Some appear to be craftsman, others merchants. At the entrance awaits a female jackal who takes us over to a table. After she leaves, an older striped hyena, the black stripes under her muzzle starting to gray, comes up to us.

"Welcome," she says, setting down a kettle of tea for us with two cups. "We're serving kebabs, stuffed peppers, and roast chicken tonight. I've got fresh tabbouleh also if you're interested in something lighter. Just tell me what you want, and I'll get it."

Naji smiles at her. "The roast chicken sounds good to me."

Only the Emir at home ever got his food brought to him like this. "I'll have the kebabs myself."

"All right. If you want anything else, just let me know." With that, she's gone.

I reach for the kettle and pour the tea. The aroma is rich and tingles in my nose. I can immediately smell the mint and honey undertones in the tea even before I put the cup up to my muzzle to take the first sip. The taste is wonderful and explodes across my tongue.

"This is amazing," I say to the hyena, as he pours his own cup.

He sniffs at the cup and tilts a little into his muzzle. "I'm sure the food is of similar quality."

I nod. "I'm excited to see Aksu," I say, to strike up some conversation as I sip my tea. "You must also be happy to be getting back."

He shrugs. "It will be nice."

"Why were you traveling through Zaptu?"

"I was an escort on a caravan traveling across the desert to Zara."

"Zara? That's quite a distance."

"It's a three-week journey once you leave the sultanate. We only made it to Banu when things kind of fell apart when the two merchants who hired me started fighting about who owed the other. I decided to take my coin and return on my own."

"That sounds like it was a disaster. How do you find work like that anyway?"

"I have a friend who works in the Grand Market who is always good at giving me leads. She knows when people are looking for guards."

"So, what will you do for work when you get back home?"

He considers. "That's a good question. Usually, I do guard work or travel with caravans, but it depends on what's available."

I frown, unsure of how to respond to that, so I fall silent. I'm going to be in a big city alone if he takes another caravan job. What will I do in Aksu when I get there? All I know is whoring and dancing for coin. I'll be away from home, and the only person I have to rely on is Naji. I hate not being able to control what happens next.

"Don't worry. I think you will like Aksu. It's a very bustling city," he says.

"I hope so. It will be a big change. I just hope the boys aren't as rough in Aksu as they are in Zaptu."

"How can you even think of doing that again?" he says, shocked.

"It's money," I say. I hope it doesn't come to that, but I wonder if it will. Like the hyena, I need to make sure I can eat, and if he's going to be back on the road soon, I'll have to figure out things on my own.

He grumbles. "I told you I'd help you find good work."

I sigh. "It's how I support myself." It's not how I want to support myself, but it's a path. "Plus, you will be leaving soon again."

He considers. "I guess I'll need to see what Naima has for me that's in town until you're settled. I hadn't thought about that, but I'll stick in town for a bit. You can stay with me until you've figured things out. My friend Fadel will know what you can do."

I'm hoping Naji is right that I can find other work, but whoring is still my fallback. There are always men looking to buy a good night for themselves. In a big city like Aksu, there will be many more of them than in Zaptu who prefer other men. If I have to return to that life, I am sure I will do alright for myself. "I'd appreciate that," I respond.

He picks up his cup of tea. "Let's drink to new beginnings."

I hate relying on people, but I hold up my cup. If I don't want to be a whore, I will have to trust he knows what he's talking about. "To new beginnings." I take a sip of my tea and we wait in silence for our food.

Mountain Crossroads
(Naji)

I lie in bed, but sleep does not come easy, and when it does, it is not restful. After a few hours, I wake up suddenly from a dream. I was back in that camp where my life first came apart, looking for the friend I lost the second time it came apart. I desperately searched the broken camp, searching for spotted fur, but I could not find him.

Steel is hard; it flexes and warps under pressure, but it will keep its shape. Push it too much, though, and slowly it will weaken until it fails completely. I think my armor is failing, as regret is starting to eat at me. If I was just faster, if I was just quicker, so many more people might still be here today. I told myself I was going to just focus on me, that I would travel alone, yet here I am now with someone, once again.

It feels like it takes the morning forever to come, and when the first tendrils of dawn creep around the shuttered window of my room, I abandon any hope of sleeping more. With nothing better to do, I go for a walk to clear my head in the dawn's light.

The inn is quiet, and I slip out the front, letting the heavy wooden door close silently except for the click of the brass lock. Outside the air is cool and chilly; the streets are deserted, but there is still life in the town. A few merchants are out, opening up their stalls. A cart carrying sacks of flour rumbles past me. The market here supplies traders from the Grand Market of Aksu, and business goes on all day. My thoughts are brooding, so I turn off the main road and head up a street that ascends toward the top part of town.

Stone houses with shuttered wooden windows line the road, while the workshops of craftsmen are dotted among the houses. Many people live on top of their stores. I don't have a specific direction in mind, so I keep climbing until I reach the upper part of town where the largest and wealthiest homes are located. Among these houses is the town's main temple, its domed roof and spire towering over the surrounding structures.

I stop to examine the intricate carvings and tilework over the entrance. The words above the door exhort all to enter and seek truth inside. I think about that for a moment before I continue on my journey. If I was a religious man, I'd stop and join the morning prayers, but I don't know what guidance that will give me. It might help some of the ghosts in my past, but I know some here would condemn me for partaking in desires of the flesh with other men. That some would think I need to suffer for that hurts, but I know I am not broken or wrong. I have always stuck to the golden rule that tells me to treat others as I myself wish to be treated. I will have to figure out the other things in life on my own.

My paws eventually carry me back to the inn. By then the front door is unlocked and the caracal is at the desk. He waves when I enter. It's still early when I return, so I take this opportunity to carefully go over my pack, unpacking and repacking it to see what provisions we have left. When that doesn't calm me, I unpack and repack everything again in order to better distribute it. It's when I'm doing this that there comes a knock on my door.

When I don't immediately respond, Zayn calls to me. "You awake in there, Naji?"

"Yes," I respond, as I set some clothes back in my pack. Aksu is a day's journey, and we have extra food. Even if the weather brings rain, the road is well traveled as it passes through two small villages.

"Should I come back?" he calls from the other side of the door.

I flick my ears. It's not like I can hide in here all day from reality. "No," I say, getting up and unlocking the door. "I was just checking on things to make sure we have enough supplies."

"Aren't we supposed to reach Aksu tonight?" Zayn asks me.

"We are, but I just wanted to make sure everything is in order," I say, returning to the pack on the bed.

Perhaps he senses my unease. "Should I let you be for a bit?"

"Nah," I say quickly, tossing a few final things back into the pack. "If you are ready, we can get some breakfast, and then we'll set out after we refill our waterskins."

Zayn nods. "Good, I'm already packed."

"Then let's go get some breakfast," I suggest. He nods his agreement, so we leave our rooms and pad across the courtyard. Zayn points toward the arch leading to where the inn serves its food, but I shake my head and lead him toward the front door.

The market is now in full swing since the sun is above the mountains, and I've always felt at home in places like this. Thankfully, the air is still cool with morning dew. We walk through the crowd until I find a vendor hawking food. Tables and chairs are set up to the side of the booth, and the striped hyena proprietor is quite affable. He waits patiently as Zayn and I discuss the food on his sign board.

After consulting with Zayn, I buy us a meal of bread and salted white cheese accompanied by tea. Taking the food to the tables, we sit and eat, watching the crowd as porters and carts roll by.

"Yokus is quite beautiful," remarks Zayn. "There is a lot of life in this city."

I'm forced to chuckle. "You have not yet seen Aksu. Yokus is a quiet town."

His ears flick. "I hope I can make the adjustment."

"You'll be fine."

Zayn's ears dip as he chews on some bread. He's likely worrying about the unknown. I should give him some reassurance that things will be okay, but it takes time to adapt. He won't have as hard a time though as I did when I first went to Aksu. I'll make sure of that.

Out of the corner of my eye, I can see his tail wagging slowly, and I take that as a good sign. His ears are perked forward in curiosity, and he's watching the crowd.

I take a sip of my tea and let it relax my frayed mind. When we are finished, we head back to the inn to get our packs.

∾

Immediately south of Yokus, the road winds through the base of the mountains. Olive orchards dot the slopes, while date palms are growing in the bottom of the valleys. We pass quite a few wagons carrying goods out on the road and stop in the late morning at a village for a brief rest.

An hour later, we're traveling through the woods where the road cuts around a large hill. Zayn is admiring all the trees when a wagon traveling fast comes around the bend. I quickly step out of the way off to the side. Zayn is behind me, and I hear him scramble toward the shoulder as the sound of clattering hooves gets his attention. Over the noise I hear a loud yelp and a curse. I turn around as the wagon passes us, and I see Zayn has slipped on the gravel on the side of the road embankment and fallen. He's rubbing his right leg. The fennec and leopard in the wagon are obviously in a hurry, because the cart bounces on down the highway past us without stopping.

"Are you okay?" I ask Zayn, reaching down to offer him a hand. "Did they clip you?"

"No, I just fell." He grabs my paw, and I pull him up. He yelps again, and I'm forced to catch him so he doesn't fall a second time. "Oh, that hurts," he hisses through gritted teeth.

I have to hold onto him to keep him from falling. "Stupid horse-cart drivers. Can you put weight on it?"

Gingerly, he tries to put some weight onto his right foot, and he winces. "I may have broken something," he says.

There isn't much flat land right here for me to examine him. "Let's get around this bend, and then I'll look at it."

He tries to walk on it, but I have to support him. "Put some of your weight on me," I say, wrapping an arm around him. He doesn't say anything as we walk down the road together. I spot a boulder for him to sit on, so I help him over there.

Once I've got him seated, I kneel down in front of him. Carefully, I start exploring his right foot. He winces and whimpers a little as I check his leg.

"I think you just twisted your ankle," I say. "Nothing feels broken."

"It really hurts," huffs the jackal.

"We'll let it rest for a bit, and then we'll see how it feels."

"I'm sorry," he says, as I get up. "I hadn't expected the ground to slide out from under me."

There is space on the boulder, so I hop up on it. "It can happen to anyone. If we have to, we can camp out on the road for the night and reach Aksu tomorrow."

"Yes, but I can't dance on this."

My ears lift, but I don't say anything.

He catches my expression. "I guess I don't have to either," he sighs and looks at his feet. "I'm just nervous I guess."

"That's only natural."

"You left home you said, right? Were you nervous when you did?"

"I don't remember that day clearly, because it was unremarkable. I had gone home to visit, but never expected what would happen later would cause me never to return. I did not think when I left it would be the last time I left, but we never know where our path will go. In the end, I found a better road for myself."

"I hope I have too," he says. "My parents taught me when I was young to always keep your eyes out for opportunities. As they always said, opportunity, like a good meal, does not last."

He's right there. "That's a good piece of advice. Opportunity is fleeting."

He puts his paws behind him on the boulder so he can lean back. "Thanks. I keep those words with me."

We rest for a few minutes, and then he tries flexing his foot again. It still hurts, but he's able to put some weight on it. We walk for a bit, slowly going down the road, but it's still giving him trouble, so we rest again, this time for an hour. I take this opportunity to find him a stick he can use.

Even before we resume walking, it's obviously Zayn can't make it to Aksu tonight. The stick helps, but he still has to stop to rest frequently. The next village is a little ways away, so when we reach a mountain stream the road crosses, I decide to stop there for the day. There is an inviting clearing surrounded by cedars nearby, their aromatic scent thick on the air, so the decision of where to camp is easy. While I gather some firewood, he dips his aching foot into the cold running water.

I want to get back home, but I can rough it another night. The road in this area runs through forest dotted with orchards and farms. While we're still in a sheltered part of the valley, I know the land opens up and runs through the foothills a few miles further on. Since I didn't plan for us to be still on the road tonight, all I have is some jerky and dates. I offer to go see if one of the nearby farms has some fresh meat I can buy, but Zayn says he'll be fine.

Making the best of what we have, I split up the jerky between us and build a small fire to make tea. It's not a big meal, but it's filling enough. In the morning, we can buy breakfast from the next village.

While I'm chewing on my jerky, I go down to the stream to draw water. Then I take the kettle and hang it over the fire. While waiting for the water to heat, I walk over to prop my back up against one of the cedars. Zayn comes back from dipping his foot a second time to sit next to me, leaning his back against the tree.

"I'm surprised how lush it is on this side of the mountains," he remarks, looking up into the canopy.

"Up here it is, but the trees give way to scrub a little lower down. We're still in a sheltered part of the mountains. Down at the bottom of the foothills, it's drier. Most of the rain in Khalin falls up in the mountains and not along the coast."

He nods, watching the fire with me in the glowing gloom. I'm about ready to get up to check the water when he speaks again. "The land here is so different from Zaptu. Back there, the soil is thirsty, and every drop of water is precious. Here? It's abundant. Even the air feels different."

I chuckle. "It's not as dry as the desert, but you'll get used to it."

His tail wags. "I hope so."

We fall silent and I watch the fire as dusk falls. The night is alive with the sound of insects, and the wind blows through the treetops. I get up and pull the kettle off the campfire then add tea leaves and sugar to brew.

"Hey, Naji?" Zayn asks me while I'm working.

"Yes?"

"Why do you work as a hired swordsman?"

"Because the coin is good."

"But why?"

I'm not sure now is the time to talk about my past as a thief having to steal to eat in the Grand Market, or the training I got back home before the war. "I was taught how to handle a blade before I reached adulthood, and I am good enough with one not to get myself killed. I didn't have a lot of other skills at the time to rely on."

The conversation dies for a moment, with just the gentle sound of the wind to fill the gap between us before Zayn speaks up. "And the reason you stay in that profession?"

"I haven't really given it much thought. I've been saving up coin. A good friend of mine, she runs a spice stall in Aksu, and I might like to open something like that when I'm older. It takes money though to go into a business like that."

"It does. Usman did that, but he had to save up first. So, you see yourself someday selling spices?"

I laugh, amused. "Oh no, not spices. I could never compete with Naima. She has a nose for good spices I could never hope to duplicate."

"This is your friend who helps you find jobs?" he asks me.

I pour out some tea and blow on it to cool it. "Yes. We go back years. She's helped me a lot." I blow on the cup again and then lift it to my lips. The tea is black and sweet. "It's ready," I say, returning to the tree, carrying the cup and kettle. I really should have bought a second cup back in Zaptu, but I have only been carrying one for myself.

Zayn takes the offered cup of tea. "It's good you have someone who looks after you like that."

Before I knew Naima I was sleeping on the streets, so I owe her my life. I'm a little jealous she was able to retire like she did, but that's not a story for today. "Yes, I owe her."

He drinks some tea, and when he's done, he passes the cup back to me, so I pour some for myself. Zayn gets up and hobbles over to the fire to poke at it. I just watch as he moves around the campsite. After we're out of tea and it's cooled, I take the kettle and our cups and wash them down in the stream. Finally, after stoking the fire so it will burn for a while, I pull out my bedroll to curl up close to the fire. I watch the flames crackle.

Zayn hesitates before setting up his sleeping mat. He starts to unroll it on the other side of the fire, before changing his mind and taking the thin mat over to where I am and placing it next to me. He then lays down, behind my back. It's like how we slept on the first night on the road, but this time we're not sharing blankets. It's quite pleasant out tonight, so there is no need to cuddle for warmth. As I start to drift off, I feel him scoot next to me and gently press his back up against mine.

I'm surprised by the motion. I don't know why he does it, but he just does. It brings me back to sleeping on the streets with friends in order to keep ourselves safe, but there is nothing out there that should find us here. I'm not sure what I should do, so I just lie there feeling the warmth against me. I almost think the motion is unintentional and that he's just shifted around in his sleep, except I hear him whisper, "Goodnight, Naji," as I'm drifting off to sleep.

"Goodnight, Zayn," I whisper back.

The Great City of Aksu
(Zayn)

In the morning, I awaken still curled up against a snoring hyena. His presence is comforting and as the sun is just starting to rise and the light is filtering through the trees, I take this time to think before he wakes up.

The hyena is certainly attracted to me, and not just physically. I've always watched out for behavior in my customers that shows unwarranted affection. It brings much more trouble than it's worth. A good whore knows he or she can't afford to fall in love, no matter how well they treat you; it gets in the way when it comes time to work. Naji has treated me well, and he's put any desires about me aside since that first night in order to help me. So why am I starting to feel attached to him?

If Naji is right, I will never again have to surrender myself to someone for the coin to buy food. I want to believe he is right, but I don't know what Aksu will hold for me. Do I even know this hyena well enough to truly let my guard down? Do I even know the difference between a liaison and a lover? Sarda is the closest I've ever had to a lover, but that wasn't love. I know that, but I'm not sure what being in love really entails anymore.

I turn this all over in my head until Naji gets up, and we proceed to prepare for the day's travel. The hyena splits up the rest of our meager food while I build a small fire. He pulls out his mortar and pestle, grinding the coffee and then brewing it with his kettle. He again serves me first, and I have to shake the cup to signal I don't want any more before he pours some for himself. The food and coffee finished, we break camp and pack up everything before we set out. Naji insists I continue to use the walking stick to keep weight off my twisted ankle. While my ankle does feel better, I still must take frequent breaks to rest.

The journey through the foothills is uneventful. Because of the stops, we don't make great time. The stream we slept by connects to the Zaharani, the river that runs from the foothills down through Aksu and onward to the coast. The road follows along as it heads down through the foothills, and the Zaharani might be the most beautiful thing I've ever seen. I want to stop so much to admire it that Naji more than once tells me we need to keep going. Around noon we stop and buy food in a small farming community before we resume our journey. Eventually, it leads us to our destination.

I thought that the mountain town of Yokus was huge with its steep, sloping streets and city wall. It was the biggest place I had ever seen, and I felt out of place in its bustling streets. The smells were overwhelming to my canine nose. Now, overlooking Aksu in the late afternoon sun, I realize my sense of scale is off.

We are standing on the side of the road as it descends from the foothills to the plains below, the city stretching out before us. Golden light from the setting sun seems to drape across the buildings like an embroidered fleece, and Naji tells me what the structures are so I can understand what I'm looking at. The river cuts right through Aksu, dividing off one large district from the rest of the city. Tall sandy colored walls protect the city, while bridges cross the river. Aqueducts carrying the water necessary to support so many people flow into this bustling hub of life. Above the walls, I can see an assortment of flat and domed rooftops that stretch across the skyline. Bits of green from over a thousand courtyards are interspersed throughout. A dozen tall towers reach above the surrounding houses, dotted across the urban landscape. These are obviously where temples are located, but the most dominating feature is the large rock outcropping the city encircles. On top sits a citadel, its fortified walls watching over the buildings below.

"How many people live here, Naji?" I ask the spotted hyena.

"A little more than a hundred and fifty thousand," he says. "This is the capital of Khalin, did you expect it to be small?"

"A hundred and fifty thousand?" I mumble nervously. Yokus has ten thousand and I felt lost in such a large place. Aksu is huge, and I feel overwhelmed just imagining how crowded its streets have to be.

The hyena smiles softly at me, noticing my hackles. "I'll do my best to make sure you don't get overwhelmed."

I let out a timid squeak. "I didn't realize so many people lived in this country."

"Aksu was intimidating when I first came here, but I adjusted with time." He points to the large fortress in the center of the town perched on top of the acropolis. "The streets can be maze-like, but the Sultan's palace in the center makes it easy to know where you are." Peeking out above the citadel's walls, I can see a complex of gardens and elaborate buildings, a symphony of color rising above the dull defensive structure.

"It looks beautiful."

"It is, but I have never been beyond the main gate. When the fennec princes came out of the southern deserts, they settled here and built their citadel at the highest point in the area. They created the city of Aksu at their feet. The rumor is they wanted a city to match the splendor of their new home, and so they made Aksu the jewel in their crown."

Naji is still talking, but I can't wrap my head around the size of this place with its myriad structures and imposing city walls. I pride myself on my personal strength and being able to stand on my own, but in Aksu, I will be just another golden jackal in the crowd. At least in Zaptu, I was someone, just not someone many cared for.

"Zayn?" he says softly. "You're shaking."

I look up at the hyena. I hate feeling powerless, but here I am at the mercy of a place beyond my sense of scale.

"It's huge," I say, sucking in my breath. I can feel myself shivering.

He reaches out and rests a hand on my shoulder. "I know, but it's going to be okay. I'll help you, and there are others like us here. I can take you to meet Fadel tonight."

I try and still my body. "I would like that." I don't know who these others are like, but if they're like Naji, that would be nice. I don't see him hanging out with someone like Sarda.

"When you're ready," he says.

"It will take me time to learn my way around this place." I take a deep breath and nervously reach down to pick back up my pack, using the walking stick to support myself. I've learned to put aside my fears, so I can do this. I'm not alone either. "Let's go."

He smiles, amused at me, and picks up his pack to start down the road to the city.

৵

Once we pass through the city gate, it feels like I've been swallowed whole by some great beast. The rattle of carts and the barking sound of hawkers echoes off the stone and

82

wood that this city is built from. The streets of Aksu are full of people going about their business. The scents of so many different bodies living close together assaults my nose, a complex milieu of smells that makes my head spin.

Naji strides forward confidently, and without him, I would be lost in the crowd of pedestrians. After traveling down the main road leading away from the gate, he turns off onto a side street where we are forced to dodge a group of wolves buying bread from a pushcart. It's quieter here on the side street, with parents tending children and craftsman finishing up their day's work. We pass a leopard carefully watching her cubs play chase in a small garden attached to a temple. The green of the neat garden and shaded space contrasts nicely with the blue and gold tilework of the shrine.

Already some of the shops we pass are closed, but peddlers are busy cooking street food for the evening crowd. To me, it feels like everyone in the city has taken to the street now that dusk has started to fall. When the traffic on the side road gets too busy, Naji turns down a back alley so narrow that if I stretched out my arms, I would feel my claws brush both walls. I would have thought this would be unused, but we're constantly having to dodge people before it connects to another main street full of traffic.

A few blocks down the road, he turns down another alleyway, and I'm forced to quickly dart after him and his retreating tail. "This city is a maze of streets. How do you not get lost?" I call to him as we pass two fennec foxes in the narrow corridor.

He laughs. "You get used to it really. I probably should have stuck to the main roads instead of taking a few shortcuts today."

As I nervously follow the hyena through narrow streets and small squares, past public wells and down narrow alleyways, I definitely wish we'd taken a path I could retrace. Finally, after ten more minutes of winding maze-like streets, we're standing in front of a three-story stone house like many of the others we've passed. This one is on a quiet street. The first-floor windows are narrow and shuttered, but the upper floors have windows covered with wooden latticework. Shutters have been thrown open to let in the evening breeze.

"I rent the whole third floor in the back," Naji says, opening the door and stepping inside. I follow, and we walk down a short narrow corridor, passing a staircase leading to the floors above. This opens into a narrow courtyard, with water bubbling into a small cistern on the side of the wall. There are arches on one side of the courtyard, and rooms overlooking it from the two-story annex of the building. Behind that, another three-story section is incorporated into the structure connected to the courtyard. Several plants grow along the edge of the courtyard in pots.

"Do a lot of people live here, Naji?" I ask him.

"It varies depending on who is renting, but each floor of the building in the front and in the back is rented out. The central part here is where the family who owns the property lives. They're a group of striped hyenas who own a leatherworking shop."

I stop to look at the water collecting in the cistern. In Zaptu, there were two wells, and if you wanted water, you went and pulled it up yourself out of the ground. Here, you can just come downstairs. The entire sultanate is awash in water, and it constantly surprises me. I reach out to touch the water. It's cool, and feels refreshing, similar to the stream I stopped to admire up in the mountains.

"This building has its own private well?"

Naji laughs and walks over to stand beside me. "It's not a well. The city is fed by aqueducts and qanats that run down from the mountains. All the water that comes to Aksu is carefully piped into the city and distributed. Water not used here is recycled into other fountains. Each connection is taxed."

I just nod at the hyena and run my paw through the water. Countless hours of engineering have gone into building this system. To live in a place where water flows so freely, I never dreamed of it.

"Come," he says. "Let me show you upstairs."

I nod, still mesmerized, and follow him to the back and up two steep wooden flights of stairs. At the top, Naji unlocks a door and leads me into his apartment. The room is dark, stuffy, and dimly lit, but after closing the door he walks over to the wall and opens each shuttered window wide. I put down the pack I've been carrying with me near the door as Naji goes window to window. The dusk light filters through the latticework. With the windows open, Naji moves to light lanterns hanging about the room, giving the house a warm glow as the night wind freshens the air.

There are two rooms in Naji's home. The largest is a living space, while the other, the bedroom, is separated by a wall. An arched doorway leads into it. A set of curtains are tied to each side of the arch, allowing the room to be closed off for privacy. The floor is covered in richly woven rugs, while tapestries hang from the walls.

In the living space, most of the room is dedicated to a majlis for seating guests. A hookah sits invitingly in the center of a group of chairs and low divan. Nearby is a cabinet with a couple of books sitting on top of it. On the other side of the room, there is a small hearth with a kettle. It's a beautiful room.

It reminds me of what my parents' house once looked like. After my mother died, I quickly ran out of money. In order to buy food, I had to sell the rugs and furniture my father accumulated over the years working for the caravans. When I started working at the caravanserai, I bought some of it back at markup in order to have an inviting enough space for my clients, but I could never afford to fully restore it.

Naji puts his pack down in the bedroom and comes over to me. "Do you approve?" he asks, ears standing up. He looks really excited to be showing me his home.

"Yes," I say. "I will sleep here on the divan?"

"If that's where you want to sleep. I can share the bed if you want, I've had to do it before, but I will let you decide what makes you feel comfortable."

"I don't mind the divan."

"Good," he says, tail wagging. "I have a spare chest you can use. I'll need to move things around, but I have plenty of space."

The hyena leads me through the arch to the bedroom. One chest is at the foot of the bed, while the other is located against the far wall by itself. Naji opens the chest by the wall and removes a few blankets, which he places on top of the chest by the bed. I take time to unpack what I brought with me into the chest. A few changes of clothes and my dancing costumes are all I have. On top of everything, I place the carefully folded shawl my mother used to wear. Her scent has faded from the bright red fabric, but I swear sometimes I can still smell her. It and the sword are the only personal possessions of my parents I still own.

Naji is busy unpacking and sorting his clothing. "I'll take stuff to the wash lady I use tomorrow, but tonight we will go out to celebrate and see Fadel."

"Celebrate?" I ask him. "Celebrate how?"

He steps over to me, smiling coyly. "Fadel runs a special place called the Blue Door. He will know where you can find work."

There is a quirk in his smile that suggests something I don't know about. "Perhaps I should use the hammam first? "

"Nonsense. The Blue Door has its own baths, and everyone there is mithly, same as us."

"There is an entire hammam for us?" I say, surprised. I have lived in a town with a single hammam and here there is a hammam for just men who love other men? Just the thought of it brings a bit of a flush to my ears. I have never been able to be so open in my life.

"Yes, and more. They even serve wine and have their own entertainment. Come, let us get ready. You'll feel at home there."

❧

Even after dusk, the city of Aksu seems to pulse with life. We stop for kababs from a vendor near Naji 's apartment before we head to the Blue Door. The meat is tender and spicy, and I quickly eat the three I've bought. The traffic on the street has thinned, but I still see many people out going about their business. A few drunks and beggars are around, but not nearly as many as I would have thought. The city streets seem very safe. When we pass a group of city guards carrying torches, I realize why.

As for our destination, it becomes clear as we walk why Naji likes it so much. While I appreciate the fact Aksu has places like the Blue Door for people with interests like Naji and myself, I am a bit nervous about this. He says the inn has a tavern inside that serves wine and hires dancers to entertain the guests. There are rooms for rent to anyone who needs some privacy. The hyena insists they don't allow any whoring inside, but it still feels too close to the life I'm trying to escape. I want to get beyond this, yet it also calls to me. This is a place I can be myself, a place to be the Zayn I always dreamed I could be. I never thought such a place existed outside of my fantasies.

The building is two stories and nondescript from the street except for a large blue lantern hanging over a set of blue double doors. The name is carefully lettered onto a sign above. Standing outside on the street, under the blue light, I stare at it in disbelief.

"Do I belong here?"

"I think you do. No one will judge you for your past, and no one will pressure you to do anything you don't want to do either. Fadel is very strict about that, and we've all got our stories."

"You sure we don't need to clean up first?"

The hyena smirks. "They have a full hammam in the back."

"When you say full, do you mean they have a steam room?" I've only heard of those before.

The hyena nods, "Yes, and a cold pool too."

This inn has its own cold pool? From the street it does not appear to be very impressive or large, but it must go much further back than I realize. When he gestures to the closed heavy wooden doors, I nod in assent, and he pulls one side open to let me in.

The arched entrance hall is invitingly lit with glass lanterns. Off to the side there is an alcove with a desk at which a fennec fox is going over a ledger. Beyond, there is a courtyard bathed in light from multiple lanterns.

At the sound of our claws clicking on the stone, the fennec fox looks up. He smiles widely at the hyena. "Naji! You are back sooner than I expected. Did the trip go well?" he asks, hopping up to walk around the desk. His big ears are the only part of him that clears Naji's shoulders.

"No. They started bickering about who was paying for what, and I decided to cut my losses and left them in Banu to argue among themselves. I got what they owed me and came back," says Naji, before they exchange cheek kisses, the fennec standing up on his toes.

After the exchange, the fennec steps back. "Well, I'm glad the journey back went well."

"I did. Better than the journey out there. I brought a friend this time. Let me introduce you to Zayn."

"You've brought a friend with you? You get slyer every time I see you," he says, turning to me and offering a hand. "My name is Fadel. The Blue Door is my establishment."

I grasp his paw and then he leans forward to give me a quick cheek kiss, still holding onto my paw. It takes me back. "Uh, hi," is all I can awkwardly say.

"Ah, perhaps I was too forward," he says, letting go of my hand.

"No, it's fine, I'm just unsure what to make of this?"

"I assume you have a sexual interest in other men?" He smiles at me.

That's far more direct than I would have said it. "Yes…, but I didn't think a place like this existed."

The fennec pats me on the shoulder. "Not everyone knows about us. Naji is family here, so if he brings you here, you are family too. We are all mithly, same as you. Are you still trying to figure yourself out? Do not be afraid if it takes time."

I shake my head. "No, I know." I've known for a while. I thought it would make the work easier, but it didn't. It just told me more of what I wasn't.

"Well, you can explore yourself here or relax. Do nothing you don't want to do, and let no one pressure you. I ask you not to fool around in the courtyard or the tavern. Those spaces are for friends. In the hammam, I don't mind, but clean up after yourself if you do that in there. Also, people will watch you there, so if you want privacy, rent a room."

I blink. "You are quite forward," I say.

He laughs and gives me a sly grin. "I know men, and I have rules that must be followed."

I know men too. They will push you to get what they want if you let them, but this is the fennec's house, and I can see that. I also know what Fadel thinks we came here to do.

"Oh, don't worry, I know how to keep them in check," I say, patting Naji's shoulder. "It's easy if you know how to manage them."

The fox's smile widens.

"Fadel is quite the ruler of this establishment," interjects Naji.

"I have to be," he says. "The Sultan rules the city, but I rule the Blue Door." He gestures toward the table and chair in his entranceway. "My throne is far more modest, yet I have all the treasures in life I could ever seek here." His tail wags with amusement.

"Fadel fancies himself as royalty," says Naji. "All the fennecs here do."

"Hardly, but I must keep the peace," says the fox.

"Indeed," says Naji. "Inside these walls, his word is the law."

He rolls his eyes. "Do I look like our dear Sultan Ghazi?" he says to me. He stretches out his arms. "As you can see, my kaftan is but simple cotton, not silk."

"I wouldn't know. I'm not from around here."

Fadel glances at Naji. "Where are you from then?" he asks me.

"A little town called Zaptu."

Fadel gives Naji a questioning look. "I've heard of it, but never been there. Well, I hope your time in Aksu is pleasant. What can I do for you two today then?"

"We'd like to use the bath," Naji responds. "Just the bath."

"Of course," says the fennec. "Ten copper fals as always, but since this is Zayn's first time here, he's free."

Naji fishes out the copper and pays the fox. He then leads me into the courtyard. In the center of the quadrangle a small fountain sits, while to the side are groups of benches with backs. A thick fabric is draped over each bench and low tables that are easily moved to serve food and drink. Voices drift out of an open door behind the tables. A few patrons are sitting outside, smoking hookahs and talking to each other. A gallery rings the courtyard, and I assume that's where the private rooms are.

Once we get out of earshot of the fox I speak up. "He thinks we're here to fuck," I say.

The hyena stops and turns to me. "I know."

"And do you think we're going to fuck?"

"Did I ever once say we were? Fadel can help you, and I needed to introduce you to him."

I walk over so I can get my muzzle in his face and whisper. "As I said, I know men."

His dark colored eyes glow, catching a little of the light from the lanterns. "You assume you are the only one who does. I also know men, but I also said I would help you. That is more important than getting my dick wet." He gestures to the people around us. "Look around you. There is community here."

There is the tickle of smoke hanging in the courtyard air. Not far away, a jackal and a wolf are playing cards while smoking hookah. There is a strong familiarity in their action. The wolf laughs at a joke I can't hear from the jackal. Near them, a mixed group of friends, two ibexes and a leopard, appear to be drinking, while in the back of the seating area, a fennec like Fadel enjoys a smoke by himself.

I look back to Naji, and I suck in my breath. "I don't know what that is or feels like. All I know is men who use you, who take what they want from you and throw you away when they're done with you. I don't know what community is."

His ears fall and he stares at me for a few seconds, blinking. "It's a shared sense of belonging. Maybe you find someone for yourself, or maybe you play around, but you can do that as you see fit. You can do what you want. "

I let myself process that. What is belonging? I don't know anymore. Did I belong in Zaptu? Not really. People avoided me once I started dancing, and outside of Usman and Farida, I was alone. Oh sure, I could spend time with Amare, but he was a coward, too afraid to admit the truth in himself. Do I belong here? I don't know yet. The hyena has treated me well, one of the few in a long time. Do I belong with him? No, but should I want to?

"That may be so, but what do you want?"

"Right now, a bath, a massage, and a glass of wine. Later, I would like to sleep off the tiredness of the road."

"I mean beyond tonight."

He shrugs. "I keep moving for a reason."

There's something about that I don't understand, something in him that pushes him forward, that I can't see. "You're running from something, aren't you?"

He regards me carefully. "Only from myself. Is it that obvious?"

"Only to one who looks for what a man really wants." I wrap an arm around him. "I can help you relax."

He tilts his head, and an ear dips. "Of that I'm sure, but is that what you want? I recall you telling me you don't want to be someone's house boy."

Old habits die hard, but they must die. I can have my own desires now too. "You said I can play around, right?"

He nods.

My ears go back. "Well, you're gentle. I like not being broken afterward."

He looks at me, searching my expression, trying to understand what's going on inside of me. "I did not take you here to do that with you."

"I realize."

His lips curl up in a smile. "Let us wash first. We both stink of dust and sun."

On this point I cannot argue, and Naji breaks out of my grasp so he can resume leading me forward.

Under the arch, there is a narrow hallway that serves as the entrance to the baths. The hallway leads to a domed room with high windows. Inside there is an attendant who gives us each a towel. We take off our street clothes in a small side room across from the attendant's desk. Naji then leads me down a hall to the warm room of the bath where a number of patrons are already in the process of bathing.

The warm room is a large octagonal space, with smaller, hotter rooms opening off from it. Basins of water with spigots line the walls. High windows allow light into the room during the day, but the lanterns lining the white walls give the space a glowing feeling at night with the reflections off the tilework. In the center of the room sits a large, raised slab of marble. A geometric pattern of tilework is inlaid on top of the slab. On it a few patrons are sitting and talking, towels draped over their laps. On the other side of the room, two caracals are receiving massages from attendants.

We sit for a bit on the edge of the slab, letting the steamy heat soak into our fur. I'm surprised to find out the stone itself is hot to the touch. After just a minute, my tongue is out as I pant.

"It's good for you," Naji says, also panting.

I gulp, trying to catch my breath. "I guess?" is all I can muster.

"You'll feel a lot better. Trust me." he reassures. This is the first time I've ever been to a true bath, so I'm not sure what the process is.

We rest for a little bit in the warm room, towels wrapped around our mid-sections, before moving to one of the hot rooms. In there I feel like my entire body is going to give out, so we don't stay long. Afterward, we return to the warm room to rinse, soap, and rinse again. Metal bowls are placed next to the basins of water that line the room, and we dip into the cold water a couple of times in order to rinse ourselves.

Next, we wait for the two attendants, who are busy with other patrons. When they're done, it's our turn. We spread our towels down on the stone and lie down, posteriors and tails exposed. The underside of my muzzle lies against the towel. It feels weird to have my backside exposed like this with it not being a job. The attendant who works with me is a heavy set, older red fox with strong, powerful arms. He instructs me to lie still and proceeds to dig his paws and claws into my neck.

Concerns of modesty flee quickly. "Ow," I cringe, as he squeezes at my shoulders. "What are you doing to me?"

"Your neck and shoulders are tight." He pinches at my neck and then reaches over to grab an arm. He pulls it back while a heavy paw rests in the center of my back.

"Go easy on him, Ales," offers Naji, grunting as the attendant massaging him pushes against his back. "He's never before met someone with paws like you have."

The fox chuckles and twists my arm, putting weight against my shoulder. I yelp, surprised.

"I can tell. Your muscles are just a series of knots. Let me do what I do best, jackal, and Ales will make you a new man. It will hurt now, but you will feel amazing when I'm done."

"I need that arm," I whimper.

Ales is already prodding at my back. "What have you done to yourself?" He's obviously noticed the scars. "Your skin is a mess."

"It's a long story."

He runs his blunted claws over my back, and I twitch. "Head back down," he says to me. The fox cracks his fingers. "I like a good challenge, and you, sir, are in need of my talents."

Ten minutes later, I feel like someone has taken a lead ball and rolled it all over my body. To his credit, when Ales finally lets me off the slab, I swear I'm standing taller than I ever have in my life. Places that even Sarda never reached ache, but the feeling is strangely pleasant. Naji has been waiting for me off to the side, his massage taking much less time than mine.

The hyena smirks as he rinses off a final time at one of the basins on the side of the room. "How do you feel?"

I dump some cool water on my head, letting it run down through my fur. "Horrible and amazing at the same time. You?"

"Better. Civilized again," he chuckles as he towels off his face. The mane of fur that runs from the back of his head down his back sticks up.

I'm just sopping wet and still panting. "I'm going to need to brush my fur out when we get back."

"Oh, they have someone here who will do that, but first, would you like to swim?" He motions me to follow and leads me to the cool room on the opposite side of the main hallway of the hammam, tail wagging. We're the last people out of the steam room, although a mixed group of mongooses and caracals enters as we're leaving. I can hear Ales chuckle at his good fortune from the hallway.

We step into a room with an arched vaulted ceiling. Green and gold tilework covers the vaulting all the way to the top. This room, like the bath, is also octagonal. A colonnade wraps around the dome over an octagonal pool. Each side of the room contains a niche with wicker chairs and tables. Lanterns hang off each column, and on each table, a small oil lamp has been placed. Naji walks up to the pool and drops his towel next to it, before slipping into it nude.

I glance around. In a niche, the caracals who were ahead of us are talking over tea. A wolf who was also ahead of us is sitting still for a striped hyena. The hyena is pulling snags out of the wolf's fur with a coarse brush.

"The water is nice. It will help you cool down after the warm room," he says, splashing in the pool.

The water looks inviting, but it also looks deep. "I don't know how to swim."

He chuckles and stands up in the pool. The water comes to midway up his chest. "See, you'll be fine. Even Fadel can stand up in this."

I let go of the towel and the last sense of privacy I have here. Gingerly I step down the stairs into the pool. The shock of the cold water stops me, but I don't dawdle long.

Naji sinks back into the water. "See, not so bad."

"It is refreshing," I concede with a shiver as my body adjusts to the shock.

He smiles and comes over. "Nice, isn't it?" he says.

I wrap my arms around myself.

He frowns. "There is no need to be shy now."

"It's cold," I say, curling my tail around myself.

He laughs. "Well, it is the cold pool now. You have to let your body adjust to the sudden temperature change."

Yes, I'm no longer panting anymore, but how is this comfortable?

"You all right?"

I exhale and let my arms drop.

"Yes."

"Your ears are down."

Damn these things and their expressive nature. I force a smile and push them up.

He lets go of me and slips backwards, kicking off the bottom, splashing me.

"Stop that!"

He smirks. "Sorry."

"You did that intentionally."

"Me?" He kicks the surface again and I get showered with water.

I growl and come after him. It's harder to walk in the water than on land. He laughs and rolls over and makes an escape to the other side of the pool.

I scramble after him and grab at his tail, pulling backwards and slipping as I do. In the ensuing chaos, my head gets submerged. Water rushes into my lungs, and I panic. What was a moment of playfulness is suddenly life or death, as I can't breathe. I have to push myself off the bottom of the pool in order to get above the water.

Breaking the surface, I sputter and cough, lungs burning.

"Okay, okay, maybe we'll get out."

"It's not my fault I grew up in the desert and can't swim!" I grumble, standing in the middle of the pool. The water comes up to the middle of my chest in this part.

"You are not supposed to drink the water now," he laughs. "Come on, let's go towel off."

I'm not sure what makes me do it, but it may be my inner pup, long suppressed, that comes suddenly to the surface. I'm not ready to get out yet, so I lunge at him and pull him down. This time I keep my muzzle closed, and when he breaks the surface he laughs, instead of being angry at me.

"You deserved that," I growl at him.

"Oh, do I? Let me show you how a good game of chase works."

I dart away, or at least as fast as I can in the water. A paw closes around my tail, and I yelp.

"Hey!"

He laughs and lets me try and pull him across the pool before he lets go. I make it to the side with the entrance. He lazily swims over to me.

"There, that's better. Your ears are up now."

"Yes, this is nice."

"I…" I'm naked in a pool of water with this man, surrounded by others. I glance around. The wolf and hyena are now talking, the brushing finished. On the other side of the room, I see a lion with a striped hyena curled up against him. They're in an alcove, but it is obvious he's fondling the hyena.

"Is that what Fadel means by playing around?"

"Yes, people fool around sometimes in this room. I've seen worse though. Done it once myself, even."

I frown. "Worse?"

He licks his muzzle. "Everyone here is like us. Use your imagination."

In the safety of the Blue Door, here in the back where clothes are not needed, the moment to enjoy each other's company likely leads to much more involved touching.

"Is there a limit to how far you can go?" I ask, curious. The hammam has been much more proper than I would have thought it would be.

"Fadel would prefer you to rent a room, but if you keep it down, he is not going to break it up. Just don't touch without asking."

I glance back at the couple. The lion has his muzzle down in the striped hyena's crotch and is bobbing up and down. I turn to Naji, who just shrugs.

"Some people are very open about it."

I don't ask the hyena if he is. Maybe I should, but I already know the hyena enough to know the answer. Underneath the layers of a whore's professional composure, buried inside of myself, I can feel my own longings. It feels both foreign and strange to me, a fire that barely lives smothered under years of wretched work. I gingerly take one of his hands, then I push myself toward him and kiss him. Deep inside, I can feel the fire gasp as it's given fresh air.

His eyes register surprise. His body tenses just for a brief moment, then relaxes. He gingerly returns my kiss. When we break off, we just look at each other.

"We don't have to do it here," he whispers.

I suck in a breath. It feels weird how open it is here, yet I know what I desire. "I… I want to."

"Then let me do for you something I doubt many have ever done."

His words are an intriguing proposition that floods my mind. I feel the rush of possibilities as he guides me over to the steps into the pool and sits me down at the top of them.

His first kiss is gentle, wetting my dry appetite with the feeling of something I rarely remember, reciprocity. I press back, and the hyena sinks down, lower half of his body still in the pool, along with my feet. I feel the gentle nipping at my throat and then my chest. His movement is nothing like the urgent need for relief from Sarda. He takes his time, teasing me with hot breath against my fur.

Slowly he lowers his muzzle and noses my crotch, his whiskers tickling my thighs. I watch, captivated as his tongue darts out to tease my sheath. I shiver in anticipation, and he wraps a paw around the base of my shaft as he begins to nose it. My reservations about doing this here fade away as my lust only grows.

My sheath pulls back, pushed aside by my growing hardness. The hyena gingerly takes my shaft into his mouth and starts to suck on the tip. My member quivers at the new sensation. His tongue is hot and moist against my sensitive skin. For as many blowjobs I've given, I've rarely had someone give me one before. The motions he's doing are familiar to me, but the sensations from being on the receiving end are all foreign.

I squirm as Naji starts to suck on my entire shaft. I moan so loudly, I shock even myself. I feel myself slipping away. I know the other people in the room are watching now, but I'm far too into this to care. Naji looks up at me from where he's crouching on the stairs as he licks up my shaft. I can see the edges of his muzzle quirk up in a smile, but he doesn't break his pace. I've given my body over to countless patrons, but it has never been like this. It was always their needs that mattered, never mine. Now, I feel myself quivering, each frayed nerve desperate and needy.

When I grab the hyena by the back of his head and force him down on my bucking body, he doesn't fight me. Instead, he lets me drive myself into his muzzle rapidly before I shoot my load into his mouth. Sagging back against the marble at the pool's edge I close my eyes, and my paw slips off Naji's head. I am spent, but the fire inside me burns brighter than I ever remember it. I have desires. I have longings, and I want to do this again. I may have just corrupted my ability to service clients uncompromisingly. I hope to hell I have.

"My god, Zayn, you cum like no one has ever sucked you off before," says the hyena. I open my eyes to catch him wiping away a trail of my seed from his muzzle.

I feel my ears warm at his concern and the warmth of the moment. I briefly consider lying before I tell him the truth. "It's been a very, very long time."

His eyes light up, but Naji doesn't say anything else. He moves to get up, but I stop him.

"You should finish," I say. "I want to watch."

"Okay," he replies, getting back down between my legs. Naji nuzzles my shaft for a minute as he plays with himself. I get to admire the view as the hyena handles himself until he climaxes at my feet. Then he swims backwards from the steps to dunk himself. Together we get out of the pool and start to towel off. After initially patting himself dry, Naji towels my back down, fluffing the fur.

The striped hyena who was brushing the wolf walks up to us with a cough and hands us both a wet cloth. He must have watched the entire performance. "Did either of you want a brushing?" he asks, holding up his wooden brush.

The question throws me for a loop. I'm holding the wet cloth in my hand to clean myself with, my towel in the other, and my spent shaft still hanging out in front of a total stranger. He, in the meantime, is wearing a simple shirt and loose pants and looks like someone I'd encounter on the street. "I think I'll be fine."

He looks behind me towards Naji.

"Of course," says the hyena, "and I think Zayn here is going to need it too."

My ears droop a little. "I don't mind doing it myself."

The striped hyena shrugs and gestures towards a stool off to the side. Naji walks over and sits on it, and the hyena proceeds to brush Naji down. He starts with his head and works his way down with an expert's care. I'm forced to watch since I don't have a brush for myself. He stops a few times to pull clumps of shed fur off, but he doesn't waste time in getting all the snags out of Naji's fur. To finish, the striped hyena stretches out Naji's tail and works his brush through it until it shines.

"You're good," he says to Naji, who then gets up. The striped hyena turns to me. "Change your mind?"

He does know what he's doing. "Sure," I say.

With a paw motion he has me sit, and then he starts to brush me. He quickly does my head and works his way down to my shoulders and arms. His strokes are deft and long. He goes all the way down to my legs before he finishes with my tail. When he's done, he nods to us both and walks off, carrying away two large clumps of different colored fur.

"You look good," says Naji, "almost glowing."

I get up and look at the hyena's handiwork. "Thanks. He's quick and smooth."

"Yes, he doesn't waste any time or words," says the hyena, leading me back to the changing room in the front. We dress, and I wish I had brought clean clothes. Walking back into the courtyard, Naji heads over to where the tables are. A few patrons are sitting outside, talking in groups or smoking hookah. Behind them, through the large open door, I can hear music, and this is where Naji goes.

Stepping through the open door, we enter a vaulted rectangular room that reaches up to the second story of the inn. Low divans are arranged in groups, flanking a low stage against the front wall. A leopard at the front of the room dances to a soft, sensual song. I slow my pace, concerned at what I'm walking into, trying to read the room. Many of the couches are already occupied, but not everyone is watching the leopard. Some people are just talking to their friends. This audience obviously appreciates the leopard's movements, but their eyes do not look like the eyes of men who have traveled far and seek respite for the night. Some even watch the leopard together, paws resting on legs or clasped together in familiar intimacy.

While I'm looking around a lion walks up to Naji who says something to him I don't catch.

"A pitcher and seating for two please," responds Naji.

The lion proceeds to usher us over to a divan in the back of the room. After a quick word and an exchange of coin with Naji, he trots off. Less than a minute later, he returns with a pitcher of wine and two pewter goblets. He sets them down on a low table in front of the couch and pours us wine before leaving the pitcher for us.

"To life, to love," Naji says, holding up his cup, his voice competing with the din of the crowd and the music.

"To life," I say, putting the cup to my lips to sip the wine. The rich liquid with its heady scent flows over my tongue and down my muzzle. It's surprisingly good, better than what I ever found in Zaptu. I set the cup down and lean back into the pillows on the divan. I see the allure this has. The dancer is slowly working his way through the crowd near the stage. The music is relaxing, and from the jovial nature of the crowd, I can tell the wine flows from the pitchers as long as you have the coin to purchase it.

After checking out the room earlier, I focus on the leopard now. He's graceful, but the music is intentionally slow so he can flow through the air. His motions aren't hurried, but he has a practiced ease with the way he approaches men for tips. His movements are perfectly timed to the two musicians sitting in the corner of the stage. For all the pampering Naji is giving me tonight, this show transports back to my dancing back at the caravanserai in Zaptu. While I never enjoyed having to whore myself out afterward, the time I spent dancing in the night air was a thrill. It made what came afterward easier.

I lean over to talk to Naji. "Do they often have dancers?"

"Some nights. Other nights they just have music. It varies," he replies.

I sip my wine and go back to watching the leopard. The couch with its pillows is very comfortable, but I've never been in this type of setting as a customer. It unnerves me a little. I identify more with the dancer than I do with the other patrons. I follow the cat as he moves around the front of the room, passing a fennec sitting against the wall with a hood pulled over his head. Only his ears and nose tip give away his species, but he's calmly smoking, watching the dancer with rapt attention. Idly I wonder who he is and what he is hiding, before I turn back to the leopard.

I'm just watching the performance, sipping my wine and letting my mind wander, when I'm woken out of my reverie by Fadel walking over to us.

"Ah, I see you two have made it out of the baths," he says. When Fadel motions, Naji shifts over, and the fennec sits down next to him. "Quite satisfied as I understand it."

Naji lowers his ears. "Yes, we did."

The fox glances at me, but I just turn and go back to watching the dancer. I'm not in the mood to be harried, and from the smile on the fox's muzzle, I can tell he's amused by what he heard about us.

It takes me a moment to notice that he's whispering something to Naji. The hyena responds back, but I can't make it out. As calmly as I can I lean over and discreetly tilt an ear.

"Tell me what is going on, my friend," I hear Fadel whisper.

"It's nothing important," says Naji.

"You are back early, and with company. There was no trouble out there?" Out of the corner of my eye, I see him move closer to the hyena, possibly noticing I may be listening.

"Those two cheetahs tried my patience, constantly back and forth with each other about money. I told them I was tired of it and cut my losses. For all I know, they're still arguing about whose cut my wages came from."

The fox chuckles. "And your friend here?"

Naji's response is clear in my ears, the force in his voice making it carry to my tilted ear. "He needed help. I couldn't let someone suffering continue to suffer the way he was."

The fennec glances at me, and I smile. His response to Naji is so low I almost can't hear it over the music. "I would pin you for a fox myself if you didn't have those spots."

The hyena shrugs and then Fadel speaks up so I can clearly hear him.

"Are you enjoying the music and dance?" he asks me.

"Yes. I find his style of dance very interesting. I'm used to more energetic forms."

"A connoisseur, I see," remarks the fennec. "Not all of my customers appreciate the artistic part of the performance."

"Zayn is an accomplished dancer in his own right," adds Naji.

"Are you now?" inquires the fennec.

"Yes, I'm quite proficient at sword dancing."

"Well, that would be a sight to see," he says, ears up. "I've never had anyone who could do that."

Before I can respond the room explodes into applause as the leopard up front finishes his routine. Many people are clapping and all the conversations in the room end as the leopard bows. This response floors me, because there is not the sense of lust from the audience I expect after dancing. After the leopard speaks to someone up front, I catch the tell-tale passing of coins to the cat before he takes his leave from the stage through a side door with a wave to the audience. After he is gone, the musicians resume playing.

Fadel clears his throat to get my attention. "As you can see, I have quite an enthusiastic audience. I'm always looking for new talent."

Quite enthusiastic indeed. "I see! I would be happy to show you my routine sometime."

He claps his paws together. "Tomorrow perhaps, in the early afternoon? If you're good, I can rotate you in as a performer."

"I would be delighted," I respond. If no one else does sword dancing, I could do quite well here. Naji makes an amused sound. I think this is what he wanted to have happen.

Fadel looks like he's going to ask me something else, but someone catches his eye. One of the servers is trying to flag him down.

"It looks like I have business to attend to. Tomorrow, Zayn?"

I bob my head in assent. "Tomorrow."

"Excellent," he gets up and points toward the doorway, where a caracal is leaning against it. "Also, look who else is back," he says to Naji.

Naji glances at the cat. "You still let him in here?"

Fadel flicks his ears. "As long as he behaves. Do let me know if he doesn't. I know he used to be your friend, but I have the staff watching him like a hawk because of last time."

"'Used to' being the key words," says Naji. The fennec shrugs, and with a polite wave to me, he walks off.

When he's gone, I pick up the pitcher and top off my cup. I could easily work this crowd like the leopard did. There's no guarantee Fadel will hire me, but it's a shot. Naji casually puts an arm behind me on the couch and relaxes.

"That worked out as I expected," Naji says.

"You think he'll hire me?"

"I don't see why not, but it's up to you though if you want to work here."

It's my old life and yet it's not. There was no bidding, and there will be no prick to service afterward. There is just the art of the dance and the sensuality of the movements to worry about. "I think I'd like it," I remark, holding up the goblet of wine to toast.

"Yes," he says, returning the toast. "I thought you might. It isn't too much like life in Zaptu though, is it?"

It is, and it isn't, but there's one part of that I don't want to give up. "Maybe, but I love dancing."

He opens his mouth to comment, but something catches his eye. He frowns instead. "Oh great, Rigel is coming over here."

The lanky caracal Fadel pointed out is walking toward us. He has a serious look on his muzzle as he beelines straight to us.

"Naji, I didn't know you had returned." His voice is soft, and yet there is something in the way he talks that bothers me.

"Just today," says the hyena.

"I see you have a friend," he remarks. "Forgive me, my name is Rigel. Would it be okay if I joined you and Naji?" he asks me.

Naji looks annoyed by this question. "I uh think we're—" I start to respond.

"Now isn't the time, Rigel."

"Why not? Do you not have time for an old friend? I was waiting for Fadel to finish talking to you."

Naji pulls his arm back to himself. "You tend to ignore me nowadays, so what do you want?"

"Can we not remember the old days?"

The hyena exhales slowly. "There is not a day that goes by where I don't think of what used to be, but the past is the past. "

"Do you?" He gestures toward me. "I wonder if you perhaps forget."

"Please leave Zayn out of this, okay? I'm helping him out."

"Is he helping you out?" he asks me.

"Yes?" I respond, confused. I wonder if there's a specific answer he is looking for.

"You don't sound convinced. Perhaps you need someone to show you a better time," he suggests, letting some fang show. "It is the least I can do."

The implication hits me full force. "Absolutely not."

Rigel laughs, but Naji cuts him short. "Why do you even suggest such nonsense? I would think at some point you'd want to do more than rip at what's left of our tattered friendship."

The caracal narrows his eyes. "I am not the one at fault here, but I thought, old friend, you might like some news. I hear that an acquaintance of yours, Aziz, is back in town, and he's looking to settle old debts with you. You should watch your shadow."

"Thank you, but I don't think that's going to be an issue."

"I would not be so foolish now. I can help you with this, should you have the sense to ask for my help."

"Again, thank you, but I think I can handle it. Aziz is my problem anyway, not yours."

The caracal shrugs. "Once again, you're not listening." The cat focuses on me. "Make sure he keeps his ears up." With that, he walks off as Naji growls softly at his back.

"What was that about?" I whisper, after Rigel is out of earshot.

"Rigel is being a dunghill. We used to be close, but we lost a friend, Isim, and our friendship has never seen the same," he says, and reaches for his wine goblet. "I wish it hadn't happened, but there is nothing I can say that will ever ease his pain. "

It's easy to tell from the way Naji's body sags there's more to this story, but I'm not going to ask. I don't want to let it ruin the rest of my night, and I can already tell Naji's eyes are wet as he takes a deep gulp from his wine. I'll have to see when the time is right to press him for more information.

In the meantime, I am excited that things are looking up for me. My tail refuses to be still as I settle down to enjoy the rest of the night.

❧

In the afternoon the next day, while Naji is out running errands, I go to the Blue Door to show Fadel what I can do with a blade. It takes me a little while to get there, but I'm able to retrace the steps from last night. My ankle is still sore from the fall on the road two days ago, but it's feeling much better. Even though I'm not able to push myself as much as I'd like, the fennec finds my performance so good he immediately offers me a chance to perform in two days. After talking to one of the musicians about the music for the dance, and noticing that I'm using a sharp sword, Fadel directs me to a nearby shop that will have a sword designed for what I do.

"Tell the owner to charge me," says the fennec, giving me a note. "He supplies us with various wares for the inn. I know he had an acrobat's sword in there, since he asked a while back if I had a use for it."

Following Fadel's directions, I go to a small shop close to the Blue Door. The lion who owns the store does indeed have a sword specially made with a dull edge, but he must dig in the back to find it. In the meantime, I admire all the various other metalwork he has. Lanterns, braziers, and bowls are stacked all over along with an amazing selection of decorative platters. When he finds the sword, he brings it out to me. The blade is similar to mine but has a different heft to it. The shopkeeper tells me it is specially made for the type of dancing I do, and after giving him the note, the lion sends me on the way with the sword.

I want to wander around a little and see what else is in Aksu, but I have to retrace my steps so I can return back to the apartment without asking for directions. When I get there, and since I have nothing else to do, I go up to the roof and start creating a new routine.

This sword doesn't feel right in my paws at first. I've been dancing so long with my father's sword and its sharpened edge that I feel like this precaution is unnecessary. While I learned the art using a wooden sword, I sold it back in Zaptu. This new blade is carefully balanced between the hilt and blade; it easily sits on my head without trying to pull on one side. The sword I own is made for fighting, and this new one is made for doing tricks with. It simply handles differently.

Naji comes back late afternoon from seeing what other jobs he can take and finds me still practicing up on the roof. He watches me for a while before he speaks up.

"The meeting with Fadel went well, I take it?" he asks.

I pause for a moment to catch my breath. "Yes. Fadel thinks I have talent, and the work pays. He's very nice. I have two days to prepare, and I want to do something different for my debut."

"That he is. He's got a big heart, but he will expect you to work hard."

I chuckle. "It can't be anywhere as bad as Zaptu. It will let me save up some coin and I can find a place for myself, he says."

The hyena doesn't say anything and just nods.

"I won't have to sleep on your divan then." Last night I fell asleep on the divan tipsy and tired after a wonderful evening.

His expression is neutral, but I can see his ears dip. "If that's what you want," he says. "You're welcome to stay as long as you want."

I really don't know what type of relationship Naji and I have now. Last night was fun, but I wanted to explore. I wanted to again feel the freedom I've given up to man after man. I'm not here to be Naji's house boy, but I never said I couldn't find love. Am I in love? I'm not sure. I know I haven't been in love for a very long time, so the concept feels foreign to me now. He's not like the many who've had me, and yet I'm not sure if this is something deeper. Even more serious, can I still love? The wounds my life in Zaptu inflicted upon my heart are still fresh.

"Thank you. I'm in no hurry to leave."

I lift up the blade again and start slowly tracing out the pattern and footwork I'm working on. It will feel good to dance again and to not do it as a prequel to selling myself. That itself is liberating. Naji watches me, but he doesn't say anything. I try and focus on the routine I'm working on, but I can't help feeling I'm performing to an audience of one as I work to refine my new routine. I hope I am.

A Traitor's Bargain
(Naji)

Since I started lodging in this apartment, I've had my rooms to myself. I could be alone with my own thoughts here, so it is strange to suddenly have someone else with me in the apartment day and night. When I did not have a job to do, I would eat when I was hungry, and go out when the mood suited me. I tend to spend my days off either at the Blue Door when I want to be social or reading at the café at the corner where the street I live on intersects the main road.

I only own a dozen books myself, but I cherish the fact I was taught to read so I could enter service to the Emirs back home. I was trained to be a solider but educated so I could become an officer. While that did not work out as planned, access to the written word has taken on a new meaning for me in Aksu. Books are still a luxury here, but the city drinks deep of the written word. Scribes are in high demand, dutifully copying the words of the great poets and writers. New works appear frequently, and if I had a steadier stroke to my hand, I could have taken up the pen instead of the sword. I have more than once been called on in the café to read for those who cannot themselves, and if I kept a steady schedule, I would likely be an institution there.

Except I don't keep a steady schedule. My life shifts like the desert sands, shaped by the winds of change. Now though, it has finally blown me into a sheltered crack in the rocks of life that I could anchor myself against, should I be willing to. I could have gone looking for work today, but since Zayn is working on his routine, I decided to take it easy. Tomorrow I'll talk to my contacts.

"Are you going to come tomorrow when I perform?" He has come downstairs from practicing on the roof and he's panting from the exertion. The strong scent of sweat and excitement fills the room. I heard him come in, but I didn't want to disturb his preparation.

I look up from the book and close it. I've read this one a couple times already with its epic poems about warriors long gone and their trials and failures at war and love. "Of course."

"I hope I get this right."

"You'll be fine. You've already been to the Blue Door today to speak to the musicians."

His ears lower. "Yes, but what if I mess up?"

"With how much you've been practicing, I doubt you are going to mess up. You are not performing for the Sultan either. Convince the audience you're good, and Fadel will give you more work."

"How will I know if they like it?"

"You saw the applause two nights ago. You'll know."

He considers for a moment and then sits down on the divan. "I still worry I won't be good enough for them. That I'm too different."

"How could you be different? Everyone is mithly."

He shrugs. "It's not that. I don't have the refinement of someone who grew up here."

I bark out a laugh. "You say that, but do I?"

"You seem to know your way around it."

My tail flicks back and forth in amusement. "I learned. I was a newcomer here once also. I came here with basically nothing and had to sleep on the street."

He glances around my apartment. "You've done well for yourself."

"Thank you. It wasn't an easy road. You'll do well for yourself, if you give yourself the chance to."

He nods. "I hope so."

"Trust me on this," I say, reaching out to take one of his paws in both my hands. "You'll do fine, and I'm going to be here to make sure you do."

He smiles then, and I feel myself smile back. I'm glad I brought him here. I think everything is going to be fine.

On the fourth day back in Aksu, I decide to pay an old friend a visit to inquire about work for myself. Waking up after dawn, I find Zayn is still asleep on my divan, curled up on top of the pillows. After we talked yesterday, he went back and practiced until dusk. I pause for a minute to watch his chest rise and fall. He is just an outline of golden fur against the shuttered windows. I've wondered if he would like to sleep in the bed with me, but if this is what he feels comfortable with, he is welcome to sleep here. I'm still trying to figure out what type of situation I've got myself into, but I think only time will tell.

I slip out to buy breakfast. Even though I'm gone less than thirty minutes, by the time I come back, Zayn has gotten up. The shutters are open, and he is in the process of tidying up and making tea. I bring back some dried beef sausage, bread, and sliced cucumber. We eat together in what already feels like a pleasant routine, talking about the Blue Door and Fadel.

After promising Zayn I will be there tonight to see him dance, I head out to the Grand Market. I don't know how long it will take and if any promising leads will come up that I need to follow up on, but I am looking forward to seeing Zayn step out onto that stage.

By then, it's already late morning, so the city has settled down to wait out the midday heat. Today, like yesterday, promises to be hot. Business in the bazaar continues, but things take on a more relaxed feeling this time of day. Only during the height of summer, when even in the shade it's sweltering, will most places close before noon and reopen in the early evening. Today the warmth is just an annoyance, but since my venture with the caravan netted me less money than expected, I need to start looking.

Located near the gate to the Sultan's citadel is the Grand Market of Aksu. It consists of a large public square where traders and traveling merchants meet to sell their wares. A large souk is adjacent to the square made up of covered streets full of small shops. Caravans from distant lands beyond the mountains and across the desert come to trade here with merchants who come from the west, across the ocean. Together the square and the souk form the commercial heart of the entire sultanate. The fortunes of many have been made and broken in the Grand Market. From this epicenter of activity, the fennec sultans have financed an entire nation.

Rows of tents cover the square. These makeshift streets are the only form of organization that can be forced upon the economic bustle of the market. The square is packed with traders and shoppers. The sound of vegetable hawkers and rug sellers mix in with the murmur of storytellers to form a cacophony of sound. Around this noise, the city thrives and the sultanate prospers. Even the scribes, carefully tucked in a quieter part of the market, have a place here.

When I first came to Aksu, I called the market home. Like many before me, I slept out in the open with the other street youth, scratching out a meager existence. Even now, the sounds and sights of the market still work their magic upon me whenever I visit. I dodge carts and camels like a younger hyena as I fight my way through the crowd in the square. This controlled chaos is a part of the city I love the most. Each day, the market changes subtly as new merchants and caravans arrive and depart.

My destination is a quiet store located in the adjacent souk. While the streets here are calmer, the shops are just as important. Many a merchant who started in the Grand Market eventually moves their business here, once they have made a name for themselves. The shaded, less crowded conditions provide a more relaxing setting to work in, but these streets are by no means deserted. The traders here make bigger deals.

Down one alleyway, past a silk trader and a carpet salesman, is a section of the souk that specializes in spices. Naima's shop, a modest affair stocked with tea and dried herbs, is located here. Walking in under the arch, my nose is tickled by the rich aromas of sage, cardamom, and mint. There are so many scents it's impossible to sort them out, and in the middle of the store, sitting in repose, is Naima. The leopard's golden eyes sparkle when I enter. She is older, with a touch of gray in her black spots, but I would not want to find myself the target of her anger. The rumor is when she was younger, Naima was the most sought-after assassin in the sultanate. I don't know if that's true or not, but I did learn the best knife tricks from her.

"Ah, good morning, Naji," she says when I enter. "I just got in some freshly dried mint and sage this morning," she adds, sweeping her paw around. "Might I interest you in some?"

"Please, Naima. How often do I come in here looking to just buy mint?"

"Perhaps then the finest tea from the farthest reaches of the east is more your speed."

"You know my weaknesses, but I'm looking to see if you have any leads for work."

"You know I'm not some recruiting agency for swordsmen. This is a spice and tea shop here, Naji." Her eyes sparkle. Naima runs a respectable business, but she's still got her paws on the street and ears to the ground.

"You still have to trade for these."

She smiles, fangs showing. "Indeed, indeed I do. Speaking of, I hear there is a caravan leaving in two days for the Banu Oasis and then all the way to Ardal. Most of what they're taking isn't high value, but they will have some saffron on them. I believe they're planning to return with nutmeg. They could use a good guard. The pay is good, and I can put in a word for you."

That's a three-month round trip under good conditions. If they're taking saffron, something worth its weight in gold, they're going to have quite a bit of money with them on the return. They'll need able men to go with them.

"That sounds excellent, but I'm looking for something closer to home. Something low key. I was just in Banu anyway. Not looking to go back."

The leopard considers. "You were supposed to be heading to Zara, weren't you?"

"Yes, but things with the job fell through. I decided to part ways with those two idiots in Banu."

"Ah… I'll make a note of that for when they return. Well, I also know someone heading down to Akara next week."

That's still a two-week trip. "I need something stable in Aksu."

"Well, there is nothing you are going to want that I know about. I can ask around though," she pauses, tail flicking. "You know they're always looking for people down at the counting house."

I snort. "The reason they can't keep anyone there is because they don't pay."

"Well, you said you wanted stable. There's nothing stable in your line of work that pays big. If you're thinking of finally settling down, why don't you see if the city guard is recruiting?"

"You know the city guard won't take me. We have a history going back. I'm pretty sure I haven't made any friends over there."

She chuckles knowingly. "True, but why are you looking for something different than what you normally do anyway? I'm sure I can hook you up with someone in need of protection if you're willing to work for someone who has reason to hide."

"I've got someone who needs my help. I can't be taking risks like that right now."

"Really now?" says Naima, getting up from her stool and coming over to me. "What trouble did you get yourself into out in that desert? Were there unforeseen problems with the job?"

"The job didn't give me any trouble like that," I say cautiously. "I'm just helping someone I met in Zaptu out till they get on their feet."

The leopard grins at me. "If you have work right now, why are you looking for more?"

"This isn't work. This is a personal favor."

She frowns. "Since when did you do favors for people?"

I put a paw to my chest. "You assume I am not capable of being a charitable soul, my friend."

"I know you, Naji, and I remember only two people you ever did favors for, besides me. One is dead and the other you aren't on speaking terms with. Now I would not say that people don't change, we both know I've taken to the shopkeeper's life, but this is a new sense of caution and charity I'm not used to seeing in you."

I grumble. "You know I stopped taking the really dangerous or shady jobs a while ago. I've helped Fadel before."

The leopard pokes me in the side. "Three people, but a favor for someone else? Is this for some boy you fancy? I can't think of a reason why else you'd be doing favors like this."

"Not really," I lie.

"By God, it is about a boy!" the leopard exclaims loudly. "Finally, someone has found the key and unlocked the great Naji's heart. Now this, this is someone I have to meet."

"It's not about that. He needed help, and I was in a position to help him."

"So, you haven't slept with him then?" she smiles.

My ears splay. "Yes, but he was a prostitute."

She squints at me. "Since when did you start frequenting prostitutes?"

"I haven't, well I have, but look, it was a one-time thing, okay? Plus, this was in Zaptu, and I didn't expect to do this. Things got away from me."

She doesn't say anything, but just motions with her hands to continue.

"I'm not sure why I bid for his attention. I felt sad for him, and then I didn't know if I really wanted to go through it, but he encouraged me, and I did. I guess I was alone then, and I wanted company." I don't really want to tell her what I thought about all the way from Banu to Zaptu when I was by myself.

"And you brought him to Aksu because…"

"He was in a bad spot, and he asked me to take him. Plus, you act as if I have no heart when I see others suffering."

"Since Isim died, you have only watched after someone else's tail if they paid you coin to do it. You've built a good life for yourself these last few years, but you also spend part of your time running away from it."

I frown. If anyone would know that about me, it would be Naima, but it still hurts to hear it. "I like to keep myself busy."

"No, you like to keep yourself preoccupied. There's a difference. But now there is someone else in your life?"

"Maybe, maybe not. I don't know yet. He's got things he needs to figure out about himself, it seems."

She shrugs. "You should bring him by."

"Bring him by?"

"Yes. I would be delighted to meet your friend. Anyone who's reached that heart of yours is a worthy man." There's a sparkle in her eyes.

"I guess," I mumble.

"Bring him by tomorrow. In the meantime, I'll ask around, find you something good. It will probably only pay half what you'd get if you take a caravan position, but it will be low key."

"Bring him by tomorrow?" I say, surprised. Naima and I both have our dalliances, but we usually have kept that to ourselves.

"Yes, yes, of course. I will need to get Femi to watch the shop while I go make the rounds for you. I have a few old friends who owe me favors."

"I'm sure you don't want to…"

She clears her throat. "Nonsense. I insist you bring him. Now, let me see what strings I can pull for you." Her eyes are shining brightly.

"You're thinking this is more than it is."

"Are you sure there isn't? Lately, you've rarely come to me looking for work in town. In the last year, I think you've spent more time outside of Aksu than in it."

I see she's noticed my habits too well. "Fine, tomorrow then," I say, nodding at her.

"Yes, yes," she says, shooing me out of her small store. "Now let me work some of my old magic. As soon as Femi is back, I will be paying an old friend a visit."

I leave her in her little shop. I'm not sure who Naima is talking about, and I don't know if she'd tell me. Sometimes it's better I don't know. She is a woman of many secrets. I am just grateful I am not on her bad side.

❧

Without any other leads, I wander the market for a while browsing the wares. I talk to some of my other contacts for jobs along the way. There are several caravans looking for people, and a few guard jobs, but nothing promising presents itself. The wink in one of my contact's eyes, a white-furred wolf, tells me exactly what type of risk the job he knows about will entail. I tell him I'll have to think about it, and he nods knowingly.

The only work in town I can find involves a level of discretion that tells me I don't want it. I've had run-ins with the city guard before, and clients have left me high and dry to face them. I need money, but that's not a risk I'm interested in taking right now. Making the rounds like this is a path I have often run before, but it feels different now. I need to be even more selective than I usually am. I may have learned it the hard way, but I know if I pick my work carefully, I can avoid most trouble. Today, nothing good is presenting itself. Maybe Naima is right, and I'm in the wrong line of work to play it safe. Maybe working at the counting house is my best bet.

Since nothing else seems to be going on for me, I stop by one of my favorite food stands. Zayn should be up on the roof practicing for tonight. It's only midday, so I'm going to bring home some roast lamb for us to have for lunch. Hopefully he hasn't eaten yet.

"Doing okay today, Naji?" comes the baleful voice of Rigel.

Great, Rigel is really the last person I want to deal with right now. "Well enough," I reply, trying to stay civil.

"Is that so?" he remarks. "I've seen you out on the street today talking to some of my contacts."

"We must use the same people," I say. "I'm just looking for another job."

"If you're interested, I might know of one. I'd take it myself, but I have already promised to go with a caravan down south in the morning."

"I thought you were working with that clan?"

"They don't need me right now, and it's a quick trip south. I'm kicking myself for being unable to take this other one though."

"Ah, well, I'm sure you know other people." The roast lamb smells delicious, and my mind is on that right now instead of this job Rigel has.

"A few. One of the merchants I know has a shipment that needs to be guarded when he's not home."

That does perk my interest. "Sounds simple enough."

"Yes, it's for a few days. Pays two gold dinars for a week's work. You interested?"

That's good money. Really good money. "Maybe," I say. "What does this entail guarding?"

"He deals in perfume ingredients and various dyes. He had some valuable stuff come in, and he needs to have his workshop kept under guard while he's out of town."

It sounds easy, and a workshop like that is worth a lot. "That does sound good."

"Well, I need to get my gear together, so if you want the work, let me take you over now."

I know my ears flick in annoyance at this statement. I really want to get some food and take it home to share it with Zayn. Still, local work is exactly what I'm looking for. "Can it wait an hour? I'd like to buy lunch and take it home."

The cat smirks knowingly. "You won't be done in an hour with that jackal."

I give him an icy look. "That's not for you to know."

He shrugs. "He asked me to see if I can find someone before I leave tomorrow, so if you want the work, I'll take you over now."

"Fine," I say, trying not to let my annoyance show. "We can go now."

He starts walking, and I follow him. "I was hoping you wouldn't be too busy to help an old friend out."

I catch the reference to what I said to him when I saw him at the Blue Door. "You are the one who became distant, not me."

"What you did that day still hurts."

"As I said many times before, I'm sorry I didn't realize Isim wasn't following me. He always was one step behind me, except on that day." That day when we lost him.

"You should have noticed."

I sigh and stop walking. "I should have noticed, but I didn't, and I've regretted that every day since. I thought he was there, but he wasn't and when he came over the wall bleeding…" I shudder. "You were gone by then, but I held him. I held him as he died. I remember the feeling of his blood on my paws, and the sound of his ragged, faded breathing. It still haunts me."

The caracal is silent.

"Perhaps it is best I find my own work, Rigel."

He reaches up and rests a hand on my shoulder. "I realize he's not coming back. Come on, let me help you out, one old friend to another."

I look at him, and in his eyes, I think I see a little of the old Rigel. The Rigel who used to be my friend. "Okay. Take me to your contact."

Rigel nods and turns to leave. "It's not that far."

&

122

Rigel's idea of far seems to be a little different than my idea of far. We have to cross to the other bank of the Zaharani. Once there, we walk through the workshops and warehouses clustered near the docks where the river boats land. This part of town is one I don't visit much anymore, but I'm familiar with it. It's where the seedier elements of the sultanate's trade are based. Even the beggars in this part of town look poorer, and the buildings here are unimpressive.

Eventually we stop on a quiet side street of nondescript houses. The windows of the house we have come to are all shuttered, even the ones on the upper story. The heavy wooden door is old and unpainted. Rigel knocks on the door. Inside we hear some shuffling around.

"Who is it?" calls out a gruff voice.

"It's me," responds Rigel. "I've got a guard for you."

I can hear the bolt being drawn, and the door opens inward. A tiger dressed in a simple tunic with a dagger tucked into his belt is standing by the door. Rigel gestures, and we enter the house. The tiger closes the door behind us.

The first thing I notice is that the entranceway is rather sparse. I sweep my eyes around, realizing everything seems to be coated in a thick layer of dust. This house has been vacant for a while, it appears, but beyond the smell of dust that assaults my nose, there is something else. A scent I haven't smelled in a very, very long time. It takes me a moment to recognize, but it's already too late.

I go for my sword instinctively, but Rigel is quick. Before I can even reach it, I feel the tip of his blade poking me in the back.

"I wouldn't do that if I were you," coos Rigel into my ear.

My body goes stiff, frozen in mid movement.

"Slowly, unbuckle your sword belt. One wrong move, and I'll cut you open."

"How could you, Rigel?" I croak out.

"The same way you left Isim behind," he says to me in an icy tone. "Now unbuckle your sword belt, Naji," he adds, pressing the tip of the blade against me so that it starts to draw blood.

Out of the corner of my eye, I can see the tiger has bolted the door and is leaning against it, his dagger out. Even if I can somehow keep Rigel for cutting me open, I'll have to deal with the tiger. There's nothing I can do. Slowly I unbuckle the belt and let the scabbard drop to the ground, the sound echoing hollowly in the entrance. Rigel kicks the blade away from me then reaches out to my other side, and without having to look, he pulls out the dagger I have tucked in under my clothing.

"Have you no honor, Rigel?" I ask, hoping this is not going to end the way I fear it will.

The caracal comes around to face me. He keeps his sword pointed at my chest. "Oh I do, but my loyalties lie elsewhere now. I trade your life so that others may live. It is not as if I didn't warn you were being hunted either. I just didn't tell you who would come for you."

I know he blames me for what happened to Isim. I blame myself, but to lead me to my own death?

"Aziz will be pleased you brought him here so easily," says the tiger, moving away from the door.

"You will do anything to make a quick bit of coin, won't you?" I say, snarling at Rigel.

I hear movement from behind me, but Rigel is quick to bring the tip of his sword up. "If you want to die right now, go ahead. Try it."

My ears fall. I know how good he is with a sword. I might get one good strike in, but he will slice me apart.

He gets close to my face and whispers quietly so that only I can hear. "You try to escape, and I will make sure your little jackal dies too. If you want to spare his life, you won't resist."

"You leave Zayn out of this," I growl at Rigel.

"If you behave for them, I will. Otherwise, what will happen to him won't be pretty, and you won't be there to protect him."

I want to wipe the smug expression off his muzzle, but I know what he's doing. He's buying my cooperation in my own death. Rigel breaks away just as Aziz comes in from the other room, accompanied by a red fox carrying a yataghan. The wolf is smiling toothily at me as the fox draws the curved blade. I narrow my eyes as I look at Aziz. He hasn't changed since I last remember, but I've only seen him twice. He walks over to where my sword is lying on the ground and leisurely picks it up.

"It really was as easy as you said it would be, I see," he says, as he pulls the sword partly out of the scabbard to examine it.

"Of course," says the caracal, as he steps away from me. "He's yours now."

"Is this the blade you killed him with," he asks me.

"It was self-defense," I say.

"You murdered my brother," says the wolf, as he pulls my sword completely out of its scabbard. "I will have my revenge for Borak's death."

It is indeed the same blade I killed Aziz's brother with. I've carried the same weapon for years. Out of the corner of my eye, I can see Rigel recognizes it. It's Isim's sword. The cat shifts his weight and looks away.

"You don't know how long I've waited for this moment," the wolf says, walking forward to press the blade against my neck. The tiger and the fox are ready to strike if I should attempt to resist Aziz. "Fitting that you should die by the same blade that my brother died from."

"Your brother," I say, trying not to cut my throat on the blade, "would have killed me had I not met his charge with steel."

"You took from me that which was dear to me. You had no right."

"I was paid to be there. He was trying to rob my client. I did what they paid me to do."

The wolf sneers at me. "I don't care. Our dispute with the Aragvi Clan was between us and them. They have paid their debt. It is time for you to offer up your payment."

Rage smolders in his eyes. It's the same look of rage he had when he saw me looming over the corpse of Borak, freshly dead after their ambush of the caravan had gone so horribly wrong for them. There will be no mercy for me.

Rigel coughs. "I believe our business here is concluded, Aziz. I went and got him. What you do with him isn't my concern."

"Ah, but he wronged you too, did he not, Rigel? Don't you want to watch the slow, painful death I have planned for this cur?"

"No," he says. "You can do that without me."

"A shame, but suit yourself," replies the wolf. "I will hold up my part of the deal."

The cat bobs his head in acknowledgment and gives me one final look. He meets my glare with indifference and a shrug before he walks behind me to the door. I hear the tiger slide the bolt open and let Rigel out. Afterward the door is locked.

The wolf steps back but keeps the sword pointed at me. "Bind him," he says with a sneer. The tiger steps up behind me. He grabs me and starts looping rope around my wrist. I struggle against him, but Aziz steps up and swings the sword, slapping me with the flat side of the blade. I stagger back against the tiger who pushes me down onto the ground. I hit the floor, then the tiger and the fox are on top of me, securing my wrists. I fight against their combined weight on top of me, but I see the flash of my own blade as Aziz points it straight at one of my eyes.

"Oh yena, I enjoy seeing you like this. Perhaps we'll start with an eye."

I stop my struggles so I can stare at the tip of the sword. The blade is inches from my face. This lull lets the tiger finish tying my hands while the fox loops a gag through my muzzle and pulls the fabric tight against my face. When he is done, he lifts me up to a kneeling position. Aziz lowers the sword and steps towards me, licking his chops.

"You will pay for what you did. I would make it quick, but I intend to enjoy this. It's taken me three years to finally get my revenge."

I square my shoulders as I look up my own sword at him. This is it. This is how I finally die. It's not the first time I thought I might die by the sword, but fate has finally wrestled me into a corner with no escape. I could fight, but I won't give Rigel a reason to go for Zayn. I will meet my death here with as much honor as Aziz will let me have. I won't see Zayn dance for the crowd tonight at the Blue Door, but he will do well, I'm sure. At least his story will end well, and some part of my life will work out as intended.

I have often wondered if my entire time here in Aksu has been bought on borrowed time, that I should have died with my old comrades back home. I thought when I saw them fall in battle, I would surely die with them, but somehow, I managed to survive. I fled the south and made a new life for myself far from home only to lose that once already. No matter how much I've tried, the ghosts of that past and the ghost of Isim keep coming back to me. Still, through luck and tenacity, I've held on when so many I knew couldn't. Today my luck has run out.

The wolf begins to circle me, then kicks one of my shoulders to knock me down. Without being able to move my arms to catch myself, I hit the floor with a muffled yelp, my shoulder slamming hard into the ground.

"You have pride I see, yena," says the wolf, towering over me. "That makes this all the better. First, I will break your pride, and then I will make you beg for your death."

I close my eyes. I feel a kick strike me in the chest causing me to gasp. He rains down blows against me in white hot rage. All I can do is curl up in a fetal position to try and protect my more sensitive parts. It's the only form of movement they've left me. I do not know if Rigel will keep his promise of leaving Zayn out of this, but it's all I can hope for now.

Apparently though, my willingness to acquiesce to my death does not satisfy Aziz. He leans down from towering over me as he casually steps on my tail, "You're not begging yet, cur."

I blink at him since I cannot speak through the gag, one eye already starting to swell shut. There is a look of madness upon the wolf's face.

He grabs me by my shoulder, steps on my back, and jerks my arm back. Pain spills out from the joint as he forcefully wrenches my arm out of its socket. I cry out, suddenly seeing stars.

"That's better," he says. "I plan to savor each of your cries of pain as I break you. I've planned a nice, slow death for you," He gets up and spits on me. "Achmed, show our guest to the room we've prepared for him," he orders the tiger. "Make sure he's properly secured. Then we can go celebrate our victory."

With that he's gone, leaving his two lackeys to take care of me.

"Do we carry him?" the red fox asks Achmed.

"No. We drag him there," the tiger replies, grabbing my bound wrists. Without ceremony he starts yanking on my dislocated shoulder and dragging me down the hall. It brings tears to my eyes, and I am forced to help them muscle me down to the makeshift cell they've prepared for me.

The Bandit's Den
(Zayn)

After spending most of the day practicing, I head out to the Blue Door. I was hoping Naji would be back before I left, but he must have found a good lead for work. It's still early when I arrive, but several patrons are already relaxing in the shade of the courtyard. I make sure to bring the practice sword with me, my dancing outfit, and a good brush so I can comb my fur out. Along the way to the tavern, I make sure to stop to eat some pita and kebabs so I'm ready to go when I get there.

Upon arrival, Fadel takes me to a small room with a door to the courtyard and a second door to the stage that serves as a changing space. Inside, there is a dressing table and a stool. A small platter of walnuts, almonds, and dates has been set out. Next to the platter is a pitcher of water and a simple cup. There is also a small hand mirror on the table to help me get ready.

"Who is this for?" I ask the fennec, pointing to the food.

"You, of course. It's a welcome platter. You are my star entertainment tonight. We still have a while before the show, and I didn't want you to have to perform hungry."

Even though I've already eaten some kebabs, my stomach rumbles for more. In the past, I danced on an empty stomach to afford the coin to eat. Now there is food for me to make sure I am comfortable? "You'll spoil me, you know, and I will not be so lithe if you start feeding me."

The fennec chuckles. "A few good meals won't kill you. You can always work it off keeping the patrons entertained."

Entertained. I will keep them entertained, but I do not have to bed any of them. It's like my old life, but better. "I'll do my best."

"Excellent. Let me tend to some things, and I'll be back. I think in about an hour and a half, after the sun goes down, we'll put you out there."

"Sure."

He leaves me be, and I take the time to dress and brush out my fur. Once I'm properly attired in a silk waist wrap and a sheer top cut to show off my stomach fur, I start warming up as best I can in the tight space.

I miss the balance of my old sword, but I'm adjusting to the new one. Father died defending his caravan from raiders with the same sword in his paws I danced with. It is nice to finally be able to give the blade the respect it deserves.

I wonder what my parents would think of my new life. I don't know if either of them would be proud of me, but I'm still here. I've survived, and tonight I will advance beyond whore to something else. I wish they could see that, but at least Naji will be here to witness it.

I know Usman would be proud of me, and if he was here, he'd tell me my parents are proud of me too. I know he is still kicking himself for what happened with Sarda. When it started, I should have told Usman what the lion was asking of me, but I thought the coin would make me independent. I wanted to be strong. I wanted to make the cheetah proud. Instead, I only hurt myself to please Sarda. Once things are settled, I will send Usman a letter to let him know I am alright and to tell him about my new life.

I'm swinging the kilij in wide arcs to stretch when there is a knock on the door from the courtyard.

"Enter," I say, panting, lowering the sword.

Fadel and the leopard who was dancing last night enter. Fadel looks at my dancing outfit and chuckles. "You are certainly showing off your stomach fur with that," he says.

I shrug. "I wanted something affirming tonight of myself and who I am. Is it too much?"

"Not at all," says Fadel. The leopard next him quirks an ear at me, and Fadel notices the movement. "I'm being rude. Zayn, this is Khalil. He wants to see you dance."

The leopard steps forward and extends a hand. "It is a pleasure to meet you."

I take his hand and we lean forward and exchange cheek kisses. The exchange isn't warm like when I met Fadel, but formal instead.

"I see you are a sword dancer," he says when we break our contact. Up close, I can see he's lean and lanky with a layer of muscle on top.

"Yes," I respond. "It's what I did to stand out."

"Stand out?" he asks. There is a wrinkle of confusion on his face.

"Work was not easy to get."

Fadel clears his throat. "I have plenty of work for the both of you."

The leopard relaxes, reassured about his own position here. Neither of them realize what I mean by work. I hesitate, but then I clarify. "It's not the dancing I got paid for."

The two exchange glances. "You worked as a whore?" the fennec asks me.

My ears droop, and I just nod.

The leopard makes a shocked face. "That must have been awful."

"Well not here," Fadel says, putting a hand on my shoulder. "I have a much better use for your skills and talents."

"Thank you," is all I can say. My tail gives a slow wag.

"Do you want to me to have the musicians do your set after their current song?" asks Fadel. "There is a good crowd already gathered."

"Is Naji here yet?" I ask the fox.

"I haven't seen him yet, so I don't think so."

"Can we wait for him?"

"Of course," remarks Fadel. "Khalil, can you go to the front desk and wait so we know when our spotted hyena friend has arrived?

"Sure," remarks the leopard, walking over to the courtyard door. "I'll check the main hall, and then wait in the front."

❧

Two hours have passed, the sun has set, but Naji still has not shown up. Fadel comes and goes from the room a couple of times. I can hear a murmur of patrons in the courtyard along with music the musicians are playing in the hall.

"Where is he, Fadel?" I ask, wringing my paws together.

The fennec fidgets with a goblet of wine he brought in. He offered me some wine earlier to help me relax, but I declined. I want to be sharp with my moves. "I don't know," he says.

"He said he would come see me dance, so why isn't he here?"

"Perhaps he found a job that needs him right away. There could be some very good coin to be made."

I scratch behind my ears. "He said he would be here."

"I'm sure he has a good reason," offers Fadel. "We can wait a little longer, if you want."

I take a deep breath. Maybe Fadel is right and Naji found work that needed him immediately. He wanted to see this, but I know we can't delay for too long. Next time, I guess. "No. I don't want to keep them waiting."

The fennec nods. He finishes off his goblet of wine and gets up from the stool he is sitting on. "Let me talk to the musicians and I'll come get you through the stage door in a few minutes. Will you be ready?"

I nod. "I just need to do my eyes."

Fadel walks over to the door into the hall and exits. I take a minute to smooth out my silks and fur. I've been trying hard not to pace, but I've still ruffled myself. After I've tended to my fur a final time, I pick up the small hand mirror on the table. For the final step in my preparation, I put some kohl around my eyes, to make them more striking.

When done, I look over myself in the mirror. My ears are sitting too low. I sigh. I need to look chipper. I don't think Naji would abandon me, not now, but I'm certainly going to need the money from this job if that's what happened.

"He must have found something that needed him immediately," I whisper to myself.

There is a knock from the other door and Fadel peeks his head in. "Are you ready?"

I take a deep breath and pick up the sword. "As ready as I will be."

He motions. "Come." I walk over to the door and out onto the little stage in front of the hall.

Immediately, the power of this moment hits me. People quickly turn to notice me. It feels like there are more people here now than when I came here with Naji, but it may just seem that way since I'm the center of attention. The din of the conversation drops as I take center stage. People's eyes follow me. I've never danced for a crowd like this. Almost all eyes are following the movement of my body. I put a little swish into my step, already getting into the role. There is appreciation and hunger in their eyes, but that is very different for what dancing in Zaptu entailed. They did not come here to see me, but they certainly want to see what I'm about to do.

"For your pleasure tonight, for the first time here in Aksu, may I present Zayn!" shouts Fadel, taking a bow. He steps off to the side and I step out. There is a soft applause. The musicians start up then. The rhythm is a song I know well. It is slow to start and builds as layers are added. This is the same song they played when I showed Fadel my moves, and I came by yesterday to make sure I had the timing down right in my head. I wait to let the soft melody of the intro fade, and at the first drumbeat, I spring into action.

The sword is light in my hands as I spin in a tight motion, the blade flashing in the lantern light. I step and duck, bob and weave letting the blade fly around me. After the first initial flurry of swings, I slow my stepping down and grab the back of the sword, the blade held out in front of me. I start to gyrate my hips as I hold the blade above me.

Usually, my motions are feminine in that I always hold something back. I never tell all my secrets. The more like a woman I can be, the more likely I am to get a customer. Today, there is no need. I can feel their eyes on me, and they're hungry for me. When I give them my backside to admire and flick my tail, swinging my hips, there is a happy murmur from the audience. These are people who want everything I have to offer, and I want to give it to them as suggestively as I can. My pulse beats quickly as I spin, and move from paw to paw, letting the blade sail through the air. It's exhilarating, even more so than I expected it to be.

When the music starts to fade out slowly, I drop to my knees, and arch my back, holding the sword out behind me. I've turned facing the door I entered through so that the audience can see the arch of my back. I shift my weight up and down, undulating my stomach, until the music stops, and I lay still.

Then with a quick roll to the left, I spring to my feet and bow to the audience. The applause is the best I've ever had. I smile inwardly as I take my bow, then stand in front of them, chest heaving, taking in the moment. I feel exhausted. I finally let my eyes sweep the crowd for Naji, but I don't see him. I do notice the hooded fennec I saw previously is in the back, and Rigel grinning slyly at me from one corner. I don't recognize anyone else.

I step over to the side where Fadel and Khalil are waiting for me.

"I'm impressed," says the leopard, genuinely smiling at me. "You are really talented!"

"You doubted I was?" I ask him.

He ears flick. "A little, but not now."

"You definitely have earned your pay," the fennec says, pressing two silver dirhams into my paw.

I hold up the coins to look at them. It's not much, but it's mine, and I earned it. There is no evening after. I will only be down on my knees tonight if I want to be. I smile to myself.

I'm so pleased with myself I don't realize Khalil has moved away until he returns with a small bowl.

"With tips like this, I should be jealous," remarks the leopard.

Fadel peeks into the bowl. "They always tip a new performer well, but they were generous tonight I see. Perhaps you two can work out a routine together."

The leopard offers me the bowl and I take it. Inside there are two dozen copper coins, a half dirham silver coin, and two more silver dirham coins.

"I get tips?" It's a stupid question since I saw Khalil get tips, but I hadn't thought about it.

They both nod at me.

I was worried I was a fool to make this journey, but I can do this. I can make it on my own. Yes, I'm still offering myself up, but it's not the same. I don't have to feel their paws on my hips. I don't have to lie there while they sate themselves in me and then leave me to cry alone. I can finally perform because I want to perform, not because I need to attract buyers.

I feel a sense of warmth inside of myself, but something bothers me. Where is Naji? I'm here with his friend, at a place he likes to visit frequently, but he's not here. He didn't bring me here to just abandon me, so, if he's not here, where is he?

࿐

After asking other members of his staff, Fadel tells me nobody had seen Naji today. Maybe he went back to the apartment and fell asleep. I don't know how long he spent looking for work. He could have walked all over Aksu and be worn out.

I'm not sure what the reason for his absence is, but I'm disappointed Naji missed my performance. This is a great moment for me, and I wish he were here to share it with me. Fadel is thrilled with my work, and even Khalil is impressed. They tell me to come back tomorrow, and I see Khalil is already thinking of ways to change his routine. I sit with Fadel to watch the leopard take a turn dancing before I go clean up, and this time he selects a more energetic trio of songs. I think we both have things we can teach each other.

After using the hammam to freshen up, and turning down a massage from Ales, I take my leave of the Blue Door, my dancing outfit wrapped up in the small knapsack I brought with me. Stepping out of the door into the night, dressed in my street clothes, I don't at first hear my name being called.

I glance around, and spot Rigel across the street, leaning against a wall. The light of the lantern hanging about the entrance to the Blue Door casts Rigel in shadows. He's wearing a hooded cloak, but his eyes catch the light, shining in the night.

"You dance well, jackal," he says.

There's something off in the way he's acting. "I'm glad you enjoyed the show," I offer.

"You are quite the artist."

"Thank you. Do you know where Naji is?" I ask.

Rigel's expression is stoic. "He's probably detained with a job."

"He wanted to come. Would you know where he might have gone off to?"

The caracal gives me a look. "He's gone."

My ears shoot up. "What do you mean gone?"

He shrugs. "He's gone and not coming back. I'm sorry, but it had to happen. It's not your concern." He turns to walk away.

"How the fuck isn't it my concern?" I growl. "I'm living in his apartment!"

The caracal pauses. "Well, I guess what's in there is yours now."

"What do you mean mine? Where is he, Rigel!" I demand, walking up to him.

Rigel stops and turns back around. "What happened isn't your concern. A price had to be paid, and Naji was what they wanted. I'm sorry."

I reach for Rigel's cotton tunic and vest to grab them, digging my claws into his chest, "Let me be clear," I snarl in his face, "it is still my concern."

I am pushed backwards suddenly by the cat as he sweeps his arms in a fluid moment to dislodge me. I fall onto the ground and land on my tail with a yelp. The pommel of my practice kilij digs into my side when it gets stuck against the ground. Rigel walks up and looms over me, smoothing out his vest

"You are a feisty one, I see. Fine, I will tell you what happened. That man I mentioned a few nights ago, Aziz, he has Naji. My guess is the hyena is dead by now."

Dead? He's dead? "You're lying," I growl.

Rigel sighs. "He's gone, Zayn. Aziz had a blood debt to settle with Naji."

"How do you know?"

The cat kneels down, and his eyes reflect the light of the lantern back at me. There's a coldness about his expression. "Aziz wants the life of the man who killed his brother, even though they are the ones who started the fight."

"And how did you get into this?"

He gets up. "That you don't need to know." He starts walking off.

"Wait!" I call, getting up quickly. My head is spinning. "Aren't you going to try and help Naji? He could still be alive."

He stops but doesn't turn around. "I can't."

"This Aziz, he must be somewhere we could find."

"He is, but why do you care?"

"Why do I care? I care because he's a good person. He's helped me out. He brought me here to Aksu."

"There are a lot of good people at the Blue Door. The hyena is not one of them."

I'm not sure what he means, but I need to know what's going on. "Please. Tell me where I can find Naji."

The caracal turns around to look at me. "Why should I let you get hurt?"

"Please, we can't just leave him there. We need to go get him."

"You don't know what you're getting into. This is dangerous."

"If you won't do something, I will," I say, my hackles raised. "Where is Naji?"

"I don't know, but if you want to find Aziz, he hangs out at a tavern near the Malhaa District, called the Silver Shroud. He won't take kindly to you asking questions. But if you want to end up dead yourself, be my guest." He resumes walking off.

I watch the cat leave, clenching my paws into fists, feeling the claws digging into my pads. I can't leave Naji in the hands of this Aziz. If Rigel isn't going to do anything to help him, I will.

⤜

I want to let Fadel know what is going on, but he isn't at his desk when I reenter the Blue Door. Naji hasn't mentioned the fennec ever being connected to the work he does, so I can only assume the hyena keeps most of this to himself. I could look for Fadel, but something needs to be done, and quickly. I don't know how I will, but I need to save Naji. I finally found someone who sees me for more than just meat; I'm not going to lose that. First though, I need to find this Aziz.

One of Fadel's staff, a fellow jackal who goes by Salim, gives me directions. He doesn't know exactly where the Silver Shroud is, but he does tell me how to get to the Malhaa District. Salim says this area contains the original market square in Aksu and while it no longer serves as the city's trade hub, it has many cafes and taverns. The square also hosts food vendors that stay open late.

After thanking him, I'm on my way. I only have a vague plan in my mind, but if I can find this tavern, I might be able to reach Naji somehow.

The night air is cool, but it does not calm the burning urgency inside of me. The homes I pass are shuttered, with only a few lanterns glowing inside. I reach the main road, which is much quieter than I've seen so far, and take the left I was instructed to in order to reach the Malhaa District. I wonder if I'll be able to find anyone out to give me directions to the Silver Shroud when I get to the market, but this worry proves to be unfounded.

Many people were still in the Blue Door, enjoying their night when I left, yet I thought the Malhaa District might be quieter. That proves to be untrue. The area is lively and bustling with street cafes packed with patrons. Many are sitting outside under lanterns drinking tea and smoking hookahs. Even more people are just out walking around and buying from vendors.

The market in the center of the area is a small square surrounded by buildings, serving food out of their first floors, and even at midnight, the Malhaa District buzzes with life. Booths have been laid out in the square. Some have already closed, but many are still hawking trinkets and food. To one side a storyteller has a small crowd around him, telling an old fable I recognize. On the other side of the square, I spot an acrobat troupe. A striped hyena breathes fire, while a fox with black fur and a white tipped tail, strumming on a lute, sings an unfamiliar ballad in accompaniment. As I pass them by, the fox calls out to me, asking for my attention and tips; I stop for a minute to watch the act before dropping two coppers into their cup and moving on.

Finding the Silver Shroud takes me some time. I have to ask two people for directions, and only the second one has ever heard of the place. It turns out to be down an alleyway leading away from the square of the Malhaa District. From the outside, it's little more than a door with a small lantern over it. A guard leans against the doorway, casually watching the street. He has a muzzle like a wolf or jackal, but his ears are bigger and rounder. His muzzle is dark, with yellow and white fur splotched at the neck and arms like an artist dipped him into different colored inks. I have heard of the painted before, but never have I seen one.

As I walk over to the door, the guard looks me over, noting the sword I have strapped on. I wonder if he's going to say something, but he nods and quirks his muzzle in a smile. I'm not sure what to make of that, but I quickly understand why once I enter. While the Blue Door is warm and inviting, the Silver Shroud is a dark and dingy affair. In a vaulted room with rows of columns, carpets have been placed over a stone floor with cushions and low divans. Against one wall, casks of cypress wood are stacked. The furniture looks shabby, and the crowd is rough. Many appear armed, and there is a general feeling of menace. I regret I have only the dancing sword and not my sharpened kilij on me.

A mongoose shows me to a small table and some cushions against the wall and I sit down there, putting the knapsack I've been carrying next to me. She asks if I want some wine. I nod and she makes sure I pay my three coppers before she gets me some. While she's doing that, I scan the room. I don't know even what species Aziz is, so I ponder my options. The mongoose brings me an earthenware jug and cup, and places them on the small table before scurrying off, not saying anything else.

I find her behavior odd, but I pour some of the wine and take a sip. It's slightly sour and probably an older vintage that's sat for too long. I drank wine like this back in Zaptu, and it's only good for getting drunk, nothing else.

I drink a little to blend in, but mostly I just sit there, trying to study the crowd. A few give me dirty looks if I spend too much time looking them over. Any one of them could be this Aziz, assuming he is even here. It's dim inside and noisy, so it's hard to get a clue who I might be looking for. I swivel my ears trying to get a clue, but they only pick up bits of conversation.

Most of the men appear to be drinking with friends, but I catch a few women in the crowd. Some are serving drinks, but a number are looking to minister to other needs. I can see the way they're appraising the customers and the way the customers watch them to know what they're looking to sell.

I'm thinking this is a hopeless task when a pretty fennec girl slides up to where I'm sitting, joining me on the carpet.

"You look lonely," she says, tail wagging slowly. "Perhaps you need some company?" She's dressed in revealing clothes, her heaving chest sticking out at me. She winks at me as she leans down over the low table so I can get a good look at her assets.

"No," I say.

That takes her off guard. "I'm not your type, huh?" she snorts. "Well, fine with me." She gets up and starts to walk away when an idea pops into my head.

"Wait," I call out. "There is something I need."

She pauses. "Oh?"

"I need some information," I say.

She laughs. "I'm not a messenger for the Sultan."

I fish out one of the silver dirhams Fadel paid me earlier tonight. "I'll pay. You just need to tell me if you know anything. I'm looking for someone."

She eyes the coin. I don't know what the going rate for whores in Aksu is, but I imagine that the money is at least attractive. She nods and make a motion for me to move over, and she sits down next to me.

"What is it you want?" she asks me. Her voice has lost the sultry elements it had earlier. She's all business now.

"I'm looking for someone called Aziz," I say.

She barks a laugh. "Aziz, huh? He's over on the other side of the room."

I look up. So, he is here! "Which one is he?"

She holds out her paw for the coin. "That will cost you another coin."

I grumble and fish out the other silver dirham Fadel paid me. I hold both coins up.

"He's the wolf drinking in the corner over there with some friends of his," She points to a table in the corner. There is indeed a wolf drinking with a tiger and a fox in the corner. "Most of the whores avoid him. They say he likes it rather rough."

She reaches for the coins, but I close my paw around them. "How much for you to forget we had this conversation?" If I'm unlucky, she's going to take my tips too.

"Discreetness is always a part of my services," she says, and I drop the two coins into her paw. She gets up. "Pleasure doing business with you." With that, she's gone and off to solicit someone else. I sit back and take a gulp of the wine before I remember how awful it is.

I glance over to the wolf, trying to ascertain what I can about him. Aziz seems to be having a good time with his friends. They're drinking, but I can't just walk up to him and start asking him questions. I need some reason to get close to him.

Pondering, I idly count how many whores I see floating around the tavern. They move through the crowd of men, catching eyes. I smile to myself. So, the whores avoid Aziz? Maybe I can use that to my advantage. I'm going to have to work quickly though before he leaves.

I take a deep breath before I get up. I never wanted to have to do this again, but if I can convince Aziz to buy my attentions for the night, I might be able to find out where he is keeping Naji.

Assuming of course there is still a hyena left to save.

꘏

When I dance, I prefer clothing that makes it clear I'm male. It's rarely misinterpreted, but I've had a customer be confused before. I don't have time to run all the way back to Naji's place to change, but I do have my dancing outfit with me that bares my stomach fur. I've used strong perfume to cover my scent and the musk of sex when working as a whore, so combined it might convince someone expecting me to be a woman. It at least would let me play up the role of a whore.

Searching the vendors in the Malhaa District square takes longer than I want, but I am able to locate a caracal selling perfume and combs. The bottle costs me half a silver dirham and two copper fals, but it's strong and smells of roses. I might have been able to haggle him down a bit, but I take the price he offers, and leave with it clutched in my paws.

I'm also able to find an alley near the Silver Shroud to change in. While my undergarments are designed to provide support, it does keep my maleness snug. I never have thought to hide it, but it might reduce the obviousness. I use the dull blade to rip my kaftan and stuff some of torn fabric under my top, hoping it provides a little cleavage under the top of my dancing outfit. In the dark of the alley, it seems fine, but I don't know if it will look believable. I also have to abandon my clothing and the sword there when I'm done, shoved into the back of the alley. There's a small gap between two houses that I manage to wedge the sword and bag into. I can't take those with me, and I'm not sure either will be there when I get back.

The whole process takes longer than I want, and the only reason I don't run back to the tavern is it will draw attention to myself. As I walk up to the building, I don't know if Aziz will still be there. I put some swish into my step though as I approach. The painted dog I saw earlier is still at the door and he looks me over.

"Can I help you?" he asks me, barring me from the door.

"I'm looking to go in for a drink."

He quirks his muzzle, and I hope he doesn't recognize me from earlier. "Are you now?"

"You wouldn't keep me thirsty, would you?" I say, letting my fangs show. It occurs to me that the woman working here might give the owner a cut. That could complicate things.

The dog chuckles. "I would, but someone inside will buy you a drink. You can't just come in and work here."

Well, there is one thing I can offer him. "Perhaps I can convince you?" I suggest. I let one of my hands slip to my side and curl my tongue in my muzzle. I don't want to have to do this, but I need a way in.

His reaction though isn't what I expect. Instead of a positive reaction, the painted dog wrinkles his nose at me. "No, you can't," he says. It's easy to read the feeling of disgust on his muzzle.

"Then what do you want?"

He crosses his arms and leans against the door frame. "I don't want anything."

Well, this isn't working. Perhaps another tactic will work. "I'm looking for a friend. I think he came here tonight."

The dog quirks his ears. "Are you now?"

I nod.

He considers me for a moment. "A friend, huh?"

I nod again. "He helped me out, and I need to," I stumble on my words, realize I'm about to say too much, "thank him. Before it's too late."

The dog scratches at an ear, looking wistfully away. I don't know what he's thinking but he considers for a minute. "Too late?"

"He got himself in a bad spot. It's a long story."

"That's not my problem, you know."

"I know, but I need to find him, please," I whine. "It's very important."

He hefts himself up from the door frame and pulls the door open. "Fine, just don't take any work, okay?"

I laugh earnestly. "Trust me, I'm not looking for work tonight."

His tail with its white tip wags. "Good."

Back inside, I can tell the crowd has thinned significantly. I glance to the back and see Aziz is still there. Also, now that I look the part, I see some eyes are upon me. I purposefully walk over to a jackal serving wine and beer to a group of men and pull out some copper coins. I wait for her to finish serving, and when she turns to me, I speak up.

"I'm looking for a strong mug of beer. It's been a long night."

She looks me over with a scowl, but unlike the painted one at the door, she doesn't ask me any questions. She does take me over to sit in the back, not too far from Aziz. I take a seat and wait for my drink, trying to look relaxed and approachable.

A few minutes later a chipped mug of brown liquid is pressed into my paws for two copper fals. I thank the serving girl and take a sip as daintily as I can. Thankfully, this is better than the wine they were serving. When she leaves, I survey the room carefully. The fennec from earlier doesn't seem to be here anymore. She probably found someone to entertain.

While I'm thinking what my next move should be, another jackal, this time a guy, comes up to me and smiles. We have a brief conversation where he makes it known what he's looking to procure from me, but I tell him I've been busy most of the night and want to relax for a few. That at least gets rid of him, but I'm still without a plan for how I get to Aziz. While I may look the part of a woman, if I let someone get me alone, it won't take them long to find out I'm not.

While I'm thinking about this, out of the corner of my eye, I see the fox drinking with Aziz get up. He starts to move in my direction, and I suck in my breath. I try not to look at him as he approaches me.

"I've never seen you here before," he says, walking up to me.

"I don't come here to work," I say in my best feminine voice. It comes off a little husky and throaty. The fox's lips quirk up.

"Well, my friend over there would love some action," he says, pointing to Aziz. My heart leaps, but then it sinks as I panic. He must know why I'm here. They're just looking for an excuse to get me out back and dispatch me. I suck in my breath.

"It's, uh, been a long day already," I say. "Is your friend willing to pay to make it worth my while?" It's the same thing I basically told the jackal who propositioned me earlier but leaving the door open.

The fox chuckles. "Oh, he's willing. The question is, can you handle a man like him?"

Aziz must be one of those clients who thinks he can own you and gets to try and break you. I've dealt with men like this before. They tend not to care if it hurts you, just what they want. I see why the whores avoid him. "I'm sure I can take care of him. He won't be complaining when I'm done with him."

"Good," says the fox. "Come with me."

I get up and take my mug of beer with me as I follow the fox over to the table where my quarry sits. Up close, Aziz's clothes are worn and dusty. He has the look of a man who thinks about sharp steel a lot—a man who is unafraid to use violence. The wolf is talking to the tiger, but he glances at me for a moment, appraising me before he finishes. Even though the low table in front of them has two empty pitchers of wine, he is still watching the room. While I should probably stand, I take the open seat so I can hide my maleness below the table. I smile, waiting to be acknowledged. The fox, with me taking the cushion he was sitting on, is forced to get one from another table that is currently unused.

"Soon enough, Achmed. First though," Aziz says to the tiger and then turns to me, "I have some other needs to take care of." He looks me up and down, tracing the lines of my cleavage. He sniffs audibly as the perfume I'm wearing hits his nose. "A little flat, but she will do nicely," he says to the fox just over my shoulder before he goes back to admiring my body.

I clear my throat. "As I was telling your friend, it's been a long day. I expect to be well paid for this." I hold out my paw. I know I said I wasn't here to work, but I need to play the part to find out what has happened to Naji. I'm also not sure what situation letting Aziz buy my attentions is going to put me in. I try not to swallow nervously. I need to stay relaxed for this to get any information at all from Aziz.

He finally looks at me in the eye as he smiles, showing me his fangs. There is an amused expression on his muzzle. "You're direct and down to business, I see. I like that." He reaches down and digs into his coin purse, pulls out two silver dirhams, and leans forward to deposit them into my outstretched paw. "Two now. Two more later if you're good."

I pocket the coins and smile as cutely as I can, sitting back. "I'm always good," I say with a smirk. Usually, I require my money up front in case there is a hitch, but I don't care about the money. I need to know where Naji is. I'm also going to need to get him talking. With luck, I'll get out of this in one piece. "So, what is it you want?"

Aziz takes another swig of his wine. "Everything." He looks me over, and he's not seeing clothes on me anymore. After three years of doing this, I know exactly what the expression he gives me means. It doesn't matter if they're after boys or girls, the look is always the same. "I have been dry for so long, I need to quench my thirst," he adds.

I can feel the fur want to crawl off my neck. He's another Sarda. "I only have two hands and one muzzle."

He laughs in a lopsided grin. "Oh, it's not just the muzzle I want. Tonight is a special night for me."

The tiger, who Aziz called Achmed, has been watching me warily. He frowns at this turn of phrase. Whatever he and Aziz were talking about, he doesn't want to bring it up in front of me. Aziz, Achmed, and the fox who dragged me over all smell of alcohol. Aziz's grin is very lopsided. Even though he has a wary sense about himself, he might be the most gone.

"Is that so? What are you boys celebrating tonight?" I ask, seeing if I can get them talking. Aziz hasn't tried to drag me off somewhere yet, so maybe I can get what I need now. Then I just have to figure out what to do with that information.

"Nothing in particular," says Achmed.

"Nonsense," says Aziz to his friend. He leans forward and breathes into my face. The strong whiff of alcohol that hits my nose tells me he's definitely drunk. "We're celebrating the capture of my brother's killer."

Capture and not killed? There may still be hope for the hyena. "Oh my," I say, still trying to keep my voice as feminine as I can. My heart is thundering in my chest as Achmed shifts his weight a little. He didn't want Aziz to say that. "I'm sorry to hear about your brother," I add in my best sympathetic voice.

"I've waited for this day for a long time. I plan to savor every moment of it," says the wolf, licking his fangs.

The fox isn't paying attention to the conversation, but instead seems to be watching the crowd. Something has caught his eye. "I think I see my own prey for the evening," he says to his friends. With that, he excuses himself and goes to wander off. I watch where he goes out of the corner of the eye, and he starts talking to a lioness.

Aziz and Achmed nod at each other, and Aziz drains his cup of wine. The wolf stands up with only a hint of sway in his body. I should have noticed it before, but there is a sheathed sword at his side, hidden under the cloak he is wearing.

"Come," he says. "I want you to prove to me you are worth those two extra dirhams."

Well, time to see what trouble I've got myself into. I get up and follow him out of the common area of the tavern into a back part of the inn. My heart beats fast. In the hallway, he grabs me and pulls me to his chest. I lean up to kiss him, and I guide his hands to my muzzle to keep him from attempting to grab my nonexistent breasts. He moans happily and pushes his tongue into my mouth, turning to pin me against the wall. This simple act makes me feel violated in more ways than I ever have. I don't know if this man has killed Naji or not, and he's about ready to try and have sex with me. He may even kill me once he finds out I'm not the girl he thinks I am. As he presses himself up against me, I can already feel his erection hardening. My blood thunders in my ears as he explores my muzzle. I don't want to do this with him. If I'm lucky, I might be able to get away with giving him a blowjob and escape with my life.

"I should put you on your knees right here," he pants, breaking off.

I could run, but I need to find some clue to find the hyena. "Perhaps in your room would be a better choice," I offer.

"Mmm, yes, but I am not staying here tonight."

"Is it far?" Perhaps that is where he has Naji.

"No," says the wolf with a grin.

I cup his crotch and lean forward to whisper. "I can get you off here, but if you want something more satisfying, we'll need to go to where you are staying." I feel only disgust, as I put my hands on Aziz to get him excited. He is good-looking for a wolf, but he has a sense of danger about him that tells me he isn't someone you want to do anything with. I inwardly shudder at how I can see him treating the women.

His tongue lolls out of his muzzle as he licks his lips. "I can tell you're someone who's made many a man happy."

I pull back and smile coyly with a small nod. I need him to take me where he is staying. He just has to take the bait I have put out.

Instead, he rolls off of me so his back is against the wall and picks at the rope around his waist that keeps his pants up. "I think I need to see a little action first."

Shit! I have to fellate him and then let him take me back to the room so he can fuck me. I was hoping I wasn't going to have to do that.

"Mmm… are you sure now? I don't want you to be spent for later." I trace my fingers against his cock through the fabric. It throbs in my paw, and I have to not cringe. I've sucked off a lot of men, but I don't want to suck this one off.

He grunts, reaches up to my shoulders, and roughly shoves me down. I fall to my knees with a grimace. "Don't worry, I can provide."

With trepidation I start to undo the rope belt around his waist and pull down his pants. He holds up his pants on the side carrying the sword. My nose has already told me he is fairly drunk, but the whiff of musk I get when I free his member is stronger than I anticipated. He has not bathed recently, and I can tell his cock is going to taste dirty.

"That's a good girl," he coos to me, roughly gripping my ears.

I suck in my breath and reach up to take hold of his shaft. It's already nicely hard in my hand. My own cock is quite flaccid. If it hardens at all, it's only because I enjoy sucking men off, not that I want to suck this one off.

The first tentative lick brings the taste of sweat and musk to my muzzle and I gag inside. He doesn't keep himself clean. However, before I can continue, there is a commotion down the hall.

"Hey, you can't do that here!"

Relief floods into me. I let go of Aziz's hard cock and turn.

"Who says?" Aziz asks. The stranger confronting us is a caracal, and he looks angry.

"I say, because I own this place. Now if you want to have a liaison with your whore, either rent a room or take her somewhere else."

Aziz grunts and I can tell he's sizing up the caracal. Is he foolish enough to attack the owner?

"Very well," he says in a snarl. "Come, we are leaving." He pulls up his pants and with a sneer, stalks past the caracal. Even though Aziz is drunk, he carries himself with purpose. I glance at the caracal and mouth a wordless apology and thanks to him.

He frowns at me since he doesn't recognize me. He catches my scent, and he tilts his head, squinting at me. I don't linger so he can find out who I am or lecture me not to prostitute in his tavern. Instead, I follow Aziz through the common room and out onto the street. The painted dog is still there, and I bob my head at him. He waves and watches as I walk away.

Aziz sets off into the night and I follow, watching the sword on his side shift back and forth under his cloak. When the right moment comes, I'm going to need to get that off of him. I still don't know if this is for naught either. If I don't go with Aziz though, I'll never find Naji.

❧

The stalls in the square are closing as we walk past them, but a few people are still walking around the Malhaa District. Nearby is the Grand Bridge, and we cross the river there. This main thoroughfare is empty, the water dark. The river calls to me, asking me to stop and listen to it, but I can't. On the other side, the streets are quiet. We see no one.

When I walk too slow, trying to get my bearings, Aziz turns and without saying anything, grabs my wrist and starts pulling me down the street. I am forced to trot after him and soon I am hopelessly lost on the far bank of the river.

Aziz is the type of customer I would never service more than once. The type I worry would leave me broken. Sarda, for all his dark interests, always paid me well. He wanted to break me but not to the point I was unable to service him again. I flashback to the joyful gleam in the lion's eyes as he

152

whipped me. I shudder a little in the cool night air. They are both dangerous customers, and I imagine Aziz will try and get everything he can from me like Sarda did. I laugh to myself. The wolf is not my customer, but my prey. I will need to be quick before he sees through my ruse, otherwise I may end up dead myself.

Soon enough, we arrive at a dark house with a heavy, unpainted door. There are no lanterns on the street or in the houses on it. All the residents of this street appear to be asleep already.

"Is this your home?" I cheerily ask him.

He grunts and pulls out a metal key. He slides it into the lock in the door and turns it. I can hear an audible click, and he pushes the door ajar enough to slip through it. I follow him in and step back as he closes the door.

A single lantern burns, turned down low, hanging on a peg in the back of the room. The moment I'm inside, I scent the air. The overwhelming smell of stale dust assaults my nose. I sniff again trying not to make it too noticeable. There is the musk of wolf, tiger, and fox. Fainter, there is a scent vaguely familiar I can't quite place, but it isn't Naji.

"Come," the wolf says, as he steps up to whisper into my ear, reaching around to grip my butt. "Let me get you a drink." He picks up the lantern to lead me through the home.

I am glad the house is dark, because my eyes narrow as I look around. I need to keep my wits about me in here.

"Just a little one," I coo to him.

He turns, and I follow him into a sparsely furnished room with a divan that opens onto a small, overgrown courtyard. He motions to the couch, and I settle upon it while he hangs the lamp from a hook in the ceiling.

Not wanting to be drugged, I watch him carefully while he pours out two goblets of wine from a small wooden cask. Taking a quick glance around, I can see that the room is littered with gear and various household items. None of it is particularly tidy. I believe this is where Aziz sleeps, since the divan smells strongly of him.

He comes back and hands me a goblet. "Drink!" he says, as he tips his own up to his muzzle.

I lift it to my muzzle and daintily sniff at it. The wine smells slightly sour like it is of an inferior quality. Under his watchful eyes I sip just a little. It doesn't taste that good either.

"Now," he says, sitting down and leaning back on his cushions, holding his wine. "Why don't you show me what you have to offer."

I flick my tail and smile at him. I have done my best to hide my bulge and make this ruse work, but if he wants me to get naked now, this ruse will be over.

I gulp and stand up and start seductively swaying my hips as I turn around to give him something to admire. I don't have anything to strip tease him with, and I can't take off anything, else my deception is up. Hopefully my tail is enough of an appetizer while I think up a plan.

"Mmm…," he says. "You are quite the lady."

"Thank you." I think it's obvious I'm a guy, but he may just be too drunk to notice.

I turn around and sink to the floor to crouch down and approach him when the scent hits me: caracal. It's weak, but I think Rigel has been in this room recently. So that's how he knew what happened to Naji. I smile and slide up to him on all fours.

"Let me take these off of you," I say as I nuzzle his crotch, trying not to gag on his thick musk.

He reaches to undo his belt, but I shoo his hand away. "Allow me."

He smiles and leans back. First, I undo the buttons of the vest he is wearing to expose his chest fur. Aziz's tail thumps in approval, so I slowly undo his sword belt while running one paw up his chest.

"You said tonight you are celebrating the apprehension of your brother's killer?" I ask him casually, as I slip his belt and the sheathed kilij off of his hip, and then pull down his pants.

"Yes," he whispers breathlessly. "He will pay for his crimes."

If I understand his words right, Naji is still alive! This hasn't been a wasted effort. I reach up and start to pull his pants down, wagging my tail slowly. He lifts himself up so I can do that. "It is good the authorities found him."

"The authorities," he barks out a laugh. "No, I found him, and I will make him pay for what he has done, slowly and painfully."

I nodded as I pull his pants, belt, and kilij away from him.

"It is a shame then." The feminine tone is fading from my voice.

"A shame?" he asks me.

"Yes," I say, sitting back and smiling. In the back of my mind, I have to ask myself, am I really about ready to kill this man over a dispute I don't have anything to do with? He doesn't appear to be a good man, but does he deserve to die at my hand? Does Naji deserve to die at his hand?

I don't know the answer, but I'm going to have to act quickly. Naji brought me here, and while he wronged Aziz, even Rigel says he acted in self-defense. The hyena has seen death before, and obviously caused it. If I do this, I will have this wolf's blood on my paws. If I don't do this, Aziz will surely kill Naji.

He scoots up on the pillows and looks at me, confused. "What do you mean?" His erection flaps in the breeze between us.

My hand traces the hilt of his kilij next to me. I do not believe there is any way I could bargain with Aziz. There's only one way this is going to end. My hand closes onto the hilt of the sword.

"The man who killed your brother… Naji…"

He blinks, but before he can react, I pull his kilij out, flinging the scabbard backwards. I swing the sword out, but he is already moving toward me. The blade slices into the side of his chest. I scramble back, keeping my grip on the sword.

His eyes go wide, panicked to suddenly meet the end of a sword. "You bitch!" he yells as he rolls off the cushions, pressing a paw to his chest "I will kill you!" he growls at me, watching the blade tip warily.

I grip the kilij with both hands. Now that I have it out of its hilt, I recognize it. This is Naji's sword, and it still has his scent on it. I didn't notice that when it was on Aziz.

My resolve solidifies and I lunge forward. Aziz attempts to dodge but he is drunk, and I am not; Aziz's reaction is far too slow, and I plunge the blade straight into his chest. With a snarl I shove the blade deep and through him. I let go of the hilt, and he falls back onto the divan, blinking in shock, looking up at me. "Who are you?" he wheezes, as he attempts to grab at the sword blade and cuts his paw pads.

The sword is implanted in his chest. This is a killing blow. When I pull back the blade, he will bleed out. I step back and pull off my top. Two lumps of cloth fall away. Beneath, my flat chest is bare.

"You're not a woman." His face twists in rage.

I shake my head. I approach the stricken Aziz and grip the hilt of the sword. "You may call me Zayn, but that doesn't matter now. Know though, that I am Naji's friend." I pull the blade out to make his death quick.

As his life fades away, he stares at me and barks out a hacking, wet laugh. "I am not the only one—" he trails off. I want to ask him what that means, but I can't. His eyes go blank, and the puddle of blood around him quickly becomes quite large, dripping onto the ground before the divan.

Sins of the Past
(Naji)

The sound of the key being inserted into the lock of the storeroom wakes me from a stupor. I've been hanging here, not thinking, for who knows how long. It's hard to be sure what time it is. The light coming in under the door is very faint, suggesting it is still night, but I feel like I've been here forever. Aziz's men chained and shackled me so I can't straighten up, and since then I've crouched, awaiting my fate. My back hurts since I've been forced into this position, and the shoulder that Aziz dislocated has gone numb. My nerves have all gone dead.

Since I've been locked up, no one has bothered to come back and check on me until now. I could hear them earlier, but the house has been silent for a while. I wonder if this is it. Will Aziz finally finish it, or is he going to keep me here for a while, beating me when the mood strikes him? My ribs are bruised, and one might be broken, but I don't have any injuries I think won't heal, yet. I'm pretty sure if he keeps me alive much longer the damage will be permanent.

The door opens. Someone slips in carrying a small lantern, and they close the door behind them. Two things hit my distorted senses: the first is the strong smell of perfume, and the second is the painful feeling of light being thrust into my face after hours of being stuck in the dark. It doesn't help that one eye is swollen shut. I squint, trying to focus my other eye.

The lantern is set down next to me, and I can feel the gag in my muzzle being loosened. When it is loose, I spit it out. The gag hits the floor silently, all of the saliva in my mouth long since gone.

"You look awful."

The voice gives me a shock. The words I try to form are just a rasp. I have to work my tongue back and forth before I can croak out the name. "Zayn?"

"Yes," the jackal whispers, looking me over. "They secured you tightly, I see."

I swallow and try and moisten my lips before I speak again. "How...," It hurts to talk, but I need to know. "...did you get in here? Where is Aziz?"

"He's dead," Zayn says, testing a key in the lock securing the chain holding one of my arms.

"Dead?"

"Yes. I killed him."

I struggle to look at him, still blinded by the light. "How?"

"Details later. First, we need to get you out of here." He tries a different key and the lock clicks. Carefully he undoes the shackle and helps me move my arm. It's gone numb, but I can feel the blood flowing back into it as I gently work my fingers. Zayn moves over and unlocks the shackle on my other arm, and I tremble in pain as my dislocated shoulder finally slips back into socket.

"Thank you," I whisper, as I push myself into a normal seating position. I fall back against the wall behind me and pant. My back is screaming for having been hunched over so long, and moving anything hurts. Feeling is slowly coming back into my body, and pain is what is flooding my dead senses.

Zayn nods and moves to unlock the shackles binding my feet. While he's trying different keys on those, I notice he is wearing his dancing costume, and I don't understand why. Did Aziz or Rigel come looking for him too?

"Why," I ask him, "are you dressed like that?"

"Hmm?" he asks.

"In your silks?"

He looks up at me, muzzle just an inch away from me. "It was the only way to get close to Aziz. It worked well," he says, bending down to test another key. This one works, and the last lock opens. "I used an old trick to fill out my chest, and he didn't realize I wasn't a woman until it was too late."

I want to ask questions, but maybe I shouldn't. Whatever Zayn did, he did for me. He pulls the shackles off my feet and with his help, I'm able to stretch my legs out. My body hurts all over; even my tail is sore.

"Will you be okay?" he asks me.

"Eventually," I respond. My sword arm's shoulder is throbbing from being out of joint. Just moving it forces me to bite my tongue to not scream.

Zayn comes and holds me, and I make a dry sobbing sound, as he cries against me. I want to cry too, but my tears are dry. Even trying to hug him hurts. I have nothing to offer. All I can do is sob, safe in his arms.

The jackal holds me for a minute, letting his tears wet my fur before he glances at the door. "We need to go before the others come back," he whispers to me, wiping at his wet fur.

I nod, agreeing, and he carefully helps me up. My legs protest, but I don't care. I don't want to stay here, that's for sure.

Zayn goes to the door and opens it to check the hallway. Motioning for me to come on, he slips out into the hallway, and I follow him. It's quiet in the house. I strain my ears, but I can't hear any sounds except for our breathing and the gentle wind outside.

"What time is it?" I ask Zayn.

"Sometime after midnight," he says. "I'm not sure exactly, but it's very late. We need to go before the others come back."

I nod. "My sword. Have you seen my sword?"

He turns to me and gives me a curious look. "Why?" he asks.

"We can't leave without it."

He fidgets, ears down. "I left it with Aziz."

"Which room?"

He sucks in a breath, then turns to head in a different direction. We cross an overgrown courtyard, and he pauses at two open large double doors that lead into a room off the courtyard. He just points through the doors.

Limping, I walk into the room. The place smells strongly of blood and vomit along with the unmistakable smell of death, faint but already present. Various things are scattered about but in the center of the room there is a divan, and on top of it, naked except for an unbuttoned vest lies Aziz, in a pool of blood. The blood has congealed, but the kill is still fresh.

So that's how Zayn managed to find me. "I must give you credit, this is very resourceful of you."

"He thought I was going to sleep with him."

"Thank you," I look for where my sword is, and I see it lying on the ground next to some vomit. I hobble over to where it is lying. "I know it doesn't help, but I threw up too the first time I killed someone," I say, reaching down to pick up my sword where it lies against the stone floor. My entire body screams in protest, but I will not leave this blade behind.

"I didn't realize it felt like… this," he stutters.

I glance to where he stands by the doors. Zayn is shaking a little, his tail dead behind him. I look for my scabbard, which I see lying thrown across the floor. I fetch that and then, without caring, I walk over to the divan and grab a pillow and use it to wipe off the congealed blood from the steel. When I drop the pillow on the ground, I look over at the dead wolf. His eyes stare up at the ceiling unseeing. His body is twisted.

"May God have mercy on you, Aziz." I say, sheathing my weapon. I turn to look back at Zayn. The jackal is leaning against the door frame, trying to keep it together.

I limp over and offer him my good arm. "Are you going to be okay?"

"The other two will come for me now, won't they?" he asks.

"If they do, I'm not going to let them find you."

"I think I'm going to be sick again," he mumbles.

I give him an awkward hug with my non-dominant arm. "It's never easy taking a life. It never really leaves you, but it was mine or his. He would have it no other way." A small part of me worries that maybe he should have left me, that I've now gotten him tangled up in the threads of my past, but I can't think about that right now. He needs me to be strong for him.

Zayn looks up at me, eyes wide and fixed in the distance. He doesn't say anything. My words aren't helping, but I'm too beat up myself to offer him much comfort.

"Come on," I suggest, gently trying to nudge him into the courtyard, away from the body. We need to get out of here before the tiger or the fox comes back. I can't protect either of us in my current state. At the edge of the courtyard, I pause to listen. "Aziz brought you back here alone, right?"

"Yes," he flatly responds. "Aziz and his friends were drinking at the Silver Shroud, and he brought me back here to fuck me. I made sure he didn't get the chance."

I flick my tail in approval and walk into the entranceway. Zayn is definitely inventive, but it's my turn to be the inventive one. If Aziz's lackeys are smart, they'll pick up our scent in here and try and track us through the city. If they come back soon, they might be able to follow it. It's a risk I don't want to entertain.

The entranceway is dark, and I approach the door, carry-ing the sheathed sword in my left hand. I want to drop into a fighting crouch, but I'm in no shape for a battle right now.

"You better take this," I suggest to Zayn. "I wouldn't be any good with it right now."

The jackal takes the sword from me, but just holds it limply at his side. I walk up to the door and listen. Carefully I open it and when I hear nothing, I peek my muzzle out. The street outside is dark, and glancing around suggests it's de-serted. I sniff the air, but nothing distinct comes to me except for the smell of the perfume Zayn is wearing and the general scent of Aksu at night.

Carefully I slip outside, and Zayn follows, letting the door bang as the latch closes.

"Shit!" he says, and then he quickly covers his mouth.

I glance around. "I'm going to have to train you on the meaning of covert. Which way did you come from?"

He points to the left and I set off down the street in the opposite direction. "Better to not go the way the other two will be coming," I suggest.

We reach the end of the street where it intersects with another one. I take a moment to see if I recognize it. When I don't, I take the branch that I think leads toward the river. This road leads to another intersection where both roads lead to a dead end. Backtracking, we take the other branch, and this finally intersects with a road I recognize.

"Do you know where we are?" he asks me as we walk past shuttered stores.

"I have a rough idea. I don't come to this part of town often. I know this road ends down by the Zaharani."

"The river?" he asks, following me.

I nod. "I hope you don't mind a late-night swim."

"In this?" he stops.

"We want to throw them off our trail. They won't take kindly to Aziz's death, and this is the best way I know to lose them. It's still too far from dawn for the crowds to erase our scent off the street."

He shakes his head and follows me. "You've done this before, haven't you?"

"I've had to make myself scarce before," I say as we hurry down the street. I'm not running, but don't want to take too long. Zayn is right behind me.

"I should point out that outside of the cool pool in the Blue Door, I've never gone swimming before," he calls after me.

I should have thought of that, but I have an answer for him. "We'll walk through the shallows until we reach the western bridge. Any way we can mask our scent will make their tracking us harder."

As we walk, I'm thinking how to chart our route back to my apartment. I can do this, and get us there safely, but what do I do after that? I'm going to have to figure this out tomorrow and quickly.

∾

My body feels awful when I wake up, but I'm in my own bed. That alone makes it better. I'm still alive, and I am not locked in that awful room. Zayn even slept in the bed with me, but his warm presence is gone now.

Getting up hurts. I have bruises all over my body and when I move, they each want to remind me of what happened last night. When I got home, I sponged down my fur to get some of the dried blood out of it, but I still look and smell awful. My swollen eye is a little better, at least; I can see out of it again. My shoulder still aches from the dislocation, but I can move my arm slowly.

I find Zayn in my majlis, sitting on the divan. The shutters are thrown open so light can stream through the arabesque in the windows. He is dressed and is staring out the window at the courtyard below. His ears flick as he hears me approach, but he doesn't move. He's leaning over the back of the divan, his eyes focused on the fountain below.

"Zayn?" I say, sitting next to him. I reach out and gently touch his shoulder.

"I want to be left alone," he responds, brushing my paw away.

"You're thinking about Aziz, aren't you?"

He turns to look at me, searching my face for something. I don't know if he finds it, but finally he sighs. "I can still smell his blood. The look of desperation in his eyes as he bled to death is bored into my mind."

I gently reach out and touch his shoulder again. "I remember the first time I took someone's life. It has stayed with me since then. Sometimes I dream about that day."

He trembles under my touch. "This isn't why I came here. I was better off back in Zaptu."

I frown. "You lived under the lash there."

"Only when Sarda came to town. It wasn't so bad the rest of the time. Now…" he stares at his paws, the digits spread wide.

I tilt my head. "First, I would disagree that it wasn't that bad." I reach down and gently stick my paw under his loose shirt, so I can run my hand up and down his flank. "You can say that, but your body tells a different story. Sarda may have been the only one who whipped you, but this was not infrequent."

He frowns. "I did what I had to do to survive."

"So did I when I was younger, but life should not be this hard. We deserve dignity. We deserve respect," I say. "I can give you a life where you don't have to sell your attentions to others."

"Naji, you are an expert swordsman, and you can't even protect yourself," he says icily.

I let go of him. "I should have seen it. I should have realized he was leading me on, but I've wanted so long to get past what happened to Isim, to reconnect, yet each time I thought we were reconciling, Rigel's thrown it back at me. I foolishly thought finally things were going to get better."

He glares at me, steel in his eyes. "And Aziz?"

I sigh. "I did what I was paid to do. He and his brother picked the fight. The fact I bested one of them in combat just meant luck was on my side that day. I never gave it much thought, but when Rigel mentioned the name, I should have become suspicious." I pause, thinking over last night. "Thank you. Every day of my life going forward is due to you. Without you, I would be dead."

He sighs and goes back to starting out into the courtyard below. "I still can't get Aziz's lifeless stare out of my mind."

"It takes time. Eventually it goes away," I say.

"Naji, I've spent my life giving myself to others. I'm just a whore. I give people pleasure. I don't take their lives," he scowls at me.

I look down at my paws. "This is my fault."

"So, what do I do?"

I scratch at an ear. "That is a good question. I don't know what Aziz's two remaining associates will do nor do I know what Rigel will do when he finds out Aziz is dead."

He considers. "What about the city guard?"

"You mean go to the guard and tell them what happened?"

"Yes. Can they help us?"

I consider it. "They wouldn't take my word about what happened, but they might take yours."

"Wait, why wouldn't they take your word at face value?"

"Who do you think the city guard found clutching the dying Isim? Me. Rigel was gone by then, and he left me to rot in that jail for six months. Naima had to get me out."

"He abandoned you with the dying Isim?"

"Yes. Rigel was the lookout, and he took off once he passed the word on."

"This sounds like it wasn't a legal job."

I chuckle. "Oh no, it wasn't legal at all, but back then I did a lot of jobs that were dangerous and not always above board. It was the only work Rigel, Isim, and I could find, but we lived together liked brothers, and I loved them both. We ate together, we slept together wherever we could find shelter, and I worked out who I was with those two. You have to realize, I was nineteen and on my own, and I wasn't from Aksu. Rigel and Isim were my world, and my only family."

"When you say loved —"

"Completely, with both my heart and my body. They knew each other first, but together we were a trifecta. I discovered who I was with them, and all the things about myself that never made sense before finally fit. I hadn't really had the time before to discover my desires, but with those two, they taught me how to love."

Zayn's muzzle is hanging open. "I can't see you and Rigel together."

"That's because the Rigel I knew back then is gone. I lived and worked with him for almost five years. Before Isim was killed, I knew the sound of the caracal's footfalls in an empty room, and the way he'd swish his tail when he laughed. He's not the same Rigel anymore. The loss of Isim hurt him deeply, and when I've tried to talk to him, tried to get past his new stony façade, he's refused to let me in. He's still Rigel, but he's not the Rigel I knew, yet sometimes I can feel that Rigel looking out at me through those eyes."

He shakes his head. "So, when Isim died, Rigel basically stopped being your friend and lover?"

I nod.

"And he blames you for what happened?" Zayn asks.

I nod again. "Yes. I should have realized Isim wasn't right behind me. I've played those moments over in my head, and I swore he was right there. Did he trip? Did he not hear me at first? I'll never know because I never got to ask him. For five years now, Rigel has held what happened that night against me.

"The job was supposed to be simple. There was a merchant who was skimming money from his business partners, and we were going to break into his house when he wasn't there and get it back. Naima had been giving us work for a couple years, but she was starting to pull away back then and was looking to settle down into something honest, so when this came up, we took it.

"The merchant's house had high walls, but on one side of the house was a courtyard. Isim and I snuck into the house by scaling the wall while Rigel kept watch outside. Together, we were supposed to search the house and return any coin we found. His business associates were keeping him busy while we did this.

"We weren't having any luck, so we split up. Isim was on the far side of the house when Rigel gave the sign someone was coming. I called out to the leopard and bolted for the wall. I grabbed the rope we used and was up and over it in no time. I thought he was right behind me, but he didn't come right over the wall.

"It turns out the merchant had hired a guard with his money and the guard returned from the market. Because we were ransacking the house, he knew immediately after he entered something was amiss. He ended up catching Isim in the courtyard as he as trying to climb over the wall. A scuffle broke out and Isim managed to escape, but the guard mortally wounded him. The moment he hit the dirt and crumpled onto the ground, I knew something was wrong.

"I can still see the leopard's face as he panted, lying where he fell. At first, I thought he'd slipped, but then I saw the dark puddle forming in the moonlight. There was so much blood then. Too much blood. I know when I reached down and cradled Isim that this was it. I had seen that same panting expression before on the dying.

"Rigel had already headed to safety, and that left me with Isim," I whisper as my voice turns hoarse. "I wanted to carry him away, but I knew the wound was fatal. I cradled his dying body in my arms until he was gone. The city guard found me clutching his lifeless form."

There had so much blood and screaming. Lots of screaming from the city guard. "They had to pull me away from him. I was covered in his blood. When the guard who killed him came out, he just shook his head at me."

"And Rigel?" asks Zayn, snapping me back from the memory.

"He left me. He never came to the jail, and I sat there for six long months, until Naima managed to pull strings to get me out. I don't think Rigel made any effort to get me released, and when I did see him after that, he blamed me for not making sure Isim heard the warning. He completely shut me out of his life. We were both devastated by the loss, but he had no room in his heart for my grief and would accept no blame in what happened. If he'd given us more warning or waited for us to get out, things might have been different, but he has never wanted to hear my side. We both grieved for the loss of Isim, but in different ways."

Zayn is silent, processing this. Finally, he speaks up. "So, he puts all the blame on you?"

I nod. "I should have been more aware, but he was the lookout. I've wanted so much to make it right for him, to at least get past this, but he's always refused to discuss it. Naima was able to get Isim's sword back from the city guard, and I considered giving it to him for a while, but in the end, I kept it to use as my own weapon to remember Isim by. I know Rigel hates me, but I don't understand why he would choose now to attempt to kill me. He's had plenty of chances these last five years."

"Sometimes hate festers like an open wound."

I sigh and look out over the courtyard. "That's true. He knows where I live too."

"So, they will come here?" he asks me, concerned.

I scratch at an ear. "Not sure. My neighbors might notice something. Scaling the outside wall would be the best option. Rigel could do it, but I don't see the other two being able to do that."

Zayn goes back to watching the courtyard.

"I should go talk to Naima. She might be able to help me understand what's going on. Rigel hasn't kept in touch with her, but she might know something."

"You want me to come with you? I don't want to be here alone."

I consider. "Rigel knows I'd go see Naima after something like this, so no. I can take you to the Blue Door," I suggest. "Fadel can rent us a room, and it's safer there."

"Won't they come looking for us there?"

"Maybe, but I would feel better with you somewhere with someone I trust while I'm with Naima. Plus, the Blue Door is a public place."

He sighs. "Is that putting too much of a burden on Fadel?"

"I think he'll understand, but if you want, I can just drop you off, and you can just hang out for a bit." I realize I haven't asked him about his debut at the Blue Door. "How did your dancing go last night?"

"It went well. Fadel was impressed and so was Khalil. They want me to repeat my routine tonight."

"Then we should at least visit Fadel, and if you are feeling up to it, you can dance tonight. It might help you settle your mind and be a useful distraction."

He fidgets with the tip of his tail. "I guess, but won't that just let Rigel find us?"

"I don't know. Fadel has done a lot to make sure the Blue Door is a safe space, so I doubt he would cause a scene there."

Zayn considers. "That does sound good…" He snaps his fingers suddenly. "The sword! I left the sword and my bag in an alley near the Silver Shroud."

"The Silver Shroud? Is that where you found Aziz at?"

He nods. "Yes. I need to go back and get the sword."

I hesitate. "I'm not sure that's a good idea."

"Is it worse than going to the Blue Door? Fadel paid for that sword. He wanted me to use a dull blade."

"No. Fair point. Okay. Let me get dressed and we'll go to the Silver Shroud. We can get some food on the way. I haven't eaten since last morning. Then I will go see Naima."

❧

It was already late morning when we left the house, and finding the alleyway Zayn used took a bit. We got lucky and did recover his sword and bag, but I wasn't able to speak to Fadel before I left the Blue Door. The fennec was busy, but Zayn told me to go. I left him with some tea in the shade of the courtyard.

As I walk down the street in the midafternoon, heading for the Grand Market, I think over what happened yesterday. I'm trying to piece it together, but something is missing. I don't understand why Rigel would turn on me now. He had many opportunities to trick me before in the past, so something must have happened, but what? Isim has been dead for five years, so that can't be it. Rigel's actions are never without reason, so Aziz has to factor into this somehow. The wolf said to Rigel he would hold up his part of their deal, but what that was is beyond me. Without some clues, I'm never going to figure it out. Maybe there's something I've forgotten Naima can clue me in on. I know Rigel might be staking out her store, so as I enter the souk, I keep my guard up, watching for anyone who might be taking an interest in me.

It is clear to me that Rigel did not do this just because Aziz offered him money. Rigel and I have not been friends since Isim died, but he's never been just after coin. Even as he was bringing me to Aziz, he seemed finally willing to reconcile. For years I've wanted to work things out with him, but apparently that was all a lie; he just wants me dead.

When I arrive at Naima's store, she is talking to a customer about how fresh her mint is. She gives me an appraising eye, obviously taking note of my rough, disheveled look, but she doesn't say anything. She nods at me to wait and stays focused on the business at hand. After a protracted negotiation, the customer buys some mint, along with tea and cardamom. Even after they've exchanged money, the jackal talks to the leopard for a few minutes about various caravans recently coming through town before he takes his leave.

"I don't see how you do it," I remark, once the jackal has left. "He would talk for an hour if I wasn't here."

"He's a good customer. He and his wife buy something from me every week." While she talks, Femi comes out from the back. The leopard is carrying a sack of paprika which he puts down next to an empty sack.

"I guess keeping him happy is important."

"His coin is good," she says. She glances at the leopard and back to me. "Femi, can you go see if Nazar has my saffron in?"

The young leopard pauses. "I checked just this morning, mistress."

"I know," she coos at him. "Naji and I have some business to discuss that would be best talked about in private. Come back in thirty minutes."

He nods then, and after dusting off his paws, he exits the store. After he leaves, Naima walks over and bolts the door from the inside.

I chuckle. "I'm surprised he doesn't ask questions."

"He's smart," the leopardess says, turning toward me. "Some might think him slow because he is slow to offer an opinion, but he's very astute. He quickly learned when it is best not to be around. He's also paid to exercise his discretion. Now," she opens her paws in a gesture to get me to talk, "what the hell happened to you?"

"I had a rough night."

"I can tell. It looks like you got into a fight after a bad night of drinking."

"That would be better than what happened to me."

She shakes her head. "Do I need to start having my friends keep tabs on you too?"

"I thought you didn't have many ties to your old business associates."

"I have enough," she smiles. "For starters, I knew you would be here today at some point, but not looking like a one-eyed beggar," she says, gesturing to my still partially swollen eye.

"So, you already know what happened? Here I was the one who thought he was coming to ask questions, but you already know the questions I seek to ask," I say.

Naima frowns and her tail lashes. In that moment, I can see the gray on her muzzle come out. The simple robe cinched at her waist covers a powerful leopardess, but the years are starting to creep up on her. "I may be old now, Naji, but I'm not stupid."

"I wouldn't call you old," I offer.

She laughs. "At least you are still polite. I must give you credit for that. But to business. You came about the news I found out about yesterday, yes?"

"News? Possibly, but I have a more immediate problem."

She walks back over to her stool and sits down. "Let's start with the news and you tell me if this relates to last night, then you tell me what happened last night. For starters, I've heard that an old 'friend' of yours is in town."

"Aziz?"

She frowns. "The only Aziz I know is a fennec who trades in black pepper and tea. Have you been getting in fights with my suppliers behind my back?"

"Remember three years ago that job I did where the caravan I was guarding got attacked, and I killed one of the bandits? The guy I killed had a brother named Aziz."

"Oh! I remember you telling me about that. No, I was speaking of our ex-associate Rigel."

"He's around. I saw him yesterday," I growl.

"Did you? I don't see or hear anything about him. Last I heard he was working with the Aragvi Clan over in Japar."

Japar is the port west of Aksu, at the river mouth. Most of the trade that flows through Aksu and heads west across the sea embarks in Japar. "Interesting. I've seen him on and off for the past year at the Blue Door, but I never know when I'll run into him. He must be traveling back and forth. He decided to help me find work yesterday. I thought perhaps there was some kindness in that black soul of his until he sold me out to Aziz."

Naima's tail becomes still, her expression dark. "What do you mean by he sold you out? You two were close once."

"Apparently, Aziz has been looking to settle the score over his brother's death. Rigel was happy to take me straight to him."

She scowls. "I realize you were adults when I met you, but I tried to teach you, Rigel, and Isim that you were at your strongest when you were together. Someone who betrays his friends will quickly have none. I'm glad you managed to get out of that situation."

I chuckle mirthlessly. The fact I was dependable impressed Naima when she first met me, but it's more than just that now. I've always appreciated her sharpness and keen observations, and being so far from my own parents, I've come to see her as my adopted mother. She took me under her wing and showed me much. "I know, but I misjudged Rigel by trusting him yesterday. Rigel left me with Aziz for whatever Aziz wanted to do to me. There was no escape available. I'm only alive because Zayn managed to get me out."

She shakes her head. "So, who is Zayn? Someone else you are working with?"

"Zayn is the jackal I met in Zaptu."

"Is that this boy you fancy? The one you are supposed to have brought by today?"

"Yes. Sorry," I say. "I wasn't sure Rigel might not be watching your shop."

She laughs. "If he's out there, he should show himself in. I would be quite happy to give him a piece of my mind or a taste of my steel. I did not mentor a traitor."

I smile. I don't see Naima carrying a weapon, but I know she's got something on herself. "Unfortunately, this has pulled Zayn into the equation, and I didn't want to see him get caught up in this. Rigel warned me about Aziz, but I didn't know this was going to become a thing."

"Naji, Naji, Naji… I told you, you need to be careful who you work for and what they want from you."

I throw up my paws. "The job seemed easy! It wasn't like they hired me to be attacked by some people, one of which would show up three years later with a vendetta against me."

"Fair point. So how did Zayn get you out of this situation?"

"Zayn tracked Aziz down after Rigel told him I was dead and to find himself a new friend. Zayn, however, managed to convince Aziz to take him back to the house, thinking he was a woman he was paying for services. He took the wolf out himself, but I'm worried that Rigel or the two people I saw working for Aziz might try and track us down."

She whistles. "Zayn sounds like he's quite the fighter himself."

"He's resourceful and he knows how to handle a sword."

"I don't think you'd be good with a man who didn't." She stops to smirk. "I wonder if this relates to what I heard yesterday."

"You mentioned you had news for me."

"I do. Rigel works for the Aragvi clan, and they've been more active recently. There are rumors they're up to something big."

"Do you know if Aziz was involved? He attacked the Aragvi clan's caravan, but I suspect he worked for them once long ago."

She thinks, tapping her claws across the counter. "He was a wolf?"

I nod.

"It's possible. I never heard the name. The Aragvi haven't had a presence here for a while, but now they're selling wares again in the market."

"Interesting. I'm sure they have been here to trade before."

"Probably, but they're looking for a few guards and they're being discreet about it. The job I found for you is a guard job with the Aragvi Clan. They're looking for some muscle to protect their shipments. I thought it might be legit, but now I'm not so sure."

I stiffen. "Really now?"

Naima nods. "I mentioned you and Rigel weren't exactly friends. The response I got back was that would not be a problem. I was told Rigel was not involved with this job."

I suck in my breath. Maybe Aziz came back to town for more than just revenge. "What are they transporting?"

"They wouldn't say, just that it's important it stay safe. They need someone discreet."

I pace across the shop, thinking. "That itself isn't unusual."

"Yes, but they pay a gold dinar a day."

I stop pacing. "This isn't legal, is it?"

"My guess is no, but it is hard to say what this is. I can keep my ears up, but I don't know what they're up to. I do know if you take this, you'll be working for Abu."

"Abu, Abu, wait, is this Abu a lion?"

She nods, gets up from the stool, and starts to pack some herbs into a small satchel. "You know him?"

I shiver. Even though the air in the shop is still and warm, I feel a sudden chill. "He's the lion who set up the job where Aziz's brother died. Somehow all this connects. Aziz told Rigel that by turning me in, he would make sure he fulfilled his end of some deal they had."

Naima considers, drumming her claws. "Abu is a good man. I've worked with him before, when we were both younger. He joined the Aragvi clan later, but he's loyal to those who are loyal to him. He follows the Aragvi creed to the letter."

"They were founded by wolves from the north, weren't they?"

"Yes, but they've diversified their membership. They're part merchant company, part muscle, but no one knows exactly what they're doing."

"This sounds risky."

"Very much so, but what was one of the first lessons I taught you?"

I recite her words on command. "It is better to be the hunter than the hunted."

She grins. "If you want to find what Rigel and Aziz were doing, then you already know what I would counsel you to do. The clan has rented a booth in the market. If you go tomorrow, you can talk to Abu. I need to reopen the shop, but I can let you know if I find anything else out."

I sigh. "Let me think first, but outside of tracking Rigel down and pummeling the answers I need out of him, I don't have anything else to do."

Naima has finished putting herbs into the satchel, so she walks over to unbolt the door. "Yes, but that won't earn you any coin. I think Rigel is on the outs with the clan now. If so, you're in luck! Or you could bump straight into him."

I snort. "You're right. I guess I'll see what Abu says and make a decision there. If it does come to clash of blades, I will be happy to pay him back for what he did to me, but I'd like answers. He owes me some explanation."

"You were always principled, and I appreciate that about you, but you must realize, if he wishes your death, no honeyed words of yours will change his heart."

"I know. I will visit Abu tomorrow."

I turn to walk out. As I pass the leopardess, she puts a hand on my shoulder. "Watch your back, Naji. Do not let Isim's death be the way toward your own. I will miss you greatly if something happens to you."

"Thanks, Naima."

She nods and hands me the satchel she has been putting together, pressing it into my paws. "And make yourself a strong cup of tea with this. It will help with the swelling. Now go, my friend, hunt well."

House Rules
(Zayn)

In the afternoon, the Blue Door is practically deserted. What patrons there are mill about under the courtyard colonnade or in the great hall to escape the heat. I considered ordering myself a hookah, but I instead settled on just baklava and water to stay cool. The sweet pastry with its chopped nuts is delicious and I lick the honey from my fingers greedily.

Fadel was busy tending to his stock of wine when we arrived, so I can't talk to him yet about Rigel, but I will when I can get him alone. Until Naji returns from speaking to Naima, all I can do is wait. I've got the practice sword and my bag, and I stretch out on the bench so I can be comfortable. This idleness annoys me, but hopefully I'll see Fadel go by so I can get his attention. For now, I'm alone with my thoughts and that's rough. Hopefully I will be in the right frame of mind when I dance tonight.

I must have dozed off from the heat, but approaching movement and the sound of someone calling out my name stirs me from my reverie.

The voice is cold and calculating. "I'm surprised to see you here, jackal."

I jump out of my skin. "Rigel," I say, surprised, and scramble to my feet so I can turn and face him. I'm unnerved that I didn't realize he approached me. I notice his hand rests calmly against his sword's hilt.

He frowns at me. "You have been busy, it seems."

He's feeling me out. "I don't like to stay put."

"No… you don't."

I shrug, and without thinking fire off a proverb my parents were fond of. "Opportunity, like a good meal, does not last."

Rigel's ears go up. "No, it doesn't," he remarks, "but I hear you apparently had quite the night last night."

"As I said, I don't like to stay put."

"You surprise me, you know. I didn't think you had it in you, but here you are dozing off as if nothing happened. I guessed right where I could find you."

He's playing with me. "The element of surprise cuts both ways. I've heard what you did," I say snidely. "You seem to have a loose definition of friend."

"I was trying to settle things, but you went and unsettled them. Now here we are again, but this time, I'm not here to mince words."

"Forgive me, but I think we're beyond pleasantries at this point."

He flicks his ears. "Indeed. So, let me lay this out for you clearly. Naji will get you killed. What you did last night is the first step on a road you don't want to be on. This wasn't your fight, jackal, until last night. Now, the hunters will come looking for you." His voice drops an octave, and his eyes are trying to bore into me.

I step forward toward him, a low growl underlying my words. "You made it my fight, cat, when you betrayed Naji. He told me what you did."

"And did Naji tell you who Isim is and how he got Isim killed?" he sneers. "Or did he not bother to tell you the whole story?"

"He told me how you left him to rot in a jail cell for six months, and how Naima had to get him out."

He considers me, his tail lashing. "He's with Naima right now, isn't he? A useful piece of information. I've wondered how much they still talk. I guess he still eats out of her hands. So, did Naji tell you Naima gave us the job? She was starting to pull back from the risky jobs, so she passed the one over to us. Oh sure, we didn't have to do it, but we needed work, and we always did the jobs she got for us. Did Naji tell you that?"

"I don't have to answer to you."

"What about the fact he saw all his friends back home die in battle, and instead of returning to his clan, he ran away?"

I have no idea what Rigel is talking about, so I just stare blankly at the cat.

"I guess he hasn't told you that one. You should ask him, see if he'll tell you about that story. You can hear about his whole time on campaign. My point is, people near him die, Zayn, because he lives that type of life." His expression softens slightly because my ears have gone down. "But I cannot fault you for foolishly loving someone like that, because Isim and I did. You can see how well that worked out for Isim."

I frown. The hyena does have a checkered past, and I need to find out more about it, but there's something else here. Something I recognize. "You're jealous. You're hurt and since you're hurt, you want him to hurt. I know what loss is and how it breaks a man, and I can see it in your face," I say.

He laughs coldly. "Oh, now you think you know me?"

"I've seen what the past can do to someone; how it can twist them and make them forget the present and any happiness they could hope for. I've felt that pain intimately." Rigel is no better than me when it comes to dealing with his life.

He walks up to me to get into my face. "You don't know what I went through, but if you want to live, if you want to ever get out of this, go back to whatever hovel Naji found you in. You've already cost me dearly with your interference, but I'll give you blind loyalty once. I don't want to see Naji get someone else killed, but I will see to it Aziz's friends find you if you stay."

I kind of already suspected that they will hunt me down, but I've also hit a nerve with Rigel. "Your pride, like Aziz's, will be your undoing."

Rigel regards me for a moment. "Unlike Aziz, I know when to keep my prick to myself. The question is, do you know when to put down your tail?"

I will not be demeaned. "The motion of my tail should be of no concern to you."

"It isn't, but it's not going to save you either."

"You expect me to leave and never come back here, never talk to Naji again, or you'll kill me?"

He smiles. "Yes."

"Go to hell, Rigel," I snarl at him, flashing fangs.

He steps back instinctively, and before I know it, he's got his sword halfway out of his scabbard. "Careful now, or I'll show you how a true swordsman works."

I stand up straighter. "No, that's how a murderer works. If that's what you're going to do, make your cut clean, for there is no honor in that." They are stupid words, but I will face him with courage. My father did not run when raiders attacked the caravan he was with. I will not run now.

The caracal breathes in steadily, the sword still half out of its scabbard, ready to strike. "You have a fool's heart, Zayn."

"Rigel!" screams a familiar voice.

Rigel rolls his eyes, and lets the sword fall back into the scabbard. He then turns to confront the fennec. "Fadel, I didn't see you there."

The fennec is standing in the courtyard with his fangs bared. Next to him is Ales. "What the fuck are you doing, threatening people in here?" asks Fadel.

"We are just talking."

The fennec narrows his eyes. "And the reason you had your hand on your sword?"

"It's none of your business."

"If it happens in the Blue Door, it is my business," snarls the fennec, walking up to him. The fox is a good foot shorter than Rigel, but he moves purposefully, closing the distance quickly.

The caracal snorts. "You don't scare me, Fadel."

"Then you don't deserve to be here. This is family here, and if you threaten one of our own, you are threatening our entire family."

Rigel laughs. "He just came to Aksu."

"And when you came here the first time, young and confused, did I not let you in?"

The cat shakes his head. "You live in a dream world, Fadel. It's a lot different out there beyond these walls. Aksu has its dark alleys."

"Then you don't deserve to be here. I welcome my guests with open arms, even if their birth families draw back from them for their tastes. You don't get to threaten people because you feel like it."

I'm not sure what to make of this scene. Fadel has approached Rigel, even though the fox is unarmed. Ales is standing behind him, arms behind his back. I think he's unarmed, but I catch the flash of a dagger hidden behind his back. Many of the patrons are standing behind Ales, watching things intently.

Rigel glances behind Fadel at Ales and everyone in the courtyard who is watching us. All eyes fixed on Rigel and me. He flicks his eyes at me, muzzle taut. Finally, he lowers his head. "I'm sorry, Fadel, but the jackal and I have a… disagreement."

The fox growls. "No one pulls their sword in anger inside of the Blue Door. Get out of my establishment, Rigel."

The cat scowls at the fennec and turns and walks off toward the entrance. Fadel walks over to me, and Ales comes up. I notice the red fox has sheathed the dagger he is carrying. "Ales, make sure everyone knows to deny him entrance."

"Of course," says Ales. He turns and trots off to follow the caracal who has disappeared into the entrance hall.

"Are you all right?" Fadel asks me.

"Yes, I'll be fine," I say.

The fennec huffs, looking toward the entrance hall. "I know he and Naji have not been friends for years, but I didn't know it had come to this."

"It's the reaction I expected from Rigel."

Fadel glances at me and scowls. "What did you do in a single day to get a reaction like that?"

I look around. "I think we should talk about that in private."

He pinches the bridge of his nose. "Do I need to speak with Naji about you?"

I chuckle. "It's the other way around."

∾

Naji growls at me. We're in the back of the Blue Door inside Fadel's apartment, two rooms on the first floor that open onto the courtyard. The fennec is seated on a chair, back against the wall in his private majlis, watching the two of us argue.

"Rigel is not to be trifled with like that. He could have killed you right there," says Naji.

I throw up my arms. "Well, what did you expect me to do? It's not like I walked up to him or anything." Naji arrived while I was discussing the events of the night before with Fadel, and I had to tell the hyena what happened with Rigel. Fadel made us all coffee and set out a dish of dates for us while I did that, but no one had yet touched their coffee or the dates.

Naji paces back and forth across the rug in the middle of the room. "Try not and antagonize him to the point he decides murder in public is a viable option."

"I don't take kindly to be threatened."

The hyena sighs, rubbing a paw through his face fur. "Nor would I."

"Was it necessary to kill Aziz?" Fadel asks me.

I grumble. I told the fennec the story earlier, but he seems displeased with my actions. "What was I going to do? Go up there and ask him to let Naji go?"

"Does it look like Aziz wanted blood money?" remarks the hyena, pointing at his still swollen eye. "He sought my death over any kind of compensation. Even if I could have paid Aziz a sum of silver and gold to satisfy him for the death of his brother, he never would have accepted it."

"No," says Fadel, "but the traditional law of an eye for an eye does not hold sway in the sultanate. He could not lawfully take your life for his brother's life without a trial."

"As if he intended this to be lawful," I remark.

"I concur," says Naji, "People like me don't get to live by those laws."

"The Sultan imposes his laws over all his subjects," says Fadel. "Since its founding, the sultanate has always followed civil law over traditional law. Even the Sultan must answer to it."

"Zayn and I are not subjects of the sultanate. He is from Zaptu, and I am from the south."

"You have lived here long enough, you would count as a subject, and while he does not enforce it, the Sultans of Khalin have always claimed authority east of the mountains and into the desert. The Emirs are nominally under his control. Thus, Zayn would be considered a subject of the sultanate under the rules of the courts."

"And the fact I killed someone?" I ask.

Fadel considers. "I could speak to the city guard. Presenting the case carefully would allow you to be cleared. I would need to talk to some friends of mine first, though, who know the courts."

"That won't stop Rigel from killing either of us," interjects Naji.

Fadel shakes his head. "No, it wouldn't, but I can intervene if you let me."

"Blood rules them, Fadel. They do not fear the Sultan," says the hyena. "I have lived by the sword my whole life. I know what they will do to me and you, if you get involved."

"And all that sword has done for you is bring you sadness. Eventually even your friend the leopardess put down her sword."

Naji snorts. "Naima was born here. She chose her fate. I was born down on the savanna under the acacia trees. I was chosen to live by the sword before I could even hold one."

Fadel scowls. "You have to let the past go. This is your life now. You can still change your course."

"Perhaps I will, but right now I need to figure out some things. We'll need to find a place to go."

"You can stay here," suggests Fadel.

"Won't Rigel come back?" I ask.

"No," says Fadel. "You would be my guests. He won't violate the sanctity of my house like that again. Rigel knows not to trifle with me. I have some connections that even he respects."

"Thank you," says Naji, inclining his head at the fennec.

"It is no problem, old friend. Let me get you the key," he says, getting up and letting himself out of the majlis to cross the courtyard.

"Do you really think we're safe here, Naji?" I ask him, now that the fennec is gone. "I know you didn't think he would come here."

He sighs. "Safer than the apartment. I don't know for sure, but I doubt Rigel would come back tonight. He does respect Fadel's authority, but I don't want to use the fennec as a shield, either."

I nod, thinking about this. A minute later the fennec returns with a round wooden key which he gives to Naji. "You know the room that backs up against the hammam with the cherry wood bed you've stayed in before?"

Naji nods.

"That is where I will put you. It's in the back near the rear stairs."

"Thank you," the hyena says, motioning for me to get up and follow him.

"Go get settled, and I will see you in an hour, Zayn," Fadel says to us as we walk out of his apartment.

Before we go upstairs, I fetch my pack from the dressing room where I had dropped it off. We walk over to the main stairs and climb to the top floor, but Naji does not go to the room. Instead, he walks over to the ladder by the trap door to the roof and climbs that. At the top of the ladder, he slips open the bolt holding the hatch closed and lifts it. After glancing around, he climbs out onto the roof.

The roof is flat, with a large square opening in it for the courtyard in the center of the inn. Against a taller neighboring building there is a rough fabric draped down to form a sunshade. A few grass mats are under it. On the other side of the building there is an alleyway that runs up the side. In the back is the hammam with its domed brick chambers and halls. The sun is starting to set, casting deep shadows into the streets below.

"Why are we up here?" I ask the hyena.

"I want to look at how easy it is to reach the roof," he says, walking over to the edge of the roof to look down on the street below.

"You think they'll try that?"

He shrugs and starts to walk over to the side of the roof with the alleyway. I follow him over. "Rigel and I had to use this trick one or twice to get into a house. I'm sure he hasn't forgotten it."

I'm not reassured by that suggestion. "You think he could get in this way?"

He looks around as a breeze ruffles the fabric of his kaftan. "Right now, it wouldn't take too much effort." He turns to face me. "It's a lot harder to do in the dark when you don't have a planned-out route already."

"You've tried this?"

"Multiple times when I worked with Naima. Twisted both ankles once. Another time I fell through a partially rotten roof. She had us do a number of breaking and entering jobs."

That sound concerning. "So often?"

"Not anymore," he says. "I was nineteen when I did those jobs. I was still a scrappy, hungry hyena back then." He starts walking over to the trap door.

"How many people have you killed, Naji?"

He stops and turns to me. In the setting sun there are highlights in his fur that aren't normally there.

"More than I'd like to admit to."

I cross my arms. Maybe I should be scared, but I need to know. "How many?"

He scratches at the back of his neck. "Seven."

"That's a lot."

"Five were in battle, and I had no choice in the matter. One of those left me this scar. The other two tried to kill me to get what I was paid to guard. I've never murdered an unarmed man."

Is that supposed to be reassuring? Aziz's blood is on my paws like the blood of the seven men Naji killed are on his. "Am I to assume you made each of those kills with the best intentions?"

He huffs. "I've done things I'm not proud of, Zayn, but if you are going to judge me for it, can you honestly tell me you have not done the same?"

"It's not the same," I blurt out.

He laughs mirthlessly. "I needed to buy food, just like you. I needed to survive. When someone charges at you, sword or spear out, you don't think, maybe I can negotiate with this person. You fight. If you are lucky, you walk away from the encounter. You have to realize, I fought in a war before I came to Aksu."

"What war?" I inquire.

"In the south against the Republic of Batu. A pointless thing if you ask me, but I was young and they said this was the honorable thing to do, so I did what they told me to do. I was on the losing side of the war."

"I didn't know."

He shrugs. "I don't like to talk about it much. My life didn't really begin until I came to Aksu, and that's why I need to find out what's going on," he says. "Naima did find out something interesting I'm thinking over."

My ears perk. "What did she find out?" I ask.

He motions over to the mats under the fabric, and I walk over and sit down with him. Together we can see the sun starting to reach the horizon over the buildings.

"The Aragvi clan are looking to hire guards. That is the same group that I was working for when I killed Aziz's brother. Rigel works for them too."

"Rigel works for the people who Aziz's brother tried to rob?"

Naji nods.

"Do they know there is a connection between Rigel and Aziz?"

"I don't know, but Naima brought up with her contact that Rigel and I were not on the best of terms. They were very quick to reassure her that would not be a problem."

I frown. "I don't like this. Either it's a trap or Rigel is working against them."

"I think it's somehow related to Rigel and what he did to me, but it's also possibly another trap. The Aragvi clan does not often hire outside help."

"When you say clan, what does that entail?"

"They are traders, but they're also a large kinship clan. Most are wolves from the north who came here for reasons I'm not exactly clear on. A few locally born wolves work with them, but they function as one big pack. I think they are involved with smuggling, but a lot of their business seems to be legit. Their reputation has faded in Aksu, but they're still around in Japar."

"What do they sell?" I ask him.

"It varies, but ceramics and metalwork used to be big for them. It may have changed."

My ears lower. "You realize this could be dangerous for you."

He looks over at the setting sun. "I know, but I need to figure out what Rigel is up to. There was a reason for his actions, and I want to know why." He looks back at me. "Whatever turned Rigel against me lies in the past, but I can't figure out what parts of my past brought us here. It isn't just about Isim. There is something more."

"I came here to get away from my past, Naji."

He wraps an arm around me. "I know. I need to stop mine from hurting your future. Tomorrow I will go see about the job."

"Be careful," I advise.

"I will," he says, and he pulls me against him. "You too. Tonight though, I want to see you perform."

I nod and together we watch as the sun fades below the horizon. It's peaceful up here, and the wind is soft against us. I can only guess at what lies ahead for us.

❧

The sword in my hand is heavy, but it is not the weight that makes it feel so burdensome. There is a tiredness about myself that reaches beyond the physical into my soul. Part of me is still back in that room, watching Aziz die. That moment is buried now inside of me, and I don't want to remember it, yet I can't let it go. Still, I step out onto the stage to an audience that appreciates me for me. I don't use the costume that shows off my stomach fur this time, and I ask for a more melodic song than the one I used last night.

I dance well, at least that's what Fadel and Naji tell me afterward. For me, it passes in a blur, my body knowing the motions while my mind is focused elsewhere. I feel like I'm a half step behind the entire time, and I'm forced to make small corrections to my footwork throughout the routine. I danced often in Zaptu in this state when I was hungry and too foolish to ask Usman for the money to eat. I feel bad for not enjoying this tonight, yet for some reason, tips are better than the night before.

After changing, I join Naji in the back of the common area while Khalil takes a turn entertaining the audience. The leopard is good, and I can tell he's changed his routine already. His moves are more carefully planned now. I'm sensing some friendly competition for tips forming here, and I like that. It gives me something to focus on.

Naji orders a hookah and a sturdy wine along with it. It's much bolder than what we drank our first night here, but it complements the tobacco smoke well. I drink sparingly from the goblet he pours me, not wanting to be caught unaware, and I know Naji does too. Instead, I just let myself fall back into the cushions, listening to the environment.

A snow leopard who knows Naji joins us to talk. He is well-traveled, and while I wouldn't mind staying to listen, I have other things on my mind. I take this opportunity to slip away for a little bit and seek out Fadel. The night before is rolling around in the back of my head, and I have questions I need answered. I find the fennec in the front, going over his books for the night. He is alone and that puts me at ease.

He looks up at me and smiles. "You are already making a name for yourself here," he remarks. "I can tell my clients like what they see."

"Thanks," I say.

"So, did you want to dance again tomorrow? If not, Khalil would be happy not to have the competition for tips."

"Not tomorrow," I say. "May I sit with you for a few minutes?"

The fennec nods and points to a chair against the wall of the alcove and I sit down in it. "I have a question for you."

"Sure," he says. "What is it?"

"I need to know more about what trouble I've got myself into. I wanted to ask you about Naji and Rigel."

Fadel sits back. "What did you want to ask?"

"Why does Rigel hate Naji so much? I understand what happened to Isim, but is there more?"

"There could be. I came to know Naji later when he started frequenting the Blue Door, shortly after I opened it. Isim was already dead then. Naji washed up in my establishment as a bitter man, but slowly he opened up."

"And Rigel?"

"Some of the same, but he hasn't been a regular like Naji."

"But they've been able to get along till now?"

Fadel smirks. "Yes. We have a way of putting people at ease here, and they've never had an altercation, although they avoid each other. Rigel did get into a shouting match six months ago with another guest, but that's been my only issue with him up until now. Today shows I can't let him back in. This is my house, and it is a space for us to meet and gather in safety. We are family here. I can't have anyone jeopardize that."

Fennecs are one of the shorter species, but their big ears try and make up for the lack of height. Even still, I can tell by the way Fadel carries himself that he is proud and unafraid of others. I'm not sure where he gets the confidence from, but it's admirable.

"Thank you," I say. I hesitate and he waits. He knows I want to say more. "How much do you know about what Naji does for coin?"

He scratches one of his ears. "I know the basics. He has told me some stories, but we don't discuss details. I usually know when he's going to be gone for a while because he'll stop by before he leaves town, but he has disappeared for weeks unannounced. Now if you asked me which of my customers he's bedded, I could give you a detailed account." He grins, showing his fangs.

"That really isn't a question I think I want to ask."

He shrugs. "It's not as many as you'd think, but I understand if you don't want to know. Naji probably doesn't want to know the details of your liaisons back in Zaptu, in your previous line of work."

It strikes me that even though he barely knows me, he's already labeled that as my previous line of work in his mind and that I've moved on. I've not told Fadel any details of my past. I'm pretty sure he'd be very concerned if he learned about Sarda.

"I doubt he would, but what have I become now?"

"Brave. Very brave," says the fennec, "but you could have told me what Rigel said. I would have helped you find Naji."

Just like with Usman, I had someone I could have turned to in a moment of need, yet I didn't. "Perhaps, but would you have been able to act quickly enough?"

He considers. "I want to say yes, but it would have been easier to have contacted the people I needed in the morning. How did you know Aziz would find you attractive?"

"I didn't start with seducing Aziz as the plan. It just developed."

He nods. "That is thinking on your feet."

I wring my paws together. "Yes, but now I have blood on my paws."

He leans over and rests a paw against mine. "Do not think of it that way. Naji is a good man, and Aziz was not. I know I said the law would have been on your side, but the law takes time to work. Time Naji did not have. What you did, Zayn, was very brave. It takes strength to throw yourself into a situation like that."

I sigh. "I don't feel strong right now."

"Strength comes from within, but even the strongest among us can doubt their own power at times. Together we are stronger than alone."

"That sounds like a lion proverb of some kind."

He laughs. "I'm sure they have one like this."

"I'm sorry about provoking Rigel earlier."

He squeezes my hands. "I don't blame you for Rigel's indiscretion, but I need you and Naji to be cautious."

"I fear this is just beginning. Naji is trying to find out why Rigel has waited for so long to finally come for him. He's taking a job with the Aragvi Clan in hopes of learning something."

Fadel frowns. "I am not surprised he wishes to know more, but these people are not to be trifled with."

I consider. There's something I need to ask. "I have another question. Rigel said Naji had been in a battle, and he fled?"

"Rigel is telling half-truths. Naji doesn't like to talk about it, but it wasn't a battle. It was a massacre. Much blood was shed for the pride of a foolish emir who thought he could tangle with the Republic of Batu. The Republic caught the emir's army unprepared. Naji was on the wrong side of the war."

Usman had friends he would take coffee with who would talk about the news from distant lands. He might have known of this, but I only heard of Batu being mentioned briefly growing up. "I don't know about that."

"It was ten years ago. I was still working as a scribe then, so a lot of obscure news like that passed my way."

"You were a scribe?"

"Yes. I was a man of letters before I opened the Blue Door. I worked in the counting house where I kept records for tax purposes. Later I worked in the palace correlating information in the office of the Grand Vizier."

I tilt my head at him. "Are you nobility?"

The fennec laughs. "Not at all. My family has no ties to nobility, and only a small group of fennecs in the sultanate are related to the noble families. That said, being a fennec has made some of my business dealings easier because people have to stop and ask themselves if I am from a noble house."

"Sorry if me asking was assuming."

"No harm in it. Others have asked before," he says, stretching. "The ears are a mark of prestige in some areas."

"Makes sense," I say and get up. "I should go see how Naji is."

The fennec nods. "Watch over him, Zayn, and watch out for yourself too. I don't want to lose either of you."

"Thank you. I'll do my best to keep us both safe," I say, as I walk off.

In the courtyard I pause to ponder Fadel's words. There is something paternal in how the fennec is talking. Usman spoke to me the same way, long ago before I made the decisions that would make my life what it became. Back then I was both proud and desperate to survive. I needed to do something, so I found my own path. Usman helped me, but ultimately it was I who stepped out dressed in silk to sell myself. The cheetah did not sell me to men for the night against my will, he sold me to men because I asked him to. That was the help from him I wanted, and in the end, I paid a horrible price. There were other ways to earn the coin I needed, but that was the way I knew I could make for myself, so that is the way I went.

Usman watched me every time I danced, knowing that I chose whoring over more direct help from him. This time, I need to not be so foolish to accept what people are offering to do for me. I have a lot to figure out. This business with Rigel and Aziz has certainly made things harder, but if I refuse to take the help offered, things are likely to be worse for me.

࿐

When I return, Naji is alone, holding the nozzle of the hookah in one hand, quietly smoking. I sit down next to him on the divan and pick up my goblet. It still has a little wine in it, but I don't want to keep drinking. The musicians are packing up now, and many of the chairs in the hall are empty.

"Did your friend leave?" I ask him.

He nods. "We talked for a little, but he wanted to head home for the night."

"It is quite late," I remark.

Naji nods and picks up the pitcher of wine. "Did you want more?"

"I'm not thirsty, at least not for wine."

He puts it down without pouring himself any. It sounds like there is another full glass in the pitcher. "You had me worried for a minute when you didn't come back right away."

196

"I wanted to talk to Fadel." I don't want to say what my conversation with him was about.

He takes a long draw on the hookah and hands me the hose. He leans back against the couch so he can look up at the ceiling as he exhales. "I'm sorry I got you into this mess."

I scratch at one of my ears. "I didn't help matters."

"What you did is because of what I foolishly let happen. I should have been more careful. I've tried so hard these last few years to keep things legal. It's why I travel more now than I used to, but even with that caution, it hasn't been easy."

"Like with my customers, you don't always know what you are getting into."

"That's true. When I killed Aziz's brother, Borak, the city guard didn't even sniff around. They were known criminals, and the fact they attacked us made the killing lawful."

"Life does not always give us clear paths to follow."

He stops staring at the ceiling so he can look at me. His ears are down. "No, it doesn't, but I'm still sorry last night happened."

I just shrug. I've dwelled on it enough for the moment. I have Aziz's lifeless face stuck in the back of my mind and a vague sense of unease about everything right now. It's why I didn't drink much of the wine. I think Naji didn't drink much either for similar reasons.

He gets up and offers me a paw. "I'm glad I got to see you perform again. The crowd seemed quite enthusiastic."

I smile, showing a little fang, and take the offered paw, letting him pull me up. "Does that bother you?"

"A little," he says sheepishly. "I saw a few sideways glances when you came out and joined me."

I chuckle and walk out into the courtyard with him. "And whose bed am I sleeping in tonight?"

"Should I have asked to get you your own room? If it's an issue I can sleep on the floor."

"Naji, it's okay," I say, gently touching his arm. My tail wags instinctively. "I don't need my own room. I don't want to be alone right now either."

He pauses by the bottom of the back staircase. "Does this mean we are a couple?" He looks at me with soft eyes, but his ears are erect and there is an eagerness upon his face.

"Let us see what happens in the next few days first," I suggest.

He smiles then, his grin broad and warm. "Sure." He starts up the stairs and I follow his tail.

"It's…" I ponder, "…weird to think about being with someone when it's not just a show."

"Isn't that a good change?" he asks me.

I can enjoy the blissful feeling of release, unworried about if I pleased him enough to earn my keep. It would be a comfortable arrangement, but there is more to it than just having an arrangement, isn't there?

My parents loved each other very much, and when my father died, I could see the spark in my mother faded. It wasn't just that she had to take on the burden of raising me alone, she missed Dad. She never had the same laugh, and as time went on, I realized a part of her had been lost. This same type of need would only grow within myself if I stayed with Naji.

"It is a good change, right?" Naji asks me again, at the top of the stairs. He's noticed I haven't responded to him, and his ears have drooped.

"Yes," I say with a smile, my tail wagging. "A very good change." I can explore now with freedom I have never had before. I've had many men, but I've never had one who I truly knew well, except for Sarda. The hyena is nothing like the lion: he's warm, he's compassionate, and he's gentle.

Naji's ears have gone back up and he smiles. The hyena walks out onto the gallery, and then two doors down to where our room is. He fits a wooden key into a hole in the lock and turns it, and the door unlocks.

It is dark inside, with just a little light filtering through the arabesque set high into the back wall. In the dark, Naji walks over to where a lantern hangs against the wall and picks up the lantern to carry it outside. He lights it from one of the other nearby lanterns hanging along the gallery.

While he does that, I let my nose tell me what has happened in here before. I was only in here briefly earlier to change. The scents are hidden under the smell of rosewater, but I can tell that there has been many a liaison in this room. I walk over to the bed, which has the strongest scents. I try and sort out the individuals, but there is a general smell of male musk and the undertones of sex.

Naji returns with the lantern and hangs it on the hook on the wall. He then closes the door and clicks the lock. The room is simple. A large bed sits on one end. There is a small table, and nothing else in the room. Surprisingly, the sheets on the bed are clean. I don't know why I thought Fadel would skimp on that, but I think that says a lot about the type of environment he wants. Even though the scent of lovemaking is present, an effort has been made to clean the room to minimize the obviousness.

The hyena walks up to me and wraps his arms around me from behind. "I hope this is okay." He nips playfully at my ear. "One so beautiful as you deserves the best."

I'm a little muskier than I would prefer, having only quickly groomed myself after dancing so I could join Naji to watch Khalil, but he doesn't seem to mind. I turn to face him. My gut reaction is to get on my knees and start undoing his pants, but he isn't one of my clients. This is something different, and I can take my time. I want to take my time. "You are just trying to flatter me."

He chuckles. "You look good in silks. You look good out of silks."

I smirk, letting my tongue loll out of my muzzle. "This isn't a performance."

He traces a paw over my chest, lifting the hem of the rough cotton shirt I'm wearing so he can ruffle my fur. "Even in your street clothes, you are beautiful."

I know quite well how to give a man what he wants. Without saying anything I reach up and pull at where my belt is holding my pants up. Silently, the fabric slips off of me and falls to the floor. The hyena looks down and licks his lips.

"No," I say, stopping him. "Not until you disrobe."

He smiles and reaches up to pull his shirt off. While he does that I get on the bed and slip off my kaftan and toss it at him, lying back. He grins and catches it, stopping to sniff it before he discards both shirts. He then undoes his pants and lets them fall. Straightening up, he steps toward the bed. His cock, now free of its fabric prison, bobs in front of him.

I catch my breath and watch as he approaches me. His spots are faint in the light of the lantern, but I can make them out. He sinks down onto the floor instead of getting on the bed. I roll over a little so I can flick my tail underneath myself. When I sit back, Naji leans forward to lick my hard sheath.

I shudder in pleasure, and I can feel my legs relaxing. His broad tongue works over my tip before going lower to tease my shaft. If he thinks I'm too musky, he doesn't say anything and instead washes over my cock with his tongue. I wiggle a little underneath him, still unused to the sensation of someone returning the favor to me. The hyena chuckles a little at the reaction and breaks off.

"Do you honestly like being entered?" he asks me.

"I am quite used to the sensation."

"Yes, but do you enjoy it?" he presses me.

This is a question I am not sure I really have an answer for. Most of my clients wanted to enter me, so it's what I have come to expect. I press all thought of the term client out of my mind then and without saying anything, I roll over. There is no time like the present to see if the new me that's slowly coming to life actually likes this feeling.

"It's familiar, but we can explore me in you later." If he wants to do that with me, I want to do it with him.

The bed creaks as the hyena gets onto it. I shiver in anticipation. I don't have any oil, but I feel a slick finger pressing into me. I turn to crane my neck and look back.

He can read my inquisitive expression because he smiles. "I got it at the desk with the key." He holds up a small clay bottle. The hyena then pulls back and presses another finger in. I feel myself instinctively relax.

The hyena removes his digits, and the next thing he presses against me isn't a slickened finger, but his whole length. I shudder and for the first time in a long time, I press back not because I'm paid to, but because I want to. He growls softly and pushes himself in, sliding in with ease.

Carefully, he starts to work himself in and out in a rhythm. I can feel my body tense and relax with each thrust. Soon, I'm pressing back to meet him. He pants a little and I can tell he's enjoying himself. My own maleness stands stiff at attention and is soon found by one of Naji's paws.

It's nice, but there is something else I want. "Stop," I say.

"Did I push too hard?" he asks me, concerned.

"No," I scoot forward and let him slip out. Then I roll over onto my back. "I want to watch you."

"Oh!" he says, laughing, and repositions himself. Pushing my legs forward, he presses himself back in. I gasp and screw my eyes shut. He wastes no time in getting going again.

When I open my eyes again, I can see that he's panting, his tongue hanging out. As he thrusts harder, I yip at the building pressure inside of myself. A stray thought comes to my mind asking me, what does he mean to me now? I grasp at it, but Naji's next thrust pushes it out of my mind and I just enjoy the fucking.

His body is hot against mine, and he plays with me, stroking me, as he fucks me. I shiver, letting myself slip into the rhythm and the joy of the moment. It goes on longer than

I expect, and when he finally gets close to finishing, he waits to make sure my cock is hard and twitching before he climaxes. His timing isn't perfect, but I can tell he tried to get it just right and that is something special. His hand strokes me quickly, urging me on, and as he finishes me off and I shoot onto myself, I feel a warm glow about myself I have rarely experienced. The pleasant tiredness that comes after sex suddenly feels new and fresh, like I've not done this hundreds of times before.

"I hope that wasn't too much," he says, exhausted.

"No, not at all." We rest for a bit intertwined together on the bed. He leans down over me and gently licks my nose and I giggle. He is sweet and special.

Once he softens a little and slips out of me, he lays down next to me to cuddle, yawning.

"You may be tired, but I am a mess," I say. "Are the baths still available at this time of night?"

"They don't heat the water late at night, but you can still get cleaned up." He yawns again.

"Can I just go downstairs looking like this?" I don't want to put on my clothes since I'm sticky, but I don't want to wander downstairs nude. I don't think anyone would like that, and I don't want to show them anyway.

Naji picks up on my hesitation. "Go down the gallery to the back staircase. There is a hallway that continues past the top of the staircase, and at the end of the hallway is a door. That opens onto a separate staircase that leads down to the baths. You enter next to the attendant's booth." He points to a cloth hanging behind the door I hadn't noticed. "Wrap that around yourself, and take your clothes with you."

Well, at least I don't have to walk through the courtyard naked. As I wrap the robe around my body, I realize I'm not the first to do this, and certainly won't be the last to make this run. I slip out of the door carrying my clothing. I glance over the wooden railing down to the courtyard. It's almost deserted now, but two wolves are outside drinking wine under the lanterns. I walk down the gallery to the hallway, and a room by the intersection sounds like it's occupied with something similar to what we just did. At the end of the hallway, I find the second staircase. Descending, I come out in the baths.

The baths are quiet, but an ibex is napping at the desk. When he hears me, he wakes up and yawns. He takes one look at me and nods and points me over to the warm room with a knowing wink. "We've already stopped heating the hammam for the night, but it will get you cleaned up. Have a good time I take it?" he asks me.

"Yes," I say, with my ears suddenly hot.

"Great. Leave your robe at the entrance to the cold room and I'll pick it up. I'll get you a towel."

"Thank you," I say to him. Under the robe, I have cum in my fur and my shaft is hanging flaccid and sticky, but we're having a casual conversation. It strikes me as a little absurd.

The room is already cooling, so I work quickly. The stone in the center of the warm room is still quite warm though, and I sit on that as I scrub myself clean. I get the sticky parts out of my fur, but the shock of the cold water washes away the warm afterglow of sex in a way I wish it didn't.

The bath attendant brings me the promised towel, but by the time I finish drying and dressed, he's disappeared. I stretch, not really tired, and walk out into the courtyard to see if anything is still going on.

The two wolves are still out in the courtyard drinking and are very much into whatever they're talking about. The fountain bubbles softly in the darkness, oblivious that no one is paying it any mind. I peek into the common room, but no one is in there. It's deserted and empty. I stroll to the front of the place to use the main stairway, and Salim is there talking to a tiger. They both give me a brief nod but make no comment or remark on what I might have done earlier in the evening.

There's a safety here I've never felt before. It isn't the fact that I just had a liaison upstairs and no one cares that strikes me either. It's that it's natural here to have the desires and attractions like I have. I've never had that type of safety before, and as I return to the room with Naji, I can feel that acceptance enveloping me. In Zaptu, I was tolerated, but people looked down upon me. Here, I belong.

There's comfort in that thought, but I also know my time here may be limited. I don't know what tomorrow will bring. Even if Rigel won't come for us here, we can't hide inside these walls forever. When I get back to the room, the hyena is already dozing, but he rolls over to hold me when I get in bed. I sleep soundly that night, although my dreams are troubled as I run down streets I don't know, stalked by the presence of the dead Aziz.

Complications
(Naji)

It is early in the morning when I wake up. Faint light filters into the room from the high-set windows. I listen to the silence for a few minutes, trying to catch any suspicious noises, but only the distant sounds of life in the city of Aksu tickle my ears. When I do finally roll out of bed, I move slowly, trying not to disturb Zayn.

The scent of sex from last night clings to the room and me. The warmth of the encounter comes back to me, and I smile. Zayn rolls over, curling into the warm spot I left in the bed, but he doesn't wake up. Wrapped up in the bedsheets, the jackal looks peaceful, tail curled under himself. Asleep, he is unafraid of what could happen to us. Being awake, I am not.

I carefully creep over to the door to listen, pressing one of my ears against the wood. The Blue Door sounds quiet, but that doesn't reassure me. Naima trained Rigel and me well. Death could wait on the other side of this door, and I would never know until I opened it.

My dreams were troubled last night. My unconscious mind was worried about what today would bring. The soft breathing of Zayn and the rich, male musk in the room is reassuring, but the peaceful feeling it brings does not extend beyond this room. As I crouch behind the door, I wonder what awaits me. Even if I am safe here in the inn, what about the streets beyond? Surely Rigel and Aziz's two men will look for me.

Quietly I dress and reach for my sword, which I buckle on. Fadel doesn't want weapons in the Blue Door, but he told me it would be fine. He's sometimes been lax on the rule, but after Rigel's confrontation with Zayn yesterday, he's stepped up enforcing it. I am glad he did not ask I check my blade at the front desk, and instead let me keep it. The only weapons Fadel keeps on premises are a dagger at the entrance and one at the attendant stand in the hammam.

With an ear against the door, I can hear only my hurried breathing. I pull out my sword and carefully unlatch the door. The bolt rubs against the wood. I freeze, ready to strike, but nothing happens. I suck in my breath and holding it, I crack open the door. After a few seconds of silence, I poke my sword tip through the open air and then quickly step out and spin around looking, searching for someone in the corridor, ready to parry an attacker.

Instead, I am greeted with emptiness. There is no one here.

I lower my blade tip and glance down to scan the first floor. One of the staff is in the courtyard looking at me, confused.

"You okay up there, Naji?" the caracal standing below asks me. His tan fur is darker than Rigel's, and he is heavier. I don't know his name, but he waits on tables and serves wine.

"Yes, I thought I heard something," I call down to him, sheathing my sword.

He tilts his head and gives me a concerned look. "Fadel mentioned if I saw you awake, he'd like to see you this morning."

"Sure, give me a minute," I say, turning back to the room.

Zayn has been roused by the conversation and has propped himself up on the bed. "Is something wrong?" he asks me.

"Nothing at all. I was just being cautious."

He yawns. "We can go somewhere else tonight."

In the bright light of morning, my fear seems foolish. I could see if we could stay with Naima, but there are always people here at the Blue Door. If the fennec says we'll be safe here, I need to trust his judgement. That doesn't mean I shouldn't be cautious, though.

"I don't think that will be necessary," I say, "but let's see how today goes. I need to go talk to Fadel."

Zayn sits up, letting the sheet that draped his frame fall away. His tawny fur is mussed, and even in the soft light of the room, I'm reminded of how beautiful he is. "If you are worried…" He trails off, waving a paw at me.

My ears flick. "It will be fine." I turn to go but realize I still have my sheathed sword. I unbuckle my sword and lay it down on the bed with him. "It's going to be okay. I'll be right back."

He tilts his head but doesn't speak. He just nods and I walk out of the room unarmed, closing the door behind me, trying not to jump at every shadow. If I let every possibility haunt me, I'll never have any peace.

⁊

Fadel is sitting at the front desk looking over the books when I find him. He's making some notes on a sheet of paper, writing down figures and sums. He looks up when I approach him.

"You wanted to talk?" I inquire.

He glances back at his work. "Give me a second to finish this," he says, dipping his quill back into the ink and scratching out a few more notes. He checks his math and, satisfied, he puts the quill down and closes the ledger. "I always like to check the previous day's ledger first thing in the morning," says the fox, leaning back and picking up a date. He tosses it into his muzzle. "Date?"

"Sure," I say taking one and letting the sweet taste fill my muzzle. "What did you want to talk about?" I ask, after spitting out the seed into a brass spittoon Fadel keeps by his desk for this exact purpose.

"The incident with Rigel yesterday has been on my mind," he says. "I've been thinking about what else I should do."

"I'm sorry it happened. I could find a place to stay down by the river. It would be somewhere Rigel wouldn't expect, and I've got a few ideas already."

Fadel frowns. "You will be fine here."

"I know that, but you have not spent these past years building up the Blue Door to declare it a fortress."

"No, but that doesn't mean I don't care what happens to you. Do you know Zayn asked me last night if I know what you do for coin?"

I blink. "What did you tell him?"

"That I don't always ask for details about your jobs. I only know the basics sometimes."

"That's true, but I've wondered if you don't sometimes ask around about what I've been up to."

The fox smirks. "I've tried not to read too much between the lines of what you've told me. I am running a respectable business here. Discretion is also important to many of my customers. I learned years ago that powerful people will ask you questions if they think you know the answers they're seeking. As a scribe in the palace, I learned to keep my muzzle out of places it shouldn't be. It's why I know not to ask certain questions, but perhaps I should be asking you more questions."

Fadel has connections, I know, but I have no idea who they are. All I know is I've seen letters on his desk with very official looking seals on them. They can't all be about taxes. "Discretion is an important skill in your line of work."

"It is, but sometimes things must be shared. I did offer Zayn an accounting of your past liaisons that I'm aware of. He declined."

"Wait, that's what you pay attention to?" I say, surprised. "You aren't nearly as proper as I thought you were."

He laughs. "People are quite willing to talk about that around here, but I also keep my ears up." He leans forward over his desk then and his tone changes to a more serious one. "And I know you are in trouble."

"Yes, that's obvious."

"Let's start with the beginning here. First, Zayn now has blood on his paws because of you. He killed for you."

"I know, and they will seek both of us out. Even if I could offer enough blood money to satisfy the debt against us, I doubt anyone would accept it."

"I agree, but it's more than that," says the fennec. "You owe Zayn protection for what he did. You put him in this spot, but I think I can help you both. I have friends who owe me favors. They can arrange a place for you to stay in the south."

"And leave Aksu?"

"I would sooner see you and Zayn happy together than see either of you dead."

"I don't feel comfortable doing that. I want Zayn to have a chance to find his own way, and he can only do that here. You have given him the opportunity to finally put his skills to good use. I will ask, but he will likely be frustrated hiding somewhere. I don't think he's someone who takes well to being idle for long."

"Probably not," says the fennec. "Cages, no matter how nice they are, quickly grow old, but the bars that keep you inside can keep things on the outside. I have to ask, do you love this man, Naji?"

"I think I have to figure that out still."

"I suggest you figure that out and soon. You've already got him tangled up in this."

I growl. "You know I never wished this upon him. He asked me to take him here, and I couldn't just leave him there. And you know I've been trying to untangle myself from these complications. I just want to live, and not have to worry about catching a blade."

Fadel folds his arms. "Not to judge you too harshly, but you haven't done a very good job at it. Some time in the south might do you good. You have lived a complicated life, my friend. To be free of your past will not be easy."

"And can you know these people won't follow me wherever I go in the sultanate?"

"I was thinking Akara," says the fennec.

Akara is a city on the other side of the mountains southeast of the sultanate. "That place is awful. They only like hyenas there."

"And are you not a hyena?" comments Fadel.

"Let me clarify. They only like striped hyenas there. I've been there before. Over half the population is striped hyenas. Their city guard followed me around simply because I had spots. Even with the reputation I have here, the city guard has never done that."

The fennec shrugs. "Even if they do that to you, they will tire of it eventually. I don't want to see the jackal dead because you got sloppy."

"I know, but whose side are you on here? You seem mad at me for things I couldn't control."

"Both of your sides, but I realize this is serious. You have more than your tail to watch out for."

I sigh. "And you think I can't protect him?"

The fennec stretches out his arms. "Naji, think about this for a minute."

"I can protect him!" I insist.

Fadel sighs and shakes his head, causing his tall ears flick back and forth. "You can't protect yourself; how can you hope to protect Zayn?"

"I..." The way Rigel played me, what happened to Isim, and even the battle back on the savanna all flash through my mind. Each time I walked away and someone else paid. "You're right, I'm not strong enough."

"You are, but you need to be careful. You can't do this alone, Naji."

I've failed all of them. This time, I need to be strong enough to see this through, even if it costs me everything. It's the only way I can make sure they don't come looking for Zayn. "Only I can make this right. I need to figure out what I can do that will get Rigel off my back. Zayn killed Aziz for me, and I will make that right for him. I am going to go meet the Aragvi Clan today. Rigel works for them, but Naima says they're looking for someone to do a job that doesn't seem to involve Rigel. I killed Aziz's brother Borak for the Aragvi clan, so I feel there's a connection with what happened with the wolf. I won't know if I don't take this job."

Fadel does not look pleased with me. His ears are back. "Zayn told me that last night. And if it's another trap?"

I get up. "I have faced death before, Fadel. But if I'm just being stupid, will you make sure Zayn is going to be okay?"

The fennec leans back to study me, drumming his fingers on top of the wooden desk. He frowns. "You don't have to rush over there. You still look rough, and happiness for you appears to be in your grasp. Why throw it away?"

"Death stalks every sellsword's life. Few of us reach old age. Always there is risk."

The fennec gives me an icy look. "I believe this is why Naima sells spices now."

I chuckle. "It is indeed."

He shakes his head. "So, what does throwing yourself into danger do?"

"It gives me a chance to find out what I'm up against. Plus, I need to find Rigel."

"You know, if you were just looking for stable work, I could hire you as a guard. It wouldn't earn you what you make now, but it's a lot safer than what you have been doing."

My ears perk. "I don't know if I could accept. You do so much for me already, and I consider you a friend, not a potential employer."

The fennec shrugs. "You've told me before I take in a lot of strays. I do have need of a guard on duty, and Rigel has reinforced in my mind the need, so what's one more stray?"

"I may always be a stray, you know."

"You say that, but I can see the growing sense of weariness in you about this. It's time to consider your own path, like the one Naima took."

"Yes," I say with a sigh. "If you want me working here, I would be happy to accept the position after I figure out what is happening."

"You sure that's a wise path?"

"No, but I need to follow the path before me so that I can find answers."

"Then try and come back alive."

"Have I ever not?" I say, tail wagging.

Fadel looks up at me. "We all only ever die once."

Fadel's words rattle around in my head when I return upstairs. I sit down on the bed to watch Zayn brush out his tail while I think. Am I being foolish for not leaving town? Will Rigel and his friends come looking for me, or am I safe here within these walls? For how long should we stay here?

I'm not one to hide, either. I am used to being the hunter, not the hunted. I've followed people down dark alleys and waited behind corners to spring traps. Now, I am the one looking over my shoulder when no one is there, greeting each corner with trepidation.

"Are you still going to go see the Aragvi Clan?" Zayn asks me.

"Mid-morning. I need to clean up first."

"And what should I do?"

"That's a good question. I guess wait for me to get back."

He frowns. "That seems boring."

"I know, I just don't have anything else to suggest," I say. "Waiting is always the hardest part in these situations, but I want to figure out what's going on."

"And I can't help with that?" he asks.

"I don't want to see you in any danger."

He sighs and puts down the brush. "What about yourself?"

"I'd rather put myself in that situation than let something happen to you."

"That seems foolish," he remarks.

I sigh. "I know, but it's all I've got, unless we want to take up Fadel's offer and head south to Akara. He said he could find us a place down there to lie low."

His ears shoot up. "That's certainly one option. Do you want to do that?"

"Not if I don't have to. I don't think it's fair to you to take you here and then be forced to take you somewhere else because I messed up. Also, the few times I've been to Akara I found it very unfriendly."

"Naji, I have something to ask you."

"What is it?"

"Would it be better if I just went back to Zaptu?"

My heart falls. "I don't think that would be better."

His ears lay back. "Safer?" he offers.

"Yes, but you have to let me try and fix this," I say, ears drooping. "I brought you here to help you. I am not going to let Rigel mess that up for you."

He frowns, looking down at the bed. "I know, and I appreciate that—"

"Listen," I say, taking his closest paw in mine. "I will not let any harm come to you."

He looks at me, searching my features. "It's not me I'm worried about."

I sigh. "I know, but all I ask is you give me a chance to make this right. I know I can't guarantee anything, but I am going to find some way to fix this thing with Rigel, Aziz, all of it. Hopefully not with my own death."

"Yes, but I can't just sit here and do nothing while you take all the risk."

I frown. "I know, but you need to be patient. I need to know what we're up against first."

"Why do you think there is something more to this than just Aziz getting even?" Zayn asks me.

"Rigel doesn't do people favors without good reason."

"Even if that is so, the reason may not involve us. You could have just been part of the bargain."

"True, but the Aragvi are the best way to find out what that reason may be," I say, getting up. "Let me go clean up, and then I'll see what they're looking for."

"Please be careful," he says.

I lean forward and plant a kiss above his eyes. "I will. I promise."

He makes a small, surprised gasp at my motion and smiles. "Good."

As I walk out of the room, I notice his tail is wagging. Seeing that gives me a spring to my step.

❧

The walk to the Grand Market goes off without a hitch. I feel jumpy, but once I get into the large crowd in the square, I relax a little. I've been here many a time, and while some find the press of people among the market stalls unbearable, I'm used to it. It's a second home to me, but it's also a second home to Rigel. I still have to keep my wits about me. Luckily, I don't spot the caracal, but it's easy to hide in the crowd. The best I can do is I try and use that to my advantage to throw off anyone who might be following me.

The instructions Naima gave me take me to a large market stall in the Grand Market under two large tents. There I find a few wolves selling various odds and ends. On one side of the tent, pots are piled high with plates, iron cookware, and other household goods on top of blankets, while on the other side, various bolts of fabric and a few rugs are laid out.

"Can I help you?" one of the wolves asks me. He was stacking goods until he noticed my approach. He is gray and cream colored and has a scar on one of his forearms.

"Yes, I hear you are looking for guards."

He glances me over. I know I'm still looking rough from the beating two days ago. "You good with a sword?"

I smile, showing him my fangs. "Quite good."

"Talk to Abu," he says, pointing to the lion who is sitting in the back of the stall on a rug. He is leaning over, reading from some paper spread out in front of him.

The wolf goes back to stacking the plates he is organizing, unloading them from a crate. With that conversation over, I walk over to Abu, careful not to step on any merchandise. Abu is an older lion with long tawny fur that has started to gray. Beads of ceramic and silver are braided into his mane, and when he looks up from the papers he is reading, the beads jingle. Abu looks me over shrewdly. I remember we met the last time I worked for the Aragvi clan; besides the gray patches in his mane possibly being larger now, he is exactly as I remember him. He's also one of the few non-wolves I remember seeing work for the clan.

"You are looking for work?" he asks me.

"Yes."

"What do they call you, yena?"

"Naji."

He frowns. "You worked for us before, a couple years ago, didn't you?"

"Yes, about three years ago."

He closes his eyes and doesn't say anything, thinking. Finally, he opens his eyes. "You killed someone for us, a wolf who thought he was our better."

I just nod in confirmation.

Abu breathes in and exhales slowly as he settles back on his rug, studying me. He strokes his chin, thinking.

"You used to work for Naima, didn't you?"

"Yes, when I was young. I heard about this job from her."

"Why do you come back?" he asks.

"I do a lot of caravan work, but I am looking for work in town."

He tilts his head. He is trying to discern my intentions and figure out if I'm lying. "Interesting," he says finally.

"Beg your pardon?" I ask him.

He waves his hand. "It is nothing, but did you get in a fight recently?"

"Yes," I respond. "The other guy got the worst end of the deal." It's true, but that wasn't my doing. Hopefully Abu doesn't ask for details.

"I see. Well, you can't get in a fight with my men."

"Oh, I wouldn't dream of it," I reply.

"Good, good. Then you are hired. I will give you five silver dirhams, for five days of work."

He's intentionally low balling me to see if I really want this. "Five? Five is a pauper's pay. I could make that carrying sacks of wheat around the market."

"No risk, yena, no pay."

"You never said what type of risk there is."

He smiles and flashes me his fangs. "Normally I pay only ten to non-clan members, but I will give you twelve. You are sharp," he says, pointing a digit at me, "and I like that. I remember you being quite reliable."

"Naima said you were offering a full gold dinar a day. There are risks associated with this, aren't there?"

"Only a little. You will help us keep an eye on some goods we're picking up, so you won't be working alone."

"And the pay? Discretion comes at a cost."

"You drive a hard bargain, but a gold as advertised."

If they're hiring guards to move something around Aksu, it has to be quite valuable. They already have a group they can trust, and the city is well protected. "Can you be more specific on the work?"

The lion shakes his head. "Just know it's important this happens."

I think he's downplaying what they need. "A gold it is then." The pay is excellent. I've only had a few jobs that paid that much for a single day's work, but the money is a secondary concern right now. It has the scent of something that will lead me to the answers I seek.

Abu gets up from the rug he is sitting on and claps me on the back. "Good. I need you to come to the warehouse tomorrow at dusk. Make sure you get a nap beforehand because I will need you till dawn."

I nod. "Sure, but where is the warehouse?"

"Ah, it has been a while since you've worked for us." He nods to himself as he talks and goes over to where the ledger book is sitting to scribble down directions on a scrap of paper. "It is across the river near the Grand Bridge, but this will tell you where. Now go. Be there by dusk."

I look over the instructions. They seem easy to follow, so I fold them up. "I will see you tomorrow then."

Abu nods and sits back down on his rug to watch the stand. I use that cue to take my leave of him, but I can tell his eyes follow me until I disappear into the crowd. With how important this job appears to be to Abu, I'm not surprised they are being selective on who they're hiring. My question is though, what are they protecting?

First though, I need to make a stop. I want to make sure Zayn is going to be okay while I'm doing this work.

In the Souk
(Zayn)

I hate sitting around feeling useless, and right now, that's what I'm doing. Naji is trying to find information, so I am just waiting. I did a lot of sitting at home in Zaptu waiting for things to happen, but not like this, not with the portent of death hanging around me. Maybe it was a mistake to come here. I could go home, get my house back—and do what exactly?

Usman and Farida would be happy to see me, but who else would care? Amare? Maybe, but our relationship was always weird. Nawra? She'd tell me I should have stayed in Aksu. Sarda?

I would prefer never to see Sarda again. I never want to feel his touch again. I think letting him bed me now would break me in a way he never truly succeeded in before.

I sigh and sit up. I've been lying on the bed naked, thinking, but the silent white plastered walls and the bed with its layers of hidden scents offer no answers. Light from the open window filters in. It faces the hammam, so only a soft murmur of street noise comes in. I can hear a few indistinct voices, but that's it. It's warm in here, but not so hot as to be unpleasant.

I guess I can go downstairs, maybe see if Fadel needs some help. It would give me something to keep my mind occupied.

There comes a knock on the door. "It's me," comes Naji's voice. I get up, walk over to the door, and unlock it, letting the hyena in.

He comes in carrying the pack I used to trek across the mountains along with my father's kilij. I have the dancing sword with me right now.

"You went back to the apartment?" I say, surprised.

Naji nods and puts down the pack. "I wanted to get you some reassurance," he says, placing the sheathed blade on the bed.

The fact I might need the sword is not reassurance. At least not to me. "I thought you said we shouldn't go back to your apartment."

"I did, but I wanted to take a look. It was untouched. I talked to the neighbors and mentioned I had a friend who was hoping to catch me at home. They said they hadn't seen him. I told them I'd likely be gone for a bit and to keep an eye on the place for me."

"Do you think that means they're not looking for us?"

He shrugs and sits down on the bed next to me. "It's too early to know."

"True. How did it go with the Aragvi?"

"It went fine. They hired me on the spot, and I'm supposed to meet them tomorrow. Abu, the guy I'll be working for, told me to meet him at the Aragvi Clan's warehouse around dusk. They're paying me a gold dinar a day for five days of work. He's the one who hired me last time."

"That's something, but where does that get us?"

"I haven't a clue. The water is still and murky. Who knows what lies below it."

"So, we wait?"

He frowns and ponders. "That's all I've got at this point. Do you have any ideas?"

I look around the room at the white walls. I'd been pondering that, while I waited for him to return. Nothing beyond leaving has come to my mind. "No, but I can't sit in here and do nothing. Fadel doesn't need me to dance every day either."

"I'm afraid waiting this out is all we've got right now. I don't know yet if this job is a trap or something completely unrelated."

"What does this entail anyway?"

"That's a good question. They were vague, and said we'd be picking up some goods. No idea what and why."

"In town?"

"It seems so."

"You said the Aragvi clan has their own people. Why would they need to hire more?"

"That is the question I can't answer yet. It's obviously something quite valuable though."

I huff. "So, I am to sit here for five days hoping that you come back and this isn't another trick Rigel has laid out for you to fall into?"

"Unfortunately, that's the only thing I can come up with right now. We could go someplace else, but that still leaves you sitting there. Probably better doing that here than at a random inn. If I come back, it will probably just be to sleep."

"This is a rotten deal."

"Waiting is the hardest part about things like this. Sadly, unless we're going to leave Aksu, it's the safest thing we can do right now."

I pick up my father's sword, tracing my paw pad over the handle. "I guess we wait and see if death comes to visit us."

He opens his muzzle to speak, but then sighs and closes it. Finally, after a minute he speaks up. "This has been a lot of my life. I've done a lot of standing around waiting for people with weapons to present themselves to me."

I grumble. "It's not a healthy way to live."

"I'm beginning to think Naima was crazy for staying in this line of work for as long as she did."

There's nothing I can suggest or think of, so we lapse back into silence. It stretches on for a minute as Naji just stares at his feet in thought.

"You know, there is an entire city out there, and I've spent most of my time since arriving in bedrooms," I remark.

He chuckles wearily. "When this all blows over, I'll take you around and show you Aksu in all her glory. We'll have a great time."

"What is the Grand Market like? My entire life I've heard about this fabled place here in Aksu."

He sighs. "I should have taken you already. It's big and full of sights and sounds. Consider what you saw in Yokus and make it much, much bigger. It was my first home in Aksu, but even today, it can still make my head spin."

"It sounds amazing."

"It is. The Grand Market is something special. There are all sorts of merchants there and storytellers and even acrobats who perform. You'll love it when we go."

I nod, wishing I could see it now. Instead, I get up to look at the clothing Naji has brought me. I pull out a kaftan of cotton and pull it on, wrapping some red fabric around myself as a belt. Below the fabric there is my mother's knit shawl. I pick it up and look at it.

I turn to Naji, who has sat down on the bed. "Why did you bring the shawl?"

He looks up and squints at the fabric I am holding. "I grabbed everything that seemed useful. Is that not part of one of your costumes for when you dance?"

I wrap the fabric over my shoulders. "No. It was my mother's. It's the last thing of hers I own."

"That's all you have?"

"That's all I didn't have to sell." I remember how desperate I was back before I took up whoring. "I was very poor before I took up the dance."

"Then may you never be so hungry again," says the hyena softly.

I take the shawl off and wrap it up, putting it back into the pack. I reach for the sword. I unwrap my belt and use it to secure the sword against myself. "May neither of us be so hungry again. It sounds like you had your own lean years."

"Yes, but it wasn't so bad once I found Rigel and Isim. We were a pack, and we shared everything we had back then in a way that only those who have never known wealth can."

"And what now? Will you kill Rigel when you find him?"

He opens his muzzle and closes it. "I still remember the old days. The way he used to laugh at the jokes Isim and I told. It will be hard, but I cannot hesitate."

I realize now there is something about Rigel's betrayal of him that Naji can't understand. He needs answers, and until he finds out what those are, he's not going to rest. I can only hope the journey to those answers is one he can survive.

"I don't think he'd laugh at them now."

"No," says Naji, with a sigh. "He wouldn't. I'm not laughing at his jokes anymore either. I will need to be ready to cut him down if the opportunity to do so comes."

∾

With nothing pressing to do, all we can do is wait. Not knowing eats at both of us, and even trying to nap, rest doesn't come to me. I know Naji gets some sleep, but I don't. The idea that I should just wait and see what happens feels weird to me, but that's all there is.

As the sun is starting to set, the hyena stirs. When I roll over, he speaks up. "Perhaps we should do something," he suggests.

"What's there to do?" I ask. Drinking wine downstairs doesn't seem very relaxing to me right now.

"I'm sure Fadel has some entertainment tonight."

"I believe Khalil is dancing tonight."

"Not feeling it?"

I shake my head. "No."

He yawns and stretches. "Aziz's men worked me over good. I'm still sore. Maybe I'll see if Ales can give me a massage, if I can get him to go easy on me."

"Does he know how to go easy on anyone?"

"Only one way to find out."

Back in Zaptu, I was lucky if I could afford to bathe more than once a month. I've already bathed thrice here at the Blue Door. I'm going to have to start conditioning my fur so it stays healthy. There are special oils I can brush in to keep my coat glossy. "I could use a good grooming."

Naji gets up and fetches his shirt. "Then let's go down."

Even though we're going to just go downstairs to get naked, we dress, although I do opt for only a simple brown kaftan. From the gallery above the courtyard, I can see the evening crowd is coming in and the murmur of voices fills the space.

Upon descending the staircase to the hammam, I notice that the baths are already quite busy. We take our towels and drop our clothes off across from the attendant. Instead of the quick wash I took by myself, we do the full process. We start in the warm room, sitting on the slab of stone soaking up the heat, before moving into one of the hot rooms. Once we're panting, we returning to the warm room to soap and rinse.

Bathed, we wait for Ales to come around. I go first this time, and he digs his paws with their blunted claws into me, pulling at my tired muscles.

"You have stress," he says to me, as he's pulling back my left arm.

"Yes, ow, yes," I say as he's working my arm around.

The fox clicks his tongue. "Do not let that caracal bother you. I never liked him anyway."

I know he saw what happened, but I don't know what Fadel has told everyone. "I'll do my best."

"Good, good. I fix you up well," he says, before he digs a paw into my back.

When the fox is done, and I get off the stone, I'm sore, but in a very pleasant way. My muscles feel relaxed, and I almost feel like I'm standing taller, which seems silly.

"Okay, Naji," says the fox, "your turn."

"I'm going to need you to be gentle with me," says the hyena, as he lays face down on his towel.

"Gentle?" laughs the red fox. "For you?"

"I got in a fight, you see."

"What is it with you two?" says the fox, starting around Naji's neck.

"It's a long story," says Naji. The fox grunts and pushes his hands into Naji's shoulders, trying to loosen the muscles. Naji yelps in pain. "Not so rough please."

Ales pulls back for a moment. "Where did they hit you?"

"Pretty much everywhere."

Ales looks over the hyena, gently tracing his fingers down his back, exploring the fur there. "Oh. I see. Okay, I fix you too, but this will take some time."

To his credit, Ales takes his time working on Naji. The hyena whimpers, but the fox doesn't push or pull as hard on him as he works the muscles in his back. By the time he finishes, he's already got three other people waiting for him.

"Better now?" he asks Naji, as he's getting up.

Naji rolls his shoulders so he can stretch his neck. "Yes."

"Excellent. Stop doing that to yourself, both of you now," he says, before he walks over to the next person and has them lay down so he can work his magic.

Both of us now refreshed, we walk over to the cold room. A lion and a cheetah are in the cold pool, enjoying a cooldown. We both opt for a brushing, which today is done by a leopard. Then Naji and I retire to one of the niches and order mint tea, which a mongoose brings to us. From here, we watch the crowd.

"Feeling better?" he asks me, once the tea has arrived.

I haven't been thinking about what could happen to either of us. "Yes."

"Good. Did you want to see the dancing tonight?"

I shake my head. "No. There will be other times."

He pours out the tea for us, and smiles. "If we sit here for a bit, we might see some things, you know."

Just looking at the lion and the cheetah in the pool, I can tell. The lion is currently holding the cheetah against himself, and his paw is trailing across the lion's stomach. "I've heard from a good source about what happens in here."

He looks away in mock modesty. "Ah yes, well, I'm sure you have."

I scoot around the bench so I can get near him. "I'm sure you've seen some stuff yourself."

His ears perk. "I have."

I pick up my cup of tea and blow on it to cool it. "Those were probably more carefree people than us who did that."

"It is still a pleasant memory," he says.

"Indeed, it was." I get close to him and sip my tea as I watch the lion start to stroke the cheetah. I'm sure Naji's shaft stiffens a bit like mine does as the two in the pool play, but I'm not in the mood. He doesn't appear to be either.

Instead, I just lean against the hyena and shift my view so I can't quite notice what the lion and cheetah are doing. Naji holds me and playfully teases my ears with nose to get me to laugh. We spend the rest of the evening just people watching in the Blue Door.

&

The need to do something the next day is even worse. Morning finds me staring at the ceiling after having slept fitfully. We only leave the Blue Door to get some breakfast and return to wait until Naji has to go. We talk throughout the day, but there's a feeling of restlessness at the back of my mind, and I can tell he feels it too. While we do talk, there is little to discuss. Naji does feel better at least, and the bruises under his fur are much less tender now.

To kill some time, Naji teaches me a game that involves capturing pieces by picking up a handful of small stones in a bowl carved into the board and moving them around to other bowls on the board. I've played this before, but the version he teaches me is different from the one I played growing up. It takes me a little time to get used to the different rules, but after a few games, I manage to come out ahead of the hyena when the stones are tallied.

In the early afternoon, Naji decides he should take a nap before he heads out to meet Abu. Seeing my bored look, he speaks up. "Go see if Fadel has some time. Maybe you two can go to the Grand Market."

"I can wait," I say.

"You might have to do a lot of waiting. Plus, with Fadel, you will be safe."

I frown. "I can't keep imposing on him."

"The fennec still owes me a few favors. He won't mind. Business won't pick up here till dusk. I don't want you to feel trapped here."

I can't say my interest about the market isn't piqued. "You think Fadel will be able to go?"

"Hopefully. It can't hurt to ask."

I nod. I do need to stretch my legs, and it would be nice to get out. "I'll go see," I say, my tail already getting excited about the prospect.

Naji nods and rolls over, trying to get comfortable. I get up and let myself out of the room to head downstairs. I go looking for Fadel, and I find him at his desk in the front of the Blue Door, going over various papers scattered about. I tell him what Naji suggested about us going to the Grand Market.

"I would love to, but I have some correspondence to write right now," says the fennec. "Perhaps tomorrow though."

My ears droop. "I was hoping to go today," I respond.

"I'm afraid I can't go right now. I have to arrange my next shipment of wine. Some things can wait, but wine is not something I can go without here," he says, with a chuckle.

"Do you think I can go myself?"

The fennec clears his throat. "That probably wouldn't be very wise."

I frown. "It's only a little past noon. How dangerous could it be?"

"The market? As long as you watch your coin purse, you are fine. It's the part about Rigel I'm concerned more about."

"I've got protection," I add, patting at my sword. "Plus, Naji is in just as much trouble as I am, but he still gets to take chances."

Fadel's large ears splay. "He does not listen to all my advice either, but he also knows the city well."

"So, I should just sit here?"

Fadel frowns at me, wanting to say something, but something catches his eye, and he raises a digit to get me to pause. Salim, the jackal I've seen who sometimes staffs the front desk, comes walking up.

"This is a private conversation," says Fadel to the jackal.

"I understand, but the man who brings the wood for the hammam is out back. Ales is negotiating with him, but he's trying to raise the price."

Fadel sighs. "He does this every few months. I'll be right there. Tell Ales to stall for me."

The jackal nods. "You got it." He heads off in a trot.

Fadel waits a minute before he turns his attention back to me. "I've got business to attend to."

"Right..." I say, ears still low. "Let me know about to-morrow."

The fennec considers for a moment. "Come with me," he says, getting up. "I have something that will keep you busy."

Unsure of what he wants, I get up and follow him. He heads back to the hammam, but at the attendant's station, we go behind a door and down a set of stairs. This leads to a narrow corridor off which the furnaces are located to heat the rooms above. Already an attendant is stacking wood for the night's firing.

At the end of the corridor, there is a set of stairs that lead up with a door at the top that opens onto a narrow alleyway on the side of the Blue Door. We can hear voices as we climb up, and as we emerge into the alleyway, Ales is talking to a male painted dog and a female caracal standing next to a cart stacked with wood a little ways away from the door.

"We agreed upon a set price last time," says Ales.

The painted dog shrugs. "We have less wood this week."

"And that changes the price why?" asks the red fox.

"If you buy too much, we won't have enough for every-one," says the caracal.

"They do this every other month to see if they can get more money out of me," whispers Fadel. "Look, go to the end of the alley and take a right. That will put you on the street behind the Blue Door. From there, you will go until you hit a major road and take a left. You'll need to take a right when the road intersects the main road that leads from the main bridge to the Grand Market. Follow the wagons, but if you get lost, ask for directions. Just say you are a traveler still learning the city."

"What about Rigel?" I ask.

"If he's watching the building, he's got someone in the front, but he doesn't know about this entrance. You'll need to come back to the main door, but I'll leave someone out front for when you come back."

The temptation to get out is too great. "Thank you."

"Keep your wits about you, and be back in an hour or two. I don't want Naji to worry."

"I can do that," I say, as I turn to walk past the cart and the ongoing negotiation.

As I go, I can hear Fadel walking over to Ales. "So, if what I understand is true, you can't get us enough wood. I should perhaps look for another supplier then?"

"There is no need for that now," says the caracal, alarmed.

"You're the one saying you can't meet my standing order…"

As I reach the end of the alleyway, the conversation fades away and I take that right onto a street. Outside, the sun is bright, and people pass by on their day-to-day activities. I see no one lying in wait for me, but I glance around to get a better feeling of my bearings. This isn't a busy street, but it isn't deserted either. I walk slowly at first, trying to make sure no one is taking an interest in me. A few pass by me, but no one stops.

I breathe a sigh of relief and pick up my pace. My couple of trips to and from Naji's apartment have only given me a rough idea of the city layout, so it takes me a while to make my way to the Grand Market, even with Fadel's directions.

As a child I always knew Aksu was rich from the robust business its traders did, but the size and scope of the activity takes me aback. This dwarfs the caravanserai in Zaptu. On one side of the large square is the counting house, a modest but ornate building. Next to it, a broad road leads to the gate of the Sultan's Citadel that covers the rocky outcropping at the heart of the city. Beyond the open part of the square spread market stalls in long rows. There are countless people going about their business, a crowd that undulates around the stores.

Just walking into one of the rows of stalls makes my head spin. People of all species are selling everything here.

The spots of cheetahs and leopards clash against the stripes of tigers and hyenas, while those whose fur patterns are more muted walk by. I even see jackals with black furred backs, something my parents said was common only in the southern lands. The bark of an amused canine mixes with the chitter of a mongoose and voices of all walks of life, weaving a tapestry of sound.

There are fruits, spices, cloth, ceramics, metalworks, baskets, carpets, and more for sale in a variety of shapes and colors. Merchants hawk goods to passers-by, while scribes patiently listen to their clients' needs, drafting and reading letters for those who cannot read themselves. Acrobats and musicians entertain crowds, while storytellers hold audiences captive with their tales. All around is the smell of roasting meat and vegetables to feed the hungry masses. This isn't just a market, I realize—this is the beating heart of the sultanate.

I wander the stalls, trying to find my way through, and am mindful in the press of people to keep my paws on my purse. A hundred different smells come to my nose, while a thousand sounds reach my ears. It's overwhelming, and I realize now why Naji wanted to accompany me here. The press of people is intense, and I can feel my heart beating faster. I'm surrounded by the crowd, and I have to push my way through at points to catch some air.

I eventually make my way through the crowd to the other side and stop to smooth down my hackles. I did not expect there to be so many here, and it's making me anxious. While I'm panting in the shade of a building on the edge of the market square, a group of striped hyenas go by chatting about iron prices, while an ibex argues with a wolf over the price of sacks of grain. A fennec passes, pushing a cart with chickens squawking irritably.

I decide after a bit that perhaps I should stick to the edge of the square. I walk around the side, just looking at the throng of people. I stop at one booth by the edge and for a copper buy an orange from a merchant. I peel and eat the fruit as I walk. It's much sweeter than anything I have ever had, and certainly much fresher than the old fruit I could barely afford back in Zaptu. I savor the sweetness, trying not to let the juice drip down my muzzle. The tang in my mouth lingers after I finish it.

Continuing to explore, I encounter something else that catches me off guard. Behind the temporary stands in the market, there is a series of souks—covered stone walkways with permanent stands lining them. Here the bustle is less intense, with people strolling along in the shade, shopping for garments, tea, and perfumes. Many of these stands are small, but they have names above their doors. I cannot fathom how much coin is exchanged here or how many goods are traded and sold. Naji told me the Grand Market also isn't the only market in Aksu, although the others are much smaller, generally focusing on a few goods.

In a quiet alleyway of the souk, I find a bookseller. Passing by, I cannot resist the temptation to step in and see what they have. Books were rare to see in Zaptu, although my father had a few. I had to sell them to Usman for coin, but he let me borrow them later to read.

Here, in this little shop tucked away off an alleyway, there are more books than I have ever seen before in my life. Some appear to be quite old, but the works of many of the great poets are prominently displayed. I pick one up with a name I have only heard of before to see what it contains. I know Naji has mentioned he reads poetry on occasion, and I would like to read more myself. It would at least give me something to do while I wait at the Blue Door.

"Is there something I can help you find?" comes a female voice behind my ear. I turn, and another jackal has come up to me. Her fur is tawny like mine, but she has different markings. She is wearing loose, white linen cloth that is pulled up to her body at her waist and falls away into a dress. On her top, she wears a tailored tunic to fit her form. Her smile is warm, and her authority tells me she owns this shop.

"I am looking to see what poetry you have."

"Is there something specific I can help you find in that area? I have all of my stock here, but if you need a specific work, I can ask around and see if I can find it."

"I don't have a specific volume in mind. I am more looking to find something to give as a gift."

"Ah, do they have a favorite poet they love?"

"I'm not sure, but I'm thinking more of a traditional courting gift."

She smiles. "Ah, I know the right thing for the woman in your life. I would suggest a traditional set of poems for your lover to read and enjoy."

I shift my weight. I'm not sure whether or not to tell her the person I am planning to give this to isn't female. "Along those lines, yes."

She walks over to where some of the books are shelved and pulls down an elaborately decorated volume and hands it to me. The calligraphy on the cover is breathtaking. "Perhaps this?"

I recognize the author's name. They're a poet my father used to love reading. I flip open the cover and skim the listing of poems in it. Some of them I recognize, and I feel myself getting excited, my tail wagging a little.

"This is perfect. I am sure he will love it."

The moment I say that, I feel my body freeze up. I didn't want to say that out loud.

"A he, you say?" She gives me a coy smile. "I will not judge you, but I have another book that might interest you then."

"Uh, thank you," is all I can manage.

"Do you have a name?" she asks me.

"Zayn."

"It is a pleasure to meet you, Zayn. My name is Safiya. Now let me show you something in the back."

She steps towards the back of the store and pulls a different volume off the shelf. This one is plain and the cover is not embossed. She comes back and hands it to me. "This writer is mithly like you and wrote about his experiences."

I look down at the book shyly as I take it into my paws. The name on the cover is not one I'm familiar with, but the title, *By the Lamp's Light*, intrigues me. I open the copy to a random page and skim it. The speaker in this one, a fox of some kind I gather from him talking about his bushy tail, is talking about a feline he fancies and the way his fur lights upon his frame. I keep skimming and some of the passages bring a bit of a flush to my fur and I stop reading and look up at Safiya.

"As you can see, his descriptions leave nothing to the imagination," she says.

"Indeed, they don't. That wasn't quite what I was looking for. Your first recommendation I know well."

"Five silver dirhams for either book. I will sell you both for eight dirhams."

I want the first work, because that is what I imagined getting Naji. The second fascinates me, but that isn't what I wanted to get him.

"Four silver for the first?"

"The price is firm on that one. The other one I will sell you at a discount."

It's not that I don't want the second, but I feel very shy about buying it. The reassuring smile though does give me some confidence that she will be discreet, not that anyone I know cares I am buying a tome of erotic prose. Still, I've never been so open about my persuasion before when not working. Even though she is welcoming, I feel hesitant.

"I think I will take just the first book," I say timidly. I want something traditional for Naji anyway, not something explicit, although once things settle down, I may come back for the second.

She nods when I hand her the second text. "Is there anything else I can find for you?" she asks me, as I fish out the five silver dirhams from my coin purse to hand to her.

"Could you wrap this up for me?"

"Of course," she says, taking the first volume and going to her table. She sets both books down and pulls out some coarse brown parchment, and proceeds to wrap them both up.

"I only paid for one book!" I say.

She shrugs. "The other has been looking for a home for quite a while."

"Yes, but—"

"Your embarrassment is obvious. Sometimes we need a nudge."

I fish out three more silver dirham. "I can pay for it."

"Or I can just discount the first one," she says, holding out the two parchment-wrapped volumes.

"That is very kind of you."

She smiles, and I take the package. "I have others when you finish that one."

My ears get really hot. "Thank you, Safiya." I say, and then walk out of her store with the package clutched under my arms.

She waves as I go, and I am swept up by the crowd outside. Even though I feel embarrassed, my tail wags as I weave in and out of the various customers shopping among the stalls. This is a courting gift, and I hope Naji enjoys it.

The jackal Salim is outside, busy cleaning the lamp above the door when I return to the inn. I am hurrying down the street quickly to reach the Blue Door before I notice him. Even then, I do not stop until I am standing by him and take this opportunity to pant.

"You okay there?" he remarks from the top of the ladder, having paused the cleaning he's doing.

"I'm good now," I say, catching my breath.

"Excellent," he says, as he goes back to wiping down the lantern. "Fadel's just inside."

"Thank you," I say as I enter. The fennec is indeed at the desk, and his ears perk at the sight of me.

"Was there any trouble?" he asks.

"No," I say. "None at all."

He makes a satisfied squeak. "Excellent. Naji was worried I had misjudged the situation."

My ears lower. "Was he upset?"

"He was concerned, but even he didn't realize we had the other entrance. To keep himself busy, he's up on the roof, sharpening his sword."

"I'll go talk to him. Hopefully this will cheer him up," I say, patting the parcel under my arm, heading for the stairs.

As Fadel said, I find Naji on the roof, sharpening his sword under the awning. He is intently studying the blade, but he looks up as I climb up the ladder and my claws click against the roof. He gets up and walks over to me to give me an unexpected hug, pulling me to him.

"You're safe," he says with a sigh. "I was worried when Fadel told me you went alone. He shouldn't have told you to do that."

"I didn't see anything to give me concern."

"I really wanted Fadel to take you."

"I may have pressed him on that."

"I realize just sitting here isn't fun, but these people are dangerous. They'll wait for our guard to go down before they strike."

"Perhaps they're not looking for us?"

He finally lets go of me. "We might not know till the knife flies toward one of us. Next time, make sure Fadel goes with you. That would make it harder for someone to grab you and pull you into a dark alleyway."

I sweep my hands out. "The city seemed pretty safe to me."

It is miserable up here; the air is still, and the sun reflects off the stone, tile, and brick roofs. We are both panting from the heat. From this height, Aksu is a field of buildings that surround the large rock outcropping upon which the Sultan's citadel sits. The river that runs through part of the city is a gash across the built-up area.

"It's not the city I'm worried about."

"I know, but should we just hide in fear now?"

He closes his eyes and mutters a quiet prayer to himself. When he opens them again, he looks me square in the face. "Isim was fine too, until I took my eyes off of him. Now he's gone."

That takes me back. "This isn't some botched robbery."

He opens his muzzle, then closes it. He shakes to settle his fur. "No, it's not, but I still don't want to see you cut down like that."

He's right, something could have happened, but I let myself get too caught up in being curious. "I wanted to see the Grand Market."

"Oh, I don't blame you. I would too if I was you. I will take you everywhere when this is over. To the Malhaa District to see its sights and sounds, and to the gardens beyond the walls. I will show you everything Aksu has to offer from the great temples to the modest cafes tucked in the oldest parts of the city."

He looks out at the city beyond before he glances over to where his sword is sitting. "I can't do that though, if one of us doesn't survive this."

"I know."

"I have faced death most of my life, yet I do not believe it does not stalk me in the shadows when I do not see it. Someday, it will find me. I can only hope by then I am old." He walks back to the awning where he was sitting when I came up the ladder.

I follow him, my ears and tail drooping. "Sorry. Perhaps I was too impatient."

He tilts his head a little to smile. "No, I understand. I would want to explore too in your position. I remember, when I first came to Aksu, how breathtaking the city felt to me then." He goes back to where his sword and the whetstone he was using are sitting.

I follow him. There's something I've been meaning to ask him. "You mentioned previously you were born under the acacia trees. How far away is that, exactly?"

He looks up at me. "It's across the Crimson Sea, where the plains meet the foothills of the mountains. It's about a month and a half journey. Aksu is my adopted home."

I sit down under the tent with Naji and put the parcel I've been carrying down next to us. Back in Zaptu, people often slept on their roofs to beat the summer heat, and I can tell some people do here also. Cushions are set up on top of an old rug under the awning. I pull one over and prop myself up so I can watch Naji work. "Tell me about it."

"About home?" he asks me, running the whetstone over a section of his sword.

"Yes."

"There isn't much to tell. I left when I was fifteen, and I haven't been back since."

"You ran away at fifteen?"

"No, I was sold by my parents when I was fifteen."

"Wait, they have slavery down there?"

"It's not slavery exactly, but the clans each provide a tax in blood to the local emirs who train the boys and girls sold to be soldiers. They taught us how to fight, how to read, and used our service to protect their interests. A son or daughter providing the service of the blood is very prestigious and raises the standing of the whole family. Wages for the child are paid upfront."

"And you never saw them again?" I say, with shock.

"I saw them again, but it was never the same. Even with the prestige of the position, I knew I wasn't free, and they had put me there. I resented them for that, and my loyalty was to the Emir of Zeway and not them."

"How did you end up here?"

"When I was seventeen, a war broke out that swept across the plains against the Republic of Batu. My emir was strong and sought to take advantage to increase his power. He pressed all his men into service. Generally, you don't fight until you are eighteen, but when emirs are desperate that can change. I had already completed my training, so I went with the army and spent a year fighting across the plains and into the mountain valleys against both other hyenas and the painted ones who reside in the mountains.

"In the end though, he overreached. The Emir took his army to attack a stronghold in the valley leading to the coast, but his enemies united against him with the Republic. Even before we reached the valley, we got word that two armies had marched against his stronghold in the south and were laying siege to it while we were besieging a mountain fortress. That night, while the Emir and the generals debated their options, they forgot to set their watches right. In the darkness, painted ones who supported the Republic of Batu came and ambushed our camp."

He falls silent for a while. I can see he's reliving the battle in his mind. He frowns and looks out over the roofs.

"The painted showed no mercy. I served with jackals, cheetahs, and hyenas, but never any Takula, as the painted dogs called themselves. Their strike was silent. They'd already reached the camp before an alarm call went out. I remember people running, people dying, and I barely had time to find my own sword in the darkness before they were upon us." He traces the scar on his flank. "Our hastily raised defenses collapsed, and the survivors ran. Dawn found me alone in the hills, lost."

"And then?" I ask quietly.

"As silently as they came, they left. I went back in the morning, and I saw death like I had never seen. They left the Emir and his generals propped up in the middle of the camp as a warning to any survivors. I know a few went back home, but what was there for me to go home to? To return and serve whoever replaced the Emir? I took some supplies and struck out on my own. I traveled north and gained passage on a trade dhow crossing the Crimson Sea. Eventually, I ended up here."

"That must have been quite an adventure."

"I had to learn quickly how to survive and stay on my feet. I rarely stayed anywhere for long. It wasn't till I met Rigel and Isim that I finally thought I'd found a place to settle down. Here, I was able to find work. Not honest work at first, but eventually I did. I don't have to steal to survive, and I no longer kill at the whims of a master. I am free once more."

I reach out to put a hand on his leg. He stopped sharpening the sword a few minutes ago and is just holding it. "I didn't know."

His voice is strained. "Why would you?"

"Yes, but… I know it has to still hurt."

He looks at me, ears pinned back. "I think about it a lot. I remember the dead faces of my friends I served with. So many died, yet for some reason I lived."

I push myself so I am sitting up. "It's okay Naji. You're here now," I say, as I lean over to hug him.

He stiffens and starts to cry. "I've lost so many friends already, this is why I can't lose you, Zayn. My life has always been broken, but if I can fix yours, I will have done something good finally in this world."

What can I say that would make it better? My parents left me, but not of their own accord. I remember holding my mother as the life faded from her when she was sick. It wasn't her choice to go, and I know she did everything for me she could. "I can't imagine how horrible this has all been," is all I manage to get out.

Naji doesn't say anything but lets his tears come silently, and all I can do is hold him. They wet the fur around my neck as he sniffles, pressing himself against me. When he's done, he wipes his eyes and breaks away. "Are you going to be okay?" I ask.

He sniffs. "I have to be." He points to the sun sinking toward the horizon. "I need to meet Abu at dusk." He picks the sword back up and starts working on the edge again.

I let go so he can work, and he keeps carefully refining the edge. After a few minutes he checks his blade. "I can do yours if you want."

"Do you think it needs it?"

"When was the last time you sharpened it?" he asks.

"I don't think I've ever sharpened it."

He frowns. "Let me see it."

I hand it over to Naji from where it's been resting in its scabbard on the carpet, and he pulls the kilij out. He looks over the edge. "Well, at least you've kept it oiled." He sights down the edge. "It's not that bad at all, but the edge could use some work."

As he reaches for the stone, I speak up. "Keeping it sharp wasn't my priority with what I was doing with it. I nicked myself a few times with the tip by not being careful."

He pauses. "It's okay if I sharpen it, right? You aren't going to go back to dancing with this, are you?"

"No, I've moved to the other sword," I say.

Naji starts working on the blade. "It will be good as new when I'm done," he says, as he starts to refine the edge. I watch silently as he slowly and carefully sharpens my sword.

"So, what did you think of it?" he asks me, after a few minutes of silence.

"Think of what?"

"The Grand Market."

"Oh!" I say. "That was intense."

"Yes, it can be," he chuckles. "Even for as many times as I've been there, it still has this heady rush."

"I found the crowd so thick, I had to keep to the edges. I found a bookseller in the souk behind it."

He is looking over the edge of the sword. "There are some good ones there."

"Indeed. I got you something while I was there," I say, pushing over the parcel.

He pauses. "You bought me a book?"

"Of poetry. Two actually, although the second one the bookseller thought I needed."

"Really?"

"Yes, she cut me a deal. The second book will make your ears hot."

He looks up at me. "Make my ears hot?"

"It's a bit," and I gesture, "risqué. The author is just like us."

He chuckles. "You bought me an erotic book."

I open my muzzle, then shut it and just nod.

Naji grins. "That's rather direct of you, isn't it?"

I scowl and stick out my tongue. "I can be more discreet if you want. Perhaps I should go back to hiding my natural scent with perfume."

"There is no need for that now," he says seriously. "I like you as you are."

I lean over and give him a peck on the muzzle. "I like you just the way you are too."

The Aragvi Clan
(Naji)

I've never had someone buy me books like this before, and certainly not as a courting gift. The calligraphy on the leatherwork of the first volume is magnificent, and just glancing at a few pages suggests this will be an enjoyable read. The second book is quite plain, but just flipping through it, I can see Zayn is quite right about the content. One of the passages that catches my eye certainly makes my sheath tight.

However, I don't have more time to savor either book before I have to go. As I'm leaving, I run into Fadel, and the fennec says he's going to take Zayn out for dinner so the jackal doesn't feel so cooped up. I fleetingly wonder if that is a good idea, but Zayn can't be a prisoner here. I feel good knowing that this time he is going out with someone I trust. Without the jackal and Naima, I don't know what I'd do with myself right now.

Dusk is starting to fall when I arrive at the warehouse across the river. Some parts of the far bank are not as built up, so this area is pretty quiet. Many of the buildings here are only one floor. No one is out that I can see.

The warehouse itself is a squat stone structure. The sigil of the Aragvi clan, depicting a square tower and a mountain, is inscribed by the door in a marble inlay. The large double wooden doors are worn, and no window looks over the street, although there is a slat in one of the doors to inspect visitors. Nothing else about the exterior of the building is remarkable.

With nothing else to do, I walk up and pound on the heavy wooden doors. There is no sound from behind it as I wait. After a minute, I knock again. Finally, I hear something, and the small slat opens.

"Go away," says a gruff voice. All I can see are a pair of yellow eyes, but my nose confirms this is a wolf.

"I'm here to work. I spoke to Abu in the market yesterday. He told me to come here."

The eyes bore into me. "Did he now? Wait a moment."

The wooden slat slides closed, and I hear a faint sound. It sounds like someone is talking. After a minute the slat slides open.

"Abu said someone was coming, but he has not returned from the market yet. Who told you we were hiring, yena?" say the eyes behind the door.

"My friend Naima. She is a spice merchant in the market. She keeps an eye out for me when I am looking for work."

"Ah, you know Naima." He turns away but doesn't close the slat. He must be exchanging nonverbal cues with whomever else is there.

"All right yena, you can come in, but I will need you to wait until Abu gets here." The slip of wood in the door closes, and I can hear a heavy bolt being drawn. The door cracks open and a wolf steps out and looks around. She—I didn't realize the speaker was female—is dressed in loose pants and a vest over her shirt. She has light cream-colored fur with streaks of white and black in it. The wolf also has a sword strapped to her hip. After she glances up and down the street, she motions for me to enter. I do so, and she closes the door behind me.

The entranceway is large and runs all the way to the back of the warehouse. Off this hall, I can see two doors to each side, likely leading to storerooms. There is also another wolf in the room. This one has a dark pelt of coal with a few lighter streaks. He is watching me carefully, sizing me up. I didn't see either of these wolves at the market.

"Hi," I say to him.

"You look familiar," he says to me.

"I have worked for your clan before, a couple of years ago." I'm not going to lie, but I hope I don't have to go into details.

"Ah, I see," says the male wolf.

"If Abu hired him, we will respect his judgment, Akay."

The male wolf walks up to me and scents the air. "It is not that I don't trust you per se," he says, "it is that I don't trust anyone right now."

"I can wait outside if you want," I offer.

"No, that won't be necessary. My name, as you heard, is Akay, my compatriot here is Ilayda."

"Naji," I reply, trying to get a bearing on my surroundings. There is a lantern hanging in the room that gives off a dull glow, and I can make out what they have in here well enough. There are ceramic plates and metal pots stacked neatly along one side of the room. There is an assortment of other small wares, and to the other side some chairs with a set of playing cards sitting on top of a low table, a few copper coins on it. Everything I see are the same things they were selling in the market, and not something that warrants having armed guards. Who knows what is in the side rooms, though.

"Ah, I do remember you now," says Akay. He thinks for a moment and his ears that have been held at attention relax. "We will wait here for Abu."

"Okay," I reply.

Neither of the wolves moves, though. Apparently, that means we will stand in place until he arrives, even though there are four chairs by the table and a kettle of tea sitting next to it.

"Can you tell me about the job? Abu said it was for just a couple of days."

They both shake their heads. "No," says Ilayda.

These two are incredibly friendly, I see. "Uh, should we stand and wait for him then?"

Akay squints at me and points over to one of the chairs, and I go and sit down. They follow and reluctantly offer me some tea. I accept the cup, but it is lukewarm.

We sit in silence for a few minutes, and I try to think of something I can say that will at least get them talking. Both of the wolves look a little nervous and jumpy, and I'm not sure why. They have not resumed their game which I obviously disturbed.

"So," I begin. "Do you both hail from the steppes up north?" Some of the Aragvi clan does.

Akay's fur bristles. "I was born here, but my parents came from the north, from the lands beyond the Empire of Roum."

I have never figured out what the Aragvi clan is doing in Khalin. I think most are refugees from wars fought by the Empire of Roum, but why they came here is unknown to me. They're also not the only ones who've come here. The empire's reach is great and while Khalin is beyond its grasp, we still share a border. The Aragvi have been here so long, most of their number are now second or third generation descendants of the original members.

One thing I've noticed is their pelts are also thicker than most of the local wolves who hail from the area around Khalin. It must be colder where they're from, but I don't know how far north that really is. The steppes are one place I have never been.

"I just am curious," I say softly to reassure them. I need these people to trust me.

"It is better you not know," says Ilayda.

I shrug. If they don't want to share their story with me, I won't have to share mine with them.

We lapse back into silence and after what seems to be almost half an hour, a knock comes at the door. Both wolves perk their ears and get up. "Wait here," Akay tells me, and he walks over. I turn to watch, and when I see him slide the panel back, I see only darkness. Night has now fallen.

"You're late," he says to whomever is outside.

If there is a verbal response, I don't catch it, but they unbolt the door, and Abu walks in with three more wolves. Two are male and one is female. All wear similar forms of dress.

"It took longer to pack up the stall then we expected," Abu says.

Akay points over to me. "You have a visitor."

"Ah, good, he is here. We need to unload the cart immediately so we can be there on time," he says to Akay. "Let me talk to our guest for a moment."

I stand up from where I am sitting as Abu walks up to me. "Good evening."

"Good evening to you too, yena. Did Akay and Ilayda keep you busy?" he asks.

I chuckled. "Not really. They said they wanted to wait for you."

Abu turns to watch as the wolves wheel in one of the carts piled high with merchandise through the large double doors and start to unload it. If they're going to be in the market tomorrow, I'm surprised they're going to unload everything tonight.

"After we unload, we will go to the quarter outside the city wall."

The tannery quarter is west of the city walls. It has the only city gate that is not closed at night and is named after the goods manufactured there. The area has a strong smell from the leatherworkers and paper mills in it, but it has always been an important area for workshops. After the tannery quarter, the Zaharani winds through farmland to Japar on the coast. There are a number of houses and inns outside the gate, but the area is the least desirable part of Aksu. The back alleyways are known for their trouble, and only the main roads are considered safe late at night.

If we're going there, with carts, we must be picking something up. "Will we be meeting someone?" I ask Abu.

"In a way, yes," he says. "Just follow my orders. Now, go help them unload the carts. We're late."

I nod and trot to where the wolves are working. They have begun stacking goods against one wall of the warehouse. I join in, picking up crates of dishes packed in straw and large platters wrapped in cloth, careful not to drop or chip anything. It takes about fifteen minutes, but we get everything out of the carts to one side of the warehouse. Outside, Akay waits with the horses. When we are done, we reattach the horses to the carts and then get on our way.

Abu drives the first cart and one of the wolves that came with him drives the other. We split up into two groups. Ilayda and Akay are with me in the second cart, while the other wolves are in the first.

The carts rattle down the cobblestone streets, bouncing us around. Personally, I would prefer if we walked. It wouldn't be that much slower, but the wolves seem happy to ride. We cross the river at the Grand Bridge and bounce down a major thoroughfare. No one seems to be talking, so I take that as a cue and watch where we're going. The wolves are all on alert with perked ears and bristled fur. The fact that whatever it is we are going to get requires this many armed guards intrigues me.

As we approach the gate, Abu passes the word back for everyone to relax and look bored. The guards by the gate stop the carts, but when they see that they are empty, they pass us through.

"You do know they're going to want to check the carts on the way back in," I say to Akay, once we pull away from the gate. The Sultan levies a small fee for each cart destined to the markets of Aksu, so we'll have to declare our goods on the return and pay.

"That we have thought of and already taken care of," he says with a smile.

Have they bribed the guards? It is possible, but most of the city guard are honest. Anyone taking money gets reported to the captain of the guard or the Grand Vizier quickly. The punishment is swift.

Beyond the walls, there are stables and some large inns. Small houses fit in between. Everything here is outside of the protection of the walls, and while the sultanate has not gone to war during my lifetime, living here with the stench of the tanneries is undesirable to most. Even though the workshops have shuttered for the day, there is a pervasive smell of chemicals in the air that burns the nose. All of the buildings are single story structures, and some are even built with mud-brick instead of the usual stone used in the rest of the city.

Abu turns the cart off the main road, and onto a narrow alley. Halfway down the way there is a gate set in a wall which we pull up to. Everyone starts dismounting except for Abu and the wolf driving the cart we're in. Akay walks over to the gate and knocks three times.

There is silence while everyone else waits by the carts. After a minute, the doors swing inward. "You're with me, Naji," Ilayda says to me.

I follow Ilayda through the gate into the courtyard. Two of the wolves stay in the alleyway, but the carts and everyone else enter the courtyard. Just inside the gate, Akay is talking to a snow leopard. I catch some of the conversation as I walk past.

"I have been waiting," says the leopard, "for you to arrive. I thought you might not be coming with how late it was, and I should find another buyer."

Akay shrugs. "Abu and the others got held up in the market."

"The boss would not be pleased, if he were here."

"Sarda is still over the mountains?"

Wait, is this the Sarda Zayn knew? My fur bristles instinctively. This is an interesting development.

"Indeed, but he has entrusted me to complete this deal. You have the money, yes?" says the cat.

"Abu has it."

The snow leopard nods and watches as the carts pull in, closing the gate behind them. There are lanterns hung around the courtyard, but a lot of it is still in shadow. Another snow leopard and a tiger are in the back of the courtyard standing guard under a lantern. Caravans stopping in Aksu use these warehouse compounds to offload and trade bulk goods.

The snow leopard walks over to the cart Abu was driving. "Jalus, it is good to see you again," says Abu to the cat.

"Abu," nods the snow leopard. "You are late. Come, let us talk business."

"Yes," says the lion, letting his mane jingle. He walks off with Jalus. Akay moves to follow, but Abu waves him back.

The wolves form up in a line next to their carts, waiting. The other snow leopard and the lion stay at their post. I can hear them talking, but I can't catch the words. They glance at the Aragvi wolves and me, but they largely ignore us.

There really isn't anything for us to do but wait. Since Ilayda called me to her, I stay by her side. I want to ask her about Jalus and Sarda, but I can't do that without raising any suspicion. Neither know who I am. I hover too close to the wolf while pondering and eventually she comments on this.

"I don't need a shadow."

"I'm sure, but I don't know what else you want me to do right now. So far, this seems to be a simple job."

She shrugs. "We will see."

Shouting from the back of the courtyard grabs everyone's attention. "No! You pay for it all now, or you can't have any of it!" Jalus has come out of the back, and he looks unhappy.

"Come on, be reasonable," says Abu.

"Get the whole lot of them out of here, and come back when you're ready to buy," the snow leopard says, gesturing at all of us while glaring at Abu.

The lion looks unfazed. "I can pay you the rest tomorrow, Jalus."

"Tomorrow, tomorrow. Tomorrow is not today. I need you to pay today."

I glance toward Jalus's guards, the snow leopard and tiger. Their eyes are fixed on Abu, and I can see their hands have dropped to their swords, ready for trouble. The wolves are also all standing at attention.

Abu grumbles. "The clan will not be happy if we don't get the goods today."

"That is not my problem," says Jalus, crossing his arms.

"I don't have time for this!"

"Waiting one more day won't kill you, Abu. I have people to pay, just like you."

Abu walks up close to Jalus and breathes down on him. "Today, Jalus. Tomorrow is too late."

Jalus says something under his breath I don't catch, and Abu starts wildly gesticulating. "It was an honest oversight! I thought we'd sell more in the market today. The clan has the money."

Jalus growls low. "Mistakes cost, and you know that. If it wasn't for me, there wouldn't be product to buy."

Abu glances at the guards at the back who have dropped into a fighting stance. "You know I'm good for it. You also don't want to be holding this any longer than you need to. I can send you the rest tomorrow."

Jalus sighs. "Yes, but I still need collateral. I would be a fool for letting you walk out of here without getting something in return."

Abu grumbles, reaches up, and unties one of the strands of beads out of his mane. Bits of silver glint as he does. It takes him a minute, but when he's done, he hands it to Jalus with a coin purse. "Will this get you off my back? You know how much this means to me."

Jalus looks at the silver and glass beads. "Very well, but tomorrow you pay in full, and do not be late."

"Yes, yes," says Abu. "Let us load it up and get it out of here and off your paws before anyone notices we're here."

Jalus flicks his tail but bobs his head in acknowledgment. The snow leopard waves towards me and the waiting wolves. "Pull the carts over there, and we can begin," he says, pointing to one of the sets of wooden doors that open off the courtyard.

By the time the horses pull the carts over, Jalus and his two guards have the doors open and are pulling out amphorae and setting them down on the ground. Abu steps over and lifts an amphora up with a grunt to see how heavy it is.

"How many amphorae are there?" asks the lion.

"Twenty-four," says the snow leopard, "as agreed upon."

"Good. Let's load them up."

First, we put down some straw to pad the amphorae. They're tall, unadorned jars with short necks and handles. Clay stoppers have been used to cork them. There are no markers on them suggesting what they contain. As I'm carrying an amphora, I catch a strong smell from the jar I can't place. Whatever it is, it makes my nose tickle. The odor is very distinct, but not something I'm familiar with. The smell is bitter and rotten with a burnt undertone. These can't contain wine or olive oil. No one would send armed guards like this for wine, even with the best vintages, so what is in these things? The gentle sloshing in the jar provides no clues.

Each cart gets twelve jars. After we've loaded the amphorae, we add more hay to keep them put, and a jug of wine is brought out and splashed around the carts to hide the smell. When that's done, we're ready to go. There's no space left in the carts, so it looks like most of us will be walking back.

With the loading complete, Abu and Jalus shake hands. "Tomorrow," says Jalus to Abu.

"Yes, tomorrow," says the lion, before walking back to the lead cart and getting up onto the driver's seat. I take this chance to glance around. The people Abu is buying from look pleased. Abu says something to Akay privately, who nods. The driver of the second cart gets up, and the rest follow beside them as the carts are driven out of the warehouse courtyard onto the street beyond.

It's already late evening when we reach the city gate. It is guarded by two fennecs and a jackal. They seem bored but wave us over to collect taxes. Abu hops down, and then passes them a certificate for the goods he's bringing into the city proper. The jackal takes the paper and looks it over. The wolves try and look disinterested in the exchange, but I walk up hoping to listen to the conversation.

"A bit late to be conducting trade, don't you think?" asks one of the fennecs.

"I had a busy day in the market," responds Abu.

"How may amphorae of wine do you have?" asks the jackal.

"Twenty-four."

He nods and looks over us all. "Quite a group you have here for transporting wine."

"I promised them an amphora to share. Everyone is looking for a good drink and doesn't want to give their compatriots a head start."

"Right," says the jackal, a bit of doubt in his voice. He squints at the paperwork by lanternlight. "Have you paid your customs dues?"

"The importer paid those already."

The jackal hands over the paperwork to one of the fennecs and then walks over to the lead cart.

"Hey, my goods are already paid for. The paper says so."

"I know what your paperwork says," responds the jackal, glancing over the cart. "Twelve in this cart and twelve in the other?"

"Yes."

The jackal nods and walks back to Abu. "Your certificate says you have twenty amphorae."

The lion opens his mouth and then closes it. "That's an honest mistake on the part of my supplier."

"Maybe it is, but you still owe the Sultan eight fals. Each amphora is two copper."

Abu grumbles. He pulls out another coin purse and digs out four fals and a quarter silver dirham. "They promised me they'd taken care of that."

The jackal squints at Abu. I can tell he wants to ask more questions, but he just shrugs. Abu counts out the money and the jackal just holds out his paw, which Abu drops the money into. The jackal glances at the coins and then hands them to one of the fennecs who slips it into a satchel, while the other fennec marks the tariff down.

"Have a good night," says the jackal, waving us through.

We pass back into the city proper, and I whisper to Ilayda. "Was that planned?"

She shakes her head. "The certificate for the wine was supposed to be right."

I nod, thinking for a moment, and then I continue. "But this isn't wine, is it?"

The wolf glances at me, and she speaks in a low growl. "It is better you not ask that question, yena."

My ears lay back, and I just nod again. Great, here I am to guard jars of who knows what exactly. They just look like ordinary wine or olive oil jars, but the smell is off. Everything about this is making my hackles rise. Seven guards are too many for transporting wine and olive oil around the Sultanate. In Aksu, it's downright obscene.

I glance around at our party. Everyone has their ears up. They walk purposefully and calmly, but I can see a slight edge to them all. Their eyes dart to look around corners, probing the streets. At first, I thought they were being good guards, but there is something else. They know what we're hauling back. I'm the only one here in the dark, but I can't puzzle out that smell.

The city though is quiet, oblivious to us. It's dark, and Aksu has moved toward late evening. We cross the Grand Bridge to the other side, after skirting around the Malhaa District. Here the city is alive with merchants and vendors in the square and cafes that serve as the city's cultural center. We don't go directly through the area though, but along the edge, shadows just outside the edge of the lanterns' light.

Surprisingly, we are only carrying three lanterns. Abu has one on the front cart, Ilayda is carrying one, and one of the wolves I don't know the name of is in the back carrying one.

As we approach the warehouse, the tension in everyone is palpable, yet it stands silently waiting for us. The street outside is deserted. Abu pulls up the lead cart and hops down.

"Ilayda, Akay, do a perimeter check," Abu calls out.

They nod and trot off. Since Ilayda doesn't motion for me to follow her, I stay put. The second cart pulls up, and the other wolves all stand around waiting, ears perked. I stand slightly off to the side, unsure what might happen.

Abu sweeps his eyes over everyone and pulls out the warehouse key. "We'll wait for the check to finish."

Everyone mills about. A minute later, Akay and Ilayda came back.

"Everything looks fine," Ilayda says.

Abu nods and walks up to the door and unlocks it, pushing open the heavy door. "Unhook the carts and bring them in."

"You're late with the delivery, Abu," says a familiar voice from inside.

"Rigel," says the lion, lashing his tail. "I wasn't expecting you here."

I'm standing near the door, but I slink back so the caracal can't see me. Hopefully the wind favors keeping my scent away from him. As my hand falls down to my sword, Akay catches my motion and gives me a confused look.

"I know, but I wanted to make sure things were going well, since you didn't hire any extra guards."

"Oh, I found someone I can rely on."

"You did?" he says, surprised. "Who?"

"An old employee of the clan. He happened to be available."

There is silence for a moment. "Who did you hire, Abu?"

"You look worried, brother, why is that? I found someone I could trust."

"Who did you hire?" He doesn't sound happy.

"My friend here," says the lion, turning to find me, "Naji."

I step forward, and Rigel opens his mouth, then closes it. He is shocked to see me. "Good to see you again, Rigel," I say.

Rigel looks at me, and his ears sweep back, and his pupils dilate, mouth falling open. "You!" he says loudly enough that everyone can hear.

Abu glances between us, surprised at the reaction. "You two know each other, I take it?"

I smile, showing my fangs, seeing if I can make the caracal flinch. "We go back years."

"Many, many years," says Rigel, gaining some composure. He reaches up to smooth down the fur on the back of his neck. "How did you find out about this job?" he tries to ask me nonchalantly, but I can tell the pitch of his voice is off.

I step closer to Rigel, just to see if he'll flinch. "Naima. Her job leads tend to turn out much better than yours."

His ears flick, but he glances at Abu. "You told Naima we were hiring?"

"No, I told Sirius. He said he would find us someone. I told him to be discreet, and he told Naima."

I don't know who Sirius is, but I don't care right now. I want to see if I can get under the cat's fur. "You don't trust our old associate, Rigel?"

He gives me a dark glance. "I don't trust coincidences."

"Nor do I, anymore," I respond.

Abu clears his throat. "You two don't like each other, I take it."

"After that business with Aziz, no."

"Aziz?" Abu narrows his eyes at me. I can see him reaching down reflexively with his hand. "You know Aziz?"

Shit, I dropped a name I shouldn't have. "Know? Not exactly."

Rigel chuckles. "He knew you, but things didn't work out between you, I hear."

"Apparently," I respond.

Abu flicks an ear. "Go unload the cart," he says to me, and I step away to help the wolves, turning this over in my mind. As I walk over to where they've already started taking off amphorae, I glance back. Rigel has his hands up, shaking his head, and I realize Abu has pointed at me. The lion shrugs and walks over to the cart we're unloading, talking to Rigel.

"We'll get everything unloaded, and then we wait until we hear word from them," remarks the lion.

"Actually, I'm not sure we want to unload," says Rigel to Abu. "Even with Naji, without Aziz, we don't have the added security we were hoping for here."

"We'll have to make do. Jalus said people have been sniffing around asking questions, but if we lay low, it should blow over."

"Right, but we talked about the risk. People know about this warehouse," says Rigel. "We should move everything tonight to the safe house before they become suspicious. I've made the arrangements already and everything is in place as we planned."

"Already? That was quick," says Abu.

"Being short staffed, I had to make do."

"Then let us make haste and be done with this." The lion speaks to all of us. "Change of plans. Let's take everything to the safe house."

Akay looks at the jar in his arms, and the wolf lays his ears back. "That's not what we agreed upon."

"If someone gets suspicious, they'll come here," says Rigel.

Ilayda chimes in. "The warehouse is well protected. It's easy for us to keep it secure."

"It's not robbery I'd be concerned about," says Rigel.

My ears flick at that. Wait, if I'm not to guard this stuff from robbers, why am I being employed here?

"Jalus is a good man," says Akay, putting the amphora back on the cart. "We can trust him."

"Jalus will sell us out if his own tail is on the line," says Abu. "He is not clan. This is a business for him. We can't expect him to hold the same loyalties we do."

Everyone murmurs their agreement, although one of the wolves who was at the market whispers something to Akay I can't catch.

"If you think it prudent," says Akay. "Though, we need to tell the elders about this."

"Of course," says Abu. "But first we need to move the goods. Let's get everything back on here."

A few minutes later, we're loaded back up. Rigel locks the warehouse up, joining our party. Surprisingly, he opts to walk with me and Ilayda in the middle of the group between the two carts.

"So…," I offer, after walking in silence for a few minutes.

He glances at me. "You and I will settle later. Now is not the time."

"I like how you think I should just pass that off."

He hisses at me. "You think you are so clever, don't you?"

I snort. "I told you, I was looking for local work."

"Well, it seems you found it," he says dismissively.

"You don't seem surprised to see me alive," I say with a lower voice.

He falters briefly in his pace, before he resumes walking. "It's not my problem anymore."

"Not your problem, huh? Is my life that cheap to you then?"

He growls. "Now is not the time, Naji."

It's not, but I can't get over what he did. "Just tell me why you did it. I think I deserve that much."

The caracal chuckles. "Sometimes you are still as naive as the day I met you. In some ways you haven't changed at all, and I am in awe of that fact."

"At least I didn't follow the path you took," I snap. I glance away from Rigel and can tell Ilayda is listening to every word we say by the way her ears are cocked in our direction.

"We're both a long way from filching food from market stalls and sleeping in dirty piles of hay. You can pretend you are so much nobler than I am, but I know you. I know your history."

"Nobler? Hardly. I have not forgotten our shared past. I've tried hard to make up for what happened, Rigel, but it can't be changed."

He shrugs and we just keep walking, falling into silence. I'm following the wagon to wherever this safe house is. We seem to be heading into the city instead of out of it. The night air is warm, but pleasant. We pass only a few people out on the street. Many houses still have lights in their windows, but the sounds are muted over the creaking of the carts.

The road we're on ends at the river, and we turn toward the Grand Bridge that links the two parts of Aksu. Usually it's busy, traffic constantly flowing across it, but it's late now. There are still people crossing under the lanterns along its length, but it's much more deserted than the two other times we crossed tonight.

As we're turning onto the bridge, Rigel speaks up. "You want to know why I did it?"

My ears fall back. "Because you still blame me for what happened to Isim," I respond.

He shakes his head. "Every day that goes by, I miss him. I loved him, and I will forever love him, but it's not Isim I did this for, and not for myself either."

"Then who did you do this for?"

"I did this for Zayn. I know you, Naji. You're just like me. I've worked with you enough to know where this all leads. We don't get to just walk away. When Isim died, I realized people like us shouldn't have lovers because we hurt them. Lovers are a liability in our line of work, and it's better not to put down roots. I did this so Zayn could get away from you before you got him killed. Apparently, it was too late to save him."

My mind balks at what Rigel just told me. "Are you insane?"

"We're cut from the same cloth, Naji. We're not good people."

"I took Zayn out of an abusive situation, a life without hope, and I've given him hope. A future!"

"Yes, but at what cost," says the caracal. "You made him a murderer, just like us."

"I... I didn't do that. You did that."

We've stopped walking and have to step aside as the second cart passes us. Ilayda is watching us silently, having also stepped aside. Her ears are pinned back. I think some of the others are looking at us, but my focus is on Rigel.

He laughs. "I only did what I needed to do to save my brothers and sisters. The fact things connected so nicely was a coincidence I couldn't pass up."

"What do you mean, Rigel," Ilayda asks him.

"I'm saving us all from ourselves. The clan needs to be protected from itself. Abu knows this too," he says pointing toward the first cart. "We just need to—"

Rigel's words are cut off by the sound of commotion and the horses panicking. Someone screams, and as I turn, I see the front wagon has veered to the side, away from a small fire up ahead. With the sickening sound of crunching wood and shattering ceramic, it tips over.

Without thinking, I'm sprinting toward it, Ilayda in motion next to me. There is more screaming and suddenly I hear the sound of steel crashing on steel. It's an ambush! I stop to get my bearings when suddenly a bright light erupts as a whoosh of fire springs from the overturned cart. On the other side of the fire, I can see two figures with swords drawn, and another that shouldn't be there. Zayn.

The Grand Bridge
(Zayn)

After Naji left, I decided to read from *By the Lamp's Light* in the courtyard. I was only a few pages in and already the fox who narrates the story was caught up in a sticky situation in bed with two other men when Fadel found me and said he could take the night off. He suggested we go out to a café he knows, and I jumped at the idea.

Now seated under an arched vault that is open to the street, just off the main square of the Malhaa District, I'm so glad we did this. A good-sized crowd is all around us talking, drinking coffee, and smoking hookah. No one is paying us any mind, and that's reassuring. The waiter delivers us a kettle with two small cups. Fadel tips him a copper coin and settles back as the waiter leaves.

"This is exciting," I say to the fennec, looking around. The café is bright and well-lit with large lanterns hanging from chains at the center of each dome that makes up the arcade. Small oil lamps have been placed on each table. Over the din of conversation, I can hear someone singing along to a lute, possibly from the street outside. On the other side of the road is a store selling lanterns that stays open late to show off their merchandise. Lamps of all sizes and shapes glow brightly in the dark, and the glittering glass is a magical backdrop.

"This has been one of my favorite places for years. It has the type of atmosphere I try and replicate at the Blue Door," says Fadel, pouring both of us coffee. "You must try this."

I pick up the small ceramic cup and blow on the it to cool it down. I take a long sip, tasting the thick, sweetened coffee. The beverage is strong, and I can feel the shock of it in my nose. The moment I set the cup down, Fadel pours more in to top me off.

"Well, what do you think, Zayn? They have some of the best coffee in Aksu here."

"It's very strong," I say, blinking at the fox. "Much richer than what we got at home."

"Well, of course. If you are going to stay up late talking business, you want a good cup."

"I'm sure. Do you come here often?"

The fox shakes his head. "Not like I used to. I don't have the time. My focus is on the Blue Door. If I want, I can make coffee at home and sit in the courtyard, but rarely will I be left alone when I do that. I come here when I can get some time to myself."

My ears fall. "You didn't have to take me out."

"I should have gone to the market with you earlier. Anyway, you wanted to see the city, and I could spare to be gone for an evening."

I'm curious what type of hours he keeps. Fadel always seems to be working. "Do you ever take a day off?"

He shakes his head. "Normally, it doesn't feel like work. I enjoy the dancers. I enjoy the atmosphere." He smiles. "I'm practically married to the place."

"That seems a bit lonely."

The fennec chuckles and waves dismissively. "I get to make people happy, and I have many of the best people I know right there with me. Why should I be upset about that? My family is there."

"I guess thinking of it like that, it isn't really work."

Fadel picks up his coffee and takes a sip. "Indeed. Like any family, it has its tiring moments, but it's a good life. I think you'll like it here in Aksu, once things settle down. The city always has new things to explore. I know the last few days have been incredibly difficult, but it will be good once this blows over."

"I'm sure it will, but I have a lot to think about."

"Of course, but in my house, you'll be safe."

"You don't have to do this for me. I'm not the only person who works for you."

He shrugs. "You are Naji's lover, and I have a soft spot in my heart for him. I have need of a permanent guard for the Blue Door, so I'm hoping he takes me up on the offer of taking the position."

"I didn't know you offered him a job."

"I asked him before he left today. The incident with Rigel makes obvious what I should have done already. I just have to find the right person, and I think Naji is it."

"You don't need to hire a guard for my safety."

The fennec chuckles. "You aren't the only person who comes to the inn whose safety I need to be concerned about."

"Oh?" I inquire, but Fadel waves his hands.

"Do not worry about it. The Blue Door is my home, and I must protect it. Most of the staff have been rejected or stigmatized for being like us. The patrons we serve are looking to find a welcoming family they can be a part of, even if for just one night, and that's what we do. The mithly have come to see the Blue Door as something special, and I'm not about ready to see that threatened."

I realize what I have done has possibly endangered everything he holds dear. "I'm sorry if I brought trouble upon your home, Fadel."

He lifts his cup up and takes a sip. "Some of the blame falls to Naji, but I gave him a stern talking to already. You got put in a situation you shouldn't have been in, and I consider what you did for the hyena very brave."

I've only known the fennec for a few days, but I can already see he has a big heart. Hell, I've known Naji for a little over two weeks and I bought him a book of poetry? What am I thinking? What am I even doing here in this mess? So much is going on it's making my head spin a little. "I guess."

"It was," says the fox, as the server brings us food. We let the conversation lapse as the server sets down a plate piled high with kebabs and another of hummus and pita. He fetches each of us our own plate, and a dish of tzatziki sauce to go with the grilled kebabs. The meat is spiced with cumin, paprika, and garlic. The rich scent makes my stomach rumble and my tail wags happily.

We thank the server, who heads to his next table. I take a kebab for myself as Fadel speaks again.

"Not everyone can think on their feet like that. It's an admirable trait."

"A good jackal is always light on their feet."

Fadel nods and takes a piece of warm pita and dips it into the hummus. "I hope Naji can figure out what game Rigel is playing. Aziz and Rigel obviously had some type of deal going on," says the fennec, waving the piece of bread at me before he pops it in his muzzle.

"Hopefully," I say, spooning some sauce onto my meat. "I have to ask this, though. Do you think the city guard will investigate what happened to Aziz?"

"If they find out they might."

My ears droop. If I hadn't come to Aksu with Naji, would this have happened? There is blood on my paws now, just like Rigel and Naji.

Obviously Fadel can see that I'm thinking about this. "Being you're not from Aksu, it could be an issue, but I think it will blow over." He looks around then whispers, "Plus, my moral compass tells me what you did was right."

"Thank you," I say stiffly.

"To put yourself out there for the one you love, it's a bold and noble thing."

"I…" I start and stop. I take a deep breath. "I could not leave anyone who reached out to me and said they could help me in my moment of need. Certainly not Naji."

He nods softly.

I consider for a moment, thinking about how much I want to say. Part of me wants to be quiet, but I also want to move on. I want to move past my old life. "Do you know what I used to do in Zaptu, Fadel?"

"You danced, and you said you worked as a whore," he says. When I don't say anything he tilts his head. "There is more?"

"Yes, there was a man who thought he could own me."

"Own you?" he says, confused.

I scoot my chair around to his side, and I take his paw. Gently I pull up my shirt and guide him to touch my back. He looks confused at this.

"Trace your digits through my fur, Fadel."

With a strange expression, he does. "You have scars."

I nod. He feels along my back. "They don't stop?"

"There are scars that cover my entire back."

"You've been beaten," he says in shock.

"No, whipped. Whipped for the pleasure of one man."

The expression across his face is a dark one. "This is why I don't let anyone touch my staff if they don't wish to be touched. All this for a few silvers?"

"Some gold dinars, but the price was just better. It was the best coin I could earn."

He shudders. "I would never allow something to happen like that."

I look at my food and then back up at Fadel. "It's taken me time to admit this, but I let it happen. Usman, the man who arranged the dances in Zaptu, would have stopped it, if I ever told him. When all you can get are table scraps to eat, day after day, you will take a beating to eat like a rich man."

"Why did you leave then?"

"I always wanted to do more than just survive. Naji said there was a path for me where I didn't have to taste the whip on my sundered flesh, so I took it." I pick up my coffee to steady myself and gulp some down. It's become a little cooler, but I don't really taste it.

"And I will make sure you stay on that path," says Fadel, gently squeezing my paw.

I look at him. His ears are focused on me, and he looks genuinely concerned. "Thank you," I haltingly say. "It's not easy for me to accept help."

The fennec's bushy tail wags slowly to reassure me. "You wouldn't be the first I know like that, but you deserve a life just like everyone else."

I nod, and we lapse into silence. After a minute he lets go of my paw, and I scoot my chair back. We eat in silence and watch the crowd. Some striped hyenas are at another table, smoking hookah and playing a dice game. Occasionally they laugh. A caracal couple that appear very much in love walk by the open-air storefront. Life feels easier here than it was in Zaptu, and yet my problems here are just as intense.

"Do you think you'll stay with Naji?" Fadel asks me.

My ears shoot up. "What type of question is that?" I say, surprised.

He laughs. "A direct one, but one I think you've pondered. With all that you've been through, I don't fault you for seeking the right path for yourself. I want you both to find what you're looking for."

"I don't really know. Everything has been happening so fast, I want to say I need time to think things through. Yet I do think I'm in love now. Just today, I bought him a book of poetry."

Fadel gives me a hearty chuckle. "A traditional courting gift, I see. That sounds as if it's becoming rather serious."

"The book seemed right," I say, looking at my half-eaten plate of food.

"Then I think it is."

"I hope so. I'm doing something I've never done here and letting myself live. Aksu is a beautiful place to do that in."

"It is the crown jewel of Khalin, but it has its problems. Like any city, this place has its rough spots."

"Of course, but the city is wonderful." There is a feeling of endless potential I've felt as I've walked these streets. There is life here unlike what there was back in Zaptu. Do I need to stay with Naji? I turn that over in my mind. My life had been cheap before he came into it. Now it has value. His simple gift of giving it back to me is something I can't just cast aside.

"Oh, don't get me wrong, I love Aksu. I've traveled to other parts of the sultanate, but this, this is home," says the fennec.

I nod and pick up my last kebab. A stray thought occurs to me. "Fadel, why are you still single with so many eligible men at your fingertips?"

The fennec smiles before he responds. "A little too fussy, I guess. I never thought I would get into a committed relationship, and owning the Blue Door, there have been plenty of opportunities for me to sample what's out there."

"Is that why you run the place?" I give him a grin, showing off my fangs.

He chuckles. "Maybe at first, but now it is out of devotion to people who are like me. There is more to life than just sex."

That I know for sure. "I was just curious, is all."

"Perhaps I will someday. I'm willing to settle down now. I already really have; I just am devoted to those around me."

His big ears are up, and his tail is wagging. "Don't worry, if Naji can find someone, I know I can."

"I'm not just someone, now, am I?"

He shakes his head and laughs. "Not at all. I see something special in you."

I don't know what that is, but maybe there is something to it. I pick the meat off the kebab and chew, thinking about it. I don't know what my future is, but it could be bright indeed here in Aksu.

❧

The river is beautiful in the night. Bits of lantern light from the distant bank reflect off the water, while stars shimmer above us. I can hear the soft murmur of the water and the sound of grasshoppers singing in the grasses that cover the river's bank. The street is quiet, a few going about their business. Fadel walks next to me, enjoying the cool night air as we stroll down the street.

"It amazes me how big the river is," I remark to the fennec.

He chuckles. "The size of the river is not something I really think about. Being born here, it's always been a part of my life."

"There is so much water on this side of the mountains, it boggles my mind."

"I guess we take that for granted here, but we shouldn't. The Zaharani gives life to the city by watering the lands around it. Without this water, Aksu would be nothing more than a dry bit of sand."

"I wish Usman and his wife could see this. Hearing stories is one thing, but actually seeing it is a completely different experience."

"The small wonders we see often lose meaning to us, while the small wonders we never see capture our imagination," Fadel remarks. "Speaking of that," adds the fennec, "I will take you to see one of my friend's stores which specializes in coffee and tea."

"That would be nice. Tomorrow?"

"Actually, his store is just up the street here," says the fennec. "Sometimes he stays open late and entertains people out of his little shop. With luck, he'll still be there."

The shop Fadel mentioned turns out to be a small, one room store near the foot of the great bridge. An awning hangs across the front and outside a few chairs are placed around a table. A small charcoal brazier is burning nearby. At the table, a red fox is sitting talking to a caracal. Both look up when we approach, and the fox waves to Fadel.

"Fadel!" the red fox calls, "out for some night air, I see."

"My friend here, Zayn, needed to get out. How goes things for you, Abdellah?"

"Oh, not good. Business is slow, as you can see," he says, sweeping his hands.

"Perhaps you should open earlier, and not stay up all night."

He chuckles. "And miss my chance to see you?"

"You could always come by the Blue Door, after you close for the day."

The fox gestures at himself. "I could not put such beauty so close and yet so far beyond the grasp of your patrons."

"I'm sure a few of them would like to try and change that."

The red fox shakes a finger at the fennec. "It would be your duty to protect me."

"It would be difficult, but I think we could manage. Now, what do you have tonight that might entice my coinage from my purse?"

"Always so forward," says the fox with a smirk, as he gets up. "I like a customer who gets down to business. You are in luck, my friend. I do indeed have something that should entice you." The red fox lets his tail flick.

"Most certainly you should," replies the fennec, following the fox inside the small store. Sacks of coffee along with bricks of tea are stacked around the room. A table with a scale sits to one side.

The red fox steps over to his table and picks up some sheets of paper. "What do you need today? I've got some coffee in from the south a few days ago, along with a couple bricks of a very high-quality black tea from the east."

"Do you have any left of your last shipment of coffee from Batu?" asks Fadel. "That was quite good."

"How long ago was that?"

"About four weeks ago. You sold me three sacksful."

He chuckles. "You are out of that already? I thought your clientele drank far more wine than coffee."

"They do, but we managed to get through one sack and are on the second. Business has picked up in the afternoon."

Abdellah glances at the wall of coffee sacks. "I've got two more. Both sacks or just one?"

Fadel chuckles. "I'll take both. Can you have your man bring it by tomorrow?"

Abdellah makes a note as he talks. "Of course, that will be two gold and two silver, due on delivery. I'll send the porter around tomorrow. Will you be staying for something to drink? I can put on some coffee."

"You know, you are wasting your talents here. You should have at least opened a cafe," remarks Fadel.

"Ah, but is that not a cafe outside?"

"I think that counts as the worst cafe in Aksu. One table and four chairs do not make a grand coffee house," says Fadel.

"Let us ask an impartial observer," the red fox says, turning to me. "Is that not the most intimate, most exclusive cafe in all of Aksu you have seen?"

I shuffle, unsure what to say. "I guess?"

He puts a hand to his chest. "As the owner of one of the most exclusive cafes in all Aksu, and with you as a guest at this establishment, I am deeply hurt by your hesitation."

"Do not pay attention to him," remarks Fadel. "Abdellah is dramatic like this about everything."

The fox sweeps his hands open. "Me, dramatic? I think you have me mistaken, kind sir, for someone else. Someone with fur redder than my own."

"Your fur is quite red," remarks Fadel.

He chuckles. "A dusty orange is not a bright red, but I would not expect a fennec to know that."

Fadel snorts, but Abdellah continues to me, "But I would be remiss to not confess to one as new as you that Fadel's accusations against my honor are not baseless."

The caracal who was outside has come inside. "Abdellah likes to put on a good show," he interjects.

The red fox bows. "I have been caught black pawed," he says, holding out a hand of dark fur.

I chuckle and shake his hand, and he comes closer. We exchange formal cheek kisses, and then he breaks apart. "I believe I didn't quite catch the name."

"That's because you were too busy putting on airs," remarks the caracal.

"Zayn," I say.

"Ah, a pleasure. I'm Abdellah, and this here is my friend Berat."

"Nice to meet you," says the caracal, and we shake hands and also exchange cheek kisses.

"If you would let me prepare a fresh pot of coffee, we shall respite."

"I am not sure I can handle more coffee. I'm already feeling the pot Fadel and I drank."

"Then a soothing cup of mint tea," offers the fox, "and some fresh air?"

"I don't want to trouble you," says Fadel. "I imagine you are going to go home at some point."

"My wife told me not to come home anymore, if I am going to keep making jokes like I have been making, so I sleep on the floor here now."

Fadel blinks. "I didn't know you were having marital problems."

"Absolutely," says the fox with a grin, "since the beginning. She married me, and it's been all downhill for her since then!"

Fadel presses his hand to the side of his face. "Oh, Abdellah."

"She is having dinner with some of her friends," offers Berat. "I'm keeping Abdellah company while she is enjoying herself."

"Very well, I might add! It has not been a lost evening though. We even just made some money selling a poor fennec coffee he probably doesn't need."

"You are in rare form," remarks Fadel.

Abdellah shrugs and fetches a tea kettle from a shelf under the table. "I don't know how she does it. Azra is a saint. I'd have divorced me if I were her, but she likes a good joke just as much as I do."

"You still could open a cafe," says Fadel.

"I'd need a different location," says the fox, as we all step outside. "I rather like my view of the traffic crossing the bridge. Plus, it brings in good business during the day."

I glance over toward the bridge. It's the same one Aziz took me across. Abdellah's store fronts the road that goes along the river. It's a few buildings down from that intersection where the street following the river intersects the thoroughfare that crosses the bridge.

"Is there a lot of traffic?" I ask. Both times I've seen it have been late at night.

"Oh, yes," Berat says, pointing to a lantern bobbing across the stone bridge attached to a pole above a cart. "Even now there is traffic. It's very busy during the day and even at night, people need to cross. I gather you aren't from around here?"

"No. I was telling Fadel earlier I'm surprised how wide the river is here. I grew up in the desert."

"The Zaharani is the lifeblood of the city," says Abdellah, as he fills the kettle from a waterskin. "If you want to go admire it from the bridge, it will take a bit to boil the water and prepare the tea."

I glance at Fadel. "Actually, I wouldn't mind doing that." I had to keep up with Aziz when we walked across. I wasn't in the right state of mind when I returned either, sopping wet after Naji dragged me through the shallows along the riverbank on our escape from Aziz's house. We also used a different bridge to cross the river then. It would be nice to go and just experience the flow of the water under my feet, peaceful and serene.

"I don't see why not," says Fadel. "A brief respite from Abdellah's jokes might be good for you."

"Hey!" exclaims the red fox, as the caracal chuckles.

I grin. "Be right back then," I say with a wag, and head down toward the main road, leaving the store. I pass a shuttered shop and a temple, with its dome and tower, that occupies the corner fronting the main road. The road is wide with a well-worn and rutted stone surface. A leopard couple with three kits in tow are coming across, while a cart carrying sacks of something is heading in the opposite direction. I follow the cart partway across and then step against the parapet, to watch the dark water flowing under the arch.

The water is quiet, but I can hear it splashing against the abutments. A little light from the stars and lanterns in the city reflect against the water, but mostly it is solid and dark. I cock my ears trying to listen to the gentle babble of the water. It's soothing and very relaxing. I feel at peace here, alone on the bridge with the stars shining above me. Aksu is my home now, and moments like this are the sweet treats that are going to help me put the last few days behind me.

I'm so transfixed by the water, I don't notice them.

"I believe we've met already," comes a voice I've heard before.

I turn. The tiger who worked for Aziz is there. He smirks, and as I move to back up. I bump into someone else.

"Oh no," says the person behind me. I freeze as I recognize the voice to be the fox who worked with Aziz. He's carrying a lantern and thrusts it into my face. "Achmed and I mean to have a word with you."

Shit, they have me cornered. Fadel is too far away at the store for me to call out and get his attention. I try and bluff. "Do I know you?" I offer.

The tiger chuckles. "It took me a minute, but I recognize your scent," he says. "You even still have a hint of that rose perfume. You're that girl from the Silver Shroud, but you aren't a girl at all."

"As you can see, I am all man."

"Come, jackal," says the tiger, walking up close, "you didn't think we were going to let you go now, do you?"

I straighten up. "So, you want to do this here?"

The tiger chuckles and puts two hands on my shoulders.

"No, but we appreciate you coming here. We're not going to pass this chance up."

I struggle against the tiger's grip, but he digs his claws in. "You'll wait with us, and don't make me cut you down. If I have to, I'll make sure you end up floating in the river."

"Bleeding, I would like to add," says the fox, getting close to me so he can keep his voice down.

"What do you want with me?" I whisper.

They exchange glances and then nod. "You'll find out soon enough, but I take your appearance here as a good omen."

I gulp. I don't want to know what they're planning. At least they can't kill me out here in public. I hope.

Ș

They usher me off the bridge the way I came, but in the opposite direction on the frontage road from where Abdellah's shop is. Once we're a couple feet away from the bridge, they stop and wait, with me squeezed between them, for something or someone. They do not talk, but watch the road, each with a hand on me. I pray that Fadel or Abdellah notices my absence and someone comes looking for me.

I'm also kicking myself for not taking my kilij with me tonight. I was so excited to get out I didn't think of it.

"I can't believe I thought he was a girl, Achmed," says the fox to the tiger.

"I can see the resemblance. You're one of those cocksuckers just like Naji is, huh?" The tiger pokes me.

"Does that really matter?" I ask him. Their friend Rigel is one too, but maybe they don't know that.

"Maybe. I've heard they're just as good, and I could give it a go," Achmed says.

I growl.

"Now you've pissed him off," says the fox with a chuckle.

I've decided if they are going to try and haul me away, I'll make a run for it. There are still a number of people crossing. Indeed, why are we just waiting here? This is a strange place to keep a hostage.

The tiger snorts. "He'd probably bite anyway." He grabs my muzzle, holding it shut. "If you bite, I will make sure you die in the most painful way possible."

I look up at him. If I get a chance, I'm going to bite his paw.

"Achmed, stop playing with the jackal. You are not going to put him on his knees."

The tiger laughs. "He doesn't know that." He lets go, but keeps a hand on my shoulder, digging his claws into it.

The fox looks back across the bridge. He keeps watching the traffic. "They're late, you know."

"Don't worry, Rigel will be along soon enough," says the tiger, flicking his tail.

Rigel is meeting them here? That makes sense why they're waiting. If I'm careful, I might learn something and get out of this alive. The tiger grip on me is firm and tight. He may have broken the skin with his claw.

"I see them!" says the fox. "Abu is riding in the front cart. I can't see Rigel, but he must be with them."

Abu is the lion Naji says he was going to work for. Why would Rigel be with the Aragvi clan? Wait, where is Naji then?

The tiger nods and straightens up. He pulls a dagger out from under his tunic. "All right, jackal, we're going to take a walk across the bridge."

The fox picks up the lantern. "Can you handle the jackal?"

"Absolutely," says the tiger.

"Time to go," says the fox.

"Just walk straight ahead, jackal, and I won't cut you open."

I nod and start across the bridge, with the two of them behind me. Near the center of the bridge, we approach a wagon, and I see a lion riding on it looking out ahead. I think this is the Abu who they mentioned, but he doesn't try and hail the two behind me. Behind the cart, a couple of wolves are walking, and then there is a second cart behind that. I hesitate, trying to figure out what's going on, and the tiger pokes me with the tip of the dagger to keep me walking.

"I see the others coming," Achmed whispers. "Ready?"

"Do it," says the fox.

From behind, I feel Achmed give me a shove forward into the path of the hooves of the incoming cart. The lion driving the cart pulls the reins of the horses to one side, and the cart veers. I'm knocked down as one of the horses hits me in the shoulder. Then I see the fox throw the lantern in front of the horses.

The two horses pulling the cart startle with panicked whinnies and pull away from the fire, kicking back. I'm on the ground trying to see what might be broken when the bucking horses pulling the cart causes it to tilt over. Amphorae fall onto the bridge and shatter. A foul, unfamiliar smell overtakes me.

A battle erupts on the bridge between my two captors and the wolves. There is shouting and I can hear steel striking steel. I am starting to get to my feet when suddenly a fire bright as day engulfs the cart, and burning liquid begins pouring across the bridge toward me.

The Guard Captain
(Naji)

As the fire spreads across the bridge, it hits me what we're transporting. These amphorae don't contain wine or olive oil, they contain war fire, a special mixture of naphtha and resin made for the Sultan's army. How it's made and the recipe used is a secret that the Sultan and his Grand Vizier protect. I don't know who stole this, but the city guard has to be looking for it.

Of course, half of it is now gone, engulfed in a growing column of flame between me and Zayn. Heat radiates toward me as the fire reaches for the sky. The horses are trying to get away from it, pulling the overturned flaming cart across the bridge until the shaft of wood connecting them to the flaming wagon separates. They go running past me in sheer terror dragging straps and wood behind them.

In the middle of this, on the other side of the cart, I catch a flash of Zayn, scrambling away from the burning liquid, against the parapet of the bridge. I sprint toward him, not caring about the shouts of the wolves or Rigel. I see the jackal scrambling, his feet on fire, and then I see him teeter, and tip over the parapet, taking a flash of flame with him.

As I reach the edge of the bridge, I hear the sound of swords clashing behind me. I glance over my shoulder, and I see hooded figures scrambling forward. I catch the sight of a dark muzzle and the white tip of a thin tail fighting one of the wolves before my attention is drawn back to the sound of panic from the water.

I can't reach where Zayn jumped due to the fire, so I scan the dark river. Light from the blaze reflects off the water, and I spot two arms thrashing about below me, fifty feet away.

Without hesitation, I scramble onto the parapet. I lost Isim to hesitation, I won't lose Zayn to it. Before I can process that thought, I'm diving into the river, hitting the water hard. The drop isn't that far, but I hit with such force it still takes me a few seconds before I get back to the surface.

"Zayn!" I shout. Where is he? I know he doesn't know how to swim.

"Na-gah!" comes a garbled reply. I can see Zayn's flailing silhouetted against the reflections on the river's surface.

I push forward through the water. When I was young, I used to go swimming back home in a pool by a small waterfall with the other kids. This is not a small pool. The Zaharani slowly flows to the sea. The channel is deep, and I can feel the current tugging at me. My sword in its scabbard and the loose clothing I'm wearing are trying to impede me, but I'm much stronger than that young pup who used to swim with friends when it was hot.

Stroke by stroke, I head toward the thrashing limbs I see in the water. I cannot fail. I would sooner drown myself than lose someone else.

"I've got you," I say when I reach Zayn, grabbing him by the scruff of his neck. Panicked, he tries to climb on top of me, pushing me down. "St—," I yell before I take a mouthful of river water. I have to push him off me so I can get my head above the surface.

I break the surface with a gasp. "Let me do this!" I scream, then I grab him from behind again, and start dragging him toward the nearest bank of the Zaharani. He stops fighting me, at least. The going is slow, and I have trouble keeping us both above water. Even before I reach the bank three figures are waving at me, and I see one dive into the river, swimming towards me. At first, I'm not sure who this is, but then I hear a voice.

"Bring him over here."

"Fadel?" I call out, and a moment later the fennec reaches me.

"Naji?" he replies, surprised, as he reaches me.

He gets on one side of Zayn and helps me get the jackal to the shore. With his help it's easier, and I feel relieved when my feet touch the slimy bottom of the river.

"You okay?" he asks Zayn as we're pulling him up onto the bank.

The jackal coughs, and I hold him as he kneels in the shallows of the bank and spits up water.

"Yes," he finally gasps. "What was that? I've never seen anything like that before."

"That is war fire," I say, looking back to the bridge. I can see the fire is already dying down, but I see a number of lanterns on the bridge now. "It's highly flammable, and if I had to hazard a guess, I'm going to say it was stolen."

"A good reason to hire guards for," says Fadel.

"An excellent reason," I say, climbing up the riverbank. It appears people have come out of their houses and are gathering, trying to figure out what happened. A red fox and a caracal wearing long kaftans are coming toward us.

"Fadel, are you okay?" says one of them.

"I'm fine, Abdellah," says the fennec.

Ah, that's why they're here. I've heard Fadel mention his friend Abdellah before.

"What do we do now?" Zayn asks me, hobbling up the riverbank.

"We should leave," I whisper to Zayn, "before the guard…" I glance toward where I hear someone running down the street. "Never mind," I add.

"You there! Stop!"

I'm certainly not going to run away. I'm also dripping wet, so it's not like I can pretend I just happened to come out at the sound of battle. I wait for the wolf hurrying down the street to reach me. "What can I do for you?" I ask him cautiously.

He looks me over, noting the sword and the fact I'm soaked. "Were you with the caravan?" he says, pointing to the bridge.

"Yes, but they just hired me to guard the shipment. They never told me what it was."

The wolf lifts his muzzle. "We'll need to investigate what you knew."

"I assure you, sir, no crime has been committed on our part," says Fadel.

"That's still to be determined," replies the wolf.

Fadel clears his throat. "I am—"

"Save it," the wolf snaps and swings the lantern to get a better look at him. "I've heard it before. Just because you are a fennec does not mean you won't answer the captain's questions. Our blessed Sultan expects us all to follow his laws, even the fennecs."

Fadel snorts but falls silent.

"My friend Fadel here was just helping the hyena out," offers Abdellah. "Zayn was just going to look at the water whenever what happened over there took place."

"Do you know this hyena?" the wolf asks the red fox.

"No," he says. "It seems like some type of misunderstanding."

"Do you know this hyena," the wolf asks Fadel.

Fadel looks at me, and I think he's going to lie, but he nods an affirmative. "For years."

"So, you are an accomplice then?"

"No! Not at all," says Fadel.

The wolf squints at him and then turns to Zayn. "And do you know either of these two?" he says, pointing to Fadel and myself.

Zayn sighs. "Yes…"

"All right, I need all three of you, come with me," says the wolf, pointing toward the bridge.

The red fox clears his throat. "Is that necessary?"

"Perhaps I should take you also," says the wolf. "Why are you here anyway?"

"I have no idea what's going on. That's my store back there," says the fox, pointing to a small storefront in a building across the road. I can see a table outside and a lantern hanging above it. "I followed Fadel out."

The wolf considers. "Then who are you?" he asks the caracal.

"Berat. I was talking to Abdellah over at his store."

"You two I don't need. Just these three," he says, turning to us. "Come now."

I turn to Zayn. He looks like he's hurt and he's walking with difficulty.

"Are you okay?" I ask.

He winces. "The pads of my feet got burned."

"Hurry up now," barks the wolf, trying to herd us down the road.

"I don't know if you saw that fire, but he barely escaped with his life," I say to the wolf.

"Oh, I saw that," remarks the wolf. "The captain will want to talk to you."

I grumble and slip an arm under Zayn to help take the weight off his paws. "Will that help?"

"Yes," he says, and we start off toward the bridge, dripping river water down the street.

I can hear Fadel behind me speak to the two I don't know. "I'll be okay, but tell Salim I won't be back right away."

"Sure," says the fox, and he watches as we go.

It takes a few minutes for Zayn to hobble over to the bridge. His feet are pretty badly burned, and he winces with each step. Even before we get to the bridge, my nose tells me what's happened. I've smelt this before, back across the Crimson Sea after the ambush: the unmistakable smell of burnt flesh and death.

I remember the dead that morning as I walked through the camp. They killed everyone, and by the morning, the crows were feeding on the dead. They had burned the tents, and some of my fellow soldiers died in the flames. And that smell. I will never forget that smell. It will always haunt me. There were so many of them. I see those ghosts when I close my eyes sometimes at night.

"Keep moving, you," says the wolf behind me.

I blink and shake my head, trying to clear it. I can't think of that. I need to get it together.

A dozen city guard are all over the bridge carrying lanterns. From these lights, I can see the lead cart is gone, reduced to a smoldering mess, flames still licking the wood. The smell is overpowering. Bits of broken, charred ceramics are resting next to the cart. Nearby there are bodies—the remnants of a battle.

"What a mess," I whisper, feeling myself shaking.

"Is this your doing?" the wolf asks me.

"No! I wasn't even in the front when the attack came."

The wolf just motions us forward, and I walk across the bridge. The first body I encounter is a tiger, a nasty gash across his chest. A pool of blood lies around him. It's the same tiger who worked for Aziz. Nearby is his friend the red fox, slumped against the bridge's parapet. It looks like he was struck by the fleeing horses.

Further down, near the cart, some of the stones in the road surface are cracked from the heat, and on one side, is a charred, steaming body. Not far from it I see Akay and Ilayda sitting, with two guards over them. Ilayda has her hand pressed against her flank, a rag of some kind pressed against what appears to be a sword cut. Akay is crying softly next to her. I realize then who the charred remains are from, and it wrenches my heart. Abu never had a chance to escape the inferno.

"I've got three more for you, captain," the wolf says to a guard, who turns around. The striped hyena looks at me and flashes her fangs.

"Kiya," I whisper. I've dealt with her before on a number of different jobs when they've gone south. I spent time in the city prison because of Kiya.

"Oh, this gets better! I see this includes you too, Naji. Been helping to steal the Sultan's property, have you?" she says to me.

"Absolutely not!"

She walks over to me and looks at me. "The fear on you is so plain. Are you worried I'd know you did this?"

"I did not do this, Kiya."

She regards me for a moment silently and then turns to look at Fadel and Zayn. "Who are these two?" she asks the wolf.

"Friend of the hyena," he says.

"Yes," says Fadel. "You are the commander of this watch?"

"That I am."

"My friend here is hurt."

"Feisty fella this one," says the wolf to Kiya.

Kiya takes a deep breath and sniffs at Fadel. "I know you. You own the Blue Door, don't you?" she says to Fadel.

"Yes."

"And you were on the bridge."

"No, I was over at Abdellah's coffee store. My friend, Zayn, went to see the bridge."

"I'm from out of town," offers Zayn.

"They had nothing to do with the attack," I manage to get out.

"Interesting," she says. "You will wait with the others while my men ask questions."

They force us to all huddle against one side of the bridge near the cart, and Kiya personally takes my sword. I decide to sit next to Akay, keeping him away from Zayn and Fadel. Ilayda is on the other side, and one of the wolves I don't know is also there. I'm not sure where the others are, but I see another body down the road.

I hear someone telling me something, but it doesn't register. My eyes are down on the stone.

"What's wrong with him?"

"I don't know."

"Why is he wet?"

I'm not seeing the stones of the bridge, but the sand and dirt of a distant land.

"He jumped in the river."

"I was drowning."

"He's still shaking."

"It's not from the water."

"Hey!" says someone, fingers snapping in front of my face.

I look up. "What?"

"So not only are you useless as a guard, you are a coward now?" whispers Akay to me, a growl in his voice.

I just blink at him. The wolf's face seems out of focus. "What?"

"Not only are you useless as a guard, you are a coward now?" Akay repeats to me.

"I am not a coward," I get out.

"Zayn was drowning. He jumped in to save him," interrupts Fadel. "Anyway, why on earth were you transporting illicit cargo in town?"

"Who the fuck are you anyway?" Akay snarls at the fennec. "Three of my friends just died."

Fadel doesn't flinch. "Someone now caught up in this."

Zayn almost got killed because of this stupid job. "You didn't tell me what was in those amphorae," I say to Akay.

The wolf wrinkles his muzzle in distaste at me. "You didn't need to know," he replies.

All I can see is his face and the lighter fur at his throat against his coal-colored pelt. I consider wrapping my paws around Akay's neck and squeezing until he stops breathing. Maybe I could rip his windpipe out with my fangs like our feral ancestors once did. It would be faster.

"Leave him alone, Akay," says Ilayda, putting a hand on his shoulder. "It's Rigel who set us up, not Naji."

The wolf glances back at his friend and then at me. "You're still a coward."

"Try and say that once I've torn your throat out and crushed your bones," I respond. It's too easy for me to imagine my jaws silencing him right now. The primal self is the only part of me really in the moment.

Akay wisely decides not to say anything else to me. Instead, he scoots away from me and sits silent for a minute before he turns to talk to Ilayda. "You know that Takula took a swipe at Rigel too. She managed to nick him good."

The dark muzzle, the white tipped tail, of course—it was a painted dog, just like the ones who attacked the camp, but why? There aren't that many Takula in Aksu. I glance around the bridge trying to piece this together. One group caused a distraction in the front while a second group attacked from behind. This was a carefully planned heist. Someone knew we would be bringing the amphora to this safe house Rigel and Abu spoke about.

"Well, there is no sign of the second cart," says Kiya, coming to talk to our guard. "It could be anywhere in the city by now."

"The runners should be able to reach the gates in time," responds the guard.

"Maybe, but it's just as concerning if they're not trying to get it out of the city tonight." The striped hyena frowns at us and walks over to where we're sitting. "None of you would happen to know who these mysterious painted dogs you spoke of are, would you?"

Everyone shakes their head.

"I figured," Kiya snorts. "We're going to be taking everyone in."

"What crime am I being accused of?" asks Fadel. "I was just a bystander."

"We're still investigating what happened, and I want to make sure everyone is available to answer questions," says Kiya.

"And how long do you plan to keep us?" he asks.

"A few days, maybe," says the striped hyena. "If you are just a bystander."

Fadel's ears shoot up in surprise. "A few days?"

"Keep better company," remarks Kiya, pointing at me.

I can see Zayn slump. He's been quiet, but I know what he's thinking about. Does she know about Aziz? If she does, I don't know if any of us are going to be getting out soon.

❧

We have to wait under guard until someone fetches enough shackles for the six of us they're taking in. They lock each of our wrists together with a chain running between us before they march us to jail. Kiya eventually leaves, letting the other guards haul us in.

I have been arrested before, but watching Zayn and Fadel as they trudge in front of me breaks my heart. Maybe this is the life I deserve, but not them. They deserve better than this, but watching both of them drag their tails, I can't bear to see it. I want to speak to them, to tell them it will be okay, but my words would be an empty promise. All I can do is march forward, head down toward whatever fate awaits me. At least once we're off the bridge, I don't have the smell of burned flesh in my nose.

The jail itself is under a guardhouse that sits near the Malhaa District. The building is a three-story stone edifice that watches over this part of the city. There are only small exterior windows to the street. We are led down into the structure, where stone blocks give way to passages cut into the stone foundations under the building.

The Aragvi wolves are split off from us there, and they put Zayn and Fadel into a cell with me. Thankfully they take the shackles back, but the cell is a small room with two simple wooden benches that act as bunks on either side and a chamber pot in the corner. Straw is scattered around on the floor. We are left with some water, and the light of a lantern left outside that barely throws any illumination through the window in the wooden door. The guards retreat to their rooms upstairs to sleep, leaving us alone.

Zayn paces back and forth in the cell once a guard locks us in. "Do they mean to just leave us in here?" he asks.

"I don't know," I say. I've spent months in one of these cells before, so I know the experience doesn't get better. You barely get any room to move, and who knows who they lock you up with.

Fadel slumps onto one of the bunks. "We didn't steal the war fire."

"I know, but we could easily disappear into the back alleys of Aksu. I don't want to defend it, but that's why they do this," I respond.

"I just hope Salim is going to be okay on his own. He could be running the Blue Door for a while."

I look over the door since I have nothing better to do. It's sturdy, and the lock is far away from the barred window set into it. I would wear my claws off and end up with stubs for fingers if I tried to get at the mechanism. Running my hand over the wood, I can feel where someone previously tried to get under the thick iron plate over the lock, but the wood is far too thick to do that trick.

"She has to know about Aziz," I can hear Zayn whispering.

"Shh, don't say that. You did nothing wrong there," responds Fadel.

Zayn did do something wrong. He stepped up and saved me when the time was right, and now we are all paying for it. Had he not done that, he and Fadel would have been fine.

"All this is my fault," I say, pulling to see how tight the door fits. To my disappointment, it doesn't budge at all. "I never should have brought you here, Zayn," I say, turning. Two sets of eyes look back at me in the gloom, bright and shining in the low light. "I should have taken you someplace better. Someplace where Rigel couldn't find me."

"You had no way of knowing," says Fadel.

"Yes, but now we're stuck here. I've been here before, but not you, not Zayn. You shouldn't be here. Places like this are for people like me. I can't hurt people in here."

The fennec interjects. "Naji, you're not helping this."

It's my fault. My fault.

"I could have stayed in Zaptu instead…"

"You two are not going to do this to me," growls Fadel. "We're in this together."

"We're in a cage," I say, starting to cry, going to sit on the bunk opposite of Fadel and Zayn.

"Yes," says Fadel, "yes we are."

Zayn sighs. "They feed us at least?"

"They give us bread twice a day and some water," I reply.

"Well, this is in a way better than my old life," he responds. "I went hungry a lot back then."

"The small wonders of Aksu," says Fadel.

"Naji, are you okay? You're shaking again," Zayn asks.

"What? No, I am fine."

"Your paws are trembling."

I look down at them. They're both shaking. "So they are."

"You were shaking on the bridge."

Oh, the bridge and that horrible smell. That battle back home. "I remember them, their lifeless faces and the smell of the bodies and the burned tents. That smell always brings back those memories and the feeling of being alone after that battle. The helplessness I felt afterwards. It came back to me on the bridge."

Zayn stares at me. "What is he talking about?" he asks Fadel.

"The ambush back home, I think."

If they say anything else, I don't catch it. I'm just staring at the floor, thinking about the battle, and Abu, and the last time I was here. I'm safe here, I can't hurt people here. I belong—

There is a paw on my shoulder. I look up. It's connected to Zayn.

"Hey, it's okay. We'll get through this together."

"Is it? It's my fault and Aziz and Abu and the attack and—"

"Shh...," says the jackal, sitting next to me. "Don't think about that."

"But that's all I keep thinking about!" I say, wiping my eyes. Wait, am I crying?

He takes one of my hands and tries to hold it. "You're hurt."

"I'm not hurt."

"Not physically. Inside. You're hurt inside."

The ghosts I keep, I shouldn't have those, should I? I shouldn't have this many regrets I can't let go of. But this is my life, this is what I've become, isn't it?

"Maybe? I'm not sure."

He reaches up and touches the side of my face. "I know what it's like to have a pain that doesn't ever go away inside of yourself, to have an emptiness inside of you that cannot be filled."

"It's always there," I say. "It never completely goes away."

He looks me in the eyes, then lowers his head and presses forward. We're forehead to forehead. "I'm sure. Mine has been there a long time too," says the jackal.

Zayn holds me for a few minutes before he finally lets go. I look back up and see Fadel is just sitting there, staring off into space.

"Fadel?" I ask.

He looks toward me. "What? You both needed some privacy."

"Thank you," I say.

"Just try and let me fall asleep before you both get handy, okay?" remarks Fadel.

Zayn snorts, but I smile at that. "Well, if we're still here tomorrow, we might have to worry about that."

"Let's hope we're not here tomorrow," says the fennec, curling up on the bench. "I'm going to try and get some sleep."

"I guess we all should," says Zayn.

"I'll try, but it's going to be hard," I say.

There really should be a third bench in here if they are planning to leave us in here, but they'll just move one of us to another cell before they do that. Fadel fits on the bench, but even though he's shorter than I am, there's not a lot of extra room on there for anyone else.

Zayn tries to get comfortable leaning against me, but he keeps shifting back and forth as I stroke his side to lure him to sleep. Fadel, for his part, seems to fall asleep pretty quickly, but it takes Zayn a while to do that. The wood is hard, the stone walls cold and unforgiving. Finally, the jackal settles in a position and his breathing slows down.

For all the horrible things that have happened to Zayn in his life, his coarse fur is still warm and soft in my arms. Eventually, the warm body against me lulls me into a fitful rest.

I think it is around dawn when I hear noises outside of the cell. There is a bit more light in the outside hallway, but I can't tell for sure if the sun is up yet or not. It could already be morning, but I haven't heard the guards come by at all. Zayn is sleeping in my lap, snoring softly while I'm sitting on the bunk. Fadel is still on the bunk on the other side of the cell, but I don't know if he is asleep or not. His breathing is even and unchanging.

I've been in and out of consciousness, but I feel more together somehow. As long as I don't think about what I saw on the bridge last night, I think I'm going to be okay. The thought that this is all my fault keeps popping up in my head, and I try not to focus on that. Being in jail, you need to keep your spirits up, or it will break you. We need to keep our morale up, and letting all my regrets hit me will make this so much worse for Zayn and Fadel. When we get out of here, there will be plenty of time to beat myself up for what I've done and all the stupid decisions I've made. The three of us are still alive, and that's what matters.

I hear something in the distance, and my ears swivel trying to find out what it is. There are voices, but they're distant. I can't understand them, but they seem to be coming closer. Eventually I can make out words.

I recognize Kiya's voice first. "You really think the saffron from the far north of the sultanate is better than what comes from Yokus?"

"Both are of a good quality, but the farms in the Anjar Valley produce a superior crop to the Ghola Valley. I would be happy to show you the difference." Wait, Naima is here taking to Kiya about saffron?

"Perhaps after this investigation is over, I will come by and see. There is still a cart of war fire unaccounted for."

"I assure you, if I hear something of interest, I will forward the information over to you immediately."

I hear the jingle of keys. "Everything you hear?" It sounds like they've stopped moving.

"Of course," responds Naima.

"I want to emphasize the importance the Grand Vizier has placed on getting the amphorae back. I would be very disappointed to find out if you lied to me. There would be consequences."

"I assure you, I had no knowledge of the job's details beforehand. I very highly doubt they told Naji what they were moving either. The surviving clan members should be able to confirm that."

Kiya snorts. "They could be covering for your friend."

"For a spotted hyena they barely know? Come on now, you know that's not true."

"I would agree, but I can't put anything past anyone at this point. The Sultan wants the amphorae back."

"I'm sure you'll figure it out," Naima says. "I will make some inquiries myself, and you have my word on this. If I hear something, I'll let you know."

"You'd better," says the striped hyena, with ice in her voice, "or I'll see you all back here. You won't be on this side of the cells either." The keys jingle again and the footsteps resume. I don't think this conversation was just meant for Naima. It was a warning to us too. Voices can carry in these stone halls, and Kiya knows that.

I hear a soft chuckle. "Let's not make this ugly. I would hate for something like this to come between us."

"I'm just making this clear to you."

"It is quite clear, Kiya. Now, the boys?"

I hear steps come forward. Zayn is stirring and looks up at me. He sits up to stretch, and I get up to look through the little window in the door. I can see Kiya and Naima on the other side. Kiya looks tired, and I'm surprised she is still awake. She must not have slept at all. Beside her stands Naima, the leopardess looking fresh and elegant in her long robe. I can see she is carrying my sword.

"All right, spots, someone put in a good word for you and your friends. They've corroborated your story," says Kiya, sliding a key into the lock of the wooden cell door.

"So, you finally believe me?"

"More or less," says Kiya, opening the cell. "I expect the three of you to stay far away from the Aragvi clan, so I won't be seeing you back here."

"Of course," I say.

"I don't want anything to do with them," says Zayn.

Fadel just gets up and huffs, dusting himself off. "I wasn't even on the bridge," he mutters.

"Thank you," says Naima, formally to Kiya, "for hearing my appeal so early this morning."

She nods and has to stifle a yawn. "Take your charges and go, please. Let's not do this again either."

"Of course." Naima turns and we fall in behind her. The leopardess has to stop partly down the corridor and wait for us as Zayn gingerly walks down the hall.

"Are your footpaws feeling better?" I ask him.

"A little, but I really need some salve for the pads."

"I should have something back at the Blue Door," says Fadel.

"I'm going to need it," Zayn says.

"What happened?" asks Naima.

"I burned my pads when the bridge caught fire," says Zayn. "Also, who are you?"

"Naima," she says, holding out a paw, which he takes, and they exchange a reserved cheek kiss. "You must be Zayn."

"Yes."

"I can see what Naji sees in you," she says, resuming her walking.

I groan. "You make me sound shallow, Naima."

"You appreciate certain aspects of the male body," she retorts.

"How did you know to come?" asks Fadel.

"Your assistant, Salim, came to me last night and told me what happened." She glances around and makes a motion for silence by raising a claw. We walk past the guards at the gate to the cells and through the guardhouse, exiting out onto the street below. The night watchman nods at Naima, making a stifled yawn.

Outside, the sun is just coming up, and the leopardess turns up the street, walking for a minute before she speaks again. "I had to pull some strings to get the details. From Kiya I ascertain some of the Sultan's war fire was stolen?"

"I'm not sure you can really steal something already stolen, but the Sultan definitely wants it back. Aziz's friends pulled a heist on the Aragvi clan. Also, they had help from a painted dog. I think Rigel was in on this, but they also attacked him," I respond. "Aziz's friends didn't make it, but the painted dogs took the remaining war fire."

"A Takula? Not many of those around here," says the leopardess.

"I know, but there are enough of them."

Naima frowns. "So, Rigel stole from the clan? That doesn't sound like him."

"I'm surprised anyone trusts him," says Zayn.

"He wasn't always like this," says Naima. "When he worked for me, he was honest and didn't cheat me out of anything. Naji, Isim, and Rigel did all the work I gave them cleanly, without issue. It's when I started winding down in the business that the trouble began. Speaking of…" She holds out the sheathed sword to me. "You should really carry a different kilij, Naji."

"You know why I carry this one," I say, taking it.

"That's why I think you should carry your old one or buy a new one. This one has a lot of memories attached to it."

"Did you have to beg Kiya to give it to you? I know she doesn't always return weapons."

"I asked for it, and she said I could return it. She's really not that bad, you know, as long as you don't make yourself a suspect in her investigations," says Naima. "This would be twice now you've brought her attention on yourself?"

"Don't remind me."

"Oh, so that's how you two know each other?" says Fadel.

"What do you mean?" asks Zayn.

"This is not the first time I've vouched for Naji to Kiya, although the last time was my fault," she says. "It's a long story, so perhaps another time. We have a more pressing issue."

"We?" says Fadel. "I have a business to attend to."

Naima shakes her head. "Salim seemed capable enough, but I won't keep you."

"Issue? You mean finding Rigel?" I ask her.

She smiles, showing some fangs. "Any good teacher would not abandon one of her students in a moment like this. Plus, it's been a long time since I've been in a good scrape."

I snort. "Selling me out and hiring the people that wanted to kill me is not exactly a scrape. It's a bit more violent than that."

"Well, you get my point. Do you know where they got the war fire from?"

"No, but I have a question for you, Zayn. What did Sarda do for coin?"

The jackal shrugs. "He traveled through town, but he was always alone. Why?"

"The Aragvi bought the war fire from a snow leopard named Jalus. He mentioned his boss, Sarda, was still away on business."

"It's possible it's him," says Zayn. "He never told me why he was in town."

"Who's Sarda?" Naima asks.

"Someone who used to travel through Zaptu on business. He always seemed to have a lot of money on himself," says Zayn.

"Suspicious, but I can ask Sirius if he's heard of him or Jalus. You remember my friend Sirius, Naji, don't you?"

I think. "Rigel mentioned that name. Wait, is he that wolf who used to travel a lot but retired from being a caravan guard? I think I only met him once."

"Yes, that's the one. He keeps his ears up, and he's been hearing odd rumors for the last few days. It turns out there is an internal dispute in the Aragvi clan. I suspect some of the elders didn't want the clan to try and smuggle the war fire north. I think Rigel may have gotten caught up in that. It's possible he got sloppy, and the wrong people heard about what the Aragvi were doing."

I ponder the information. "Rigel said he was saving everyone just as the attack was starting. It seems pretty dangerous to use fire to stop a cart loaded with flammable liquid. I'm sure Abu would know what happened, but he died in the attack."

"Abu had been with the clan for a long time. Killing him will bring the clan down on someone, whoever planned the attack. They'll want revenge. Of course, that assumes Kiya doesn't hunt them all down first," says Naima.

"I wonder if they never planned to steal both carts. It's quite possible this attack was set up so that all the attention would fall on the Aragvi," I say.

"It would make sense," says Fadel. "The Grand Vizier will be after the culprits. I imagine it is easier to smuggle something out of town if the focus isn't on you."

"There's too many loose ends here and a lot of people involved. There's no way to be sure who did what exactly or why. When it comes to trickery, my primary rule is very simple: run no scheme without thinking of the consequences of your actions. It's best we leave what happened on the bridge to Kiya to unravel."

"So, what about Rigel?' Zayn asks. "Is he still going to be after us?"

"You know, I'm not sure he cares that you killed Aziz," I say. "He was more concerned about protecting you from me in his strange, twisted logic."

"How does what he did protect me from you?" asks Zayn.

"Selling me out to Aziz and his two lackeys was to take me away from you, but that just left you alone. With all three of them dead now, it is a moot point. How Rigel thought this would benefit you, I don't understand. I'd have to find him to ask."

"I imagine Rigel is in hiding now," says Naima. "He'll likely be impossible to find."

I think for a minute. "That actually is surprisingly easy. I know where he'll be."

Naima looks at me, surprised. "You do?"

"Whenever Rigel needed to go think, he had a spot he'd go to on the city walls where he used to like to watch the sun rise. I bet he went there this morning."

"Are you going to go looking for him?" Fadel asks.

"Yes. I'd like to settle things with him. This is the only chance I'll have to find him. He'll disappear after this, and who knows when he'll show back up."

Fadel frowns. "You're not still hoping to patch things up with him?"

"No. I never will be able to." I take a deep breath. "I have questions, still. I need to find out if he's trying to kill me, but there's something else I need to do too. I need to say good-bye."

The three of them look at me, confused. Fadel blinks at me, and Zayn is staring at me wide-eyed. Naima has tilted her head trying to puzzle out what I'm saying.

"I'm taking the job with Fadel. I'm getting out of the mercenary business, and I think it's time I finally kick Rigel out of my life for good."

"I thought you wanted to murder him," says Fadel.

"I do, but it wouldn't ever feel right. I loved him once, and I know, deep down, if I killed him, I would never forgive myself for it. If I am to finally let go of my past, I need to let go of things and start forgiving myself."

The leopardess claps a hand on my shoulder. "I too had to put a lot of things behind me when I bought the store. I will come with you. We can go pay him a visit together."

"Thank you."

"That feels silly," says Zayn, "but he wasn't ever my friend."

"I mean, if he wants to try and kill me, I need to be prepared for that, but I think this won't result in more bloodshed. I hope at least it won't."

"Hard to say," says Naima. "Fadel, can you take Zayn back to the Blue Door? I'm hoping an escort isn't necessary right now, but if you think so, we can take you there first."

"I think we'll be fine," says the fennec, turning to Zayn. "Just be careful, both of you."

I glance up at the sky. "We better hurry," I say to Naima, starting off. "The sun is already up."

"I'm coming with you," says Zayn from behind me.

I stop and turn. "You already got hurt once, I couldn't bear to see that—"

"I'm just as much a part of this as you are," growls the jackal.

"We need to hurry—"

"I can still walk," says Zayn, gingerly taking a step forward on his own.

"Zayn, I can see that—"

"I'm coming with you!" he growls.

"He's got spirit," says Naima, with a chuckle. "I like that."

I protest. "While I don't believe this will be dangerous, you don't have a weapon to protect himself."

Naima sweeps the folds of her robe back and with a flourish produces a short dagger in a leather scabbard. "I usually carry an extra," she says, holding it out to Zayn. The jackal takes the weapon and pulls it out to check it. It's only about a foot long, but carefully oiled and sharp.

"Take notes, Naji," Fadel remarks to me. "We're going to need to check guests for weapons like this at the Blue Door once you start working for me."

"A lady never tells all her secrets, even to her pupils," says the leopardess, grinning.

"I'll see if she can give me some tips, Fadel," I say, walking back over to Zayn to help him.

"I'll walk on my own," says the jackal.

"Those pads looked awful."

"I'll be fine."

"Okay, okay." I take a deep breath. "Let's do this then," I say, setting off down the street.

"Be careful," calls Fadel.

This is either a brilliant idea on my part or another trap I'm walking straight into. I'm hoping this time it's brilliant, but lately my luck hasn't been holding up well. I will need to be on my guard. I can't afford to lose someone else close to me due to my inattention. I also need to get past all this, and I'm not going to be able to do that if Rigel is still trying to get me killed.

Upon the City Wall
(Zayn)

The walk across town is painful, but somehow not as bad as the beatings Sarda gave me. The pads on my paws are burning and itching like mad. It feels like I'm walking on two stumps. As I hobble down the street, I wonder if perhaps I should have gone with Fadel, but I also need to see this through. Pain is something that I'm used to having inflicted on me by others, and in this case, I'm doing it to myself.

Naji and Naima have grim looks on their faces and do not talk. We walk through parts of the city I've not seen before. Around us, people are beginning their morning routine. We pass artisans opening up their businesses, a cart selling fresh bread for breakfast with cheese, olives, and eggs to go with it, a school beginning the day's instruction, and a temple open for morning prayers. All around us, the city is coming to life with porters and carts rolling down the streets, people hurrying about their business.

The city is full of life, but for us there is the grave possibility of death. I can feel it in the way Naima moves and see it in the thin line of Naji's muzzle along with the stillness of their tails. They are hunting, and even for his peaceful intentions, they both know this circle may only be closed with death. I do not fault Naji for wanting answers, but blood has been drawn. Sometimes, when a wound is infected, the only way to save the victim is to cut the limb off.

The tension makes my heart clench in my chest. This could be the last hour of my life, here in this giant city, so different from the dry hills and the desert's dunes I was born to, so different from the land my parents inhabited their whole lives. My father died by the sword, but to live, I have been pierced by a very different kind of sword for the last three years. Today, I will step forward and meet fate with a blade in my own paws.

Under the tension, there is something else. Something I did not expect to be there. Already I have used a blade to taste blood, and I feel something else inside me under all the tension, something that has not been there before. It scares me.

This is a hunt, and while I may be following the lead hunters, I too am hunting. I too am upon this path, and I want to be here. Deep down, I feel something that quickens my pulse beyond the tension or fear of death. There is a thrill to the hunt, and I can feel it inside of me. My ancestors stalked the sands for generations, and now I stalk through Aksu like they once did between the desert dunes.

After walking for a while, we turn down an alley that dead ends against the tan stone of the city wall rising above the nearby houses. A square tower is built into the wall, and the alley must have been built to access it.

"We're here," Naji says, glancing up at the sun. "We're probably too late. Even if he did come here to think, he likely left already."

Naima and I both look around. The houses here are quiet. They're small two-story structures along with a small tavern still shuttered before the day's business. The alleyway is deserted. "Where would he be?" I ask Naji.

He points to the wall. "He would be up on the ramparts."

"This exact stretch of wall?"

"Rigel knew the owner of the tavern. The owner kept a key to the tower on hand for the city guard, should they need access and not bring their own. Rigel liked the view of the river from here, so Rigel had a copy of the key made at some point. That said, that doesn't mean he came here or hasn't found another stretch of the wall to sit and brood upon."

Naima nods. "He can be a creature of habit. Do you wish to take the lead?"

Naji nods and starts down the alleyway toward the tower. A heavy wooden door with iron binding is set into the base of the structure. Naji walks over to the door and traces a paw against the wood before he kneels in front of the door to sniff. "He came this way," says Naji, crouching on the ground.

"How recently, do you think?" I ask, walking up behind him.

He points to the ground in front of him. "Since the attack at least. There is dried blood on the ground and a little on the door handle."

Naima has been watching the street behind us, but now she walks up and inspects the stains. "It's not fresh."

"No, it's not." Naji stands up and draws his kilij. He reaches for the door, takes a firm hold on the handle, and depresses the lever on the metal lock. The mechanism gives an audible click. "It's unlocked."

"Brace yourself," Naima says to me. She steps to the side and then reaches into the folds of her dress and produces a yataghan. The short, slightly curved saber glints in the morning light.

"You came prepared," I remark, as I unsheathe the dagger.

The leopardess shrugs. "Just because I've retired doesn't mean I've gone soft. Now stand over behind me to my right," she says. "We don't know what's on the other side of this door."

Naji nods. "No, we don't. Ready now?"

"Yes," I say.

Naji pushes the door inward and then steps to the side to get behind the wall. The iron hinges creak as they turn, but it opens smoothly. He waits, ears perked, but nothing emerges from the darkness inside of the tower.

Naima waits with her breath held, and then carefully looks around the door frame. "It looks like it's just stocked with supplies," she says in a low whisper.

"If you want to go in, I'll be right behind you," replies Naji.

She nods and ducks into the room quickly. "It's safe," she says.

Naji enters the room and I follow, stepping cautiously as my eyes adjust to the darkness.

"They keep this war fire stuff so readily available?" I ask. The interior of the tower is about thirty feet square, and all the goods inside make the room cramped. A ladder against one wall leads to the floor above. Naima is scanning the baskets, chests, and amphorae inside.

"No, that's under guard. Most of this is odds and ends plus some arrows and torches. Just basic things that they would need if there was a siege."

Naji makes his own circuit of the room, finding nothing of interest. "We should probably close the door."

"It will be as dark as a tomb in here," whispers Naima, glancing up at the ladder that leads to the next floor. The trapdoor above is open.

"There is a window upstairs," Naji says.

She looks toward him and makes a motion for him to wait and points up. Then she climbs up slowly, trying to keep it from creaking, one hand holding the yataghan. She freezes when the wood groans, then ascends the rest of the way. I hear a thump above when she reaches the floor, then nothing.

"It's deserted," comes her voice from the opening.

Naji closes the door, and it shuts with a creak. It is indeed nearly pitch black in this room, but I can see the small bit of light filtering through from the opening in the floor above. I sheathe the dagger I'm carrying and climb upstairs, followed by Naji. My burned paws hurt immensely at the pressure the ladder's rungs put on my paw pads.

There is a slit window in this room that provides a small, piercing ray of light. Naima is by the next ladder going upstairs, looking up, but she glances at me when I come up. "With a small weapon like I gave you, you should keep it in your paws in a situation like this," she whispers to me.

"Force of habit," I reply, reaching to pull the dagger back out.

"Always the teacher," says Naji, as he comes up behind me.

Naima shrugs and studies the opening above. She ascends the next ladder. This one creaks against the wooden floor, and she moves quickly to scale it.

"Also clear," she calls down, "but the next trap door is closed."

Naji and I ascend. This time I do it with the dagger, and I'm even slower as I try not to cut myself. Naima makes it seem effortless the way she moves. I feel like I'm dead on my paws right now. Climbing up is agony.

Naima is studying the ladder. There are actually two slit windows here. They look over the town and don't offer a view of the walls.

"There is dried blood on this ladder," she remarks, sniffing it. "The scent is faint, but I can tell Rigel came this way."

"He could be upstairs," whispers Naji.

"If he's expecting us, he would be," says Naima.

Naji frowns. "Let me go first."

"No, let me. Your kilij is too long," the leopardess says, taking hold of the ladder.

I can see Naji wants to protest, but he doesn't.

Naima again climbs the ladder and gets to the top so she can listen. I wait, holding my breath, my heart beating fast. This could be it. Naima slowly lifts the heavy trap door. It creaks loudly and she freezes, with the hatch partially lifted.

"Well, so much for surprise," she mutters. She waits ten seconds and then just pushes it open all the way. It screams in protest, but no other sound is heard. Carefully she climbs up and Naji follows her, leaving me to go third.

The fourth floor of the tower is different. Another ladder leads up, this time to the roof. The trap door is also closed. The room has two slit windows that overlook the area beyond the walls, and a single window facing the city. The other two walls have doors that lead to the ramparts, and Naima is standing by one that is ajar, looking outside. She's pointing to something on the ramparts and Naji has joined her.

"He's just sitting there," she whispers when I come up.

I crane my neck so I can see around them. Sitting in the shade of a merlon on the city wall is Rigel. He's got his back against the rampart's wall and could almost be sleeping.

Naji glances around and motions us both back. He steadies himself, kilij at the ready, and opens the door. He steps out onto the battlement and starts walking toward Rigel.

The cat stirs and glances at him. He sits up but he doesn't move to get up.

"I should have known you'd come," he rasps, and he glances past Naji as I emerge with Naima behind me. "And you brought company."

"They weren't going to let me come alone." Naji stops about ten feet from Rigel. The caracal's shirt hangs loose, torn with a bandage wrapped around his side. Some blood has soaked through it. "I see the Takula on the bridge got you good," remarks Naji.

The caracal shrugs. "She got the jump on me. It's deep, but I guess that's not going to matter."

Naji looks back at me, searching my face, before he takes a deep breath and turns back to Rigel. "This is where we differ. I don't want your blood on my paws. Too much has been shed already. I came here because it is time we say good-bye, but before we do I have one question, Rigel. Why did you do this?"

He chuckles wetly. "So noble of you, but possibly a wasted gesture. I already told you why."

"I get why you sold me out. I think it's sick, but if that's what you believe, then I can accept that. I don't get why you sold out the Aragvi clan."

"I didn't sell them out."

"You got Abu killed and two other clan members."

Rigel sighs and slumps back against the merlon. "They weren't supposed to die."

"So, it was supposed to be a peaceful heist?"

The caracal shakes his head. "There wasn't supposed to be a heist. There was supposed to be a sale. Abu and I were concerned the war fire was too hot to hold. The city guard were already looking for it. Getting it to the port of Japar would be tricky, but the clan elders wanted to ship it north to rebels fighting the Empire of Roum. Personally, I didn't know if we could get it out of Aksu, let alone the sultanate. The elders were insistent, but I thought if we could resell it for a good profit, things would work out. It's easier to send money than goods anyway.

"Arranging the pickup with Jalus started to drag on while we waited for it to be delivered from the southern part of the sultanate. His boss had to leave on other business. There were just too many loose threads, so I suggested the sale idea to Abu. He agreed it was better, and we didn't want to be caught with the goods. If we could find a buyer that let us flip the war fire, we'd be in the clear with the clan. I know Akay and Ilayda wouldn't like it, but it was all we had."

Rigel pauses to cough, and the sound is wet and heavy. It sounds bad. The cut in his side must be deep.

Rigel continues after he stops coughing. "I had to discreetly ask around, but I found Aziz knew a buyer back in Japar and was willing to transport the goods himself. Word of the theft spread, and he came to town hoping to procure the war fire for this buyer himself. I just took advantage of the opportunity. He wasn't the type of person I wanted to make a deal with, but I didn't have a lot of options to fence the goods. I told him as long as we got the cash up front, it wouldn't matter who he sold it to. The handoff was going to be at the safe house I arranged for. Aziz would be hired to watch the goods, but instead his men would come and pick up the goods and we'd walk away with the profits. Anyone in the clan who wanted to argue could easily count the coins after the fact.

"Then we heard Jalus was going to raise the price, and I panicked. It was still under what we were selling it to Aziz, but it wasn't going to be as profitable as Abu and I hoped. I went to the Blue Door to blow off some steam, and after talking to you, it clicked. If I offered you to him, I could make up the difference. He agreed to raise his price, and I just told Abu I was able to get us an increase to cover the difficulty we were having in getting the delivery. When Zayn killed Aziz, I thought the whole deal would be off, but Achmed said he could follow through with it. I just needed to get the goods to the safe house, and we'd make the deal. Looking back, I don't know if Aziz always intended to take it by force or not."

Naima shakes her head. "You should never have made a deal with someone like Aziz."

"Obviously," says Rigel, rolling his eyes. "I didn't set this up so they could stab me in the chest, but that's what happened."

"Had you come to me, I could have helped you," Naima said.

"No, you couldn't. You'd have told me what I already knew. Don't buy stolen goods the city guard are looking for. Don't let your friends buy stolen goods like that either. I voiced my concerns with the clan and was overruled. I hoped this would go smoothly, and we could all move on, but the risks escalated."

The leopardess huffs. "There are ways to handle situations like this."

"Says the woman who took her money and invested in a spice stall."

Naima growls, but Naji puts up his hand. "You aren't going to convince him that stepping away from the sword was wise."

"On the contrary," says Rigel, pushing himself up again. "Naima did what I always wish I could. She got out. She found a legal line of work. She stopped running deals for people trying to circumvent the law. I have to ask you though, Naji, why are you still in this game?"

"Me?"

"Yes, you. I found people to work with, but you have stayed on your own."

"You know what happened back on the savanna, and what happened to Isim. Why should I put other people in this?"

"Indeed, why should you, but—" The caracal shifts his head to look at me. "—you did."

"No," I say, lifting my head, "I put myself in this."

Rigel looks at me and coughs. "Indeed, you did, because Naji got sloppy, again."

I see Naji tighten his grip around his sword. His hackles are standing up. "No, Rigel," he says, shaking his head. "You caused this. Zayn only stepped in to save me. He never would have gotten involved if you didn't think I was worth some coins to Aziz. I trusted you, and you betrayed me. I can only imagine what Isim would say if he were here, but it would not be kind."

The caracal doesn't say anything for a minute. "I imagine he would be angry at me."

"Very angry."

They lapse into silence for a bit before Naji sheathes his sword. "So, this is it. It's time we part ways."

"Forgive me if I don't get up for this."

"Goodbye, Rigel. I don't wish your death, but know that if you come looking for me, Zayn, or Naima with any malice, I will not stay my hand a second time. I will make sure you die by my blade."

"That is a fair trade for what I've done."

Naji lowers his head. "May peace find you." He turns and walks past where Naima and I are standing.

Naima hesitates for a moment and nods. She sheathes her yataghan. "There's nothing I can think to say that makes this better. You will have to face what happens on your own. I know you have always treated me more as Naji's friend than yours, but I tried to keep an eye out for you."

"I know, but I always felt it best to keep my distance with how close you two are. Anyway, once I joined the Aragvi they had plenty of work for me."

"Then I have nothing else I can say."

"Take care of yourself, Naima. You don't know how lucky you are to have found a new life for yourself."

"Thank you," she turns to leave. "Zayn?"

"Give me a minute," I say.

She walks off, leaving me alone with Rigel. I walk up to him and look down at where he's sitting. He's got his sword, but it's still sheathed, and it would be difficult to draw it in this position. If I wanted to, I could kill him easily, just like I killed Aziz. There would be more blood on my paws then. I already don't know if I will ever be able to feel like they're clean now.

"I know what you're thinking. If they don't want to do it, you shouldn't take up the slack. Anyway, it's possibly a moot point with this wound."

"You have a strange definition of friendship," I say.

Rigel squints at me. "You get that way when you've seen what happens to people like me enough."

"I remember being broken. Maybe I still am, but I think I know how to put the pieces of myself back together now."

I can still see the way Aziz's body jerked when I ran him through with the kilij. The panic in his eyes. The thrashing as I held the blade in. I too know death like the others. Before this I knew only hunger and pain. Now I know death. "You haven't made that easier," I say.

"I guess I haven't," he rasps, "but being a sellsword is never an easy line of work. Sometimes it gets complicated."

I glance back down the rampart. I can see Naima waiting at the tower door. Naji is behind her, waiting inside. "No, I imagine not, but neither is being a whore. We're both moving beyond our pasts though. You should too. I think you have your own pieces of yourself to put back together."

He is silent, thinking, but finally he speaks up. "I'll have to see if I heal first."

"Are you just going to stay here?"

He holds up a wine skin. "For the moment. I already went to the physician, and he sewed me back up. Now it's a matter of waiting to see if it heals. I'm not one to wait at home for death to come to me. Anyway, I like the view up here."

I look out over the city that spreads beyond. A tangle of streets and alleyways stretch out. The Sultan's citadel dominates the view on one side, while flat roofed houses are interrupted with domes and temple towers. From here the river is hidden, only a gap in the houses showing where it runs. I turn and look out over the ramparts. Fields of grain and palm groves stretch away from the walls. The river sparkles as it flows down from the mountains through the rolling hills.

"It is a nice view," I offer.

"Yes, yes it is," he says. "I'd like to be alone now."

There's not really anything else I can think to say. I give him a nod and turn to limp back to the tower. Naima watches me as I walk past. Once he sees me, Naji heads inside and starts down the ladder in silence. I follow him and Naima comes last. The leopardess closes the top trap door but leaves all the others open.

At the bottom, as Naji is closing the door to the tower, I speak up. "Is that it?"

"Hopefully," he says. "I don't think Rigel is going to bother us, at least."

"I'll let you know if I hear anything about the Takula," says Naima, "but I have to ask. How are you feeling?"

"Unsure and yet relieved," says Naji. "It was time to close that part of my life."

"You didn't tell him you were taking the job with Fadel," I say.

"He doesn't need to know that."

"True. Not like I want to see him or Sarda again. Best to get clear of this whole sordid mess. Are you sure spices don't interest you, Naji?" I ask him.

Naima laughs. "I like you," she says and leans forward and gives me a cheek kiss. She exchanges cheek kisses with Naji. "I must go now. I have a market stall to attend to. Femi will be wondering where I am."

"Take care," he says, and she starts off down the street.

"I think I've had enough fun for today, and my feet hurt." Now that we've finished with Rigel, I feel exhausted. I didn't really sleep last night in the jail anyway. "I guess we should go to the Blue Door and get the salve Fadel has. My pads are killing me."

Naji nods and gets an arm under my shoulder. "Let's just go home, and once I get you comfortable, I'll go get the salve."

ȣ

"Hold still so I can apply the ointment," grumbles Naji, as he's trying to work the thick cream into my paws.

I know I need this, but I keep twitching. "They hurt really bad." Naji came back with the salve from Fadel along with some food. He wanted to put it on first, but I insisted we eat. Now he's trying to tend to my footpaws after washing them.

"If we don't get them bandaged well, they won't heal right. You'll never be able to dance again, and I don't think you'll like that."

I sigh and try to lay back on the bed. Naji's apartment is as we left it three days ago. It feels like a lifetime to me. So much has happened, and yet it remains unchanged.

"You do want to dance again, don't you?" he asks me.

"Of course, but I'm not in a hurry. I need to still think through the last few days. It's been a lot, and some quiet time would be nice."

"Of course," he says. "Fadel will understand. When you're ready, you can go back."

"Thanks," I say. He reaches for some bandages and starts wrapping my paws. The fur on my feet protected most of my legs, but my pads are pretty rough. Walking on them afterward didn't help and they've been throbbing since we got back.

"As I was getting the salve, Fadel asked when I wanted to start the job. I told him in a few days. While I could use some coin, I also need to clear my mind. I guess the Aragvi owe me money, but who knows if Akay or Ilayda are ever going to get out of jail."

"We're lucky we're not in there ourselves. I've got coin if you need some. You don't have to buy all our food."

"Thanks." He flicks his ears in thought. "You know, I've been thinking about what Rigel told me, just before the attack on the bridge and on the wall today. He thought selling me out to Aziz would protect you from me."

My ears fall. I've been expecting him to bring this up. "Little good his twisted sense of kindness did me. I rushed in to save you from what Rigel did."

"I know." Naji finishes bandaging my paws and nods to himself, satisfied. He crawls over and lies down next to me. "I wanted to protect you, to give you something better than you had, and I failed at that."

I shake my head and turn to look at him. "You can't always protect me, Naji. I have to be able to protect myself."

He pushes himself so he can look at me, a series of emotions flickering across his face. "Maybe you're right. You've done better at protecting me than I have at protecting you." His ears go flat. "Maybe Rigel is right about me."

"Do you want to make Rigel right?" I ask.

"No, of course not. I worry though that when Rigel says he and I are cut from the same cloth, he's right. We both aren't good people."

"I know what not believing you are worthy of a good life feels like. I have the scars to remind me every day of what I've been. If I let them define me, how can I ever be someone better?"

He looks away from me to think. "I don't know. I worry a part of me is still back on the battlefield, and I can't get past it."

"Scars don't always go away, but sometimes they will fade with time. Don't ever let that be the only you."

He sighs. "You make it sound easy."

"It's not. If I close my eyes, I can still see Aziz's lifeless eyes staring up at me or feel Sarda's lash upon me. I don't know if I can ever forget those moments."

"I guess a part of me is always going to be on that battle-field."

"And a part of me will always be a whore under Sarda's lash, yet is that who we want to be?"

"No. We can be more than that. We don't need to be our pasts. We can be our futures."

Now I have to think. What is a future? Do I have one? I haven't had one before, but do I have one now?

"I don't know if I've ever had a future. Maybe when I was young, but once I started dancing, my tomorrow was whatever the coins being pressed into my paw were for. One of the dancers when I first started, Nawra, would say how when she stopped dancing in the caravanserai, she was going to get married, and that's just what she did. She always thought of the work as temporary, even though she did it for years. I guess I didn't. I never had an after planned for myself."

"And now?"

I think. I can dance at the Blue Door for a while, but what about when I get older? What would I be like at Usman's age? I'd be slower, maybe fatter, but would I be happy?

Not by myself, but what about with Naji in Aksu? Could an older me live here with him, tending tables at the Blue Door or running a stall for kebabs like Amare did back in Zaptu? It wouldn't be an exciting life, but it would be a stable life.

It could be everything I never had in Zaptu.

I turn and look at the hyena with his black muzzle and brown fur on his face. Every day I would see this face. "I think I do."

He smiles. "Good. I'm glad I could give that back to you."

"Hopefully it won't be as tiring as the last few days."

He chuckles. "Well, I don't want to ever repeat this again."

"Not at all. I'm a bit too charred for my own taste."

"You should rest."

I am tired. "What are you going to do?"

He yawns. "Some of the same. I didn't really sleep in the jail cell last night. What I did get wasn't restful."

I lean forward and give him a kiss. "Then get some rest."

He beams. "As you insist."

I get comfortable on the bed and look at the shuttered windows. Afternoon light is drifting in. It's warm in here, but it's not too bad right now.

Naji settles down next to me. This is nice, and just lying down, I can feel myself finally let go of the tension inside of me, since I don't have to worry about Aziz or the others coming to look for me. The only person who will be crossing swords with me now is Khalil, in order to see which of us is the better dancer. Once my feet are healed, we'll have to develop a routine together.

Already Naji's breathing is starting to become slower. I lie there for a bit listening to him, and I realize how quickly I can get used to this. After that, sleep comes quickly to me.

∾

I awake early in the morning with the light of dawn just starting to come through the window. I didn't expect to sleep through the afternoon and night, but apparently, I did. Naji got up at one point, but I wake to find he has an arm draped over me and is snoring softly. It takes me a minute, but I gently squirm my way from under his arm and out of the bed without waking him.

I walk over to the windows, my bandaged paws complaining. They feel better, but they're still sore.

When I reach the windows, I throw open the shutters to let the predawn light in. I can't see much beyond the courtyard below and the rooftops beyond, but I can hear distant sounds, too faint for me to really ascertain. I breathe in deeply and close my eyes.

The city is just waking up around us, and the merchants are probably busy setting up in the Grand Market. Across Aksu, shops are opening, craftsman are getting ready for work, and from somewhere comes the smell of chicken cooking.

Naji stirs and mumbles my name. "Zayn?"

I turn around and open my eyes. The hyena is still in bed. "Yes?"

"Just seeing where you are is all."

I walk over and sit down on the bed next to him. "I am here, my love."

He smiles and leans up to kiss me. We exchange a simple kiss, and he then lays back down, pulling a blanket over his muzzle. "Give me a few more minutes. Okay?"

I nod and trace my hand across his curled-up form. "Of course."

After he dozes back off, I get up and walk back to the window. The dawn light is stronger now, the sun having cleared the rooftops. This is my home now, and while there has been a lot of excitement these last two weeks, I think things will quiet down now. It isn't everything I hoped it would be, but I know I will be happy here.

Being happy is the most important thing in life, and as I stand by the window, I smile. I am finally free of the shackles my old life had placed upon me. It's not been an easy road, but I have a future to look forward to now. Whatever happens next, I can meet my fate standing on my feet.

Acknowledgements

It took me eleven years to write and edit this book. I have not worked on it constantly this entire time, but it proved to be something I was either poking at or needing to get back to for many years. During that time, the work grew and changed from the initial short story I wrote until it became a novel. This wasn't meant to be my first novel, but it turned out to be the story I needed to write.

A work like this also isn't possible without support from others. At the top of the list is my partner of all these years, Othello Rysingson, who kept encouraging me to finish the book. My *Dissident Signals* co-editor Slip-Wolf read the first complete draft of the book and provided a much needed early look. Critical feedback by Gullwulf gave me important suggestions that helped shape and smooth out issues in the novel. Thank you to G.M. Rader for reading the book and telling me I needed to publish it. I also must thank my friend Utunu who provided feedback and copy-editing to ensure my propensity to create new, exciting mistakes while fixing things did not occur.

Thank you to the Regional Anthropomorphic Writer's Retreat (RAWR), the Anthropomorphic Writers Outreach Organization (AWOO), and the Furry Writer's Guild (FWG) for providing networking and social spaces to help me pull this thing through. RAWR especially helped me develop as a writer and get to where I am now. I also must thank Fur the 'More for selecting me as their Guest of Honor in 2021, which became 2022 due to COVID-19, for first recognizing me as a writer of short fiction and also giving me a personal deadline for when this novel needed to come out. Thank you also to Hibbary for her fantastic covert art and Teagan Gavet for illustrating the map of the Sultanate.

Researching a book like this also required quite a bit of reading to capture the setting the way I wanted it. If you're interested in reading up on the Muslim world, I have four suggestions for you. *Before Homosexuality in the Arab-Islamic World, 1500–1800* by Khaled El-Rouayheb provided a historical perspective on homosexuality. *Another Morocco: Selected Stories* by Abdellah Taïa is a personal look about growing up gay in Morocco. *For Bread Alone* by Mohamed Choukri is an unvarnished, personal look at growing up in poverty in Morocco. Lastly, *Arabian Sands* by Wilfred Thesiger, with its extensive talk about traveling through the Arabian Desert, helped frame the environment of the novel.

Finally, thank you to all my readers, patrons on Patreon, and everyone over the years who asked about when this book would come out. It has been a long journey, and I am glad to have completed it and have it in your hands. Thank you all.

NightEyes DaySpring, January 2022

About the Author

NightEyes DaySpring is a known troublemaker who is rumored to have a penchant for coffee and an interest in dead, ancient civilizations. He has been writing furry fiction for over twenty years. His stories have appeared in various anthologies, including *Werewolves vs. Fascism*, *Heat*, and *FANG*. Currently, he resides in Florida with his boyfriend where in his spare time he masquerades as an IT professional, plays board games, and doodles.

Visit his website, *nighteyes-dayspring.com*, for more about his writing. For day-to-day nonsense, follow @wolfwithcoffee on Twitter.